NIGHT TREMORS

Also by Matt Coyle

Yesterday's Echo

NIGHT TREMORS

A Novel

MATT COYLE

Longboat Key, Florida

ISBN: 978-1-60809-149-2

Published in the United States of America by Oceanview Publishing
Longboat Key, Florida

www.oceanviewpub.com
10 9 8 7 6 5 4 3 2 1

PRINTED IN THE UNITED STATES OF AMERICA

For Kimberley Cameron:
Agent, advocate, friend
Without your belief, hard work, and support,
this book would never have been published

ACKNOWLEDGMENTS

Very few books are created by an author in a vacuum. They require input and guidance from a variety of people behind the scenes. *Night Tremors* is no exception.

Hearty thanks to the following:

Pat and Bob Gussin, David Ivester, Frank Troncale, Emily Baar, Connie Brown, and Kirsten Barger at Oceanview for the support and for making the book better coming out than it was going in.

The talented writers from the Saturday critique group: Carolyn Wheat, Cathy Worthington, Judy Hamilton, Linda Schroeder, and Karine Chakarian for always putting the betterment of each other's work first and egos second.

My family for unrelenting support and continued guerrilla marketing: Charles Coyle, Tim and Sue Coyle, Jan and Gene Wolfchief, Pam Helmer, Tom Cunningham, my sister Jennifer Cunningham for an essential late read, and, finally, my brother-in-law Jorge Helmer for convincing me not to fictionalize the town of La Jolla in the first book of the series. Stellar advice.

Nancy Denton for a much-needed early line edit.

Deborah Scipione for continued support of my writing.

Maddee James and Jen Forbus for creating and maintaining the best-looking website in the mystery world.

Robin Borrelli for information on the residential real estate business.

Sarah M. Chen for support and information on private investigations.

Joyce M. Aiello, Los Angeles County Assistant County Counsel, for extensive information on the criminal justice system.

D. P. Lyle for his remarkable forensic knowledge.

Sergeant Ken Whitley of the Garden Grove Police Department for information on the California prison system.

Any errors regarding real estate, private investigations, the criminal justice system, prisons, or forensics are solely the author's.

Finally, retired deputy sheriff, author, and friend, David Putnam, for being on call twenty-four hours a day to answer my police procedure and crime-scene questions. Blame me for anything I got wrong.

NIGHT TREMORS

CHAPTER ONE

The woman's back arched and her head jerked backwards. Blinds cut shadows across her naked body. She stood splayed, her arms pressed against the wall. Her shoulders shuddered and she twisted towards the window, exposing the man's bald head. His face, a tight grimace that only pain could produce. Well, pain and sex.

Click.

I got the shot I needed. The proof required to trip the adultery clause in the prenup and open the divorce settlement vault. It would be the last one I showed the man's wife, right after the establishing photos of her husband walking into the La Jolla Inn motel room with his mistress.

The adulterer drove a late-model, black Cadillac Escalade. He probably liked it because it was a status symbol and a smooth ride. I liked it because it was roomy under the chassis. Plenty of head room when you had to lie under it and shoot pictures up through slanted motel window blinds of cheating hearts and bodies. My Nikon D7100 got me the shot without a flash lighting up the cool, moonless December sky. It was early evening, but winter and clouds darkened the ancient inn's parking lot.

I crawled on my belly along the asphalt out from under the SUV and stood up. Tiny pebbles and dirt clung to my jeans and dark-blue hooded sweatshirt. I tried to brush them off, but the dew in the night air smeared the dirt into grime and stained the clothing. My mind wandered back to my time as a cop. Way back then, I'd never envisioned this as a career. A well-paid camera jockey, cataloging the weaknesses and bad decisions of others.

A snoop. A Peeping Tom. A private investigator.

I was good at what I did. Maybe the best in San Diego. The stakeout specialist with the steady hands and quick camera finger. I could sit, or stand, or lie in wait forever for people to do what they shouldn't. Then, click, I had their wrongs captured for posterity. Or infamy. I did my job so well that I never talked about it when friends asked what it was like to be a PI.

I swallowed down my introspection and headed across La Jolla Boulevard to the strip mall where I'd left my car. The mall had a Häagen-Dazs ice cream shop. Bright and shiny and full of sweet, creamy sin that went down a lot easier than self-analysis. On the drive home, after I'd chomped down the last of a waffle cone topped with two scoops of mint chip, I hit my boss' number on my cell phone.

"You get it?" His voice vibrated the Bluetooth in my ear.

"Hello to you too."

"I'm with a client." His voice now hushed. "Just give me the news."

"In flagrante."

"You got a knack, Bullet. Print them in the morning, and we'll show them to the client tomorrow afternoon."

Bob Reitzmeyer had dubbed me "Bullet-head" when I was a kid with a military crew cut. I'd listen to his cop stories when my dad brought him home for dinner after their shifts together on the La Jolla Police Department. Thankfully, he'd dropped "head" from the moniker when I graduated from the Ventura Sheriff's Academy and became a cop in the Santa Barbara Police Department. A long time ago.

"Will do."

"Good work. You're turning into a crack peeper. Your pop would be proud."

He hung up, saving me from having to hold my tongue. I doubted my father would have been proud that his son was a "crack peeper."

Dessert already consumed, I was still hungry for dinner. I drove north until I hit La Jolla's restaurant row, Prospect Street.

I rolled past towering palm trees, neon and glass edifices with ocean views and an aging cement rectangle sunk below street level with a view of the office building blocking its view of the ocean. Muldoon's Steak House. My former place of employment.

Before my life changed.

Muldoon's was stuck in a 1970s steak-house time warp: lit in permanent dusk, redwood slats and brass on the walls, salad bar buffeting an open grill area. It had once been a second home to me. Now it was just a place where I ate dinner a few times a month.

A hostess I didn't know greeted me in the entry.

"Is Turk in tonight?" I asked.

"Mr. Muldoon?" Her voice had a lilt that made sense matched with her big brown eyes.

I nodded.

"No. He may come in later. I'm not sure."

I felt guilty that I was relieved not to have to see my former best friend. Two years ago, Turk had saved my life before I finally saved myself. But I hadn't saved Turk, and he'd paid for my life with his mobility. A debt I could never repay. He'd been a casualty of a bad decision I'd made. There'd been other bad decisions.

And other casualties.

* * *

I'd just pushed my empty dinner plate away when a shadow crept across my table. I raised my eyes and saw an old piece of Texas in a tailored, western-style suit wedged up under a cowboy hat.

"Mr. Cahill." The twang in his voice had been muted by years under the Southern California sun but it still had some Lone Star state left in it.

When I first met Timothy Buckley his wardrobe looked like it had been piecemealed together by Goodwill. He'd spent his time shaking hookers and junkies loose from the legal system on the ugly side of San Diego. Now he hung his shingle in La Jolla, a jagged slice of paradise cut along the coast. The closest he got to hookers and junkies was protecting trust-fund babes from *Girls Gone Wild* videos and their silver-spoon brothers from DUI charges.

"I think we're past misters, Buckley. You can call me Rick."

"Well, there it is, Rick." He took off his hat, allowing a braided, gray ponytail to fall down onto his back. "I've called you three or four times at your office, but you never call me back."

"Nothing for us to talk about."

"Son, I know we got off to a bad start way back when." He scratched a two-week-old gray beard and squinted watery eyes at me. "But you're 'bout as ornery as a polecat with his tail up."

"Then why the phone calls?"

"Sometimes a skunk spreading stink around is the only way to flush out the truth."

"You seem to have gone a little more country since I last saw you, Buckley. Is that for my benefit?"

"I'm afraid it's out of habit. My upper-crust clientele expect an attorney from Texas to be folksy. I aim to please." He threaded the brim of his cowboy hat through his fingers. "Mind if I sit down, Rick?"

I weighed hearing Buckley out against the possibility of seeing Turk hobble in on his cane. I gambled and nodded to the right side of the booth. Buckley slid in, set his hat on the table, and steepled his fingers.

The waiter came by and asked if he could get me anything else. By the way Buckley wetted his lips, it looked like he had his mind set on the first nip of the day.

"Just the check. Thanks." I looked at Buckley. "Despite the fact that I ignore your phone calls, you keep making them, and you somehow track me to a restaurant I only decided to eat at an hour ago. What the hell do you want?"

"I'm not trying to pester you, son." He spread his hands open over his hat. "I heard you eat back at your old haunts every now and again. It's important that we talk."

"It's important to you."

"I know I put a burr under your saddle during that Windsor mess, but I was just protecting my client. And everything turned out okay come closin' time."

The "Windsor mess" had ended two years ago, but it still haunted my dreams.

"It turned out okay for you. A change in clientele and zip codes." I slowly nodded my head. "But, come closin' time, three people were dead." And one left walking with a cane.

"Actually, four people died." He avoided my eyes. "If you include the one you killed."

"Why are you here?"

"Fine. We'll put the brass tacks on the table." He leaned forward. "You remember the Eddington boy?"

"Randall Eddington?"

"Yes."

"The murderer?"

Randall Eddington had been eighteen when he killed his parents and younger sister. The murders went national as the networks' tragedy of the month. Every three-letter combination of the alphabet had news vans in La Jolla for the trial later that year, even though the judge wouldn't allow cameras in the courtroom. It had been good for Muldoon's business for a month or so. Even breathless reporters with nothing new to report had to eat after the red light went dark.

"Well, the jury found him guilty. That's true." Buckley's eyes had a little hang dog in them. "In the first trial, anyway."

"First trial? I only remember one."

"One so far." Buckley wiped his lips like that phantom drink couldn't come soon enough.

"So, what does getting a psychopath a new trial have to do with me?"

"I don't believe he is a psychopath."

"Okay. Let's just call him a kid with anger-management issues." I leaned forward and crossed my forearms on the table.

"But why me? There are plenty of private dicks in San Diego with more experience who can fudge up some evidence for you."

"I'm not looking for a prop job, Rick." He put a leathery hand on my arm. "I'm looking for the truth. And if the Windsor case proved anything to me, it's that you're a truth seeker."

"I'm a guy who peeks through windows and snaps photos of married men locked onto unmarried women."

I slid down the leather bench opposite Buckley and stood up outside the booth.

"You gonna do that for the rest of your life, son?" Buckley grabbed his hat and stood up next to me. "Or, do you want to work a case that matters? Something that won't make you want to scrub yourself with a wire brush in the shower at the end of the day."

"I use Comet and sandpaper." I strode around him down into the main dining room. "See you around, Buckley."

The moon still hid behind the clouds, and the ocean down below Prospect Street pushed up a heavy breeze that poked cold fingers in my face. I'd almost made it to my car when I heard boots clomping behind me. Cowboy boots.

"Rick!" Buckley was out of breath, his cowboy hat clenched in his hand when he caught up to me. His face was red, either from wind or exertion. "Just hold on one dang minute and hear me out."

"I've heard enough, Buckley." I opened the door to my car. "I'm not interested. The kid got what he deserved."

"Cops make mistakes, Rick. You and your ex-girlfriend are proof of that."

"Sometimes they get it right." I slid into the car.

"Tony Moretti was lead detective on the case." Buckley let his bloodhound eyes droop a little lower. "You still convinced the boy got what he deserved?"

Moretti was now police chief of the La Jolla Police Department. He'd only been a detective when he tried to pin a murder on me a couple years back. But just because Moretti had been wrong about me didn't make the kid innocent.

"Look, Buckley. I couldn't help you even if I wanted to." I closed the car door and rolled down the window. "I work exclusively for La Jolla Investigations. I can't freelance. You want our firm on it, talk to Bob Reitzmeyer."

"He's not the right fit. We want you."

"Sorry. Can't help you." I turned the ignition key. "Good luck, Buckley."

I started to roll up the window, but Buckley's hand on it stopped me.

"Randall's grandparents remember you from that article in *The Reader* about the Windsor murder. The one about you being the fella who really caught the killer. The rest of the media got it wrong and made Moretti out to be a hero. *The Reader* got it right."

"I'm sorry for the grandparents, but there's nothing I can do." He was wrong about *The Reader*. It didn't get it right, either.

"They've got their life's savings liquid and ready to pour out to the man who'll find the truth about what happened to their family. They just want to make sure their grandson gets a fair shake."

"Are you more interested in the fair shake or the liquid assets?"

"You don't know me very well, Rick." His watery eyes went dry and all the Texas hospitality left them.

"I know you well enough, Buckley." I pulled out of the parking spot and gunned it down Prospect Street as the cool, moonless night drew down around La Jolla.

CHAPTER TWO

The sun burst free from the morning fog and bathed the day in a crisp, winter shine. The kind of day you wanted to spend playing golf, biking a trail, or shooting hoops. Not thinking about jailed killers, bent cops, or cheating spouses. But, after my talk with Timothy Buckley last night, they were all tangled up in my head as I entered La Jolla Investigations the next morning.

LJI is located on the ground floor of the three-story law office of DeFreitas, Helmer, Cunningham, and Alpert. The firm is prestigious but relatively new in old-money La Jolla years. The building, sharp angles of copper and brass, sits two blocks back from the coastline. The law partners all have views of the ocean from their third-floor offices. LJI has a shingle out front and our own office tucked in the back behind the first-year associates on the first floor.

I didn't spend too much time at the office, operating mostly out of my home and, of course, under cars at night in dusty parking lots. But I checked in a few times a week to meet with clients and access the computer system's databases. We dealt with the wealthy elite, and even though we were the help, our boss didn't want us to look like it. I wore a blue blazer over a burgundy knit turtleneck and tan slacks. My wingtips needed a shine.

Bob Reitzmeyer sat behind a mahogany desk splattered with mementos from his thirty years at the La Jolla Police Department. Framed photographs and commendations crept up the wall behind his desk. He started LJI shortly after he retired from La Jolla PD eight years ago.

The memorabilia was supposed to be there to impress prospective clients. But I bet that Bob liked having his past within reach of his fingertips too. Most ex-cops were proud of their years on the force.

Some, the force wouldn't let be proud.

"You get the photos printed yet?" Bob stroked a trim, more-salt-than-pepper Van Dyke. He wore a tailored suit that hung from his LA Fitness frame like a "Sixty Is the New Forty" advertisement out of GQ. "Mrs. Bengston will be here in a couple hours to see the evidence."

"They're ready." I folded my arms and leaned back in a leather chair in front of Bob's desk. "Her husband's in the starring role."

"Funny way to make a living." Reitzmeyer gave a smile that had made three ex-wives and hundreds of other women blush over the years.

"Hysterical." My face kept its Irish pale.

"What gives, Bullet?"

Timothy Buckley's crack about peeping through motel windows had bored under my skin. It got deep enough to scrape a nerve I'd spent the last two years trying to ignore. I'd found a niche and I was damn good at it. If I made a mistake, feelings got hurt but nobody died. Or ended up crippled. Now it felt dirty. A greasy residue on my fingers that I couldn't wash off.

"When can I get off adultery duty and do something else?"

"I thought you enjoyed the detail."

"Only a pervert enjoys that detail, Bob." My shoulders pinched in on my neck. "I enjoy doing something well. I just think I can do other things too."

"Well, it's a great source of revenue for us. You're the best peeper in San Diego and an important part of the team." He leaned back in his chair and stroked his Van Dyke. "But I understand how watching all that infidelity could wear you down. It certainly wore my three exes down."

He gave me the grin again, and I couldn't help but smile.

"Give me a little time and I'll see what I can do. If business stays on the upswing, I'll bring somebody else on and move you over to something else. Maybe you could be like a utility infielder for a while until we find what fits you best."

"That would be great, Bob." My shoulders relaxed. "Thanks."

"Hey, I need a favor. Something big from upstairs just blew in, and I have to get right on it." Bob folded his forearms and leaned forward. "I need you to meet with Mrs. Bengston solo today. Give her my apologies and say I had an emergency. And soften it up a little. You'll have to be the shoulder if she needs one to cry on. This will be an opportunity for you to do something different."

Not that much different. I'd still deliver the bad news in color prints, but I'd have to hold hands through the tears and show empathy. Not my strongest suit. Not even in my deck. But Bob was right. This would be a chance to show him I was ready to do something else.

This new case must have been big. Bob never missed a sit-down with a two-timed spouse. The client truly came first with Bob. It went back to his days on the force. Even as a kid sitting at the kitchen table listening to his cop stories, I could tell that Bob cared about the victims of crimes. My dad saw being a cop as a job like any other. Bob Reitzmeyer saw it as his life's mission.

"What's the new case?"

"Darren Waters has been accused of rape."

"The ace for the Padres?" Waters was the Padres' top pitcher and had just signed the biggest contract in club history.

"Yes. No arrest, yet, if ever. Waters was having an affair with the woman, and Ed thinks it will go civil because of all the money the kid's making now."

Ed was Edmund DeFreitas. Former La Jolla district attorney and founding partner of the law firm that threw La Jolla Investigations all its business. He'd retired a few years before Bob had and started up his own law firm. He and Bob's business had been intertwined ever since Bob started La Jolla Investigations.

"Can I help out on this one?"

"Yes. I think I'll need you. According to Waters, the accuser likes it rough. We may need some bedroom clicks to verify his story."

"I was hoping I could do something other than the peep detail. Maybe interview some witnesses."

Bob leaned back and pursed his lips. "I know you're eager, Bullet, but your time will come. Right now, I need you to continue doing what you do best."

What I did best was starting to cost me sleep. I already had that part of my life covered. I didn't need any more help.

* * *

Kate Bengston was in her late forties but could pass for mid-thirties. Head-turning beautiful mid-thirties. Her husband hadn't found someone more attractive than his wife to play with on the side, he'd just found someone else.

Kate wore a conservative olive-and-tan pantsuit that didn't diminish her athletic beauty. Blue eyes above a fine, straight nose inspected me. Her blond hair was knotted into a bun. She was all business, but I knew from experience that the reserve was a brace against impending bad news.

She sat at the large mahogany table in our conference room. The walls of the room were decorated with the law enforcement and investigative histories of Bob Reitzmeyer along with each LJI investigator's police department rookie photograph, commendations, and photo holding a California Private Investigator's license while standing next to Bob.

I had two pieces of information on the wall, my rookie photo and the one of me next to Bob holding my PI's license. I didn't do anything of note or stay on the Santa Barbara Police Department long enough to accumulate any commendations.

"Hello, Mrs. Bengston. My name is Rick Cahill. Bob asked me to, ah, present our findings to you." I sat down at the head of the table. "He had an emergency and wanted to apologize for not being here."

"I'm not sure I'm comfortable with that." Her eyes and

mouth narrowed into slits. "I've been dealing exclusively with Bob. It's a very private matter."

"I understand, ma'am. Bob's been very discreet. He and I have been the only people involved with your case."

Kate Bengston had suspected her husband was having an affair for the reasons most women grasp onto. Nothing as obvious as lipstick on the collar or the hint of a woman's perfume hiding on his neck. No. It's change. Tightened abs, a break in the old routine, a sudden new routine. The couple's weekly coupling dwindles down to bi-weekly or monthly. He suddenly has to work late on a regular basis and travel more on the weekends.

Change. When spouses notice it and their questions get laughed off as paranoia, they call us. And ninety-nine percent of the time, we prove their suspicions correct. They sometimes thank us, and always pay us well.

Kate Bengston was beautiful, sophisticated, and wealthy. For her husband, that and his oath before God were not enough to keep him from poking around in the dark with someone else.

"Well, I guess we should get started. Here are your husband's credit card charges and a list of phone calls made from his cell phone that Bob discussed with you yesterday." I pushed a manila folder in front of her containing the paper trail of her husband's deceit. I kept a second folder, harboring the smut photos, in front of me.

She studied the documents silently for five minutes. The only hint of emotion was revealed by her tightened, colorless lips.

"There's more, I trust, Mr. Cahill."

"You may want to prepare yourself for the photographs you're about to see, Mrs. Bengston."

"I'm prepared."

They always thought they were prepared. They were always wrong. I placed the other folder in front of her.

She opened it and saw photos of her husband's Escalade parked in the La Jolla Inn parking lot. Her husband and a woman entering a room at the Inn. Finally, the coup de grace, photographs of them entwined, naked, caught through the window blinds.

I stared down at the table, but let my eyes sneak an occasional side glance. She held the last photo down on the table in tight fingers. Her face flushed, in anger or shame. Her eyes stayed pinned to the picture. Her chest rose and fell quickly as her breaths broke the silence in the room.

I readied my shoulder for her tears. Bob's job. He was as natural at it as a Southern politician. Bob was the buffer between the pain and the evidence. I was merely the mechanic, the lens, the truth. I felt for Kate Bengston. I felt for all the women and men whose spouses' deceit I had to lay before them in living color. But it was my job, and I'd grown a coroner's distance from the pain brought from photos of a marriage's death knell.

"Do you get your kicks sneaking around in the dark, taking pictures of naked adulterers, Mr. Cahill?" A jagged edge hung off her voice. "I noticed there's no ring on your finger. Is this how you get back at whoever broke your heart?"

Now it was my face that turned red. She'd caught me off guard, and the sadness I'd always felt for spouses in this room suddenly turned to shame. I tried to erase the flush from my face.

This was a job that she'd paid us to do. If it hadn't been me, it would have been someone else.

Still, the gnaw dug deeper into my gut.

"I'm very sorry to have to show you this evidence, Mrs. Bengston." I caught her eyes and all the pain that her husband had caused spilled out onto me. "I take no pleasure in this. You hired us to find the facts. I'm sorry that they are what they are."

"Well, you did your job." She kept her eyes lasered on mine, slowly stood up, and pulled a checkbook from her Gucci purse. She scribbled down our fee and her signature and tossed the check on the table in front of me. "You should be very proud."

She hung her bag from her shoulder, focused her eyes straight ahead, and walked right past me like I wasn't even there.

Like I'd never been there.

CHAPTER THREE

I set my third empty Ballast Point IPA bottle down onto the wooden deck next to my patio chair and looked out at the view of the bay and downtown San Diego. It was really only a wedge of a view pinched in between Soledad Mountain above Interstate 5 and the sloping side of Rose Canyon. Not the view you'd get from a house on a hill in La Jolla or even one you'd get from a lot of other homes here in Bay Ho. But it was my view, and I'd paid a lot for it. Not nearly what it was worth, but a lot for me.

Bob Reitzmeyer had worked on LJPD for thirty years and run his own private investigations firm for another eight. Over that time, he'd collected a black bag full of favors. One of them involved an ex-politician who needed to sell his home in a hurry. That's how I got a house with a view for two hundred grand under market value. Bob even loaned me ten grand to help boost me up into twenty percent down.

I guess that put me on his favor list too.

Until a year ago, I hadn't thought about owning a house for over ten years. Back when I was married to Colleen in Santa Barbara. When our love was open and unforced. When we looked to the future and dreamed of kids and backyards and family barbeques. Then my arrogance and hubris got in the way and almost destroyed my marriage. Before I could put it back together, Colleen was murdered.

So, with hopes for a family long ago left to die, I bought a three-bedroom house. A place to retreat to, without having to share a wall with a neighbor. Without having to share anything with anyone. I made one bedroom into an office. The third bedroom I left empty. Sometimes, late at night, I'd open the door and look inside and wonder where a crib would go and a bureau, and where to hang a mobile. Not very often, but sometimes.

I took my eyes off the view and stared at my dog. Midnight stared back. He'd rested his head on my thigh and given me the soft-eyed Lab look. I scratched his square black head, and he slowly wagged his tail.

The calming presence of Midnight couldn't quite do its trick tonight. Kate Bengston's hurt, anger, and words still bounced around in my head. They'd been there all day. Reminding me how I paid for my house with the sliver of a view. It hadn't been a revelation, but coupled with Buckley's comments and my own creeping regret, it landed on my chin like a haymaker.

I pulled my cell phone out of my pocket and called Bob Reitzmeyer.

"Bullet, I'm ass to ankles in the Waters investigation right now. Can this wait until Monday?"

"It'll just take a second, Bob. I may need to take some vacation time."

"Starting when?"

"Maybe starting Monday. I'll find out in the next couple days."

"You got some new gal you're going away with?" Ebullient. "That'll do you some good."

"No. Something else." I took a deep breath and let it out. "Would you mind if I used the time to moonlight on another case?"

"You mean for another agency?" Shock.

"No. Freelancing for an attorney. It will give me a chance to do some of the other work we talked about. On my own time."

"I—hold on. Ed's calling me on the other line." He put me on hold. A minute later. "I've got to go."

"What about vacation time and moonlighting?"

"Go ahead. As long as you're available to help out with the Waters investigation if I need you."

"You mean if you need some bedroom clicks?"

"Yeah." A hint of irritation. "Like we discussed. I've got to call Ed back. Be ready if I need you."

He hung up.

Not a ringing endorsement, but he'd given me the okay. I called Buckley and told him I'd meet with him and the Eddingtons, and then decide if I'd take the case. No matter how much I wanted to do something other than bedroom clicks, I wouldn't agree to try and free a murderer from prison. Not unless I was certain he was innocent. I'd been a cop and so had my father. We'd left behind a legacy of disgracing the badge. But setting murderers free was not in my DNA. Murder was the one sin for which there was no second chance. God had the grace to forgive.

I didn't.

CHAPTER FOUR

Jack and Rita Mae Eddington lived in La Jolla. Just not the part of La Jolla where I'd expected the founder of a golf club empire to live. They lived on La Jolla Boulevard in a condo complex that looked like a 1960s apartment building. Concrete. Square. Mini-balconies staring down at an oversized, kidney-shaped swimming pool.

The Pacific Coast Estates.

The coast was a mile away and a nine hundred-square-foot box hardly qualified as an estate in La Jolla. I'd expected the Eddingtons to live in a mansion overlooking the ocean. Maybe they'd exhausted their wealth on attorney's fees for their grandson.

The Eddingtons lived on the third floor. I knocked on their front door in a hallway full of front doors.

Jack and Rita Mae both greeted me at the door. They were in their mid-seventies and looked it. No stretched smiles or tight eyes. I guess grief doesn't leave room for vanity. Or maybe the Eddingtons were that La Jolla rarity who didn't worry much about image.

Jack had been tall once, but life had pulled down his shoulders and pushed his head forward. His gray hair, where there was any, was wispy. Rita Mae was short and trim and wrinkled around the edges. There was a faint gleam in her brown eyes that could probably light up a room a few years back. Before her grandson grabbed a golf club one night and beat her son, daughter-in-law, and granddaughter to death.

The Eddingtons led me into their clean, but dated, living room. Its focal point was an oversized family portrait of Thomas

Eddington's family mounted on the wall adjacent to the sliding glass door that led out to the balcony. Everyone in the picture had big, easy smiles, and Randall Eddington's hands rested on his father's shoulders, who sat beneath him. He looked to be about seventeen. The photograph must have been taken about a year before everyone in it, except Randall, was murdered.

Opposite the portrait, Timothy Buckley, cowboy hat in hand, sat on a wilted floral-patterned couch. He stood up, thanked me for coming, and gave me a hard-clinched Texas handshake. I followed Buckley's lead and joined him on the couch. Before my ass hit upholstery, Rita Mae had a plate of chocolate chip cookies on the coffee table in front of me. She wore a yellow summer dress even though summer was six months away. I had the feeling she'd gotten dressed up for my visit.

"Can I get you some milk? Or water? Or soda?" Her voice was sweet, but fragile. Like it might break if she was forced to speak harsh words. She looked at me with expectant eyes, waiting for me to accept her hospitality. Waiting for me to agree to take on the cause of her grandson.

It was going to take more than milk and cookies to convince me to try to spring a convicted murderer from prison. And acceptance of the former might give false hope for acceptance of the latter.

"Milk would be great." Well, the cookies were homemade, and I'd had a small breakfast.

"Timothy, here, speaks very highly of you. Says you're a man of integrity." Jack Eddington pushed forward in an overstuffed chair next to me. His eyes had less plead in them than his wife's, but the same amount of pain.

He wore a collared shirt, covered by a sweater vest. Knobby knees poked out under his vintage golf slacks. Neither the shirt nor the vest bore the logo of the golf company he'd started some forty years earlier, before he had finally handed the business down to his eldest son, Thomas. Interesting.

"That's mighty generous of him." I shot a glance at Buckley.

I guessed he'd pumped me up to give them hope. Probably a bad idea, since I hadn't decided to take the case yet.

"We read about your involvement in that murder investigation a few years ago." Rita Mae set a large glass of milk down on a coaster atop the coffee table. She stepped over to her husband and leaned against the arm of his chair. "The police took credit for it, but you were the one who solved those awful murders."

"I wish it were that simple." Nothing was simple about those murders, and neither would my decision be whether or not to take their grandson's case.

"You were nearly killed, but you wouldn't quit until you found the truth, because an innocent person was in jail." Rita Mae clasped her husband's hand. "That's all we want, Mr. Cahill." She looked at her husband and then back at me. "Someone to find the truth so our grandson can be set free."

Well, that didn't seem like too much to ask. Just find new evidence about an eight-year-old murder case and free their grandson from prison.

"Why now?" I grabbed a cookie.

"Why now, what?" Jack asked.

"The trial was eight years ago. Why the push to reopen your grandson's case now?" I took a bite of the cookie and fell in love.

Jack looked at Buckley, and the cowboy lawyer took his cue.

"Actually, the, ah, deaths were eight years ago and the trial seven. But some new evidence has come to light." Buckley tugged on a ten-dollar bolo tie above a thousand-dollar suit and leaned forward. "Exculpatory evidence that, if we can just verify, might be enough to get Randall a new trial."

"What is it?"

"Well, son, it would be unethical to discuss the case with you unless I knew you were ridin' our horse."

"If you don't mind, Buckley, I'd like to see the horse before I mount it."

"Son, you're pushing me up 'ginst a cactus."

"Maybe it would help you to learn a little bit about Randall."

Rita Mae bounced from her husband's side, bent down under the coffee table, and came up with a photo album. She set it down next to the glass of milk and the plate of cookies that was now short two.

Rita Mae hovered over my shoulder as I thumbed through the album. She smelled of vanilla and baby powder, and offered a running commentary of each photograph. The pictures were familiar to anyone with a family. Randall riding a bike with training wheels, opening gifts with his parents around a Christmas tree, kicking a soccer ball, swinging a cut-down golf club, hugged by adoring grandparents, later holding his baby sister, class pictures, sitting in front of a computer.

In the pictures, Randall seemed like a normal kid. Big smile when he was young, a little distant as a teenager. He had dark hair and a melon face atop a doughy body. Black horn-rimmed glasses framed intelligent brown eyes. By the time he'd reached his teens he'd thinned down, but still had a soft outline. He now had the looks and bearing of a nerd. But nerds' status had changed since my time in high school. Now it was chic. The only thing unusual about the photos was that the earliest ones of Randall were as a five-year-old.

"He seemed like a happy child." I closed the photo album. "But, if you don't mind me asking, why are there no baby pictures of Randall?"

"When Thomas met Alana, she was a single mother and Randall was already four." Rita Mae returned to her husband's side. "But Thomas adopted him and grew to love him like his own. We all did. He was a wonderful child."

"Randall's real father didn't fight the adoption?"

"Randall never knew his real father." Jack Eddington shifted in his chair. "At least that's what Thomas said Alana told him. It didn't matter. Thomas was the perfect father for a boy in a situation like that. And Randall respected and admired Thomas."

Respected and admired. What about loved?

"How did you feel about Alana?" I'd noticed Jack's mouth tighten when he'd mentioned his late daughter-in-law's name.

"I liked her just fine, Mr. Cahill." Anger flashed behind the pain in Jack's eyes. "But I don't see what that has to do with getting my grandson out of prison."

I glanced at Rita Mae, and she'd started slowly wringing her hands.

"Just getting background, Mr. Eddington. And you can call me Rick." I grabbed my third cookie. "What made your son the perfect father for Randall?"

Rita Mae jumped in before her husband. "He was loving and kind, and taught Randall how to behave like a gentleman."

"I'd imagine a boy from a broken home might have to learn a lot of new behaviors to fit into society." The kid and his father were just too perfect. That's not how I remembered my childhood. If I was going to find the truth that nobody knew, I needed to start with the truth that Jack and Rita Mae already knew.

"Randall was a wonder—"

"The boy wasn't a saint." Jack cut off his wife. "He had some problems when he was young. It was to be expected. But Thomas showed him a firm, but fair, hand, and Randall grew into a fine young man."

"What kind of problems?"

"Mr. Cahill, it sounds like you are working for that corrupt police department and not us." Jack's face flushed a leathery pink. "Maybe we should find a detective who will be on our side."

I suddenly changed my mind about reaching for that fourth cookie.

"Now, Jack." Rita Mae patted her husband's thigh. "Mr. Cahill is just doing his job."

Jack let go a breath and nodded his head. "I guess you're right. Proceed, Mr. Cahill."

"Please, call me Rick." Hard to feel like a mister while eating milk and cookies. I turned to Buckley. "Tell me about this new evidence."

"Son, we're still at a Mexican standoff. I can't tell you anything until you agree to take the case."

"If this evidence is so compelling, why wouldn't I take the case?" I caught myself reaching for a cookie and redirected my hand to scratch my knee. Four cookies would have been rude without agreeing to join the team.

"Rick you have to appreciate the situation we're in." Buckley gave me a half smile of creamed-corn teeth. "Chief Moretti built his reputation on arresting Randall. That and the Windsor case helped propel him to becoming police chief. If he got wind of our new evidence, I believe he'd do just about anything to stop us before we got started."

"You don't have to tell me what Moretti's capable of, Buckley. He and I are hardly friends. Anything you tell me won't get back to Moretti."

"Well, ah." He twirled his hat in his fingers some more. "Your boss, Mr. Reitzmeyer, still has a fairly close relationship with LJPD."

"You contacted me, Buckley, and you told these nice folks that I was a man of integrity. Apparently, you didn't mean it." I stood up and looked down at the Eddingtons. "I'm sorry, but your grandson was convicted of murder. I didn't become a private investigator to set murderers free. Unless you can give me a reason to believe Randall is innocent, I'll have to thank you for your hospitality and be on my way."

Rita Mae's hands did the spin cycle as she and her husband traded a long look.

Jack turned his attention from his wife to Buckley. "Tell him what he wants to know, Timothy. My wife seems to trust Mr. Cahill. That's good enough for me."

"I meant no harm, Rick. I know you're a good man. Please, sit back down." Buckley shifted on the sofa like his ass was suddenly sore. "A witness has come forward with information that a suspect has bragged about the murders."

"Does the new suspect have a record?"

"Drunk and disorderly, and drug possession."

I shot a glance at the Eddingtons, huddled together for support. The look in Rita Mae's eyes had weakened from hope to desperation.

"Mr. and Mrs. Eddington." I stood up. "Would you excuse Mr. Buckley and me while we talk out on the balcony?"

"Of course." Jack Eddington stood up and walked over to the sliding glass door and opened it.

Buckley looked at me with wide eyes and a pinched mouth and sectioned up to his feet. A low groan accompanied the movement of each section. He put on his cowboy hat, smiled at our doorman, Jack, and joined me on the balcony that overlooked the pool three stories below.

"Is this private confab really necessary, Rick?" The homespun country had left his voice and been replaced by the ragged edge of big-city irritation.

"This is for your benefit, Buckley." I walked to the far side of the balcony that was hidden from the Eddingtons' view by their curtains.

Buckley followed me with a sour look smeared across his face. "What the hell's that supposed to mean?"

"I didn't think you'd want those nice folks in there hear me call you a con man." I fought the urge to punctuate my words with a finger to Buckley's chest. "Is this how you're supporting your new wardrobe? Fleecing retirees out of their life's savings by playing on their desperation?"

"Listen to me, you Peeping Tom." Buckley surprised me with a quick step toward me. He got so close the brim of his hat bounced off my forehead. His face burned crimson under the hat. "I'm not pocketin' a red cent above expenses unless we get that boy a new trial."

I took a step back, leaned against the balcony's iron handrail, and looked down at the 1960s pool area. The December sky hung heavy and gray down on the afternoon. The pool was empty except for a lone, swim-capped geriatric pushing through the winter chill.

I'd never seen Buckley in court, but if he could fake the sincerity he'd just shown me, I wanted him on my side. And, if he couldn't fake it, I wanted him on my side too.

"All right, Buckley." I turned from the pool to face him. "I apologize for questioning your motives. Just tell me you have more than a small-time hood bragging about what a big man he is."

"He ain't a small-time hood. The convictions were plea deals." Buckley's color faded back to its normal ash gray. "He's a capo with the Raptors, by the name of Steven Lunsdorf."

I'd never heard of Lunsdorf, but I had the Raptors. They were a violent biker gang that trafficked in drugs, extortion, and murder for hire. The case suddenly got interesting.

"You got anything else?"

"The witness claims the suspect told him where he hid the murder weapon."

"Did you check it out?"

"Not yet." Buckley scratched his beard. "I don't know enough about the witness yet to show the police my hand."

"Give me the file, and I'll run a background check on the witness, then pay him a visit."

Buckley smiled, but I held up my hand. "If I don't believe the wit's story, I reserve the right to back out. I'll understand if you and the Eddingtons can't live with that and walk away now."

"I'll explain the situation to Jack and Rita Mae later. Let them enjoy the moment right now. They haven't had much to enjoy for a long time."

Back inside the condo, I shook Jack Eddington's hand, accepted Rita Mae's hug, and grabbed the last chocolate chip cookie off the plate before I left.

CHAPTER FIVE

When I left the Eddingtons, Buckley gave me a file with the affidavit from the supposed witness, Trey Fellows, along with what he had on Steven Lundsorf, the supposed confessor. During my short time in the Santa Barbara Police Department, I found that most witnesses of street-level crimes weren't Boy Scouts themselves. I needed to run a background check on the wit before I interviewed him to find out where he scored on the "upright citizen" scale.

The sun had finally burned through the gray and pushed Southern California's version of winter into the background. The La Jolla Investigations building shimmered like a bronze mirage. I pulled down into the underground parking lot. There were a few luxury sedans and high-end sports cars that belonged to lawyers from the firm on the third floor, like there were every weekend, but no sign of Bob Reitzmeyer's BMW.

I took the stairs up to the ground floor, used my key card to get into the LJI offices, and walked to my cubicle. I turned on the computer, accessed a national criminal database check, and found one drug possession bust for Trey Fellows. Nothing else.

I did some digging around on a people-finding website and discovered Fellows had a sister who lived in Ocean Beach, just a few miles from his Pacific Beach home. His parents lived out of town.

The file Buckley had given me also had the police report for the Eddington murders. I'd planned to read it at home, but when I'd tossed the witness information back into the folder I noticed the corner of a photograph that had been jostled out from under the police report.

Dark red. Blood.

I hadn't expected murder-scene photos. Buckley was thorough. Maybe too thorough. I hadn't been one of those cops who thrilled to the sight of blood. But it pulled at me now. Daring me to look at the wrath of evil. I pulled the photo out and looked at it. My breath caught in my throat. A man, or what once was, lay crumpled on a bed. The left side of his head crushed in like a Halloween Jack-o'-lantern dropped from the second floor. A crown of red-black blood stained the pillow underneath. Across from the man, another blood-streaked pillow and a bare foot propped up above the foot of the bed.

The next photo was of a woman facedown on the floor, her leg extended up against the bed like she'd tried to escape but hadn't made it. Her head, hair matted with blood, had been beaten, but not crushed into a grotesque mask like the man's. At least not the back of it.

There were two photos of the daughter, Molly Eddington. The first was of her completely under the sheets on her bed. No sign of blood. In the next one, the sheets had been pulled back. Molly, on her side, looked peacefully asleep, except for the bloodstain pooled under the left side of her face.

There were other photos of the horrific scene. I scanned them quickly. The photos told the story that the report no doubt verified. The man, Thomas Eddington, had been killed first. Next, his wife, Alana Eddington. Probably awakened by the sickening sound of the first few blows to her husband's head. Without reading the forensics, I'd guess that after killing Alana, the killer went back to Thomas and beat his head into inhuman gore.

Rage. Hatred. Personal.

Photos showed blood spray along the wall next to the door of the master bedroom.

Molly.

She'd been awakened by the murders and had come to the sound. The killer killed her and took her back to her bedroom, then covered her up because he couldn't look at what he'd done. Again, personal. But this time, regret. Shame. The killer most likely knew the victim.

Family.

Randall.

I'd only seen the crime-scene photographs and already the evidence all pointed to him. The police report would connect the dots. Randall Eddington had murdered his family. I doubted an eight-year, after-the-fact hearsay confession would be enough to convince me otherwise.

Suddenly, I felt a presence behind me.

"I thought you were on vacation."

I startled. The photos had creeped me out and now a lone voice in the empty building. I swiveled my chair and saw Bob Reitzmeyer.

"Sort of," I said. He didn't acknowledge me, his eyes pinned to the photos on my desk.

"The Eddington murders." It wasn't a question.

"Yeah." I turned back to the desk and shuffled the photos back into the folder.

"What are you doing with those?"

"I...ah." I stuffed the folder into my backpack and stared at my desk.

"That's what you're working on?" Up a couple octaves from his normal tenor. "Some slimy lawyer is trying to get that psychopath a new trial?"

Buckley's warning about Police Chief Moretti and Bob's relationship with LJPD pinballed in my head. Discussing the specifics about a case to anyone but the client and the agency was a fireable offense here at La Jolla Investigations. Now Bob was asking me to breach that ethic.

I continued to stare at the desk.

"Rick, I understand you wanting to branch out from infidelity surveillance." Calm. Fatherly. Arms folded across his chest. "But this isn't the way to do it. That kid murdered his family. Butchered them. There's no doubt."

"This was eight years ago. I thought you'd already retired." I stood up, hoping to exit the office and the conversation soon.

"No. I was still on the force."

"Did you work the murder?" Now I wished I had already read the police report.

Bob's eyes drifted over my shoulder, lost in thought. Then, "No, but that doesn't make the kid any less guilty. You read the report yet?"

"No."

"Do yourself a favor." He put a hand on my shoulder. "Read the report and then decide if you want to try and help get that monster out of prison."

I was way ahead of him. "Okay."

"Let me tell you a little story that's not in the report." He sat down in the chair in the next cubicle and motioned me to sit. "Three months before the murders, Thomas Eddington called me to investigate a series of thefts at his house. He said he thought the nanny had been stealing jewelry and cash. He didn't want her arrested, so he asked me to investigate off the record."

"Was he a friend of yours?" I doubted "off the record" was part of Bob's MO as a cop. Although, it had been mine. And, apparently, my father's.

"I used to play in the Eddington charity golf tournament that he sponsored for LJPD every year at La Jolla Country Club. I got to know him a little. We weren't buddies, but he invited me to play golf a few times outside the tournament."

Charity golf tournament. LJPD must have loved Thomas Eddington. And been eager to catch his killer right away. "Did you catch the thief?"

"Yes and no." Bob leaned toward me in his seat, like what he was about to tell me was a secret. "I knew the nanny was innocent as soon as I questioned her." I also knew it was an inside job, so I snooped around in Randall's room while he was in school and Thomas was at work. I found a stash of weed and one of his mother's necklaces taped to the underside of a drawer in his dresser."

"Wow." Randall as an innocent victim was looking less and less likely.

"It gets better. I confronted Randall with the evidence when he got home from school." Bob shook his head and let out a breath. "He really came across as dumbfounded and innocent. A nice, polite kid who'd been framed. He said he thought he'd smelled marijuana on the nanny once and that she'd recently been wearing nicer clothes."

"Did you believe him?"

"Almost. I was debating whether to re-question the nanny when I decided to use an old interrogation trick. I lied and told him I'd fingerprinted the necklace and baggie of weed and that his were the only prints on them."

"He fell for it?"

"Not right away. That kid was smarter than ninety-nine percent of crooks I'd questioned in the box. He said he'd never been arrested, so LJPD couldn't have a record of his fingerprints. But I told him that we'd matched them to prints we'd found in his bedroom and on his golf clubs. He wasn't smart enough, yet, to ask why there wasn't print powder all over his room."

"Did he confess then?"

"He never confessed. But his whole persona changed. I swear, his eyes went from brown to black, and he became very confrontational. He was a big kid and I thought it might get physical. I was glad I had a gun."

"How did Thomas Eddington react when you gave him the news?"

"That was the thing." Bob stood up. "He didn't react at all. He thanked me, and that was it. I had the feeling he'd asked me to question the nanny to verify what he already knew. That his son was the thief. Three weeks later, everyone but Randall was dead."

"Did you testify at the trial?"

"No. The judge ruled the incident inadmissible, but the DA didn't need it anyway. The jury got it right. Read the report, Bullet. Then take a real vacation. You deserve one."

I left LJI convinced my vacation wouldn't involve helping get a convicted killer a new trial.

CHAPTER SIX

Midnight greeted me at the front door. I gave him a Milk-Bone and let him outside. I watched him through the sliding glass door. He cantered around the backyard sniffing the ground, the air, the bushes. He knew how to enjoy the little things in life. I should have taken notes.

I went upstairs to my office and put the police report on my desk. A photograph on the corner of the desk caught my eye. It often did. The photo was of Colleen and me on the Rubicon Trail above Lake Tahoe. I'd set my camera on a tripod and we'd taken a selfie years before they became ubiquitous via smartphones. The lake glistened behind us, the translucent blue matched in Colleen's eyes. Her smile, open, inviting, joyful.

Some days, the picture made me happy. Some days, sad. Today, sad. The light in Colleen's eyes that would never shine again. The horrific photos in the police file on my desk. Sad reminders that death takes us all. And that evil is ever ready to slaughter innocent life to satisfy its desires.

I opened the file and read about evil unleashed.

The report began with a call to 911 from a neighbor, Ruth Costa, who had heard the Eddingtons' dog howling for over half an hour and went to investigate at 12:15 a.m. The neighbor often dog sat when the Eddingtons were away, so she had a key. After knocking on the door and ringing the doorbell, she used her key to enter the house, and found the dog with blood on its paws. There were bloody paw prints in the foyer and the living room, which was as much as she could see. She checked the dog's paws and couldn't find a cut. She then called out to Alana and Thomas

Eddington and got no response. She called 911. Two uniforms arrived ten minutes later and discovered the bodies as shown in the gruesome photos I'd looked at.

Detective Hailey West was the first detective to arrive and managed the crime scene until Detective Moretti arrived at 12:35 a.m. The FSU—Field Services Unit—arrived at 12:40 a.m. and photographed the crime scene and the bodies in situ.

The coroner arrived at 12:50 a.m. and rolled the bodies, then took their liver temperatures. The coroner determined the times of death to be between 10:00 p.m. and 12:00 a.m.

Moretti's partner, Detective Dan Coyote, arrived at 12:55 a.m. Dan had been a sometime golf buddy before I got tangled up in an LJPD murder investigation two years ago. He quit the force after LJPD put a happy face on the fiasco. Moretti went on to become chief of police. Dan and I hadn't talked since.

Moretti had Coyote question the neighbor, Ruth Costa, and other people in the neighborhood. Moretti acquired telephonic search warrants to search the house, cars, and front and back yards. The neighbor gave Coyote the names of the Eddington family members, and at that time the detectives discovered that Randall was the only one missing.

The coroner released the scene at 1:40 a.m. and transported the bodies to the coroner's office.

The forensic specialists from FSU collected and cataloged DNA and fingerprint evidence.

Moretti searched the inside of the house. No murder weapon was found. However, the master bedroom had been staged to look like a burglary had taken place. Clothes were strewn about and all the drawers of the dressers had been pulled open. The dressers were the key to the staging. No one starts from the bottom drawer to search a dresser. You search the top drawer first, then close it and start on the next one down. The second drawer can't be searched if the top drawer is open. The only drawer that would be left open is the bottom one.

Bleach residue was found in the drain of the shower in the

master bath. This suggested that the killer took a shower to wash off blood and then dumped bleach down the drain to destroy possible DNA evidence.

Detective West searched the two Eddington cars in the garage, the garage itself, and the front and back yards with the help of a uniformed patrolman. She didn't find the murder weapon or any incriminating evidence. However, she discovered that the sand wedge was missing from Thomas Eddington's golf bag in the trunk of his car.

Although the murder weapon was never found, the medical examiner later determined that the wounds to the victims were consistent with those made by a sand wedge.

Randall Eddington arrived at the crime scene at 2:00 a.m. He became agitated when he was prevented from entering the house by uniformed patrolmen. Detectives Coyote and West helped calm him down and suggested they get away from the house and go to the police station where they could talk. They drove Randall to the police station at 2:15 a.m.

Coyote questioned Randall about his whereabouts for the night. Randall said he had dinner with his family around 7:00 p.m., watched some TV, and then went alone to see the 10:00 p.m. showing of *Spider-Man 3* at the La Jolla Village Cinemas. He produced an electronic ticket stub time-stamped as being purchased at 9:41 p.m. Randall said he stayed for the whole movie, getting popcorn and a soda about half way through, and left the theater around 12:30 a.m. He then went to a party at La Jolla Shores until around 1:45 a.m., then went home. Randall was not charged and was picked up by his grandparents at 4:15 a.m.

Detective Moretti attained a telephonic search warrant for Randall's car, which Randall had driven to the scene at 2:00 a.m. and left there when he went with Detectives West and Coyote to the police station at 2:15 a.m. Detective West, who had returned to the crime scene from the police station, searched the car and discovered a sock that had what appeared to be blood on it. The sock was later tested, and blood from both Thomas and Alana Eddington was found on it along with Randall's DNA.

Later that morning, Coyote checked with the crew that worked at the movie theater the night before and showed them a photo of Randall. The girl working refreshments remembered Randall from the picture and verified his story that he'd bought a Coke and popcorn sometime around 11:00 p.m.

However, Coyote learned that the *Spider-Man 3* projector had malfunctioned at 11:15 p.m., and the showing was delayed about fifteen minutes until the projector was fixed. The movie ended about 12:45 a.m., fifteen minutes later than when Randall said it had.

Coyote went over to Randall's grandparents' house and again asked Randall what time he left the theater. He, again, said 12:30 a.m. Coyote then asked him if anything unusual happened during the movie and Randall said "no."

Moretti and Coyote arrested Randall six weeks later when the lab results came back for the blood on the sock found in his car.

The trial only took a month, the jury, a day. Guilty. I couldn't find anything in the report that made me question the verdict. Of course, the police report was only one side of the story. The jury had heard both sides and made their decision.

Now, I'd made mine.

I'd eaten an entire plate of Rita Mae Eddington's chocolate chip cookies on false pretenses. I couldn't try to free her grandson from prison when I thought he was a murderer. New third party confession or not.

I pulled out my phone to call Buckley and give him the bad news. Then I'd remembered I'd promised to talk to the witness before I decided whether or not to take the case. I doubted the wit could change my mind, but it was the least I could do for Rita Mae Eddington after eating all those cookies.

CHAPTER SEVEN

Midnight barked from the backyard. Someone hard-knocked my front door. I went to the door and checked the peephole. I saw the top of a woman's head and opened the door.

"Rick Cahill?" Her voice sounded like pocket change rattling around in a clothes dryer. Loud. Jarring. Unexpected.

She couldn't have been taller than five feet or weighed more than ninety pounds. Brown eyes the size of coasters took up most of her face. Lips took up the rest. Auburn hair in a bob cut. Late thirties, early forties, but wearing it easy. Everything fit together. Not pretty, but attractive. She wore jeans and a gray sweater.

"Yes." I expected her to shove a piece of paper at me and tell me I'd been served.

"Why do you have to be such an asshole?"

Not the first time I'd been asked that question. But never upon meeting someone for the first time.

"If I knew who you were, I might have an answer for you."

"You cost me a job!"

"I don't know what the hell you're talking about." I'd dealt with crazy before. Sometimes I played along. Sometimes I called it out. Either way, I'd yet to come home and find Glenn Close waiting for me with a knife in my bathtub, so my reads had been good so far. I needed braille to read this one.

"The Cowboy Lawyer hired me and then fired me because you wanted to play Hamlet."

Oh. Not crazy. Just pissed off. And rightly so.

"Buckley didn't tell me he'd already hired someone else. Sorry."

"I passed on another job to take the Eddington case." Her Betty Boop eyes narrowed in accusation. "Now, I don't have either."

"You may be in luck. I'm still playing Hamlet." I opened the door wide. "You want to come in or just yell at me on my porch?"

She tilted her head and half-eyed me, then walked into the house.

"You want a beer?"

"I guess I could have a beer since I don't have a job anymore." This was going well.

I grabbed two Ballast Point IPAs from the fridge. Maybe alcohol would help defuse the burning stick of dynamite standing in front of me.

"You got a name?" I handed the woman a beer.

"Moira MacFarlane." She didn't stick out a hand or give me a smile. I swept a hand to the sofa in the living room. She sat down. She had to point the toes of her boots down to reach the floor. "You said something about Hamlet and me being in luck."

"I think I'm opting for 'not to be.'"

"You really are Hamlet. First you say 'no,' then you say 'yes,' now you say 'no.'" Moira smiled for the first time and shook her head. "You're worse than a woman."

"You read the police report?"

"No."

"The kid did it."

"Of course he did." She flattened a smile and shrugged her shoulders. "You're opting out because the client's guilty?"

"I draw the line at murder."

"If I pulled down six figures at La Jolla Investigations, I might draw the same line. But I can't afford to be so picky." She took a swig of beer and looked at me without blinking for so long that I thought we were playing a game of blink. Finally, "A lot of people in this town think you draw the line right after murder."

"Is that what you think?" A harder edge in my voice than I expected. "That I murdered my wife?"

"It doesn't matter what I think."

"You're right." I stood up. "It doesn't."

"But I don't think you did." Moira remained seated.

"Either way, now we're even." I remained standing.

"No." She set her beer down on the coffee table and finally stood up. "That was inappropriate. I let the job thing get the better of me. That wasn't fair. You didn't do anything wrong."

Her Kewpie Doll face dropped and she headed for the front door.

"You insult me and then leave behind a half-empty beer?"

She turned around.

"Sit down and finish your beer, and I'll see if I can get you back your job."

Moira went back to the couch and sat down. "I'm all ears."

More like all eyes.

"I owe Buckley and the family an interview with a witness. Anything short of a video showing someone else murdering the Eddington family, I'm off the case."

"Funny you should mention a video."

"Why?"

"The Eddington clan is an interesting group." She hit her beer and leaned toward me. "I'm going to tell you a little story because you're not the asshole I thought you were."

"I'm a different kind of asshole."

"Exactly."

She held up her beer bottle and waved it. I went to the fridge and got her another. A hint of pink had slid under her olive skin. She seemed a bit buzzed. Maybe that's all it took when you weighed ninety pounds.

I sat down on the recliner. "Give me your story."

"About six months before he died, Thomas Eddington hired me to tail his father for about a week."

"Jack?" She had me. "Why?"

"Thomas didn't tell me. The gig was to just follow the old man and report back daily." She took a swig of beer and smiled at me. A nice smile. "Turns out Jack liked the ponies. Every day after he left the Eddington Golf warehouse in Carlsbad, he'd drive south to the racetrack in Del Mar."

"How did he do?"

"Never saw him leave the track happy." Another swig. Another smile. "One day, I'm following the old man after he leaves the warehouse, and he goes north on I-5 instead of south to the racetrack or his home in La Jolla. I tail him all the way up to a golf store in LA's Koreatown. He parks around back and starts unloading long thin boxes from his SUV to a Korean guy."

"I'm guessing Jack Eddington didn't drive ninety miles to LA to make a delivery for Eddington Golf."

"Guessed right. The Korean guy didn't even put the clubs in the store. He put them in his own SUV. Then he handed Jack a thick envelope. Got it all on video."

"Cash for clubs, then onto the black market. How did Thomas take the news?"

"I showed him the video and his expression never changed. Wrote me the biggest check I'd ever earned and showed me the door. A month later, I saw a story in the paper that Jack Eddington had retired as CEO of Eddington Golf and that Thomas had taken over. Five months later, Thomas and his wife and daughter were dead."

"Did you tell LJPD after the family was murdered?"

"Yeah, but they had their narrative and evidence." Another gulp of beer. A goofy smile. "Anyway, the kid did it."

"You tell all of this to Buckley?"

"Hell no! Jack Eddington is bankrolling the investigation." A burp, then a giggle.

This put a new spin on the ball, but not enough for me to jump on the "Free Randall" bandwagon. Maybe Trey Fellows could give me another nudge.

CHAPTER EIGHT

Trey Fellows lived in Pacific Beach. PB, La Jolla's slacker little brother to the south, was a sandy strip of beach dotted with dive bars and panhandlers. Everybody was laid-back until after midnight or the sixth beer. The bums sometimes carried eight-inch butcher knives under their Goodwill camo jackets.

Fellows lived in a cottage behind a house two streets south of Garnet, the main drag. A beach cruiser bicycle was chained to a fence on the left side of the front patio. I hadn't called for an appointment. I wanted to get Fellows' story unrehearsed. It was ten a.m. on a Sunday, but the heavy skunk smell of marijuana smoke seeped through the doorframe.

I knocked on the door and it opened in a puff of smoke. A tall, wiry man appeared when the haze cleared. He wore faded board shorts, flip-flops, and nothing else except a smattering of tattoos on his chest and shoulders. Red rings around blue eyes on a long face. A tangle of mud-blond dreadlocks fell down past his shoulders. Fine, if you're a musician in a reggae band or a third-year philosophy student. Not so much if you're a thirty-eight-year-old white dude. But, hey, this was PB. Maybe I was the one who looked out of place.

"This is medical, bro." He held a two-foot-long glass bong in his hand with a wisp of smoke still trailing out its mouth. His words came out in the lazy cadence of a SoCal surf dude. "I got a doctor's prescription I can show you."

"Do I look like a cop?"

"Yeah."

"Close." I handed him my La Jolla Investigations card with

my cell number scribbled on it. My paper badge. "I'm a private investigator working for the Eddington family. May I come in?"

The glaze burned out of his eyes and he blinked a couple times. Then his eyes rolled up and I worried that he might be having a seizure, but decided he was just thinking. Finally, he swung the door open.

"Yeah. Sure."

The cottage was a fifteen-by-fifteen square-foot room. Tiny kitchen with dishes overflowing the sink. Surfboard in the far corner opposite an unmade bed. Bathroom door next to a hall closet in a home without a hall. Hardwood floor under discarded clothes. Coffee table with a baggie of weed, a lighter, and some surfing magazines. A lone picture of a suntanned couple in their thirties hung on the wall. The musk of marijuana bud and smoke hung in the air like Elizabethan curtains.

Fellows grabbed a wet suit off a frayed green loveseat and tossed it onto the bed. I sat down, and he did the same onto a duct-taped leather recliner that didn't match the loveseat. He pinched a tiny bit of weed from a large bud in the baggie, stuffed it into the bong's glass bowl, brought the open end to his mouth, and lit the marijuana with a Bic lighter. The water in the bong gurgled and smoke filled the cylinder until Fellows pulled off the bowl and vacuumed up the smoke. He held his breath as long as he could before a cough spat smoke out of his mouth.

"You know, that stuff can hurt your memory."

Not to mention your ambition and IQ. I spoke from experience. After my wife was murdered and I quit the force in Santa Barbara, I tried anything I could get my hands on to help me forget. The ambition went, but the memories stayed.

"I got a bad back, bro. Helps the pain." He set the bong down onto the coffee table and averted his bloodshot eyes.

If this was the magic witness the Eddingtons hoped could free their grandson from prison, their dream was burning up in a puff of marijuana smoke, and my vacation started tomorrow.

"What do you do for a living, Mr. Fellows?" Brain surgery was out, but I hoped that he at least had a job.

"I've been on disability for six months."

Perfect. This guy would come across as credibly as a politician at a fundraiser. I guessed his back only hurt when he worked but not when he surfed. A couple of hits off the bong and he was as good as new.

"Where did you used to work?"

"UPS shipping center in Kearney Mesa." He put a hand on his lower back and Method-acted a wince. "Until my back went out."

"I understand that you contacted Jack and Rita Mae Eddington with information that you think could help free their grandson from prison."

"Yeah." His eyes hit mine, then moved down to the left. "I heard someone brag about murdering the family and getting away with it."

"Steven Lunsdorf?"

"Yeah."

"Where and when did you hear this?"

"The Chalked Cue in Clairemont last Monday night."

The Chalked Cue was a dive bar known to attract bikers. That seemed like rough trade for this wannabe Rastafarian to hang out with.

"Is Lunsdorf a friend of yours?"

"More like an acquaintance."

"And he just blurted out to an acquaintance that he murdered a family eight years back?"

"No." Quick. Defensive. "I guess we're more than acquaintances, but we don't really hang out. I see him at The Chalked Cue sometimes. Anyway, we were shootin' pool and he was pretty drunk. There was a show on TV about some kid in the Carolinas murdering his family. Steven said those family murders don't always go down the way they say they do on TV."

"That's it?"

"No." He reached a hand out to reload the bong. "He said it

could have been just like that Eddington family eight years ago that the son got blamed for. Maybe someone else did it. Someone like him."

"And you believed him?"

"Not right away." He hit the bong again and blew out a skunk cloud. "I said, 'Sure, bro, whatever you say.' Then he got mad and told me he could take me to the hillside behind the house and show me where he buried the golf club he used to beat the family to death."

"Did you take him up on it?"

"No, man." He set the bong back down. "I was kinda freaked out. Steven's a member of the Raptors, and I didn't want to be down some hill with him when he dug up the murder weapon and decided I knew too much."

The Raptors were white supremacists born out of the California prison system who sometimes partnered with the Aryan Brotherhood. If Fellows was telling the truth, I can't say I blamed him. The Raptors were armed and usually skittering on meth. A volatile cocktail.

"So you expect the Eddingtons to hire somebody to dig up the hillside behind their late son's house until they stumble upon the murder weapon?"

"No. I think I know where it is. Steven kept rambling on all night about it. He told me it's buried under a cactus fifty yards below the house."

"Did anyone else hear the story who can corroborate it?"

"I don't think so." His eyes skirted from the curtained window to the door, like he was expecting someone to peek through or walk in. "We were at the back table by ourselves."

Convenient.

"You said he was drunk. How drunk were you?"

He hesitated. Probably gauging his believability if he copped to being smashed. "I wasn't drunk. I'd only had a couple beers."

"While he was rambling on, did he tell you why he murdered a family of perfect strangers with no apparent motive?"

The crime scene had been staged like a burglary, but the police never bought it.

"He said it was a job. Nothing personal, but he wished the little girl hadn't walked in when he was doing the parents. He felt bad about killing her."

Hit man with a heart of gold.

"What do you get out of all this, Trey? There was no reward offered for information on the crime. This thing had been put away cold for eight years until you called the Eddingtons with your little story."

"It's not a story! It's the truth!" His red eyes got big. "Why you giving me a hard time when I'm just trying to do the right thing?"

"So, you're just a Good Samaritan with nothing to gain."

"Just because I smoke pot and don't work, doesn't mean I don't care about people. I felt sorry for the kid and the grandparents."

A stoner with a heart of gold. I'd put him up on the pedestal right next to the gold-hearted hit man. Maybe two years of peeking at people betraying their spouses and their vows before God had made me cynical. Or maybe it was just a lifetime of questioning my own motives, but I doubted Fellows' heart was anything denser than gold leaf. However, right now, I was just there to collect the story.

"So, after eight years, the Eddington case was fresh enough in your mind to remember the kid and the grandparents?" I asked.

"I followed it every day on the news. Something like that doesn't happen every day around here. Especially in La Jolla."

"If it comes down to it, you'll testify in court about everything you just told me?" The Raptors might have a say in it if they got the chance.

He eyed the picture of the couple on the wall and took a deep breath, then let it out slowly. This time, no smoke came out. Just a whiff of fear. He finally looked at me and nodded his head. "If it comes down to it."

CHAPTER NINE

Buckley met me at his office in La Jolla in the late afternoon. He sat with his cowboy boots propped up on the desk next to a bottle of Maker's Mark bourbon, staring out the window at the Pacific Ocean half a mile away. He could only glimpse a thin strip of blue above hotels and restaurants that hugged the coast. Still, it must beat the view he had of boarded-up businesses back when he worked in southeast San Diego.

I sat opposite his desk in a leather chair angled so I could enjoy the view too. Buckley nodded at the Maker's Mark. I shook my head. Early for me. Not for Buckley. I'd just given him a verbal report about my interview with Trey Fellows.

"So much for the nuts and bolts, Rick." He dropped his boots to the floor and leaned toward me. "What's your gut tell you? Is this guy legit?"

That was the question I debated with myself on the ten-minute drive from Fellows' house to Buckley's office. "Legit might be a strong term for a guy who smokes his disability money through a bong when he's not surfing."

"This isn't a worker's comp fraud case." Buckley studied me with worn gray eyes under a beige Stetson. "So he's on the dole. Doesn't make him much different than a lot of folks these days. I need your gut on the story. Does it pass the stink test?"

"On the surface." The debate from the drive over still churned in my head. "I would have to try and find someone to corroborate that he and Lunsdorf played pool at The Chalked Cue last Monday night. But the story mostly plays. It has a lot of details that ring true."

"Mostly plays." He took off his hat and his ponytail tumbled down his neck. The hat left an imprint across his pale forehead. "What's leaving a hole in your belly? You look like you got a cow in the squeeze chute but can't find your branding iron."

"I'll pretend I know what that means, Buckley." I looked out at the line of blue below the orange horizon. "The story seemed a little practiced—"

"That's to be expected. He told his story to the Eddingtons, to me, and now you. People like to get the facts together in a nice neat row. I've seen it hundreds of times with witnesses. It's human nature."

"I know, but Fellows doesn't come across as a hero or a glory seeker. It takes a lot of courage to accuse a Raptor of anything, much less murder. And if you actually get a new trial, it will blow up in the media 24/7. I don't think Fellows would welcome that kind of scrutiny."

"Scrutiny equals celebrity. Every swinging dick and dickette under the age of forty can't wait for their Warhol fifteen minutes." He closed his eyes, pursed his lips, then looked back at me. "Sorry, Rick. Didn't mean any harm. I know you got more time under the hot lights than any man deserves. Even a guilty one."

The last breath of fire from the sun snuffed itself out at the edge of the ocean.

"No worries, Buckley. I don't even think about the past anymore," I lied.

"Good work today, son." Buckley put his hat back on. "You got good instincts, an active mind. I know the money at La Jolla Investigations is better than anywhere else, but you're wasting your talent snooping on strangers playing mattress rodeo. 'Bout time Bob Reitzmeyer figured that out."

He was right, but that was between Bob and me. I'd never publicly criticize the only cop who showed up at my father's funeral. I also had the feeling that Buckley had laid it on a bit thick to give me an extra nudge to stay on the case.

"I'm still not a hundred percent."

"Life rarely gives you a hundred percent of anything, son." Buckley's red-rimmed eyes zeroed in on mine. "What's it gonna take to get you to ninety percent?"

"I want to meet Randall."

Buckley scratched his beard and raised his eyes to the ceiling. Finally, "I guess we could make a trip up to San Quentin and talk to Randall."

"I'll go alone."

"Oh?"

"Nothing personal, Buckley. I want it to just be me and Randall face-to-face between the glass."

"I'll make the arrangements. How soon can you go?"

"I already booked a flight this morning." I stood up. "I fly out on Southwest tonight and see Randall at eight tomorrow morning."

* * *

The flight from San Diego to San Francisco took about an hour and a half gate to gate. Less than an hour in the air. Not much time to travel 500 miles. Plenty of time to unlock painful memories.

San Francisco used to be one of my favorite cities. Not anymore. Not for a long time. My late wife, Colleen, had grown up in Mill Valley in Marin County, just a short drive over the Golden Gate Bridge from San Francisco. The last time I'd been up there had been for her memorial service ten years ago. I'd just been released from jail in Santa Barbara after being arrested for Colleen's murder. The DA had dropped the charges. Not because he thought I was innocent, but because he didn't think he could get a conviction.

Colleen's father had tried to use his local influence and giant wallet to keep me from attending the service. It hadn't been enough. He would have had to kill me to keep me from being there. An idea he'd no doubt explored.

The Episcopal Church that Colleen had attended as a kid was filled past standing room only. People stood shoulder-to-shoulder along both outer aisles. A murmur trickled through those standing near the door when I entered the church. The murmur built to a vibrating hum, and heads snapped toward me as I weaved through the crowd to the front of the church.

Colleen's family took up the first few pews. No one had saved me a seat. I stood next to the first pew at the front of the crowd. Colleen's parents, brother, sister, and grandparents sat directly to my left. No one jostled over to squeeze me in.

John Kerrigan stared hatred at me. Pure, malevolent, visceral. In his mind, I'd murdered his daughter, and now had come to desecrate her memory. I held his stare and took it. Let him bore his anger, hatred, and pain into me. It was the only thing I'd ever be able to do for him and his family.

Colleen's younger sister, Christy, now seventeen, sat next to John. Beautiful, with Colleen's blue eyes and blond hair. She'd always been a tagalong whenever Colleen and I visited her family. Colleen had called her my biggest fan, always taking my side whenever John Kerrigan spoke ill of me. I gave her a slight nod.

Christy looked at me with her father's eyes. Hatred. And betrayal. I could take her father's venom, but not hers. He'd never liked me. His daughter's death, the sad outcome of my unworthiness, low character, and now, depravity. I turned away. The air sucked out of me, leaving me empty. Of everything.

Again.

The minister came to the pulpit. Behind him were blown-up photos of Colleen. As a child, a teenager, a woman. The last one of her had been the one taken on the Rubicon Trail above Lake Tahoe. The impossible cobalt blue of the lake lifting the azure blue of Colleen's eyes. The photo I now kept on my desk at home. My favorite picture of us together.

In the blown-up photo on the easel in the church, I'd been cut out.

The minister prayed and quoted the Bible. Then John, Christy, and a handful of childhood friends solemnly trudged to the pulpit, one after another, and told remembrances and stories about Colleen. No one asked me to speak, and I didn't volunteer.

I stood and cried silently, swallowing the wails that erupted from me when I mourned alone. No one offered me a kind word or a pat on the shoulder.

I was the reason everyone had to suffer through the day. The Santa Barbara Police Department had released me, but refused to clear me. I was the murderer who'd gotten away with it. I had taken Colleen away from all of them and then had forced them to feel my presence. Forever tainting their memories of Colleen.

Per her wishes, Colleen had been cremated. I let her family have half her ashes. Later, in a private ceremony, they spread them in Carmel Bay, a couple hours south of San Francisco. I did the same a few days later. Alone. We'd gone to Carmel on our honeymoon, Colleen's favorite vacation spot as a child. It became mine too. The most beautiful stretch of scenery along the California coast. Now it had become a cemetery. The forever resting place of a lost life.

* * *

The night before my meet with Randall Eddington, I stayed in a high-rise hotel in Union Square. Far fewer panhandlers than Market Street, but close enough to the Tenderloin to keep an edge on. I walked through Chinatown with its red and gold banners to Columbus Avenue and its Italian flags in North Beach. I had dinner in a hole-in-the-wall joint that had a great spaghetti carbonara and a view of the street. And the restaurant across it where Colleen and I used to eat when we visited the city.

I could have picked a different restaurant. I could have walked to a different part of town. I could have forced myself to go to the place across the street.

I ate my pasta, stared out the window, watched, and remembered from afar.

CHAPTER TEN

San Quentin State Prison sat on the choicest piece of real estate in the world that ever held a prison, unless there was one on the French Riviera. Even then, it would have been a toss-up. The prison was on twenty-two acres of land on the shoreline of North Bay. The inmates would have had a hell of a view if not for the high walls, razor wire, and sniper towers.

Randall Eddington was no longer the doughy kid in his grandparents' photo album. The dough had turned to iron, and the intelligent eyes of a nerdy kid, still framed by black horn-rimmed glasses, had hollowed out into the thousand-yard stare of a grown man doing life. But prison would change anybody. Even a murderer.

I sat down opposite Randall, safe on the other side of the glass, but still locked behind prison walls. I'd walk out a free man. Whether I'd try to help Randall do the same depended upon the thirty minutes we'd spend together.

I picked up the handset to the phone that connected us through the glass. "Hello, Randall."

"Mr. Cahill." He held the phone to his mouth and looked me straight in the eyes. The thousand-yard stare slowly dissolved.

"You know why I'm here?"

"I know Mr. Buckley and my grandparents hired you to help with the effort to get me a new trial." He held my stare. "But I think you're here to find out whether or not I killed my family."

"Did you?"

"No." Direct. No challenge or fake outrage. He kept the eye contact, didn't blink.

"Why do you think you're here?"

"Because I let my lawyer convince me not to testify, and Detective West planted the sock with the blood on it in my car."

Randall didn't look, sound, or act like a criminal. He sat upright in his chair instead of the nonchalant slump and spread-legged posture of a thug. His words clear and grammatical instead of slangy and laced with F-bombs. His eyes direct without the malice or challenge of a streetwise punk. It could have been residue from his wealthy upbringing. It could have been a con to look good for the PI who might help set him free. Or, it could have been who he was.

"I don't understand why you didn't testify when the prosecution had such a strong case. The blood on the sock with your DNA and the projector breaking at the movie did you in." I leaned back in my chair. "I can't get past that."

"I wouldn't either if I was on the outside looking in." He shook his head and then zeroed his eyes back on mine. "Did you see photos of the inside of my car at the crime scene?"

"No. Why?"

"I've been a neat freak my whole life. Ask anyone who knows me. My car was immaculate. If I'd killed my family and dropped a bloody sock in my car, I'd have seen it and disposed of it."

"It was under the seat."

"Was there anything else under there?"

"I don't know."

"There wasn't. No trash, ever, in my car. Nothing, ever, under a seat. I was neurotic about cleanliness. I still am. Even here."

"I was a cop, Randall. You'll have a hard time convincing me that a detective is going to risk jail time to frame an innocent man."

"They didn't think I was innocent. They were convinced I was guilty right away, but knew they didn't have evidence to prove it." The first emotion he'd shown rolled through his voice. A plea. "Why did Detective West listen to my interview at the police station and then go back to the house and be the one who searched my car and find the evidence?" He air-quoted the word "evidence." "She was the detective who first managed the crime scene until she turned it over to Detective Moretti. She had access to the bathroom hamper where I always put my dirty clothes and she had access to the crime scene."

"She would have had to get the sock from the hamper and plant blood on it even before you arrived on the scene, meaning she pegged you for the murderer before anyone even collected evidence."

"I don't expect you to believe me." This time he didn't hold my stare. His eyes fell, but it didn't read as deception. It read despair and resignation. "I don't know when she did it or why she did it or if she did it alone. All I know is the sock was planted."

"Okay." I leaned forward and rested my elbows on the wooden shelf below the glass, two feet from Randall's face. "What about the blown alibi at the movie theater? The jury didn't buy your lawyer's story in closing arguments that you fell asleep in the movie and slept through the broken projector interruption. Especially after you had just bought a Coke and popcorn from the snack bar."

"That's not what happened." Randall wouldn't raise his eyes to meet mine. "My lawyer convinced me not to testify after I told him what really happened."

"And that was?" I had gone from a one percent chance that Randall was innocent before I arrived at the prison to close to fifty after listening to him and watching him. Now my belief bottomed out again.

"I...I used to have a thing for Kirsten Dunst." Eyes still pinned to the floor, he ran his free hand over a tight prison buzz cut of black hair. "I was a dorky eighteen-year-old with hormones raging who'd never been with a girl."

If Randall's freedom hadn't been on the line, I would have asked him to stop talking right there.

"I saw her in the movie and she kind of got my motor running." His pale prison face glowed pink. "So I...I...went into the bathroom..."

"And jerked off."

"Yeah." He wouldn't look at me.

Whether the story was true or not, I now understood why Randall's lawyer didn't put him on the stand. Sexual pervert. Lack of impulse control. Risky behavior. Not the qualities you wanted to showcase when the defendant was on trial for a rage murder. Still, something didn't ring true.

"When I was eighteen and in the pole position, it didn't take me fifteen minutes to finish the race."

"I'm glad you can make a joke with my freedom on the line." Randall finally looked at me and the shame turned to anger. Not homicidal anger, just everyday pissed-off anger.

"You can take offense, but you haven't answered my question. What took so long?"

"I made a mess on my jeans right in the crotch. I washed it off and spent the next twenty or twenty-five minutes trying to dry my jeans with paper towels. I didn't want to walk around looking like I wet my pants."

Better a lack of bladder control than impulse control. But, taken by itself, the story sounded plausible for a hormonally out-of-control eighteen-year-old. Unusual, but not unreasonable.

"LJPD surely tested your clothes from that night for blood. Traces of semen would have shown up under an ultraviolet light. Why isn't it in the police report?"

"They probably left it out because they didn't find blood. The lab report is in the discovery documents. Ask Mr. Buckley."

Even if it was, it didn't mean the semen was from that night. And if the semen was from that night, Randall still could have murdered his family. Yet, an embarrassing story to make up. Randall could have told me he stayed up all night high on cocaine the night before and slept through the movie. At least as plausible as the semen story.

"Why did you tell the police the movie let out at 12:30 a.m., when it was really 12:45 a.m.?" I asked.

"I didn't check my watch. I was in the bathroom during the projector breakdown and didn't know about the delay. I just assumed the movie let out at the normal time."

Back to fifty percent.

"Did you steal jewelry from your mother and money from your father?" One last barrier to hurdle to get Randall above fifty-fifty.

"You mean the night they were murdered?" High eyebrows.

"Anytime."

A long silence that answered the question. I waited to hear if his words matched his silent response.

"I was a pretty horrible kid before my family died. Prison has made me a better person and I'm thankful for that. Ironic." Sad eyes stared past me. "I stole from both of them, but never admitted it. I was supposed to go to Stanford in the fall. Dad told me he wasn't going to pay my tuition and that I had to move out of the house by the end of summer. Told me he was going to dissolve the trust he had set up for me. Pretty simple motive for murder, huh?"

Tears pooled in his eyes.

"Did you kill them, Randall?"

"I wanted my dad dead. I fantasized about it for weeks. But I didn't do it. I could never do that. I wish he and my mom, and Molly—" His voice cracked and tears broke loose when he mentioned his sister's name. "I wish Molly could see the man I am now. I miss her so much."

He set the phone down and put both hands to his face and sobbed. I let him cry. An emotion he could never show outside the visitor room. Finally, he wiped tears from his eyes and picked up the phone. "Sorry. Sometimes it sneaks up on me."

"No need to apologize." Randall was either San Quentin's version of Tom Hanks or he was telling the truth. "How did your father and grandfather get along?"

He wiped his tears away with the sleeve of his blue prison shirt. "Pretty well, except the last year...that my dad was alive."

"What happened to put them at odds?"

"I don't know, but something changed between them. It was sad."

I stood up. "Take care of yourself in here, Randall."

"Where are you going?"

"To find the truth."

CHAPTER ELEVEN

I called Buckley from the airport.

"You still on board, son?" He sounded like it mattered.

"You have the discovery documents from the first trial?"

"I don't have them here. My two first-year associates are going over them at the University of San Diego's law library. Don't have room for everybody at the office. What do you need?"

"Have them check if LJPD found semen on Randall's pants the night of the murders."

"Semen? Why the hell for?"

"I'll explain later." I checked the time on my phone. "My plane doesn't take off for a half hour. Call me when you find out."

I called Bob Reitzmeyer.

His greeting, "Thought you were on vacation."

"Kinda, but I have a question for you." Mostly true if visiting San Quentin could be considered a vacation. "When you investigated the thefts at the Eddington house, did you notice anything unusual about Randall's bedroom?"

"You didn't drop the case?" Annoyed.

"Still making up my mind." If Bob didn't corroborate what Randall had told me, I might go Hamlet one more time. "Was there anything unusual about his room?"

"I'm busy, Rick." Sharp edges. "I don't have time for games. What do you want to know?"

"Was his room messy or neat?"

Silent. Either in thought or letting the steam build. "Neatest room I've ever seen for a teenager. Doesn't mean he didn't slaughter his whole family."

But it was one more nudge to make me believe that maybe he didn't. Unless he had a maid who did all the work, Randall had told me the truth about being a neat freak. Maybe the rest of his story was true too.

"Thanks, Bob."

"The next time you call, it had better be about LJI business." He hung up.

Bob had been short with me before, but never angry. He's always seemed to cut me slack because he'd been my father's partner. The reins felt tight now. And brittle.

My phone rang before I could contemplate what my latest decision may have cost me. Buckley.

"Sure as shootin', there was semen on Randall's pants." A chuckle. "Pardon the pun."

"Thanks, Buckley."

"What does it mean?"

"It means that I'm still on the case." Another call beeped in my ear. "Gotta go."

I hung up and answered a number I didn't recognize.

"Did you talk to the Cowboy Lawyer yet?" A salt gargle of a woman's voice. Moira MacFarlane.

"I'm staying on the case." I doubted she liked sugar coating on bad news. "Sorry."

"You're a bigger asshole than I thought."

"Maybe, but I could use your help tonight. Get you a few hours of work and then maybe more down the line."

"Fuck you, Cahill. I don't need your charity." She hung up.

That went about as expected.

* * *

I pulled out the canvas gun case from under my bed. It had two years of dust on it. I'd never fired the Ruger .357 Magnum inside the case. I'd killed a man with another gun. A man who'd murdered three people and almost made me number four. The man with the dead black eyes staring at nothing forever, who invaded my dreams and robbed me of sleep almost every night. I killed him in my dreams just as I had in real life, but he wouldn't stay dead. He'd rise up and point his gun at me and I'd freeze. He'd pull the trigger and I'd wake up tangled in sweat-soaked sheets.

I'd been a cop long ago and had seen death up close. Gang-bangers lying dead in front yards after drive-bys. Homeless bodies twisted by rigor in fetid alleys, already on their final journey home. An eight-year-old boy bleeding out in my arms. All the deaths had bothered me, and some brought nightmares for a while, then went away.

But I hadn't caused those deaths. I hadn't taken the one thing from someone that you can't give back. Two years ago, I hadn't had a choice, but the nightmares reminded me that I'd still played God.

I hadn't touched a gun since the night I killed the man. I never planned to again, but tonight I needed one for insurance. I unzipped the case and pulled out the weapon. It felt heavy. Heavier than I'd ever remembered a gun feeling. I sighted it on the door handle of my bedroom with my finger against the trigger guard.

Images of the dead man in my nightmares flooded my head. Me shooting him. A slight tremor filled my hand and my breath double-pumped.

I put the gun in my coat pocket and hoped I wouldn't have to use it tonight. Or ever again.

I entered The Chalked Cue at 9:30 p.m. The biker bar where Steven Lunsdorf supposedly confessed to Trey Fellows that he'd killed the Eddingtons. The bar looked about the way it sounded. Long, chipped, wooden slab for a bar. Leather-clad hard men and hard women on stools hunched over it. A few scattered tables. Old-fashioned jukebox in the corner playing Steppenwolf. Three pool tables and a shuffleboard in the back. The stench of spilled beer, sweat, and testosterone hung in the air like invisible smog.

My leather bomber jacket didn't match the room. But that was okay. Better to be seen as a civilian than as a rival biker. Although, I wished Moira had taken me up on my offer. A suburban couple taking a walk on the wild side. Most of the other jackets had "Raptors" across the back above a picture of a velociraptor dinosaur sporting leather and sunglasses. Some of the younger men had shaved heads. The older ones mostly had long hair and long beards. But this wasn't a ZZ Top audition. Swastika and SS tattoos ran down exposed arms and necks. Some made of dark-blue ink, the fingerprint of the California prison system.

I scanned the bar and the bar scanned me. Conversations died and hard-pebbled eyes in the mirror behind the bar challenged me. I put my hand in my jacket pocket and fingered the Ruger .357 Magnum like a two-year-old clutching his blankie in the dark. But a two-year-old never had to worry whether he had the nerve to fire a gun at a human being.

Steven Lunsdorf had had a shaved head in the five-year-old booking photo I'd seen in the report Buckley had given to me. Five years was plenty of time to grow out his hair and sprout a hillbilly beard, but none of the eyes in the mirror looked familiar. Trey Fellows wasn't in the bar either. That made things easier. I wasn't ready for Lunsdorf yet, and didn't have to worry about Fellows accidently giving me away to the bikers.

I grabbed an empty stool at the bar where it L-ed off to the right and ordered a Budweiser. I really wanted a microbrew, but when in Rome—or SoCal redneck heaven. The bartender had brown hair pulled back in an unmade bun and a leather vest over a black Harley Davidson t-shirt. She gave me the same eyes that still stared at me in the mirror.

The eyes gradually left me and the conversation volume rose to match the music from the jukebox. I kept to myself and drank my beer like I belonged, even though everyone in there, including me, knew I didn't. The bartender came by with round two and a tiny smile.

"If you're working undercover, you haven't quite pulled it off, Five-Oh." There was a lot of cigarettes and gin in her voice, but she had a nice smile. Ten years ago she must have been a looker. Before life on the back of a motorcycle.

"I'm not a cop." I smiled, but kept it low wattage in case her boyfriend was in the bar. Didn't want a barstool upside the head.

"Oh, you just play one on TV?" Her smile was bigger now and she leaned in just a bit. Maybe her boyfriend wasn't there tonight, or maybe she was in between. "You look more sports bar than dive bar."

"Just bad genes. I'm actually waiting for a friend."

"What's his name?" She glanced down the bar, either to check drinks or make sure no one was looking. "I'm here five nights a week. If he's a regular, I'll know him."

"Trey Fellows. He'd stick out like a sorer thumb than me here. Blond dreadlocks, skinny, talks like a surfer."

"Sure, I know Trey. A little goofy, but a nice guy. Seems like a strange match for you, though."

"Well, you never can tell with friends, can you?" I raised the wattage and leaned in a bit myself. "I know him as a surfer who likes to get high, and you know him as a dude who hangs out in a biker bar a couple times a week."

"No. I guess you never know." She straightened up to leave.

"After you make your rounds down the bar, why don't you come back here with whatever you like to drink and pour me one too."

She squinted down one eye and looked just over my shoulder. "Well, okay. But I can tell you it ain't going to be a Bud. Get your wallet out and find the big bills."

I made a move like I was going for my wallet. She laughed, then started her way down the bar.

I was wrong about the gin. She came back and set down a bottle of Courvoisier VSOP and two snifters in front of me. I'd eat the beers, but the Courvoisier was going down on an expense report.

"Cognac seems a little out of place here," I said.

"You mean like a cop-looking guy in a biker bar?" She poured us each two fingers.

"Touché."

She raised her snifter. "To old friends who never show up and to new friends who do."

"New friends usually trade names." I raised my glass and clinked it off hers. "Mine's Rick."

"Sarah." She took a drink and I did the same. Smooth, hint of vanilla, expensive. "You got a last name, Rick?"

"Cahill. You?"

"Lunsdorf. Sarah Lunsdorf."

The police report on Lunsdorf had him as single, never married. But it was five years old. I shot a quick glance at Sarah's ring finger. Empty.

"Trey's mentioned a Lunsdorf he knows a couple of times. Scott. Or maybe Steve?" I took a sip of the Courvoisier and studied her over the rim of the snifter.

A quick blink, then deadpan. "Steven. My brother."

"Trey said he shoots pool here with him sometimes. In fact, he said they got pretty drunk together here last Monday night."

Sarah's eyes looked down to the left, and she hesitated just a fraction before she spoke.

"Oh? I don't remember seeing them together." She set her snifter down and studied me. A crooked smile split her lips.

She was lying. The body language, the hesitation. It was enough. Fellows and Steven Lunsdorf had been together in The Chalked Cue last Monday night. I'd gotten what I'd come for. Time to leave with the lead.

"Thanks for the drink, hon." She picked up the bottle of Courvoisier. "Hey, I take a smoke break in a couple minutes. Care to walk me outside?"

I'd gotten what I'd needed tonight, but I might need Sarah down the line. "Sure."

I left the rest of the Courvoisier in the glass. Two beers and an ounce of cognac in less than an hour. I'd blow over the legal limit if I got stopped. No need to push my luck.

I watched Sarah make her rounds and chat casually with the leather-clad men. I caught more eyes in the mirror. These belonged to a massive head full of black hair and beard. It sat atop shoulders that would have fit right in among the Sierra Nevadas. A scar slashed across his eyebrow. These eyes didn't challenge, but looked away when I held their gaze.

Two minutes later, I escorted Sarah out the front door. She'd put on a leather coat collared with fake fur and lit up a cigarette.

"Can you walk me around the back, hon? The owner doesn't like us smoking out front."

Something flipped over in my gut. The ancestral echo of fight or flight that was built into our DNA back when we were both hunter and prey. The world went modern, but the DNA stuck around to warn us that life was still dangerous.

"I really have to—"

The click of a double-action revolver behind my head silenced me and the rest of my world.

My mouth went dry and my underarms wet. Time stopped and the metallic click of death reverberated throughout my body.

Two years ago the man in my nightmares had pointed a gun at me, and I'd killed him to survive.

Two pairs of hands grabbed my arms from behind and pushed me forward before I had a chance to reach for the Ruger .357 in my pocket. Sarah led me and my invisible escorts into an alley behind The Chalked Cue. The only light came from a low crescent moon and the cherry of Sarah's cigarette. The hands shoved me up against a dumpster and patted me down. A hand ripped the gun from my jacket pocket and another one grabbed my wallet from my pants.

"You always come armed to meet a friend in a bar?" Sarah asked.

"In a bar like this." I should have brought ten of me in full riot gear.

"At least you told the truth about your name." The sound of exhaled smoke. "Rick Cahill, private investigator."

The hands spun me around. Sarah stood between the dark outlines of two mountains. Both had beards. One had a gun pointed at me. Sarah flicked one of my business cards at my face.

"Sarah, I'm working a case. Trey Fellows isn't a friend, but the rest is true."

"Fellows is where you made your mistake, Rick. You said he and Steven were drunk." An inhale. A smoke ring. "Trey doesn't drink."

The kind of research I didn't have to do when I was sticking cameras through motel windows. I missed those days already.

"Did he send you?" The one with the gun asked. His voice, twelve miles of gravel road.

"Who? Fellows?"

The gun sliced through the night and the butt smashed against my forehead. It staggered me against the dumpster, but I stayed up. A warm trickle rolled down against my brow and leaked past my eye.

"One more try," the mountain holding the gun said. "Did he send you?"

"I don't know who you're talking about. Nobody sent me." I put my hands up like it was a stickup so I could block the next blow. My head pounded and I fought to stiffen my wobbly legs.

"I'm working a worker's comp fraud case against Fellows. Going to his known hangouts, talking to friends. That's all. Call my agency and talk to Bob Reitzmeyer. He'll tell you."

"What's Steven got to do with it?" Sarah said.

"He's listed as a friend of Fellows." I looked at Sarah, but checked the gun in my peripheral vision. Out of reach and too risky. "Look, it's a crappy little comp case. I'll quit it tomorrow, and you'll never see me again."

"Here." Sarah reached my wallet out to me and, just as my hand touched it, the gun came down on my temple.

Concrete.

Black.

I awoke to a gun barrel in my left eye. I fought the instinct to go fetal and beg for my life. If they'd wanted me dead, I'd already be there. I studied the figure bent over me with my right eye. Long dark hair and bushy beard. Black in the shadow of the night.

A scar bisecting his left eyebrow. The man who'd been studying me in the mirror before I walked Sarah out. I'd remember him. Not for a description to police. For next time. When I'd be the one to come up from behind.

"Something's not right about you, Cahill." The gun stayed in my eye. "I don't believe your bullshit little story. You send word back to him that we're onto him. We know his game. And we'll settle it when the time comes."

The gun left my eye and a boot exploded into my ribs.

By the time I got my breath back, the man was gone. I crawled on all fours to the dumpster and used it to pull myself upright. Rotting food, stale beer, and blood filled my airways. The blood was mine. It rolled down my face and splatted onto my shoes. My head felt like someone was inside it using a sledgehammer to get out, and my ribs grabbed at me with each breath. I didn't know if I needed a doctor or just a new job. Or, maybe, my old job back.

I snailed past a row of Harley Davidsons to my car, wondering what had happened to my simple witness-check case and who the hell "he" was.

CHAPTER TWELVE

Halfway home, I vomited out the window of my car. The pain in my head almost closed my eyes, and I had a hard time steering the car in a straight line. Every breath felt like a left hook to the ribs. I rubbed my hand over my temple and felt a mushy lump. A hematoma. Probably a concussion. A couple miles from home, I made a right instead of a left onto Genesee and headed for Scripps Memorial Hospital in La Jolla.

It was a quiet night in the emergency room. No one was moaning, and I was the only one bleeding and walking sideways. After filling out forms and waiting forty-five minutes, a doctor finally stitched me up, iced me down, and delicately probed my ribs.

Concussion. Bruised ribs. Seven stitches.

Treatment: a lot of ice, Tylenol, and an alarm clock to wake me every couple hours.

The doctor insisted I shouldn't drive, so the nurse called Kim, an ex-girlfriend, to come pick me up. She was waiting for me when I came out from my curtained-stall consultation with the doctor. She wore jeans and a sweater that only hinted at the curvy, athletic body beneath. Her green eyes and mouth made "Ohs" when she saw me. Not the good kind. I thought I was doing just fine, but I couldn't seem to keep my hand off the wall as I walked.

"Rick!" She hurried over and wrapped an arm around my back and got her shoulder underneath my armpit. "My God! What happened to you?"

My groan stopped her. My stitched forehead was visible. My ribs were not.

"I'm sorry!" She backed away from me like I was a quail egg teetering on the edge of a nest. "I didn't mean to hurt you."

Most women never do.

"How can I help?" Her hands were open at her side, palms outward like she was defending against a bounce pass or waiting to catch me when I fell out of the nest.

"Other side would be great."

She delicately assumed her earlier position, now on my right side.

"What happened, Ricky?"

"Short story." I let her take some of my weight and it felt good. "I'll tell you later. Sorry you had to come pick me up."

"Don't be ridiculous."

We shuffled outside and Kim leaned me up against a "No Parking" sign and went to get her car. She drove up in a BMW 335i convertible. On warm days when she dropped the top and let her blond hair fly in the wind, she looked like just another beautiful daughter of privilege. That is, until you looked a bit closer and saw the intelligent gleam in her eyes. I slid into the leather seat and my ribs hurt. But not as much as if I had sat down onto my own car's seat.

When I first met Kim five years ago, she'd been a bartender at night and learned the real estate biz during the day. She'd learned well and now sold homes in La Jolla. Even in a down market, the leased Beemer hadn't been an extravagance. Easier to sell homes when you look like you belong in the neighborhood. And now, with her success, she did. Much more so than on the arm of a restaurant manager, where she'd been until I broke her heart.

The first time.

But that had been three years ago and she had rebounded well. Dating the top realtor in La Jolla. He smiled at me from bus stop benches all over town. A grin saved just for me. "You screwed up, pal." I couldn't argue.

"Take the 5 south."

"I know the way to your house." She patted my hand. "I was your real estate agent. That concussion must be really bad."

"We're not going home yet."

"Why?" Her voice rose in concern. "Where are we going?"

"To talk to a wannabe Rastafarian."

On the drive over to Fellows' house, I told Kim only that I'd been on a case and had been jumped outside a bar. Not what bar. Not what kind of case. Not that I'd had a gun barrel stuck in my eye. I trusted Kim with my life, but clients trusted my discretion. Besides, I didn't want to make her worry even more.

We circled Fellows' street and ended up back in front of the house he lived behind. No motorcycles in sight. I had to find out if Fellows had set me up. And, if not, I needed to know who the "he" the bikers thought had sent me was.

"Just drop me a couple houses up and park where you can find a space." I pulled the bag of ice the nurse had given me from my head and dropped it onto the car floor. "Wait in the car. I won't be long."

"You should be home in bed. Can't this wait a few days until you're better?"

"Five minutes, tops." I held up my hands.

I slow-motioned out of the car. Walking had been easier with Kim under my arm. The vise squeezing my head cinched down another notch. My ribs throbbed with each wobbled step.

Maybe I should have listened to Kim.

I made it back to Fellows' cottage. His bicycle was still out front. No motorcycles. I crept to the door and put my ear to it. The murmur of a TV, nothing else. I took a deep breath that hurt like hell and knocked on the door.

Fellows didn't have a peephole, so I'd get a chance to read him when he opened the door.

Muffled footsteps, then the doorknob twisted and the door opened, exposing a triangle of light.

Adrenaline pushed all my pain aside and I stood up straight, chest out.

Fellows' red-rimmed eyes went round. Genuine surprise. His eyes stayed on me, up to my jagged forehead then back down to my face. No side glances or eyes to the ground.

"Dude! What happened to you?" Sincere.

If he'd set me up, he should move to LA and start auditioning. Still, I needed to be sure.

"Mind if I come in?"

"Yeah, no problem." He stepped back and swung the door all the way open. "You don't look so good, bro."

I stepped into the studio and got the marijuana ambience. The bong and weed were still on the table, but there wasn't any smoke in the air. There didn't need to be. It was in the furniture, the curtains, his clothes. I made sure I didn't bump into him on the way in so I could avoid a contact high. A flat screen in the corner was paused in mid-Housewife. Orange County, Beverly Hills, or Miami. Some city where reality was as fake as the boobs and hair color.

"I met some of your friends tonight." I found the loveseat I'd sat on earlier and pretended that my body didn't hurt like hell when I lowered myself down into it.

"Who?" A confused smile. He sat down in the recliner.

"The Raptors."

"What?" He stood up. Terror took the place of the smile. "You didn't talk to Steven, did you? Tell him what I said?"

"No. He wasn't there, but his sister and his friends were." I pointed at my stitched forehead.

"What did you tell them?" He was pacing now.

"That I was checking you out for worker's comp fraud and wanted to talk to some of your friends."

"Why'd you have to do that?" His eyes ballooned. "They're not my friends."

"Then why do you hang out at their bar?"

"I like to shoot some stick and have a beer every now and then." He kept pacing but hid his eyes from mine.

Sarah Lunsdorf, the bartender who orchestrated my beating, had said Fellows didn't drink. Someone was lying. I stood up and almost broke a molar hiding the pain caused by the movement. Fellows stopped pacing and let out a little breath as if the inquisition was over and he could get back to his Housewives. I walked toward the front door, then made a quick left and into the tiny open kitchen. Fellows moved toward me when I whipped open the refrigerator door. No beer bottles. Just some milk, fruit, veggies, condiments, and a couple to-go containers.

This seemed to put the lie on Fellows. I started to shut the door, then stopped. The gold lids of nine or ten large mason jars pushed behind the produce and milk on the bottom shelf caught my eye. I took Fellows for a bit of a nature boy, his TV taste notwithstanding, but I doubted he canned his own preserves.

"What's up, bro?" Tiny quake in Fellows' voice. "Do you need something to drink?"

I could feel his breath on my neck.

Fellows had a surfer's body, lean, long ropey muscles, and skin too tight to pinch. If he had the heart and the know-how, he might present a challenge. I doubted he had either, but I was already battling a concussion and bruised ribs.

I turned to face him, and deliberately put my hand in my bomber jacket pocket where my .357 Magnum had been at the beginning of the night. "Go sit down, Trey."

He looked down at my pocket, then up at me. His eyes were a question mark. Mine were certain. He let out a "Dude," then went and sat down in the loveseat.

I bent down, swallowed the pain, shoved my hand behind the fruit and veggies and came out with a mason jar. Full of marijuana buds. I set the jar down on the kitchen counter. Fellows stood up, but didn't make a move toward me.

"Medical, bro." High pitched. Nervous. "That's medical."

"Only if half the glaucoma patients in San Diego live here." I pulled out the other nine jars and put them on the counter. "There has to be over four or five pounds here. Possession with intent to sell. Even with California's ever-changing weed laws, that'll get you jail time, bro."

"Dude, I can't...you gotta give me a break." He edged toward the front door. "I can't do time."

"Sit back down." I pointed my pocketed hand at the loveseat. "Let's talk about this."

"Whatever you want, man. I can cut you in. Whatever."

Two years ago, another drug dealer had offered to cut me in on his business. I flushed his stash down a toilet and broke his nose. Back when I had a temper. And thin skin.

"So you deal weed for the Raptors. That's why you hang out at The Chalked Cue and how you know Steven Lunsdorf."

"No...I..." He shook his head and his eyes blinked like hummingbird wings. "They're not...I don't deal with them."

"I used to be a cop, Trey. I got friends on the force." I lied. About the friends part. "You want to talk to them or me?"

A pause like he was actually thinking about it. "You, I guess."

"You lie to me again," I pulled my cell phone out of my jeans. "And I'll have a couple narco detectives here in five minutes."

He gulped and nodded.

"I don't care about the weed. I just need to know how tight you are with the Raptors, and if your Lunsdorf murder story is bullshit."

"It's all true, man." Whiny. Like a kid alibiing to his parents.

"Uh, uh." I pursed my lips and shook my head. "The Raptors have you scared shitless. No way you'd rat one of them out without a better reason than you just being a good citizen. The assholes who jumped me thought somebody had sent me. Somebody who wasn't you. Is that who put you up to this? This mystery man the Raptors are scared of?"

"Nobody put me up to anything! I don't know what you're talking about." He sounded like he was about to cry.

"You're lying, Trey." I held up my phone and slid my thumb across the screen to unlock it. "Time to talk to the police."

"No!" He jumped up. "I'm telling the truth! You gotta believe me."

"Okay, okay. I believe you." I didn't, but put the phone back in my pocket anyway. He was going to hold onto his story, and I had no intention of calling the police. "Just sit back down. Take it easy."

Fellows did as told. He put his head in his hands and shook it back and forth. My own head was wobbling a bit. Nausea crept up my throat. I couldn't break Fellows. Not tonight in my condition. Maybe not ever. Could he be telling the truth?

"How long you been dealing for the Raptors?" I still needed to tie up a few loose ends.

"They just supply me the gange." He pulled his head from his hands and glanced at the wall opposite him. "I don't really deal for them. I do this to make a living. I can't live off disability for the rest of my life."

"Call it what you want. How long?"

"About four years."

"Three and a half years before you went on disability." I said that just so he knew I wasn't buying all his bullshit. "How did you get hooked up with the Raptors?"

"One of them used to work with me at UPS."

"Name." I put my hand on the counter and tried not to show that my legs were shaking.

"I can't give you his name!" His eyes went round. "You don't understand, dude. These guys will kill me!"

My ribs and head made me a believer. The room started spinning, sweat pebbled my forehead, and bile shot up my throat. I stumbled over to the kitchen sink and puked into it. Then the ceiling crashed down on me.

"Dude!" Fellows stood over me, his dreadlocks spiraling down.

"I'm okay." I wasn't. I reached a hand up to grab the counter, and Fellows grabbed my arm and hoisted me up until he could get his shoulder under me. My ribs screamed, but I managed not to.

"I'll take you to the emergency room, dude. You're messed up."

"No." I tried to straighten up on my own but still needed his shoulder to stay upright. "Just help me outside. I've got a ride waiting for me."

Fellows and I did a drunk shuffle-walk out to the street.

He held tight, and never once tried to grab the phantom gun in my jacket pocket. Kim's Beemer's engine revved on, and she pulled away from the curb where she'd parked when she'd dropped me off.

I broke away from Fellows and stood on my own. "Thanks."

"Be careful, dude." He turned and went back to his tiny cottage just as Kim pulled up.

As I opened the car door, a thought spun around my already gyroscoping head. Maybe this guy *was* a Good Samaritan. Could he really be willing to risk his life just to do the right thing?

CHAPTER THIRTEEN

Kim helped me upstairs to my bedroom. The banister worked as a crutch on one side, Kim on the other. Midnight wanted to help, but all he could do was walk up a couple steps, then look back and wait until I caught up. My head throbbed constantly, and each step up the stairs was a kick to the ribs. We finally made it, and Kim shuffled me over to the edge of the bed and eased me down until I could sit.

"Bedtime for Ricky." She took off my shoes and socks and then my pants. When we were together, Kim had undressed me before bed a few times. Usually, right after I'd undressed her. There wouldn't be any reciprocation tonight. Or probably ever again.

She delicately removed my jacket and slowly pulled my shirt off over my head.

"Oh." She gasped.

"What?"

She stared at the scar on my shoulder just below the clavicle. Residue from the bullet shot through me by the dead man in my nightmares. Kim and I had both almost died that night. She credited me for saving her life. A hero, I wasn't. My bad decisions had put her in danger, but somehow hadn't gotten her killed. She'd been the lucky one.

"I've never seen it before." Emerald-green eyes. Beautiful. Delicate. Sad.

We were long past seeing each other undressed when I took the bullet. For me, the scar was a reminder of actions I'd taken and hadn't taken that resulted in people dying or being scarred for life.

"It's not a badge of honor."

"It is to me."

"Nuh."

Kim slowly steered a finger at the scar, like it might hurt us both if she touched it. She finally did. A jolt shot through me. Not pain. Warmth. And more.

"Does it hurt?" She slowly traced her finger along the scar.

"No." More tender than discomfort. The pain was in the memory.

She bent down to me, our foreheads almost touching. "There's so much pain in your life, Rick."

Her scent enveloped me. Fresh and clean, like the first sunrise in winter. Memories bubbled up of lazy days with Kim. She'd been my first and only steady girlfriend after Colleen. She'd been perfect. But she hadn't been Colleen. Her ghost had hovered over the two of us. All memories of how our relationship hadn't worked at the end, forgotten. Only the good remained.

Unattainable, because it wasn't real.

My guilt for not matching Kim's love, a wedge between us. She gave me all of herself. I gave back measured amounts. Not enough for either of us. Finally, it ended, but the friendship remained. Always with the promise of something more.

"Kimmie." I touched her cheek.

She held my face in her hands and slowly pressed her lips to mine. Old and new came together. Better. The pain in my head moved to the background. I unfolded back onto the bed and pulled Kim down on top of me. She maneuvered to avoid my ribs. Still, they grabbed at me, but I ignored the pain. I held Kim tight against me, and our mouths explored old paths found anew.

Kim suddenly pulled away and rolled over onto her back. "Rick, I can't do this."

"I'm not sure I can in my current physical condition, either." Bad humor was all I had.

"This is wrong." Sadness pulled at her face. "I have Jeff now."

"I understand. We just got caught up in some good memories."

"It's not that. Rick. Not for me." She rolled onto her side and looked at me. "We're just wrong. We'll never be right."

She was being kind, as always. We were wrong because I was wrong. We both knew it. If she slept with me tonight, she'd never go back to the real estate king. She'd end it tonight because she wouldn't lead a life of cheating and deception. Not even for a day. All I had to do was commit to her in full.

I couldn't. Even in the throes of desire, I knew down deep I wouldn't be able to give her all she needed. So the decency that was left in me, tucked behind the neurosis and stupidity, wouldn't allow me to make false claims that would ruin her life.

"You don't have to stay and babysit me." I patted her hand. "I'm fine."

"No. You told me the doctor said you need to be awakened every few hours to make sure your mental acuity is up to par." She got off the bed and walked around to my side.

"I'm starting with a deficit to begin with."

"I know." She gave me a sad-eyed smile, and I felt guilty for putting her in this position. I wished for the thousandth time that I could be the man she needed me to be. The man I should be.

She helped get me under the covers and kissed me on the forehead. Just long enough for me to regret all the bad decisions I'd made to get me to this point.

She turned off the light and left me alone in the dark.

Kim woke me up before the nightmares could. I'd take staring at her through the dark over a gun pointed at me in my dreams any night. She asked me a couple questions to make sure I hadn't gotten any stupider. I passed the test, and she walked to the door to leave.

"You stay here and I'll sleep on the couch." I swung my legs out of bed and my ribs punched at me.

"Get back in bed. The couch is fine." She put her hand on the light switch by the door, but paused and looked at me. "Why haven't you put a bed in the guest room? It's just an empty space."

I thought of the nursery that would never be. "I guess I never expected to have guests."

"This is your home, Rick. A place to start new memories." She turned off the light and left.

Kim stuck around until morning to make sure I hadn't died in my sleep, then left without having breakfast. Said she had a busy day, but I think she wanted to get away from what almost happened last night as quickly as possible.

After breakfast, I called LJPD and tried to report that my gun had been stolen. I didn't want the police involved in my business, but I couldn't have the gun show up at a crime scene still belonging to me. If the Raptors wanted to frame me for something heavy, I wouldn't make it easy for them. I'd already been their punching bag; I wasn't going to be their stooge too.

Only problem was, LJPD wouldn't take the complaint over the phone. Some police departments would. Police Chief Tony Moretti's wouldn't. That meant I had to get dressed. Alone. Getting out of bed was hard enough. I made it into slacks and a shirt without crying. If I had to put on socks and shoes the tears would have flowed. Thank God for loafers. I slipped my feet into a pair without having to bend over.

I hoped my meeting at LJPD would go just as smoothly.

CHAPTER FOURTEEN

The La Jolla Police Department was housed in an old two-story, white brick building that had once been a library. Cops called it the Brick House. I hadn't been inside in two years and I hadn't missed it. Or the people in it.

I didn't expect a warm cuddly feeling when I walked through the glass door entrance, but the cool trickle of sweat down my spine surprised me. I guess the compartment I'd pushed that piece of my past into had overflowed. No problem. I took a deep breath and opened up another chamber for the spillage.

The desk sergeant, mid-fifties, had a buzz cut and a military demeanor. He checked the stitches above my eye before he spoke. "May I help you?"

"I need to report a stolen handgun."

"Name?"

"Rick Cahill."

His chin went up and his eyelids pinched down. Exactly why I didn't want to come down here. I didn't know the desk sergeant and he didn't know me. But he knew my reputation.

He frowned and shook his head. "Have a seat and I'll call you when an officer can take your complaint."

I went over to a wooden bench and eased myself down. My ribs cried out during the slow motion descent. A few minutes later, a woman in a navy blazer and gray slacks approached me.

"Mr. Cahill, I'm Detective Denton." She was on the far side of forty, had dark hair and eyes with tiny gold flecks in the irises. Desk work looked to have filled out what was probably once an athletic body. She was pretty in a full-faced sort of way.

A detective? This wasn't standard operating procedure. Normally, a uniform would handle something minor like a stolen weapon report.

She stuck out a hand and I stood up to shake it. A little too quickly, and a low groan involuntarily left my body.

"Do you think you can make it up the stairs so we can file a report?" She put a hand on my shoulder like I was a toddering old man.

"Stairs might be a little tough right now." Chief Moretti's office was upstairs. Today was hard enough. "I can just give the information to one of the uniforms down here and save you the trouble. Sorry you had to come downstairs."

Detective Denton glanced at the staircase, then at a large vacant room to the right of the front desk.

"I guess we can go into the roll-call room."

Not the answer I'd been hoping for. I just wanted to report the gun to a uniform and get the hell out of there.

She led me past the front desk and cop cubicles to the roll-call room. She held the door open for me, then ushered me to a chair connected to a half-moon desk. The kind kids sit in at school. There were about twenty of them in the room. The only other piece of furniture was a podium.

I'd spent a lot of late nights in a room like this back at the Santa Barbara Police Department, getting briefed on the bad guys roaming the streets as I prepared to go out on the graveyard shift. It had been ten years ago, but I still felt a surge of adrenaline as I sat down at the desk.

Detective Denton sat down at the desk next to me. She pulled out a pen and notepad from her blazer and got the basic information from me, then asked me to tell her what happened.

"Someone stole my gun." I handed her my concealed weapon permit that had the make, caliber, and serial number of my .357 Magnum Ruger SP101.

She frowned and made a few notes, then handed me back the permit. "I need details, Mr. Cahill. When did this happen? Where was the weapon when it was stolen? Where were you when it was stolen? Do you have any idea who took it?"

Not only did I have to get a detective, I had to get one who didn't have better things to do than get every detail about a stolen gun. I didn't want to tell her about the Raptors or about the case. If I told Detective Denton, she'd probably follow up and ask people questions. The Raptors might reach out to Trey Fellows and hurt him or scare him enough that he would change a story they didn't even know about yet. I might not yet be 100 percent convinced of Randall Eddington's innocence, but I was close enough to go all in on the case.

I had to lie. It wouldn't be the first time I'd lied to the police. Not even the second. But the other times things hadn't turned out too well.

"I noticed this morning that it wasn't in the trunk of my car. I'd left it there a few weeks ago and forgotten about it until today. I'm not sure when it was stolen."

Detective Denton frowned. "So, the injury to your forehead and the pain in your movements have nothing to do with the theft of your gun?"

"No." All in. Technically, I'd just committed a misdemeanor if my lie inhibited a police investigation. But I had my own investigation to worry about.

"How did you receive these injuries?"

"I fell down some stairs at home."

She stared at me and drummed her pen on her notepad. I knew she didn't believe me. I didn't know what she'd do about it.

"Please wait here a minute." She grabbed her notepad and left the room, closing the door behind her.

I could have left. No law obligated me to remain. Just my curiosity and good manners. I stayed seated.

When the door opened again, I wished I hadn't.

Police Chief Tony Moretti walked into the room. My headache just got worse. Moretti hadn't changed much in two years. Deep tan, slicked-back black hair, coal eyes, oxen musk cologne, and a '70s porn mustache. Only his clothes budget had changed. He'd gone from tailored American suits to Italian ones.

"Rick." He surprised me by sticking out a hand that didn't have a gun or handcuffs in it. I struggled up from my grade school chair and shook it. "You okay? You look a little beat up."

"Fine. Just a little accident at home. Thanks."

"You always did have bad luck. Didn't you?" He leaned against the podium. "Please, sit down."

He knew that would cause me more discomfort than remaining standing. I sat anyway and ate the pain.

"Rick, I'm willing to start fresh." He tried a sincere smile instead of his usual smirk. It was close, but not quite convincing. "You obstructed my investigation during that Windsor affair a couple years ago, but I'm willing to forget the past and move forward."

"Me too." What choice did I have?

"This is my town now. Crime is down, and everyone's happy. Let's keep it that way."

"I'm all for keeping the peace."

Moretti used to be as direct as a straight right to the nose. His newfound diplomacy must have come with the office and the title. I liked it better the old way. You could see where the punches were coming from.

"That's what we do, Rick. Keep the peace. That's our job. Your job is like that of a lawyer, sort of a necessary evil. You find dirt on people for other people who are dirty themselves." He came around the podium and parked his ass on the corner of the desk next to me. "This department could be a help to you in your career. We know where all the dirt is buried in this town."

I didn't say anything and waited for the hammer to drop.

"But we try to help people who help us. Who know how to play ball. People who don't try to make us look bad." His coal eyes hardened on mine. "You know why crime is down, Rick?"

"No."

"Because we arrest the bad guys and lock 'em up. And we want to keep them locked up. In fucking cages where they belong.

So they can't come back to civilization and murder someone else's family."

Bingo. He knew about my investigation of the Eddington murders. And there was only one person who could have told him. Bob Reitzmeyer.

"I'm all for keeping the bad guys behind bars, Chief." My anger at Bob bled over to Moretti, who was doing fine on his own at pissing me off. "But your record isn't exactly a hundred percent in separating the good from the bad."

"Listen to me, you stupid prick." His finger was in my face and he was all teeth like a snarling wolf. "You think you're gonna play hero again. Swoop in with your toy PI license and save the day. But you are dead fucking wrong this time. Lightning won't strike twice in your lifetime. That kid up in San Quentin is a stone killer. He's evil. But you weren't a cop long enough to know what true evil is."

"What's your worry, Chief? If you made a righteous collar, then the streets of La Jolla will stay crime free and everybody will be happy." I stood up.

"You want to keep that paper badge, you better play by the rules." Moretti now had to look up at me, but still showed his teeth. "If I find you even thinking about bending the law, you're gonna see what the bars look like from the inside. Then your bullshit career playing fake cop will be a bad memory just like your career as a real cop was."

He stormed out of the room and slammed the door behind him.

Moretti was worried. A confident man wouldn't have threatened me for chasing a fool's errand. Not even one who hated me as much as Moretti. That, along with everything else I'd already learned, hadn't yet convinced me that Randall Eddington was an innocent man. But now I was certain that something was wrong with the case LJPD made against Randall in the first trial.

I just needed to find out what it was without getting arrested.

CHAPTER FIFTEEN

I e-mailed Buckley a report of my adventure at The Chalked Cue and subsequent interview of Trey Fellows, then planted myself horizontally on the sofa. With remote in hand, only hunger and the need to urinate would compel me to get up. Midnight sat next to the sofa and leaned in so I could scratch his chest. I hit the power button on the remote, then Midnight growled and someone knocked on the front door.

Shit.

I got off the sofa and went to the front door with the speed and urgency of the continental drift. Midnight shadowed me, ready to defend me from whoever was behind the door. I checked the peep hole and hoped I wouldn't need defending. I opened the door and let in Bob Reitzmeyer. He bent down and scratched Midnight and was rewarded with a tongue to the face.

"Get you a beer? Something to drink?"

He stood up and looked at the stitches in my forehead.

"Are you okay?" Concern echoed in his deep voice.

"Yeah."

I forced myself to swallow the pain and walked as normally as I could fake into the kitchen. I opened the fridge and thanked God I kept the beer on the top shelf. I pulled one out and handed it to Bob, then sat on one of the high stools at the butcher-block kitchen island. The emergency room doctor told me no alcohol for a few days. Too bad. I could use a beer right now.

Bob sat down opposite me. "What happened to your head?"

Bob had been to the house a few times, but never unannounced. Not a coincidence that he dropped by after I'd been to the Brick House. Bob was most likely playing for the other team now, on a mission to find out what I'd discovered. I could lie to the police and live with it. But I had never lied to Bob.

Had he ever lied to me?

"Did someone at LJPD tell you that I'd reported my gun stolen today?" Better to charge ahead than to backpedal.

He rubbed his Van Dyke and studied me with cop eyes. "Yeah. Detective Denton. Said you were pretty beat up, so I came by to see if you were okay."

"Why would she call you?"

"She used to be my partner at LJPD. She knew you worked for me and was concerned about your well-being."

"Did you talk to Chief Moretti?"

"No." No blink or avoiding eyes. But maybe a bit too quickly. "You going to tell me what happened?"

"I took a tumble." I didn't care about lying anymore. Neither did Bob. "Thanks for checking up on me."

Bob stood up. Irritation pulled at his mouth. "Did you read the Eddington police report?"

"Yes."

"If you know he's guilty, why are you still working the case?"

"I'm on vacation, Bob."

"Let's hope it's not a permanent one." He set his beer down and walked out the front door.

I didn't know if Bob got what he needed, but I did. He and LJPD were on the same team, and they were worried about what I might find on the Eddington murders. If I kept digging, I may or may not help free a man who was innocent or guilty, but I'd probably lose my job. And the new house I was supposed to make new memories in.

* * *

I met Buckley in his office at one p.m. the next day. I still had a 24/7 headache and a knife in my ribs, but both had dulled a bit from yesterday. The day and a half of relative inactivity had me on the mend.

The view of the ocean over Buckley's shoulder was a gray muddle. Fog hung low and dulled the afternoon. Buckley didn't look much better. Bloodshot eyes above deep circles. Gray hair, long and frizzed, hung down over his shoulders like a dirty mop. He looked older than the last time I saw him. I took him to be in his late sixties, but with a bourbon drinker you never can tell. The aging spins faster as the years slow down.

I eased myself down into a chair opposite him. My ribs grabbed at me, but not enough to make me go fetal. "Rough night, Buckley?"

"One in a long string of many." His shoulders stooped and his head dropped. "But, hell, son, you look worse than I feel. I'm awfully sorry about you getting waylaid the other night. You didn't have to come in today. How do you feel?"

"Better. Thanks."

Buckley walked over to a maple credenza against the far wall of his office and grabbed a rectangle tin. He brought it over and set it on the desk in front of me. The tin had a Norman Rockwell picture of a boy sitting on Santa's lap and had to be sixty or seventy years old.

"What's this?"

"Open it."

I did and found homemade chocolate chip cookies. I had a pretty good idea who had baked them.

"I told Rita Mae Eddington that you got hurt on the job, and she brought them over yesterday." Buckley sat back down behind his desk. "Said she'd make some for you every few days until you're all healed up."

"Tell her thanks." I took a bite of a cookie and fell in love all over again.

Buckley pulled an envelope from his desk drawer, walked around and handed it to me.

"What's this?"

"Payment for the work you've done." He smiled and patted my shoulder. "I added an extra week in case you have to take time off from La Jolla Investigations to recuperate from your injuries. You done good, son."

"Did you already replace me?"

"We've got someone in the bullpen. I just have to make the call."

I'd come over to talk to Buckley about the case, not to walk away from it. But maybe this was the out I needed and would be smart to take. I could tell Bob I was off the case and keep my job. Then I thought of Jack and Rita Mae Eddington and their grandson. They'd seen the state of California's justice as blind and blunt and cruel. Unwilling or unable to follow any path that didn't rest on the edge of Occam's razor—the simplest answer is usually correct. Randall had the most to gain financially from the death of his parents, so he's the one who murdered them.

As a kid, worshipping my father before it all went wrong, I was convinced the police never made mistakes. Even after my dad was pushed off the force, I still believed in the police. I just stopped believing in my dad.

After I became a cop in Santa Barbara, I saw that police were human. We were human. We made mistakes, but we tried to get things right and correct them when they were wrong. Then my brothers in blue arrested me for murdering my wife.

Occam's razor.

Even after they released me, SBPD kept the spotlight on me, and all other leads grew stale. Colleen's murderer was alive and free and still out there somewhere because the police made mistakes.

Two years ago, a blackmailer named Adam Windsor was murdered. LJPD rushed to judgment, made mistakes, then covered them up. People died because of it.

I thought of why I became a PI. To help people the police had overlooked or didn't believe. Or those who couldn't ask for the police's help because they'd done something wrong in the law's black-and-white eyes, but not in the gray world where people lived. People who had no place else to go. I wanted to help those people because I'd been one of them.

Bob Reitzmeyer had hired me at LJI because he thought he owed it to my late father. I was happy and lucky to get the job, but his clients didn't need me. They had enough money to buy justice or enough to keep it at arm's length.

Jack and Rita Mae Eddington had that kind of money once, but not anymore. They'd come to me because they had no place else to go. I was their last hope on a fool's errand. But I knew from personal experience that LJPD made mistakes, and right now the cops in the Brick House were worried.

"Don't make the call, Buckley."

"You're a fine investigator and I'd love to keep you on, but do you think you're up to it right now?"

"I'm ready to go." Almost. "But there are a couple new developments you need to know about."

I told him about Bob Reitzmeyer seeing the Eddington crime-scene photos and learning that I was investigating the murders, and that La Jolla Police Chief Moretti knew too.

"They had to find out eventually, but this is much sooner than I'd planned." Buckley ran his hand through a tangle of gray hair.

"I know. I'm sorry." I shook my head. "I should have been more careful with the photos, but there's a silver lining."

"What's that, son?" Buckley looked at me through red-ringed eyes. "All I see are storm clouds on the horizon."

"They're nervous. There's something about this case that has them worried, and I think it's the blood on the sock. Without that, they never would have gotten a conviction."

"That may be true, but you can't get a new trial with scatter-shot theories. You need new evidence, and we have that with the confession by Mr. Lunsdorf." Buckley's eyes brightened. "If we can find the murder weapon, we can get that boy a new trial. Stay focused on the job at hand."

"You're the boss." I saluted. "Now hold onto your Stetson, because I have new information which may tie into that new evidence. Seems Jack Eddington liked to play the ponies at Del Mar and wasn't very good at it. A few months before the murders, he loaded golf clubs from the Eddington warehouse into his SUV and drove them up to a golf shop in LA's Koreatown."

"He could have just been making a personal delivery. Maybe the golf shop owner was an old friend." Buckley seemed to be talking to himself as much as me. I don't think he convinced either one of us.

"The clubs were loaded into another SUV, and the owner gave Jack a thick envelope."

"Say this is true and Jack was stealing from his own company. Do you think Thomas found out about it?"

"Yes."

"Why?" Buckley scratched his beard.

"Because the person who gave me the information was hired by Thomas to follow Jack and gave him a video of the transaction. A month later, Jack retired and Thomas took over as CEO of Eddington Golf. Five months after that, Thomas, his wife, and daughter were murdered."

"Who gave you this information?"

"Can't tell you, but the person is believable." I'd knocked Moira MacFarlane off this case. The least I owed her was a professional courtesy.

"Don't you think I should be the one making that decision, Rick?"

"In a perfect world, Buckley, but, even in La Jolla, nothing's perfect. Sorry, you're just going to have to trust me."

Buckley rubbed his hands on his face like he was trying to scrub away the information he'd just heard. Finally, he dropped his hands in his lap and his cheeks matched the color of his bloodshot eyes.

"Well, that don't make Jack a murderer. What did he gain from the death of his son?" Buckley began ticking off the fingers of his left hand with the index finger of his right. "He didn't get his job back. It sure don't look like he got anything out of the will, judging from where he lives now. And we still have the matter of a biker gang enforcer confessing to the murders."

"Look, Buckley, this case is hardly a sure winner." I leaned my forearms onto the desk. "All you have is a hearsay confession eight years after the fact, supposedly told to a drug dealer. Even so, let's say it's true. Aside from drug sales and extortion, the Raptors are known for loan-sharking and contract murders."

"Son, I appreciate the hard work, and you climbing back up on that horse after it bucked you off and kicked you in the head, but you're letting your imagination run wild. Jack Eddington hired us to find new evidence and get his grandson a new trial. You think he'd do that if he put a hit on his son and family?"

"No, but Rita Mae would if she took the phone call from Trey Fellows. Jack couldn't tell her to let the matter drop once Trey called them with the Raptor confession." I bit into another cookie. "All I'm saying is, we can't ignore the information."

"Jack has lived in La Jolla for over fifty years." Buckley lifted his hands up, fingers open. "How is he going to come across a contract killer from a biker gang? I doubt the Raptors attend black tie affairs at La Jolla Country Club."

"Ever been to the racetrack, Buckley? There isn't exactly a dress code."

CHAPTER SIXTEEN

Rita Mae Eddington picked up on the fourth ring. Damn. I'd hoped Jack would answer so I could set up an interview with him alone. The only number I had for him was his home phone. I hadn't told Buckley I'd planned to talk to him. That way he couldn't tell me not to and I could avoid defying him.

"Thanks for the cookies. Just what I needed."

"Oh, it's the least I could do." Warm. Grandmotherly. Real. "Are you feeling better? Do you need some more cookies?"

I had half a tin left. That would last me two days, max. I thought about asking for more.

"I'm good for now. Thanks." I had some sense of decorum. "May I speak with Jack?"

"He's up at the golf course."

"La Jolla Country Club?" I'd wait out Jack until he finished his round, then talk to him alone.

"No. We haven't been members there for years." Sad. "He's up at Torrey Pines. He likes to use the putting green when he doesn't golf with his friends. Should I tell him you called?"

Those country club monthly fees add up when you don't have the cash flow from stealing from your own company anymore.

"I'll call back. Thanks."

"Is it about Randall? We sure appreciate all you're doing."

I doubted she'd appreciate it if I told her why I wanted to talk to Jack. "No. It's nothing important. Thanks."

Afternoon on a weekday, and I still had to circle the Torrey Pines Golf Course parking lot for five minutes until a space opened up. Financial setbacks, probably Jack's gambling habit, had forced the Eddingtons to give up their membership to one of the most exclusive country clubs in Southern California. Now, Jack had to play the muni tracks like the rest of us. But if you have to play a public golf course, Torrey—with its ocean views, cool sea breezes, and rare Torrey pine trees— is hardly slumming it. The PGA holds a tournament at Torrey every year, and the USGA held the 2008 US Open there with another scheduled for 2021.

Two large, sloping, practice putting greens sat between the parking lot and clubhouse. I spotted Jack on the northernmost one. He practiced alone, putting three balls back and forth between two holes. He wore brown slacks and a sweater sporting the Eddington Golf logo. He didn't wear the logoed clothes at home but did in public. The company he'd founded, built into an empire, and then been kicked out of by his son.

His murdered son.

"Hi, Jack."

He popped his head up with a ready smile for whoever recognized who he once was. He saw me and the smile repositioned with less wattage. "Hello, Mr. Cahill."

"Do you have a minute to talk?"

"Sure." He stooped down and picked up his golf balls. "Let's go over to the café."

The café opposite the clubhouse had a red brick patio, and we sat at one of the outside tables.

"You enjoying your retirement?" I panorama-ed an arm. "Not a bad place to spend it."

"Yes."

"You still a member at La Jolla Country Club?" Conversational.

"No." Wary.

"That's too bad. I know the waiting list is a mile long for people wanting to join. Why did you give up your membership?"

"Does this have anything to do with Randall's case, Mr. Cahill?" A vein pulsed under the wrinkles in his neck. "Because I'm not much for small talk."

"Yes, it does." I leaned across the table invading his space. "How many trips to Koreatown did you make before your son caught on and forced you to retire from Eddington Golf?"

I expected a reaction. Just not the one I got.

Jack reached into his pocket, and for a second, I thought I might have made a dangerous mistake. He pulled out a coin and placed it on the table between us. It had "Gamblers Anonymous" and "5 Years" on it.

"I've got five years without laying a bet of any kind." His ears flashed red and his eyes challenged me. "I use that coin as a ball mark when I play golf to remind me that I can't play in a game of skins or even make a Nassau bet. Anything else you'd like to know that will help free my grandson from prison, Mr. Cahill?"

"Yes." So, Jack got straight three years after his son had been murdered. Didn't mean he hadn't hired the killer. "Who took the phone call from Trey Fellows about Steven Lunsdorf's confession?"

"I did."

* * *

My phone rang just as I left the parking lot. Buckley. That didn't take long. I answered.

"What the hell do you think you're doing?" No folksiness, just raw anger.

"Searching for the truth."

"Fuck you and your truth. I told you to stick to the plan. The confession and the murder weapon are our only path to a new trial." A swallowing sound. The desk drawer with the bottle of Maker's Mark must be open. "The rest can be investigated if we ever get the damn trial. Pissing off Jack Eddington does nothing to further the cause of getting his grandson out of prison."

"Did it ever occur to you that if Jack did hire Lunsdorf to murder his son, that he might try to sabotage your effort to free his grandson at some point?"

"You don't give me much credit, son. Thanks for the work. Expect a check in the mail tomorrow."

"Hold off on the check, Buckley. I'm taking Trey to find the murder weapon tomorrow. If we don't find it, I'll walk. The case will be over anyway."

If I walked now, I'd still have my steady, good-paying job. If I followed the case to its conclusion, I might not. All for a case I wanted no part of less than a week ago. But I couldn't quit now. Buckley's words from the first night he approached me hung in my head: "a case that matters." I finally had my teeth into one and I couldn't let go now.

"It's done, son." The anger was gone. He just sounded tired now. "Jack wants you off the case."

"Just get me a day, Buckley." A hint of desperation hung off my words and surprised me. Maybe I needed this case more than I even knew. "Tell Jack you need me and that I won't talk to him again. I need to see this thing through."

"Sometimes being a truth seeker can be a hard journey." Silence. I waited. Then, "I'll get you a day. Then, no promises."

"Thanks, Buckley." I let go a breath I didn't realize I'd been holding. A day might be all I needed. The case hung on finding the murder weapon. "Also, I'm going to need an extra set of hands to videotape the search tomorrow."

"I'll be in court tomorrow for another client. I guess I could hire the detective I was fixin' to replace you with for just the day."

"Fine. Tell her I'll pick her up in front of your office tomorrow at nine-thirty."

"How do you know I'm hiring a woman?"

I thought of Moira MacFarlane and her machine-gun voice. "Just a hunch."

She might get more work than just the one day if Trey Fellows didn't back up Jack Eddington's version of their first phone call.

CHAPTER SEVENTEEN

I knocked on Trey's door. No answer. His bike was parked in the small patio in front of his house and the old Volkswagen van registered to him was parked on the street. I peeked in the small window on the side of the house. No Trey, but his surfboard was leaning up against the far wall. That eliminated one possibility of where he might be.

I pulled out my cell phone and called him. Straight to voicemail. I left a message to call me. Trey could be anywhere, but I feared he might be out peddling weed. If he got busted, Randall's shot at a new trial was over. Trey was a questionable witness now. Tack a drug bust onto him and his credibility became a quick toilet flush.

I went back to my car and put on a knit beanie and a faded Charger sweatshirt that I kept in the trunk. I already sported a two-day growth. With the rough cheeks, the beanie, and the sweatshirt, I could pass for one of the disassociated former youths that cruise the bar scene in PB. It might give me enough camouflage to sneak up on Trey if I spotted him. Late afternoon at a bar in a town where few people held regular jobs figured to be as good a place as any to make a weed connection. I figured under any scenario, Trey wouldn't be happy to see me and would rabbit.

The first bar I hit on Garnet had surfboards on the wall and a lot of wicker furniture. If one of the tiki torches on the patio fell over, the whole place would go up like the King of Pop's hair in a Pepsi commercial. A lot of sun-bleached blond hair and board shorts, even in winter, but no Fellows.

The next stop was more upscale, with music too loud to talk over and too synthesized to dance to unless you were European with an open shirt and a lot of chest hair. No Trey here, either. He would have been as out of place as I was.

The next bar was a dive. Old and dark and populated by middle-aged run-downs who sat in silence and threw back shots of hard amber-colored whiskey. There wasn't any fruit-flavored vodka behind the bar and the jukebox in the corner didn't have any songs in it penned after 1975.

On the surface, not a likely place for Trey's wares, but I'd met a lot of children of the '60s on the job in Santa Barbara who still played with childish things when it came to marijuana. I grabbed a stool on the corner of the bar so I could get a look at the tables and booths in the darkened rear area. The bartender was gray all the way around and looked like a Dead Head or a '70s Berkeley professor gone to seed. Maybe both. He wasn't much on conversation, so I ordered a scotch rocks and peered into the back of the bar, waiting for my eyes to adjust.

When they did, I saw something that made my stomach knot up, and made me eye the bottles behind the bar looking for a weapon. A sunglassed velociraptor stared at me through the darkened bar. The hip predator was on the back of a leather vest of a biker faced the other way in one of the booths. The man was so massive that his upper back and shoulders showed above the top of the booth.

Pain echoed along my ribs. A memory from the ambush beating I took two nights ago. My neck flamed hot, and I clenched my fists. I eyed a bottle of Jack Daniel's behind the bar. JD had given me plenty of headaches over the years. Time for it to give one to someone else. The hard way.

I took a deep breath, let it out slowly through my nose, and relaxed my hands. Maybe I should find out who the Raptor was talking to before I acted out a bad Patrick Swayze movie.

I nonchalantly angled my head back around and eyed the murky mirror behind the bar. It probably hadn't been cleaned since the Rolling Stones were young, but I could just make out the biker in its reflection. Pacific Beach with its surfers, college-age kids, and homeless, didn't seem like the hang for a biker gang member. I didn't see any other bikers in the bar, and they rarely traveled alone. Maybe the person he was talking to in the booth was another biker and they were scouting out new turf. My view of the person was blocked by the massive back of the Raptor.

Five minutes later, the mountain rose up and headed in my direction. He had a lumberjack beard and a mane of dark-brown hair. He looked familiar and could have been in The Chalked Cue the other night. One thing I was sure of, he wasn't the man with the scar who had cracked my ribs, given me a concussion, and stolen my gun. Him, I wouldn't forget. And if we met again, I'd make sure he wouldn't forget me, either.

I kept my head tilted down over my glass, another boozer lost in thoughts of happier or unhappier times, and eyed him in the mirror. He lumbered past me and out the front door, and my barstool vibrated on the wooden floor like an earthquake's after-shock had rolled through.

I pinned my eyes to the mirror and focused on the booth in the back to see if the person the Raptor had been talking to would follow him out of the bar. He didn't. He sat staring down at the table through his blond dreadlocks.

Trey Fellows.

Was this a business arrangement? The place they met to make deals? Maybe, but I doubted Trey needed to buy any more weed right now. Two nights ago he had five pounds in his refrigerator. That would take him a while to move, even to the stoners in PB. Maybe he was here to talk about something else. Could the Raptor have been warning him about me dropping his name at The Chalked Cue to get information about Steven Lunsdorf? Or maybe he was there to thank him for setting me up, and to plan another trap. Paranoia? Probably, but I'd been ambushed enough in my life to justify it.

Trey finally raised his head. I couldn't nail his expression through the shadows in the back of the bar, but I thought he looked sad. The view of his hands was blocked by the top of the booth, but I could tell by the movement of his shoulders that he was doing something with them. A second later he put a cell phone up to his ear. At the same moment, my own cell vibrated in my pocket. I was thankful that I made a habit of turning the ringer off when I worked surveillance. A ring in the bar now would have zeroed Trey's eyes on me. I wasn't ready to give up my identity just yet.

I let the vibration tickle my leg and kept my eyes on Trey's reflection. After the buzzing stopped, he mouthed words into his phone. No doubt, leaving me a message. I was a bit surprised that he'd returned my call. I'd expected him to be running scared and that I'd have to track him down.

He slid out of the booth and started walking toward me. I shot my eyes back to my scotch and felt him pass behind me, then watched him go out the door. I stood up, dropped a ten on the bar, and followed Trey outside.

The sun pushed down on the horizon, trailing dusk behind it, and a winter nip rode in on the breeze off the ocean. I followed Fellows on foot as he headed in the direction of his home. I stayed back a half block and on the opposite side of the street. He went home without any stops along the way. I went to my car, tossed my surveillance get-up into the trunk, and put on my bomber jacket.

I listened to Trey's message on my phone. He said he was sorry that he'd missed me and that he'd be available for the rest of the night if I needed to reach him. A lot more agreeable than I'd expected. Something didn't fit. A sharp-edged puzzle piece that scratched me when I tried to force it together with the other pieces.

Trey opened his door in a halo of marijuana smoke. It hadn't taken him long to start the evening bake after his talk with the Raptor. Because he was trying to settle his nerves, or because it was what he did every day?

"Come in, bro."

I sat down on the loveseat and he sat on the recliner opposite his bong on the coffee table.

"How you feeling?" he asked.

"Better. Thanks." I nodded at the baggie of weed next to the bong. "Is this medical or from your Raptor stash?"

"Dude, I want to help with your investigation." He held his hands out open in front of himself. "I'll do whatever you and Mr. Buckley need me to. But can you give me a break on the weed? I can't take a hassle with the police, man."

"We'll see how things go." I had no intention of reporting Fellows to the police, but I wasn't going to give up my leverage. Not yet. "You keep cooperating, and I'm sure everything will turn out okay."

"I'm cooperating, man." He slumped back into the recliner, a hurt child look on his face.

"I know you are." I nodded some reassurance. "Hey, when you called the Eddingtons about the confession, who did you talk to?"

"The old guy. Jack." Steady eyes, no sign of deception. "Why?"

"Just checking something. Did he answer the phone or did a woman?"

"He did."

"Did you just call them the one time?"

"Yeah." He gave me wide bloodshot eyes, wondering where this was going.

It wasn't going anywhere now, and I probably owed Jack an apology. If he'd hired the hit on his family, he would have sat on the information Trey had given him. I doubted Trey, having once risked his safety to bring the confession to light, would follow up if nothing came of it. One conspiracy theory put to bed and a meal of crow soon to be ordered.

"I need your help tomorrow." Time to finish the job I'd been hired to do. "I'll pick you up around ten a.m. Okay?"

"What are we going to do?" A slight waver in his voice.

"You're going to take me to the place where Steven Lunsdorf said he buried the golf club he used to kill the Eddington family."

"Okay." No hesitation.

Not what I'd expected. The Trey puzzle piece scratched a little more. I looked at the refrigerator and remembered another piece that didn't fit. During my first interview, Trey had told me he had a couple beers with Steven Lunsdorf the night Lunsdorf confessed to the murders. Lunsdorf's sister, the bartender at The Chalked Cue, told me Trey didn't drink. I'd checked his refrigerator the other night looking for beer and instead found marijuana. No beer.

"It's been a long day, Trey." I motioned to the refrigerator. "Would you mind giving me a beer so I can start the night early?"

"Sorry, bro, I don't—I'm all out." His face flushed and he shot up from the recliner. "I can get you a guava juice."

"That's okay, Trey. Sit down." He did as told, and I stood up and looked down at him. "You don't have to hide the fact that you don't drink alcohol. It's commendable."

He just stared at his bong.

"Why did you lie to me the other night about drinking a few beers with Lunsdorf?"

"I didn't think you'd believe that I hung out in a bar if I didn't drink." He fired up the bong and sucked in a hit.

"So you lied to me in order for me to believe the truth?" Trey and I had that trait in common.

A long exhale of indoor smog and then a cough. "Yeah. Sorry, but the rest is true. All of it."

The puzzle piece still didn't fit. I'd caught him in one lie. I'd give him a chance to tell me another.

"What were you doing when you ignored my call this afternoon?"

"I didn't ignore it. I was going to pick it up, but I...I was down at the beach and just needed to chill. This whole thing with the Raptors is kinda scary."

Lie number two.

"Have they hassled you? Tried to talk to you?"

"No." Lie number three. He shot a glance up at the lone picture on the wall.

I let his latest lies lay. I'd confront him after a little more recon. I started to have the feeling that the puzzle pieces that didn't fit might belong to a whole new puzzle.

"Ten o'clock tomorrow. Right?"

"I'll be ready." He took a deep breath. His first one without marijuana smoke in it.

I opened the door and was hit by fresh air for the first time since I'd entered Trey's smoke den. I swung the door back and forth a few times to remind Trey what fresh air smelled like. I caught him looking at the picture on the wall again.

"Who's in the picture, Trey?"

A long pause. "My sister."

"That her boyfriend?"

"Yeah." He looked down at the coffee table.

"Buddy of yours?"

"Not really."

"What's his name?"

"Brad."

"Brad what?" I felt an edge in my voice.

He looked back at the coffee table and scratched his scalp. Finally, "Larson."

"He and your sister still together?"

"Why all the questions about Brad?"

The only photo Trey had in his house was of his sister and Brad Larson. No pictures of girlfriends, present or ex, none of his parents, none of his sister alone. He looked at the picture when he got nervous and he was defensive about Larson. Trey was hiding something. Sooner or later, I'd find out what it was.

"I like to be thorough. What's the big deal?"

"It's my sister's business to talk about. Not mine."

I already figured I'd have to talk to Sierra Fellows, but not before I had a story from Trey to line up against hers.

"So they broke up?"

"No. I don't know." His eyes got big and rolled around the room. "Listen bro, it's none of my business."

I decided not to press him anymore. He still had to lead me to the supposed murder weapon tomorrow morning. I didn't want him to run and hide before I got back here.

"See you tomorrow at ten a.m."

He had the bong back to his mouth before I made it out the door.

CHAPTER EIGHTEEN

I pulled in front of Buckley's office building. Moira MacFarlane stood on the curb, arms folded across her ample chest, frown pulling down her puckish mouth.

She whipped open the Mustang's passenger door and jumped inside without a word.

"Morning," I said, and gave her a big smile.

"You think this makes us even?" She reassumed her street posture with her arms crossed.

"No, but I really appreciate you helping me out."

"Let's get something straight, Cahill." The marbles in the blender again. "I'm here because Mr. Buckley hired me to be here. I do what my employer asks and don't go off on any tangents of my own."

Sounded like Buckley had given her instructions to try to keep me in line and, maybe, report back to him when I veered off.

"Fine." I took a left onto Prospect Street and headed toward La Jolla Boulevard, which would lead me to PB and Trey Fellows. "I just want you to film the search today, but keep an eye on Fellows. I want to know what's in your gut. Is the guy believable? What's going on behind his smoke-stained eyes?"

"Why?" She relaxed her arms and softened the edge on her voice. "You think he's lying?"

"I don't know. I just want your gut on him."

"Okay." She nodded her head. "But I still think you're an asshole."

"Of course." I side-glanced her and caught a tiny upward curl to her lips.

We arrived at nine forty-five a.m., fifteen minutes early, as I had planned. I wanted to keep Trey slightly off balance. Keep the edge on. Then somewhere down the road, I'd let him get comfortable and see what came out of his mouth. Maybe a few more pieces to that side puzzle. The one I knew was out there, but wasn't supposed to be working on.

I found a rare parking spot outside the main house and left Moira in the car. Trey opened on the second knock. His eyes were clear and the smell of marijuana smoke was faint, like he hadn't smoked since last night. Probably a personal record.

"You ready?"

"I think so." But his eyes weren't sure. I caught a whiff of BO under deodorant. I had the feeling he'd been waiting there in his cottage since nine a.m. Sitting, straight-backed, in the recliner, flop sweat moistening his armpits.

Why so nervous? This was the time to test his story. Was he afraid because it was a lie? Or because it was the truth?

Hopefully, we'd find out today.

I led him out to the street where my car was parked. He saw Moira in the passenger seat and froze.

"Who's she?" His voice, high and tight. He stopped walking.

"She's another investigator working for Mr. Buckley."

"You didn't tell me there'd be anyone else coming."

"She's on our team, Trey." I turned and faced him. "You're going to have to get used to talking to other people about this. You knew this day was coming. Can you handle it?"

He looked down at the ground and slowly stroked his dreadlocks. Then he looked back at me. "Yeah. I can do this."

He didn't sound convincing, but I wasn't the one he'd have to convince. Not yet.

Moira opened her door, scooted her seat up, and pulled the seatback forward so Trey could get in. She could have pulled the seat forward all the way to the glove compartment and she'd still have leg room. She didn't offer him a smile or any small talk. Maybe she'd already made up her mind on him.

We drove through the heart of PB until we hit Mission Boulevard, which became La Jolla Boulevard. The homes grew nicer and the trees out front, larger. Nobody said a word. We could have been strangers on a bus or relatives in a funeral procession. But the funeral had already taken place eight years ago.

The Eddingtons had lived on a long cul-de-sac atop one of the many hillsides of La Jolla. The death house was at the bottom of the cul-de-sac horseshoe.

I parked next to the curb, one house up. Something instinctual kept me from parking in front of the Eddington house. Moira gave me a pop-eyed look, but I ignored it. I opened the car door and looked back at Trey as I got out, "Time to go to work."

He followed me out the door, and the three of us stood in silence and looked at the death house. The architecture was hardly spooky. A large, rambling ranch house, painted white with brown trim that sat out on a bluff, separated from its neighbors. The right side of the house had a fantastic view of the Pacific Ocean a mile away. The landscaping was well-kept, and the house would have been cheery if three people hadn't been bludgeoned to death in it.

It had been eight years. The blood-soaked carpet and splattered walls had long since been replaced and scrubbed clean. Another family had moved in and made it their home. New happy memories made. A different set of lives in full bloom. Still, none of us said anything or moved, until we each bowed our heads in our own contemplation or prayer.

Respect for the dead.

"Let's get a move on." Moira was the first to break the trance.

Trey started walking toward a dirt path to the left of the house that ran along a neighbor's hedge and meandered down below the houses, rimming the hillside until it made a steep drop to the street at the bottom of the bluff. I opened the trunk of the car and handed Moira a video camera. She followed Trey. I grabbed the metal detector from the trunk and brought up the rear. I stopped just below the right side of the Eddington house, which faced the ocean.

The view was magnificent. A tree-filled swath of residential La Jolla spread out below until the ocean filled up everything but the horizon. This was why people lived in La Jolla. Views that added a million-plus dollars to every home and a climate to enjoy it year round. It took a lot of hard work to live this kind of life of leisure. Or someone up the lineage chain willing to do the work so you wouldn't have to. Thomas Eddington had had the luck of birth, but had worked to earn his spot. A jury said he hadn't been as lucky with his choice of lineage.

I went down the dirt path and caught up with Moira and Trey. They had stopped next to a raised sewer pipe just above the path, about a hundred yards down from the Eddington house. It was cement, except for the iron cap, and protruded about two feet out of the dirt. The cement was painted blue. Moira aimed the video camera at the pipe, then swung it around to film the terrain below the path. It was mostly scrub brush dotted with clusters of nasty-looking cactus.

"Lunsdorf said he shoved the golf club under a bush next to a cactus plant about fifty yards below the blue sewer pipe." Trey looked out at the mass of bushes and cactus below.

"Did he get any more specific than that?" I asked. "There's a hell of a lot of bushes and cactus within fifty yards of the sewer."

"That's all he said." He stroked a dreadlock and kept his head tilted downhill. Fifty yards below or not, I started at the top of the hill to be thorough. The first bush was about ten yards below the sewer pipe. Like all the bushes on the hillside, it was dense and surrounded by overgrown weeds and cactus. It was too well protected to get down on hands and knees and stick a head or hand into it. Even with my denim coat and leather gloves, I was certain to be punctured by cactus needles. I'd save that discomfort for when I got a hit with the metal detector. I turned the detector on and moved the wand in tight figure eights over the bush. Nothing.

We repeated the procedure from bush to bush down the hill and came up with more nothing. Not a single beep. The detector was supposed to work from as far away as four feet for something above ground. I wondered if I'd been doing something wrong, so I ran a test with a quarter. Beep, beep, beep.

Moira had kept the film running the whole time, occasionally eyeing Trey while she kept the camera trained on the search. He seemed to get more and more nervous with each negative reading. Once again, I got the nagging feeling that he was working on a different puzzle than the rest of us.

We went all the way down to an asphalt path that ran along the bottom of the hill. More nothing. It had taken two solid hours. It was a cool day, but I was sweating, and my side reminded me that a biker had tried to punt me a few nights ago.

"I guess we struck out. Should we call it a day?" Moira asked.

"Not yet."

Moira frowned, and I caught a hint of relief in Trey's face. I led them up the path to our starting point and began the search all over again. This time I stuck the metal detector into any opening I could find in each bush. My mobility was limited and cactus needles impaled my jacket arm and glove. I moved the wand in as close to figure eights as possible, but mostly I was only able to shove it in small, back-and-forth movements. Halfway back down the hill and still nothing.

Trey got more and more twitchy. He stroked his blond dreadlocks so hard and so often that some of the dread was coming out of the lock, resulting in some straight, flyaway hairs. Audible exhales left him with each empty search. It seemed almost as if he were trying to unearth evidence that would free him and not some convicted murderer in San Quentin he didn't even know.

We were at least one hundred yards from the blue sewer pipe and Moira's exhales of irritation were starting to match Trey's ones of anxiety. I was tired of the whole thing too. Each jab into a bush brought a fresh array of needles stuck into my clothes and, occasionally, into the skin of my wrist when my jacket separated from my gloved hand. But I pushed on. The life of a kid who'd grown into a man in prison may depend on it. However, two times down the hill was going to be it. I had about another third to go.

The next patch of bushes was practically jailed by a group of cactus. I looked for any opening that wouldn't force me to push my whole body up against the cactus. I finally found one down low. I had to get down on my belly, angle the wand just inches off the ground, and stretch my arm out as far as possible. Cactus needles bit into my wrist as I tried to move the wand in tiny circular motions.

Beep! Beep! Beep!

I pulled out the wand and then slowly pushed it back in. Nobody breathed. It could have been anything. Some change. A screwdriver, a false positive.

Beep! Beep! Beep!

"Holy shit!" An explosion out of Fellows.

I looked up at him. He was playing hot potato with his feet. Then he stopped and his shoulders dropped. The realization hit him. If we'd found the murder weapon, he'd have to testify. Against the Raptors.

"You get this?" I asked Moira.

"Yeah." She pulled her face from behind the handheld video camera. She looked surprised, but excited too.

We may have found the prize.

Still on my belly, I peered through the tiny opening into the bush. I couldn't see anything but weeds, dirt, and dark. I didn't have enough protection to wade through the cactus into the bush, but I had an idea.

I stood up, picked the cactus needles out of my wrist, glove, and jacket, then brushed the dirt off my clothes.

"Moira," I tossed her my car keys. "Could you go up and grab the duct tape out of the tool kit in the trunk?"

"Why do you need duct tape?"

"To tape my phone to the metal detector and see if we can get video of what's in the bush."

"Why don't you just use the video camera?"

"I can't reach all the way in, and the opening is too small to get the camera through."

"Okay." She headed up the path.

I turned to Fellows after Moira was out of earshot. "If there's a golf club in there, you gonna step up and testify?"

More dread pull and no eye contact. "Yes."

I looked up the hill to the blue cement sewer cap that was a hundred or so yards away. "Lunsdorf told you fifty yards from the sewer, right?"

"Yeah. Maybe he got confused because it was at night."

"Yeah. Maybe." I studied Fellows, and he continued to avoid my eyes. "Is there some kind of award for evidence that the Eddingtons are offering that I don't know about?"

Fellows stopped stroking his dreads and his blond eyebrows pinched together. "I don't think so."

He looked like the thought had never even occurred to him. This dope-smoking drug dealer was going to risk his life to testify against a biker gang member solely because it was the right thing to do. Maybe that was the puzzle, and I was just too cynical to understand.

Moira returned with the tape a few minutes later. I taped my iPhone to the bottom of the circular coil at the end of the metal detector's wand, careful not to tape over the tiny camera or camera app. The phone's metal would have set off the metal detector's annoying beeping, so I turned off the detector. We'd already found whatever was made of metal under that bush. Now we just had to see what it was. I turned the camera on to video, made sure it was recording, then threaded it through the opening of the bush.

I tried to duplicate the movements that had earlier set off the detector, then held it steady in various positions. When I pulled out the device, I had four eyes staring at me and, again, no one breathing. Including me. I flipped up the wand, turned off the camera, and cut away the tape with mini-scissors from a Leatherman tool attached to my keychain.

Trey looked over my shoulder when I hit "play" on the phone's camera app. Moira wedged in next to me. The display was almost completely dark and the first images were blurred as the camera had been unable to auto-focus as I'd moved the wand back and forth. It came to the section where I'd held the phone steady. Dark images came into focus: weeds, rocks, thin branches, leaves, dirt. Nothing that looked metal or man-made. Another blur as the camera moved to another steady position. More of the same.

Trey blew locomotive breaths over my shoulder. Moira shook her head. There were probably some coins hidden under the debris on the ground or a long-ago-buried aluminum can that had set off the detector earlier. Steven Lunsdorf's third-party confession was nothing but inadmissible hearsay without the golf club. The fool's errand began to feel foolish.

The final steady position came into view. The same as the others. Nothing but organic crap that you'd expect to find under a bush. The only difference was that the images were a little lighter, as this final static shot was closest to the opening of the bush. The image blurred again as I had started to pull the wand out of the bush. A tiny splash of rust color flashed at the edge of the screen. It could have been a tiny rock, but it was just different enough from everything else on the screen for me to take another look. Fellows and Moira had already backed away.

I went back to the last image just as the picture blurred and hit pause. The rust color wasn't a rock. It looked to be a splash of color on something else. Something long and thin. I spread my fingers across the face of the phone and the image grew larger but more blurred.

Blurry, but clear enough. The rust color was rust on a cylindrical piece of metal.

A golf club shaft.

CHAPTER NINETEEN

"Moira. Call Buckley."

I heard feet shuffle behind me. Trey's breath, again, pistoned over my shoulder. "Holy shit."

Moira burst over and grabbed my hand holding the phone. "Oh my God. Is that really what I think it is?"

"I've played enough golf to know that it can't be anything but." Our eyes locked and hers went bigger than usual. "Call Buckley."

She took out her phone, hit Buckley's number, and offered the phone to me. "You should tell him."

After pissing off Buckley yesterday with my interrogation of Jack Eddington, I welcomed the chance to be a hero and an opportunity to stay on the case. I settled, instead, for being a decent guy. "No. You got it."

She smiled, and her tough-girl image melted into something nice. Two seconds later, "Mr. Buckley, we found a golf club." The marbles left the blender and she sounded like a schoolgirl saying "yes" to the prom.

I could hear Buckley's hoot through Moira's ear. Sounded like he'd called the cows home.

She gave him the details and the name of the streets of the intersection below us, Draper and Gravilla, which were closer and would give easier access to the bush than from the death house on the cul-de-sac up the hill.

While Moira talked, I e-mailed the video to Buckley's and my e-mail addresses. I wanted copies in case something happened to my phone.

"He wants to talk to you." She handed me the phone.

"Good job, son." Buckley sounded happy and sober. A rare combination. "Our Hail Mary may have been answered and we can free that young man. I wish I could get over there, but I'm on lunch break at court."

"We have it covered." Although I wasn't sure if I still had a job.

"Stay there and protect the scene. I'll call Chief Moretti and give him the good news. I'm sure he'll be overjoyed." A dusty chuckle. "He may go to the scene himself. The Eddington case helped put him on the road to becoming the chief. That and the Windsor mess."

Moretti. He'd be thrilled to find out that I'd helped to unravel his most famous arrest. I didn't look forward to feeling his rat eyes on me while crime-scene technicians dug up the murder weapon. The one never found eight years ago that was likely to get him a headline in the *San Diego U-T* newspaper. And not a flattering one.

"I'll leave Moira here to protect the scene and take Fellows home. I don't think we want him hanging around when the other side shows up."

"You're right. We want to keep him under wraps for as long as we can. Once the police see his affidavit, they'll be all over him like horseshit on a stablehand's boot."

"I'll get him home and tell him to lie low. You talk to Jack about me?"

"I got you today. The golf club may get you to the end."

"Thanks, Buckley." A thought that had been itching me since we found the golf club wedged its way back under my skin. "What if they find Randall's and his family's DNA on the golf club, but no one else's?"

"You sure know how to float a turd in the punch bowl, son."

Fellows didn't say a word on the drive to his house. He sat slumped down, peering out the car window like he was hiding from the world. Getting a jump-start on the rest of his life.

I pulled into the driveway of the house that fronted his cottage. He started to get out without a look or a word. I stopped him with a hand on his arm.

"You got somewhere you can hide your stash for a while?"

"Maybe." He gave me wide eyes and raised eyebrows. "Why?"

"Once the DA reads your affidavit, the police are going to take an interest in you. Time to take a break on dealing the weed and lie low."

"That's my livelihood, man."

"Keep it up, and you won't have to worry about food or rent or freedom for a long time."

"I gotcha, bro." He nodded his head and got out of the car with the energy of a geriatric who'd lost his walker.

It was nearing one o'clock and I was hungry for lunch. But I wanted to keep an eye on Trey. See if anyone came by, or whether he met with the big Raptor dude again. Even with today's find corroborating his story, I wasn't yet convinced that Trey was a piece of only one puzzle. Food would have to wait.

I lucked into a parking spot a half block from Trey's house. I pulled my binoculars out of the trunk and set up in the backseat, spying out the back window.

After a half hour my neck had a crick in it and my stomach was a grinding hole. My only solace was that I wasn't peeping through motel windows at naked bodies and breaking up marriages.

Trey hadn't come out to the street, and no one had gone through the driveway back to his little studio. Another half hour passed. The crick in my neck had turned into a wrench and the hole in my belly, a chasm. Sore and hungry, I could handle, but stupid had started to creep in. I dropped the binoculars on the seat next to me and slowly rotated my neck. It crackled like a biodegradable bag of potato chips. I was about to climb out of the backseat when a yellow Volkswagen Beetle pulled into the driveway fronting Trey's cottage. I picked the binos back up.

A blond woman got out of the Bug. I only got her profile, then her backside as she walked behind the main house, presumably to

Trey's cottage. She wore a Lycra workout outfit that showed off a fit body. She looked familiar, and I tabbed her for Trey's sister from the picture on the wall of his cottage.

I waited, the binos pinned on the driveway. A few minutes later, Trey and the woman came out to the car. He carried two duffel bags. Each big enough to carry his stash of weed. One bag for the weed, the other for his clothes? Looked like he hadn't just found a hideout for his weed, he'd found one for himself too. Smart. If the Raptors or the police came looking, they wouldn't find him at home.

Trey and the woman got into her car and it backed out of the driveway. I had to follow them and find Trey's new hideout in case he planned to hide from Buckley and me too.

I slid over the console into the driver's seat and started up the Mustang. The Bug made a left onto Jewel, heading toward Grand Avenue. I eased my way behind the car, staying half a block back to avoid detection.

The Bug turned left onto Garnet at the light and then north on Ingraham, heading out of the north end of Pacific Beach into La Jolla. Trey's sister lived in Ocean Beach, 180 degrees in the opposite direction.

I was pretty certain the blond woman was Trey's sister. I was pretty uncertain where she and Trey were going. The Bug made a right on La Jolla Mesa Drive and climbed the long hill up into La Jolla. Halfway up the hill, it made a right turn onto Lamplight.

I turned onto Lamplight and caught a glimpse of the Bug up on Candlelight Drive. It pulled into a driveway five houses up the street. I turned right on Candlelight, parked in front of a house on the corner, and watched Trey and his sister exit her car and go into the house.

I U-turned the Mustang and drove slowly up the hill, noting the address of the house Fellows had gone into as I passed it. 5564 Candlelight Drive. The home had a big bay window that, thankfully, no one looked out of as I drove by. A nice home in La Jolla that didn't match the address I had for Sierra Fellows in Ocean Beach. I needed to know who owned that house.

I knew how to find out, but didn't know if it was still fair to ask. I U-turned at the top of the hill, parked four houses above 5564, and pulled out my phone. As a realtor, Kim had access to homeowner information in San Diego County. She'd helped identify the owners of homes over the last two years, through which bedroom windows I'd had to peep.

Old habits were hard to break. She answered on the fourth ring.

"Rick." Not the usual enthusiasm. "Are you feeling better? Is everything okay?"

"Much." I suddenly wished I knew another realtor. "Thanks again for taking care of me the other night. Someday, I hope to repay half of all you've done for me, Kimmie."

"I'm not keeping score." Soft. "Besides, you saved my life. I can never repay that."

"We both know I put your life in danger." The guilt from that night and the whole Windsor mess clung to me like a shadow. Grasping tighter after the sun went down. "So, please let go of that."

"You came for me in the worst moment of my life, Rick." Sad. "I'll never let that go."

I knew she should, but, selfishly, was glad she hadn't.

"How's the real estate king?"

"Now I know you need a favor." Matter of fact. "Need another name of a home owner?"

She knew me too well, yet still remained my friend. No point in pretending. "5564 Candlelight Drive in La Jolla."

"Give me a few minutes." Click.

I shouldn't have called. I shouldn't have let her go the other night. I should have given her what she needed a long time ago.

Five minutes later, my phone rang. Kim.

"Dianne Elizabeth Wilkens is the name on the mortgage. Two n's in Dianne. Kevin Christopher Wilkens died three years ago and his wife, Dianne, became the sole owner. Well, she and the bank."

"Thanks, Kim." I wanted to tell her what she needed to hear. Three years ago. "I'll try not to bother you for a while."

Silence. Then, "You never bother me, Rick. Call me anytime. Now please take care of yourself and stay out of the emergency room."

"I'll try. You can call me anytime too."

"No, Rick." An uncomfortable pause. "You have to make the call. Bye." She hung up.

I had to make the call whether to screw up her life some more, leave her alone, or let her save me. I knew I could do the first. I wasn't sure about the other two. But first, I had to figure out who Dianne Wilkens was, and how she was connected to Trey and Sierra Fellows. Maybe it didn't matter in the effort to free Randall Eddington. But maybe it did. Until I could find out the real story about Trey Fellows, everything mattered.

I kept my eyes on Dianne Wilkens' house. A couple minutes later, Sierra Fellows emerged and got into her Bug. She headed back the way she'd come. I followed her all the way to her apartment in Ocean Beach.

So, it looked like she wasn't staying at the house on Candlelight, but now her brother was, and he'd left his car back home. If anyone went snooping around his house they'd see his car and think he was still there. He'd taken my advice about hiding his weed and done me one better. He'd hidden himself.

Well, from everyone but me. Hopefully, it would stay that way.

CHAPTER TWENTY

I got a bite to eat and made it back to the crime scene around three. The crime-scene techs were already there and had roped off roughly a fifty-by-fifty-foot square with yellow crime-scene tape. I watched from the asphalt path at the bottom of the hill with a group of on-lookers behind a line of four uniformed cops.

Moira stood up the hill just outside the tape, filming the crime scene techs who were filming on their own. Two uniformed cops stood off to her side to make sure she didn't try to enter the crime scene. The lab-coated techs had just extracted the golf club from the cactus and the bush when I arrived. The shaft of the sand wedge was almost all rust, and the grip had eroded to a few small patches of rubber. The techs tagged the wedge and stuffed it into a long paper bag. I didn't get a good look at the heavy head of the wedge which, although the shortest club, made it the heaviest.

And deadliest.

Detective Denton, the cop who had taken my stolen-gun report, stood outside the crime-scene tape on the opposite side of the square from Moira. A tall, bald detective whom I didn't know stood inside the tape near the techs taking notes. No sign of Chief Moretti. The second best highlight of the day only behind finding the golf club.

I showed my PI license to the patrolman nearest me and asked if I could join the other PI up the hill. He led me a few feet down the path and caught Detective Denton's attention up on the hill-side. The patrolman pointed at me then waved the OK sign with one hand and held his other up, palm open. Denton nodded and the patrolman let me walk up the path to the taped-off crime scene.

I caught Detective Denton out of the corner of my eye while I walked up the hill. She watched me with cop eyes. Unfriendly cop eyes.

Another fan from the Brick House. I'd have to start a club.

By the time I made it up to Moira, a crime-scene tech had already secured the golf club in the CST van. Two more techs examined the area around the cactus, and a third continued to film.

"I can take over and you can go home," I said to Moira.

"You kidding? I'm on the clock." She kept the video camera on the techs. "Gotta pay the rent and show the Cowboy Lawyer that I'm valuable."

"I think he already knows that."

"Hey, what did you do to the lady homicide dick?" She nodded her head at Detective Denton while holding the camera steady.

"Nothing." Except for lying to her on a police report. "Why?"

"She asked where you were when she arrived, and I got the feeling she wasn't a fan. Then she glared at you when you walked up here." She gave a slight nod. "Still is."

I looked over at Detective Denton. Moira was right. She lasered her eyes on mine, and even at twenty yards, I could see the hatred. I gave her a flat stare back with nothing in it. No anger, no amusement, no fear. Just a sponge to absorb her hate. The intensity of it surprised me. If she'd been a dog, she would have had bared teeth and drool hanging off a snarl. I would have expected that kind of hate from Chief Moretti. I'd earned it from him. Given it time to build, deepen, and fester.

I hadn't known Detective Denton long enough for such enmity. Sure, I'd lied to her when we both knew I was lying. That was cause for dislike, but such upfront animosity? Maybe I'd gotten her into a beef with Moretti. There had to be something more.

I broke my eye wrestle with Detective Denton and watched the techs.

"Mr. Cahill." Denton's voice. A command. She might as well have said, "Stop. Police."

I obeyed the command and looked back at her. She curled a finger at me to come. I looked at Moira, who gave me bug eyes.

"Tell Buckley to give my last check to you if Denton shoots me."

"Done."

I walked around the yellow tape over to Denton. "Detective. What can I do for you?"

"Do you know what that kid did to his family, Mr. Cahill?" She invaded my personal space. Bagel and cream cheese breath blew up at me.

"I know what someone did to that family. You don't have to convince me of its savagery. I'm just not sure 'that kid' did it."

"LJPD, twelve jurors, and the State of California were sure." The gold flecks in Denton's eyes burned the reflection of the sun. "What the hell do you know that they didn't?"

"I'm just following the evidence, Detective. If LJPD had such a locked-down case, you have nothing to worry about."

"You're following a made-up story about a hearsay confession, and wasting the State of California's time and money."

Buckley must have had to give LJPD just enough information to get them to examine the scene.

"Wasting taxpayers' money? That would make me a politician, Detective." I smiled at Denton. "I take great offense."

"This isn't a joke. You're trying to set a vicious killer free." Her nostrils flared like she smelled something disgusting, and it was me. "I don't find any humor in that."

"If Randall Eddington is truly the killer, then the DNA on the golf club should only prove that. Why is everyone at LJPD so nervous, Detective? What am I going to find if I keep digging?"

"You're going to find yourself in a deep hole without a way to get out." She turned and walked along the tape in the direction of another detective.

Was that a threat? I'd already been threatened by Moretti,

but he had something to lose if Randall's conviction was over-turned. He had worked the murder and was now chief of police. With the constant threat of a voter initiative to dissolve LJPD and farm out policing to the San Diego County Sheriff's Depart-ment, any bad press could put Moretti's job in jeopardy. He'd be forced to retire as a scapegoat to save the department.

What did Detective Denton stand to lose if Randall was set free? Her job, like all the other cops, if LJPD was dissolved. But that was a long shot. This seemed more personal to her. Why? She hadn't worked the original Eddington investigation. There'd been one female detective mentioned in the police report and that had been Detective West. Detective Denton had been Bob Reitzmeyer's partner, and he hadn't worked the case. If Denton had, Bob would have too.

Denton might be right about me being in a hole if I kept dig-ging. But I had the feeling that I'd uncover a lot of LJPD secrets before I hit bottom.

CHAPTER TWENTY-ONE

Buckley had called for a meeting at his office at six p.m., which gave me a couple hours to kill. I went home and threw a ball with Midnight in the backyard for a while. As much as he enjoyed it, I think I enjoyed it more. Watching Midnight sprint after the ball and nab it like a Gold Glove shortstop kept my mind off the Eddington case, my long-term job prospects with La Jolla Investigations, my messed-up relationship with Kim, and, always, Colleen. But reality and responsibilities clawed at the edges of my idyllic respite, and I soon went back inside the house and up to my office.

As helpful as Trey Fellows had been to the case—without him there was no case—I still didn't trust him one hundred percent. Or even fifty. I needed more info on him, his sister, his sister's boyfriend, Brad Larson—the guy in the lone picture on Trey's living room wall that Trey inadvertently glanced at a few times when he was uncomfortable—and on Dianne Wilkens, the owner of the house where he now hid out.

I googled Dianne Wilkens first and found nothing about a woman with that name in San Diego. The name came up on Facebook, but the person didn't live in San Diego. Next, Brad Larson, San Diego. Hundreds of links came up and even a few pictures. None matched the picture on Trey's wall, and none of the links seemed like a match for Trey or his sister.

Only eighteen Brad Larsons listed on Facebook. None matched the picture on Trey's wall. I'd searched Trey on both Google and Facebook after I decided to take the case and hadn't found a match. Dianne Wilkens, Trey, and Larson should give classes on how to avoid your fifteen minutes of fame in the Internet age.

I typed Sierra Fellows on Facebook. There was one who lived in San Diego. Her profile picture was taken down by the Ocean Beach pier. It was her. The woman in the photo on Trey's wall and the one who drove him to Candlelight Drive in the yellow Bug. Big blue eyes, tan, long blond hair with natural ocean-air waves in it.

I searched Sierra's Facebook photo albums and didn't find any photos of Brad Larson. Not in the last three years. I finally found some in the album from 2011. The picture of her and Larson was there along with many others. There were also ones of Larson and Trey at various beaches. The two of them smiling in wet suits, flashing mahalo fingers. All the captions used only first names. I clicked on Larson's face to see if he'd come up with a Facebook page under another name. Nothing.

So, Trey had lied about being friends with Larson. Lie number...too many to remember. Either that, or they'd had a huge falling-out in the last four years. I doubted it, not with the photo of Sierra and Larson still on Trey's wall. Why the lies from the man Buckley was balancing his whole case on to get Randall a new trial? There was always that other puzzle he was working on, and I didn't know where the pieces fit.

I went back to the more recent photos in Sierra's albums. No more photos of Larson or anyone to replace him. I now noticed that her smiles weren't as big and easy as the ones in the earlier years with Larson. Where was he now, and what had happened between Sierra and him?

* * *

Buckley's receptionist, Jasmine, greeted me in his outer office. Well, greet was a bit generous. She grunted something monosyllabic. Jasmine was pretty in a semi-Goth sort of way, but with hard dark eyes. Skin ink peeked out from an open button just above her cleavage. I'd always figured she wasn't just a wannabe tough chick, but really had a story. I'd never asked Buckley about it. Some people don't want their story told, especially by someone else.

Jasmine didn't seem to like me, but maybe she didn't like anybody. I was used to both. She ushered me into Buckley's main office. Moira MacFarlane stood talking to a stunning young woman with long blond hair wearing a short tight dress. I'd never seen the woman before; I would have remembered. A short man with curly black hair and horn-rimmed glasses stood a step back from the women and listened to their conversation. I don't think I'd seen him before either. If I had, I wouldn't have remembered.

I was surprised to see Moira. I thought her gig had only been for the day. Maybe she was there to replace me and my reprieve was over.

A card table sat in the middle of the room with appetizers and booze on it. Buckley-style appetizers: cheese and crackers, mini pigs in a blanket, and little wedge quesadillas. Buckley held three fingers of Maker's Mark in one hand and a blanketed pig in the other.

He spotted me. "Good, everybody's here. Rick, grab a drink and a nibble, and let's get started."

He introduced the two younger people as Melinda and Jacob, his first-year associates. They had been working on the law behind the scenes while I'd been snooping around prisons, biker bars, and crime scenes.

Buckley sat down behind his desk and gave us the rundown on the case now that the police had the golf club. Once they had it booked into evidence, their lab would determine whether there was human DNA on the club. If there was, we would be given a sample to test at an independent laboratory.

Buckley anticipated LJPD dragging their feet, so he had Jacob write a brief for a judge to demand that they turn over the sample to Buckley tomorrow. Once they did, he would get it to the lab. State DNA laboratories could be backlogged for months, even years. Buckley said the private lab could provide results in a matter of days. If the sample came back positive for the Eddingtons, we knew we had the murder weapon. If it came back without Randall's DNA, but with someone else's, coupled with Trey Fellows' testimony about Steven Lunsdorf's confession, we probably had a new trial.

If the golf club came back with Randall's DNA on it, case closed. An argument could be made that he had used his father's golf clubs when he played golf. Under normal circumstances in the first trial, that might have been enough to cause reasonable doubt. But, the bar to get a judge to throw out Randall's conviction was much higher. There couldn't be any doubts lingering about Randall's participation in the crime.

Buckley wanted Moira and me to trade off keeping eyes on Trey Fellows to make sure he'd testify when needed. My turn to chime in.

"Fellows has taken up residence elsewhere."

"What?" Buckley leaned over the desk. "How do you know that?"

"I saw him load two duffel bags into his sister's car and drive off with her." I didn't mention that I'd probably put a scare into Fellows by telling him that the police would soon be interested in him and that he ought to curtail his marijuana sales.

"Where'd they go?"

"To a home in La Jolla owned by a Mrs. Dianne Wilkens. Husband deceased. Sierra Fellows left alone about an hour after arriving."

"You just happened to be at Mr. Fellows' house when his sister picked him up?" Buckley stroked his gray-bearded chin.

"I had just dropped him off after we located the golf club."

"So, Mr. Fellows knew you'd followed him to this house in La Jolla?"

"No. I staked him out and tailed him."

"What am I missing here, Rick?" His usual syrupy Texas twang now had a burr in it. "It sounds like you're running your own investigation again."

"I'm using my instincts. What you're paying me for. Or were, at least." I was all in now, so I gave him the rest; Trey's meeting with the Raptor in the bar yesterday and the Brad Larson mystery.

"Well, son, I appreciate you being thorough. I suppose." He scratched his beard. "But it seems to me that a drug dealer meeting with his supplier is not exactly the Kennedy assassination when it comes to conspiracies. And the mystery of Mr. Fellows' sister's boyfriend...well, that ain't Watergate."

Moira tried unsuccessfully to hide a smile, and the two associates suddenly took interest in the carpet. I didn't care. I was long past shame.

"Look, I know Trey's story is mostly matching up so far, and we found the golf club that Lunsdorf told him about. But there is something off about it. There's something else at play that I can't get my hands around, but I will. Soon." Maybe.

"Ms. MacFarlane, do you agree with Mr. Cahill's razor-sharp instincts?" He looked at Moira, who tried not to giggle.

"Not exactly." She kept her Kewpie Doll eyes on Buckley and wouldn't look at me. "Fellows is a little jittery, but I think anyone would be under the circumstances."

"Let's stick with the original plan for now." Buckley fished out a toothpick from the pocket of his snap-button cowboy shirt. "Keep an eye on Mr. Fellows for the next couple days. You two can rotate shifts to, say, ten o'clock at night. I think that should be late enough."

"Do you think we should just call him and see if he tells us on his own that he's moved?" Moira asked Buckley.

I jumped in before Buckley could answer. "I wouldn't do that. If he's really hiding out from everyone, including us, he might spook and try to hide somewhere else. Forever."

Moira's entire face pinched in on itself.

"Well, Rick might be right." Buckley smiled like a dad trying to correct his daughter without hurting her confidence. I guess he didn't see me as a son, despite the number of times he addressed me that way. "Let's watch him for now and then decide how to proceed."

I hoped we'd be the only ones watching.

CHAPTER TWENTY-TWO

I took the first night of surveillance of Trey's hideaway on Candlelight Drive. I parked up the hill where I had earlier that day, well out of Trey's view but an easy distance with the help of binoculars.

Christmas lights hung from the eaves and trees of most of the homes on the block. Multicolored old-school teardrops, modern icicles, and single-color themed homes. Twinkling trees in front of open-draped windows. The Christmas season was in full bloom in La Jolla. Except for Trey Fellows' hideout.

I pulled some binoculars from my backpack and pointed them towards 5564 Candlelight. The front of the house came into sharp view. The driveway sat empty. A planter box with geraniums fronted the big bay window that was probably part of the family room. Closed white curtains gave off a soft backlit glow. No light on the porch, but I could make out that the front door was closed.

An hour in, a beat-up Ford F-150 pickup truck made a left at the bottom of the hill and roared up Candlelight. I hit it with the binoculars. A wide stack of shoulders with a buffalo head of beard and sagebrush hair took up the driver's side. The man-mountain could have been the same biker I saw talking to Trey in the dive bar yesterday. Also may not have been. Those bikers all looked alike to me. A man about half the size of the driver sat in the passenger seat. Beardless and mostly hairless, he looked like Jeff to the driver's Mutt.

The truck wasn't going fast enough to be worthy of its roar, but its muffler was either broken or had been removed. It Y-turned and stopped in front of Trey's new place, and the odd couple got out. The mountain wore a leather Raptor jacket and jeans. His sidekick was older and wore slacks and a blazer. He carried a briefcase with him. I grabbed my camera out of my backpack and snapped off a shot of the mountain and the thin man and the truck.

They went up to the front porch, and I could just make out the big one knock on the door. A couple seconds later the door opened and Trey stood backlit in the doorway. I couldn't make out his face, but he didn't hesitate to let the men inside. His body movements gave off neither fear nor surprise. He'd been expecting his guests.

I replaced the camera with the more powerful binoculars, zeroed in on the truck, and jotted down its license number on a small notepad. Then I called Moira.

"You have a friend at LJPD or San Diego PD who can run a plate for you?" I didn't have any friends on any police departments. Not for over ten years. Bob Reitzmeyer always made the phone calls for me when I needed car registration information while working for LJI.

"I got somebody in La Jolla." She sounded relieved that I hadn't asked for a bigger favor. She wouldn't be for long. "Give me the plate number."

I read her the letters and numbers off my pad.

"I'll call you back in a few minutes." She hung up.

I brought the binos back up to my eyes and focused on the house. Five minutes passed. No action. No phone call from Moira. On the job for Reitzmeyer, I'd spent hours waiting with binoculars pinned to my eyes. Watching people commit marital sins or waiting for them to. Sometimes, in uncomfortable positions. Sometimes, relaxed. I knew how to wait. But waiting was only worth it if you were gathering information. Short of Moira's call with the name of the owner of the truck, I'd gotten all the information I could sitting in my car. Guests had dropped by a house that Fellows had made his hideout. They looked like invited guests. Time for a little reconnaissance.

I plugged earbuds into my already muted iPhone and put the phone into my right pants pocket. If Moira called, I'd take the call through the earbuds. I toggled the Mustang's overhead light switch to off and got out of the car.

The night had a bite to it. Winter cold for Southern California. Early spring for the Midwest. I wore dark-blue jeans, a bomber jacket, and a black Callaway golf hat. Not easy to pick up in the dark, but a resident just out for a stroll if headlights hit me. I walked, hidden under the golf hat, down the sidewalk toward Fellows' new home.

The light from the streetlight down the block ran out of illumination by the time it made it up the hill to Trey's house. Dark was good. The garage door had a series of square windows across the top. I pointed my cell phone flashlight through the window and peeked inside. Empty. The owner of the house most likely wasn't home and Trey was staying there alone. Except for his new guests.

I went over to the sidewalk and glanced into the back and cab of the F-150 pickup as I walked past it. The back had a built-in toolbox and a couple of loose chains. The chains were probably for securing motorcycles, but I could envision a Raptor using them for something more colorful. And painful. The cab was empty except for take-out food wrappers.

I kept moving and glanced up at the house. Curtains closed. Same glow from behind that I'd seen when I pulled up over an hour ago. I slowed after I passed the house and checked both sides of the street up and down the hill. Nobody out walking and nobody peeking out at the street through windows.

I moved under the cover of an elm tree and looked back up at Fellows' house. I caught the corner of the family room from the angle where the front window and the one to the backyard came together to form an edge. A wood-slat fence blocked all but the upper quarter of the window to the backyard. From that angle, there was a sliver of a view into the living room between the curtains and window. From down below, all I could see was a slice of the ceiling. If I got closer along the fence on the same level of the house, I'd be able to see if anyone was in the family room.

I scouted the street and the windows of the neighborhood houses again. Clear. I walked over to the fence like it was the most natural thing for me to do at night in somebody else's neighborhood and followed it up along the front lawn. I kept my head just below the top of the fence. When I got to within a yard of the window, I slowly pushed my head up so that my eyes just peeked over the top of the fence. I saw a shadow rising up to the ceiling. I raised my head an inch and moved it slightly to the left. The man-mountain stood with his oak-tree arms crossed, staring down at something. I looked to the right and saw that he was looking at Fellows and the thin man sitting at a table.

The thin man's briefcase was opened on the table. Fellows looked down at something in front of him. I couldn't see what it was.

The thin man stood up and closed the briefcase. Fellows stood up and shook his hand. The guests were about to leave. I ducked my head down, but something on the wall above the fireplace caught my eyes just before they went below the fence. It was a photo that looked familiar, but I didn't have time to look at it again.

I backed down the slope away from the fence to the sidewalk. Then I sprinted up the hill toward the Mustang. My phone vibrated in my pocket right before I made it to my car. I tapped on the microphone/call receiver that was on the cord to the earbuds and answered.

"Yeah." Out on a rush of breath.

"Why are you out of breath, Cahill," Moira asked. "What are you up to now?'

"Explain later." I gulped in some air. "What did you find out?"

She paused. I waited. "The truck is registered to a Helen Grant."

Hadn't expected the owner to be a woman.

"Has a brother named Eric Schmidt." She sounded triumphant, so I knew there was more coming. "Has a rap sheet for assault and drug distribution. Known to be a member of the Raptors."

The information just confirmed what I'd already figured out, but now I had a name to attach to the mountain.

Moira sounded like she wanted a pat on the back. I didn't think getting the info was anything above and beyond. Any PI would have gone further than Helen Grant, but I patted her anyway. I needed a favor.

"Nice work, Moira. Thanks."

"You sound surprised."

"Not at all." I turned on the ignition, but left the lights off. "But I need your help. There's another dude with Schmidt. Looks like a lawyer. I think we should find out more about him. He and Schmidt are about to leave, and I'm going to tail them. I need you to come over here and watch the house while I'm gone."

"Did you run this by Mr. Buckley?" Little sister voice about to rat out her big brother. Even though she had me by at least five years. "You're supposed to stay and watch the house, not follow people who visit it."

"No time. You want to earn Brownie points with the boss or do some real PI work?"

"You're an asshole, Cahill."

"We already established that. Call me when you get to the house." I hung up.

Schmidt and the thin man left Fellows' hideout and got into the truck. It coughed to a start and took off down the street, turning on the first right the way it came in. I knew the street had a stop sign instead of a traffic light. The cross street wasn't a particularly busy one so Schmidt wouldn't have to wait long before he turned. Still, I kept my headlights off as I rolled down the hill.

By the time I got to the turn, the truck was already gone. Red taillights shone two hundred yards down the hill to the left. They seemed too close together for a truck. I gambled and turned right, leaving a streak of rubber as I pushed the Mustang hard up the hill. I pulled my foot off the gas, slammed my fingers down onto the electric window buttons and the windows slipped into the doors. I strained to listen past the gentle hum of the motor. Then I heard it. The distant rumble of the truck up the hill, well beyond the bend.

I pushed the gas pedal back down and turned on the lights. If I came up on Schmidt now, I was just another vehicle on the road. I caught the truck's taillights and followed it all the way up and over Mount Soledad and onto La Jolla Shores Drive up the winding hill to La Jolla Farms Road. The Farms is where the real money in La Jolla lives. The homes are mansions on huge estates. The values of the real estate is added up in multiples of five million. Rich company for a biker gang member driving a run-down pickup truck.

I began the left turn onto the Farms when a Maserati Gran Turismo blew through a stop sign. I jammed on the brakes and the Maserati did too, fishtailing into a one-eighty right in front of me, blocking my entry into the Farms. The window went down and a middle finger came out. Yeah, asshole, it was my fault. The Maserati burned rubber in reverse, then slammed into first and sped past me to go and ruin someone else's night. I finished the turn and searched for the truck's taillights.

Lost them.

I goosed the accelerator and wound around the street. The truck appeared beyond a bend, backing out of a driveway. From the angle, the truck looked like it might have just completed a Y-turn. No pedestrian visible in the driveway or on the street. I went past the truck and pulled the brim of my cap down to block the headlights and peeked at the cab. I caught a glimpse of hair and beard pointed in my direction, but the passenger side looked empty.

I slowed and continued down the street a couple houses until the truck's taillights disappeared behind me. I did my own Y-turn and stopped in front of the house where the truck had done the same. I guessed that Schmidt had either dropped the thin man at this house or at the one across the street. I wrote down the addresses for each and called Kim after I'd promised not to bother her for a while.

"Rick." She answered on the fifth ring and didn't seem happy about it. The clock may have run out on her "call anytime" offer.

"I hate to bother you again, but I need another favor." No point beating around the bush this time.

"Don't expect me to be surprised." Her voice, cold as her words. I must have caught her at a bad time. Unless I was becoming the bad time.

"Sorry. I wouldn't have called if it wasn't important."

"Important to you." A man's voice murmured in the background. The voice of the man whose picture was in the foreground at every bus stop in La Jolla. "I'm a bit busy right now, Rick."

She could have ignored my call but picked up to tell me she was busy. Was that for Bus Stop Man or for me? Either way, it made me odd man out. Where I belonged, but had never been relegated to before tonight.

"Well then, I guess it can wait. Thanks."

"I'll call you back in a little while. Good-bye, Rick."

CHAPTER TWENTY-THREE

I made it back to my perch above Fellows' hideout by 9:10 p.m. Moira was parked on the other side of the street. She flipped me off and drove away as soon as my car came to a complete stop.

Kim hadn't called me back yet. Maybe she wouldn't until tomorrow. Or never. Something had changed with her. Maybe she was upset about the other night. Upset that we kissed or, maybe, upset that we stopped. Either way, I now truly felt like an ex. I'd stayed just close enough after our breakup to remain a part of her life. Even with the new boyfriend, we'd talk at least once a week.

I could have found another real estate source. She could have spent more time talking to her boyfriend. But we had still fit and we still liked each other more than we liked most anyone else. Until now?

Ten o'clock. Still no call from Kim. My detail was done for the night, but I had one last thing to do. I pulled my backup binoculars from my backpack. They were about the size of opera glasses, small and not as powerful as the larger binoculars I'd been using earlier. But that was fine. I wouldn't need too much range.

I checked the streets. Empty. I got out of my car and walked down the sidewalk toward Fellows' house. When I got to the house's property line, I sidled up along the fence like I had earlier. The light was still on in the living room. I peeked through the curtains. No sign of Fellows. That was fine. He wasn't my target. I scanned the wall above the fireplace and found the photograph that I'd spotted earlier before my quick retreat.

I had time now. The picture was among a collage of photos in a large, wrought-iron frame. It looked like a smaller version of the picture of Trey's sister and her boyfriend at Trey's house. Brad Larson. I used the binos to get a closer look. It was the same photograph. But why was it on the wall of Trey's hideout? His sister lived in Ocean Beach. The owner of the house was Dianne Wilkens. Who was she to Trey and his sister? And who was Brad Larson to her?

I zeroed in on the other pictures in the collage. Larson was in three of the other thirteen photos. Maybe a couple more if he was the blond-haired kid at various stages of childhood. So, Larson must have been Dianne Wilkens' son. Maybe she'd been married more than once. Thus the different last name. Sierra was just in the one photo. Trey wasn't in any.

I walked back up the hill to my Mustang and called Trey's cell phone. The call went to voicemail. I hung up and called again. Fellows answered on the second ring this time.

"Has anyone from the La Jolla Police Department contacted you?"

"No, man. Shit. Are they going to?" Jumpy.

"Eventually, but you knew that." Calm, a friend checking up. "Just want to make sure they don't drop by while you're swallowing smoke, and they decide to search your house and find your stash. You know, the Mason jars?"

"Yeah, yeah." Quickly. "I took care of that."

That wasn't quite a lie. He had moved his stash when he moved himself. I didn't expect him to volunteer the last part.

"Everything else cool? You haven't seen or heard from any of the Raptors, have you?"

"No. Why would I?"

"Just checking to make sure they haven't caught onto anything." Even when I expected it, I didn't like being lied to. I fought the urge to call him on it and make him tell me what was going on. But I deferred to Buckley's wishes. For a change. "Call me if anybody contacts you. Keep it tight. You're doing the right thing."

So far, and for reasons I couldn't figure out.

A couple breaths of silence. Finally, just above a whisper, "I hope so."

"I'll be in touch." I hung up.

Trey had chosen to keep his secrets to himself and kept pushing off lies. I knew about the lies, but not the secrets within them. He was playing a game even more dangerous than the one he was playing for our team. I just didn't know what it was yet.

I didn't see the cop car pull up behind me, but I felt it. I had my head down, stuffing the camera and binoculars into my backpack. The car's light bar vibrated rainbows and winked at me in my rearview mirror. If I'd had my police scanner on, I might have heard the dispatch call to investigate the man with binoculars in the Mustang GT on Candlelight Drive.

I sat very still with my hands at my sides. Every cop stationed out of the Brick House hated me. I didn't want to make a sudden move and let one of them turn me into a martyr.

"Put your hands on the steering wheel where I can see them and don't move." Loud speaker from the car.

I did as I was told. I eyed a second cop inching up in a crouch along the driver's side of the car through the side-view mirror. Two handed grip on a sidearm pointed at me. These guys weren't joking and neither would I. The second cop stopped just behind my left ear.

"Slowly put your hands out the window." He sounded young and anxious. That made me feel old and anxious.

A light flashed in from the other side of the car behind me. The cop on my side whipped open my door.

"Slowly step out of the car, please." His gun was back in his holster, but he kept his hand on the butt.

I did as I was told.

"License and registration, please." He was probably less than a year out of the academy, and looked like he spent most of his free time bench pressing continents.

"I have to get the registration out of the glove compartment. Okay if I reach back into the car and get it?"

"Just give me your driver's license."

I pulled out my wallet and gave it to him. The other cop had circled around to the back of my car, outlined in colored shadows from the light bar.

"Do you mind telling me what you are doing sitting in a car at night staring at homes through binoculars, Mr. Cahill?"

"And those binoculars wouldn't just happen to have been targeted on any bedroom windows, would they, Cahill?" The other cop jumped in before I could answer. Not that I had a good one. He came out of the shadows and nodded the junior officer to the squad car, no doubt to run a warrant check on me.

The senior cop wore sergeant's stripes and his gold nameplate read Castro. He was in his early fifties, losing hair and gaining pounds around the middle. I didn't know him but had the feeling, by the way he said my name, that he already knew all about me. And probably my father before me.

"I'm a private investigator working surveillance on a case. I can show you my PI license if you like." I took the license out of my wallet.

"And just what case is that?"

"It's confidential." I didn't want to alert them to Trey Fellows.

"You may have come here for legitimate reasons, Cahill." He snatched the license from my hand. "But once you got here, you fell back into your old routine of peeking through bedroom windows hoping for a show. Pretty sick gig, getting paid to be a Peeping Tom."

Yeah. He knew me and he knew my specialty. I had a reputation at the Brick House, but I thought it was just for being a multiple murder suspect, a bad cop, and the son of a bad cop. Now my private investigations forte was part of the tale? I doubted it. Something else was at play.

"Well, if you have a complaint then take me to the Brick House. Otherwise, let me get back to my job."

"You got pictures of high school girls taking showers in that camera you just put in your backpack? Or something worse?"

If I showed him what was on the camera he could figure out

what house I'd been staking out, as well as get a look at the men who went into it. If he decided to investigate, Trey might panic and get busted with five pounds of weed, or flee before I could tail him. If I didn't show the cop, he'd probably continue with his intimidation con game.

I rode the con.

"Not even their mothers."

Castro eyeballed me and smiled. Not in a friendly way.

"Any paper, Ives?" Castro yelled back at the patrolman in the car.

I looked over at the young cop sitting at the dashboard computer of his police car. The young cop shook his head. No warrants with my name on them. For now.

"Stay put, Cahill." Sergeant Castro walked back to the patrol car and said something to the kid.

I leaned against my car and folded my arms across my chest. I could front it off to the cops that this was just another day at the office, but, inside, my nerves twitched and my stomach sucked in on itself. The kid eyeballed me without expression. A pretty decent attempt at a cop stare for a rookie.

I noticed a triangle of light coming from a window across the street. And the silhouette of a head in the middle of it. While I'd been watching 5564 Candlelight, someone had been watching me and then called the police. Only a week removed from peeping on cheaters and I'd already lost my edge.

Castro made a call on a cell phone, then got out of the squad car and walked over to me. "Cahill, hop in the backseat of the cruiser so we can head over to the station."

"Are you arresting me?" The words came out steady but my heart wasn't.

Castro put his hands on his hips and the kid stepped in close.

"I will if you don't play nice."

"On what grounds?"

"How about peeping through people's windows and jerking off in public?"

I stared at him and shook my head. He had the badge. I had the binoculars. His word stood for something no matter what he said. Mine would always be tinged with guilt. At least, until my wife's murderer was caught. And maybe even after. Somebody at the Brick House wanted to talk to me. I was going there one way or another. At least this time, I had a choice.

I walked over to the cruiser, and the kid opened the back door and guided me in. Castro disappeared, then I heard the Mustang's door close and he returned to the squad car with my backpack in his hand. In it, my camera and photos of Trey's hide-out, the Raptor, and the man with the briefcase.

"You have a warrant for that, Sergeant Castro?" I tried to sound cocksure instead of nervous that he might look at the pictures in the camera.

"Just taking it for safekeeping during your little visit to the Brick House. Wouldn't want anyone to steal it while you're being a good citizen."

I stayed silent for the ten-minute ride to the police station and prayed my visit there wouldn't end in a room with bars for windows.

CHAPTER TWENTY-FOUR

Officer Ives led me up the back stairs of the Brick House to Robbery/Homicide and Sergeant Castro lagged behind. With my backpack. I'd made this trek two years ago with a couple detectives. Sweat pebbled my hairline. It hadn't been a good memory. I hadn't had a good memory in a police station for over ten years. I'd had enough bad ones since then to erase all the good ones that had come before.

We stopped outside the door of Robbery/Homicide. Castro stuck his head in. "We have a package for you, Detective Denton."

Denton. This could be a long night. The detective appeared at the door and looked about as happy to see me as I was to see her.

"This time we'll talk in an interview room, Mr. Cahill." She nodded to Sergeant Castro and he led me down the hall to the same tiny square room I'd been in two years ago. Now I felt sweat under my arms and down my back.

I hadn't done anything wrong. Not this time. It didn't matter. Being on the wrong side of the table in a square white room could make any innocent man feel guilty.

"Thank you, Sergeant. I'll take it from here." Sergeant Castro smiled at Detective Denton, then handed her my backpack and left, closing the door behind him. It was just the two of us now in the small room with a buzzing fluorescent light overhead. She pointed to a tiny desk surrounded by three chairs in the corner. "Have a seat, Mr. Cahill."

I took the chair facing the closed-circuit camera over the door. I knew if I'd taken either of the other two, she would have asked me to move. Like I said, I'd been there before. The only thing missing was another detective. They sometimes worked in pairs. Maybe I only rated one.

Denton sat down opposite me and set the backpack in the empty third chair. Nobody had time to see the pictures in the camera. Yet.

She wore olive-green slacks and a tan blouse covered by a navy blazer. Her black hair was pulled back in a tight ponytail, and she wore just a hint of eyeliner and no lipstick.

All business.

"Can you tell me what you were doing, loitering in a car with binoculars and a camera in a residential neighborhood in the middle of the night, Mr. Cahill?" Her face went up one shade of red, and she bit off the words like I'd personally offended her. But she hadn't turned on a tape recorder and the light on the closed-circuit camera hadn't turned red.

Our little chat wasn't being recorded. At least, not yet. Why not? Because it wasn't about me peeping in windows. Not even Sergeant Castro believed that. It had been a ruse to get me down to the Brick House to talk to Detective Denton about something else. Randall Eddington.

"I'm working surveillance on a case." I leaned back in my chair like I owned the room. The sweat under my arms trickled down my side.

"And what case is that?" Denton leaned back too. Either to mirror my body language or settle in for a long night.

"Confidential."

"Your case is a dog, Cahill." She folded her arms across her chest and her eyes went black. "Randall Eddington killed his family, and you're only adding to his grandparents' grief by giving them false hope. Are you proud of the way you make a living, Rick? By sucking money out of other people's sorrow?"

I'd graduated from Peeping Tom to ghoul. Denton wasn't covering new ground, but she wasn't going to guilt me into quitting the case. She couldn't teach me a thing about guilt. I'd earned my masters in it ten years ago. Still, I didn't like the accusation.

"Is LJPD really that worried, Detective?" I leaned toward her across the table. Only an inch or two, but just enough to let Denton know that I could ask questions under the white lights as well as answer them. "Afraid that the golf club is going to come back with DNA from everybody but Randall Eddington? Including the real killer?"

"I know that club is going to come back with the Eddington family's DNA on it. And you're right about one thing. Randall's DNA won't be on it, but neither will some other killer's." She had air-quoted the word "killer's" with her fingers. "The kid used latex gloves. There was a box of them in the garage. Didn't Bob tell you that?"

"No. Why would he know that?"

Her eyes shot down to the table. She'd tried to catch herself from giving up too much. Too late. She'd cracked out of turn.

By Bob, she meant Bob Reitzmeyer, my boss. For now, at least. But Bob told me he hadn't worked the case and, according to the police report, neither had Detective Denton. The only detectives listed on the report were Tony Moretti, Dan Coyote, and Haley West.

"It was a high-profile case." Eyes back on me. Composure restored. "Everyone was interested in it."

Apparently, you too. "Why weren't the latex gloves in the police report?"

"They were in the discovery documents for the trial." She gave me a smirk that would have made Chief Moretti proud. "The DA didn't need the gloves because we didn't have the murder weapon to check for prints or DNA. But we had the blood on Randall's sock. An open-and-shut case. Now you're wasting everyone's time, and those poor people's emotions and money trying to unlock a shut case."

"Well, I guess we'll wait and see when the DNA comes back. Anything else, Detective? It's past my bedtime."

"Why were you peeping in La Jolla? I know you're not working an infidelity detail for Bob Reitzmeyer." She leaned back in her chair and folded her arms.

"Confidential."

"Do you really want to spend the rest of the night in a jail cell protecting information for a monster who murdered his family eight years ago?" No more smile. Hard eyes and pinched lips.

She didn't have anything worthy of locking me up. Sergeant Castro might play the public indecency card, but LJPD wouldn't want to take me to trial. Castro may be willing to perjure himself on the witness stand, but I doubted that freshly minted Officer Ives would. And if he did, it was a conspiracy. Too much to lose for such a minor charge.

The rivers of sweat flowing down my sides only heard "jail cell." I hoped Detective Denton wasn't close enough to smell the fear wafting from under my arms.

"Does LJPD really want to risk a lawsuit for wrongful arrest, conspiracy, and extortion, when its very existence could be on the line with a petition from the people of La Jolla?"

All my chips were on the table. I folded my arms tight across my chest so Denton couldn't sniff out the bluff.

"You're right, Mr. Cahill." The smile came back and my gut tightened. "Just so there is no misunderstanding, please check your backpack to make sure nothing's missing from it."

I looked at the backpack, at Detective Denton, then up at the closed-circuit camera above the door. Still no red light. Still off the record. But still in a small white room of the Brick House where everyone had guns and badges but me. Nothing would be missing from the backpack. Just something added. Something planted to put me in jail that night, or worse.

"That's okay, Detective." I smiled but could smell the fear of my own sweat. "I'm sure the backpack that's been out of my possession for a couple minutes has only my camera and two sets of binoculars. That's what I'm certain I had in there when Sergeant Castro took the backpack into his custody."

"Open it, Rick." She drilled down on me. Granite eyes and white lips. "As I said, I don't want there to be *any* misunderstanding."

She'd keep playing this game until it worked out the way she wanted it to.

"I think I'd be more comfortable with my lawyer here when I open it."

"Okay." The smile. More sweat. "I can wait. I'll make sure the camera is turned on just so we can have everything on record."

I wanted to spend the night at home in my bed. I had the feeling that wouldn't happen unless I risked spending it in jail. I grabbed the backpack off the chair and unzipped the main pocket. Camera and binoculars still there.

And a baggie a quarter full of tiny, white granulated crystals. Cocaine, or something worse

My heartbeat double-tapped, and a rivulet of sweat broke free from my hairline and ran down into the corner of my left eye. I left the baggie where it was, zipped up the backpack, and set it back down on the empty chair.

"Everything accounted for?" Denton cop-eyed me.

"Yes." I tried to steady my breath. "And someone put a baggie full of some white substance in there."

"Well, let's leave that where it is for now." She got up, grabbed her chair, and set it down at the end of the table about six inches from me, then sat down. "Are you hot, Rick? You're sweating. You could use a shower." She waved a hand in front of her nose.

"Tell me what you want, Detective."

"Give me the name of your witness and what you were doing in La Jolla tonight, and you can take your backpack and go home and take a shower."

They'd have Trey's name as soon as Buckley petitioned a judge to throw out Randall's conviction. Did I want to risk going to jail to give Trey a few extra days of anonymity? He'd have to face the cops sooner or later. If he was going to crack, what difference did it make if he did it now or later?

"I don't know his name. Buckley doesn't trust me."

Maybe Trey would crack, but the few extra days would give me time to find the holes in LJPD's arrest that they were so worried about. So worried that they were willing to falsify evidence

and put me in jail. Had they done the same to Randall Eddington? The harder they squeezed me, the more I believed Randall
was innocent.

Detective Denton had the badge and the power. Her and Sergeant Castro's word against mine. I didn't stand a chance. Except that
they'd be risking LJPD's entire existence if the truth ever got out.

I was all in.

"Why in the world would Buckley hire you if he didn't trust
you?" She leaned in so her face was two inches from mine. All-
day coffee breath. "You think I'm stupid?"

No. Just not smart enough. "The Eddingtons made him hire
me. They think I'm a hero because of the Windsor thing a couple
years ago. Buckley hates me, but doesn't have a choice."

"If you really were a hero, you wouldn't have taken the case,
spared those poor people added grief." She stared at nothing.
"They've suffered enough."

"If it wasn't me, it would be someone else."

"But it is you." She focused her stare back on me. "And I
think you're lying."

"Call Moira MacFarlane. She's the lead. I'm just window
dressing to keep the Eddingtons happy. You met her today at the
crime scene. The witness only talks to her." I pulled Moira's card
out of my wallet and put it on the table. "Give her a call if you
want and ask her about me."

A gamble, but the whole night was. Besides, the little I knew
about Moira, I got the feeling she liked authority about as much
as I did. I gambled she wouldn't give Denton anything.

"I got her contact information at the scene." She slid the card
along the table into my lap and gave me the stone eyes. "Who
were you staking out up on Candlelight Drive tonight?"

"I can't tell you."

"Fine. Go ahead and call your lawyer." She stood up. "I'm going to go turn on the camera."

I waited until she was a yard from the door. "Okay. Shit. I

was...ah...keeping track of my girlfriend." I put my hand to my forehead, squeezed, and closed my eyes.

"Your girlfriend." A question without the question mark.

"Ex."

"Gee, I wonder why. I thought you were kind of creepy. What's her name? Does she have a restraining order on you yet?"

Hooked her.

"No." More head squeezing and some heavy breathing. "Kim Connelly. She's a realtor in La Jolla."

"Wait here, Cahill." Denton left the room.

If she called Kim, I had faith that Kim knew my relationship with LJPD well enough that she'd cover for me. I checked the light on the closed-circuit camera. Still off. I grabbed the backpack, opened it, and used my shirttail over my hand to pull the baggie out and toss it onto the table.

Detective Denton came back into the room with a cup of coffee just after I'd dropped the backpack on the chair and settled back into mine. I held the hangdog look. She looked at the baggie, then at me. She set the coffee down on the table and picked up the baggie full of tiny white crystals.

"Oh, here it is." She gave me her Moretti smirk, opened the baggie, took the spoon out of her coffee, stuck it inside, and doled out two spoonfuls of the substance into her cup. "Can't have my coffee without sugar."

I blinked a couple times and shook my head to let her think I felt stupid for giving up something to her. I did feel stupid. Just not as stupid as she thought I did.

"Things aren't always what they seem, Rick." She took an exaggerated sip of coffee. "Until they are. That's when you have to be worried. Keep your backpack close, and enjoy the rest of your evening."

She turned and left the room, leaving the door open and her threat hanging in the air.

CHAPTER TWENTY-FIVE

Castro and Ives drove me back to my car. The kid drove and Castro grinned at me over the front seat. They were a happy crew down there at the Brick House. A lot of smiling. When they weren't cop-eyeing you, intimidating you, or planting fake drugs on you, they smirked at you to try to make you feel small. It hadn't worked on me. Only made me sweaty.

Castro broke the silence. "You enjoy your talk with Miss Hailey?"

"Hailey?"

"Detective Denton."

Hailey had been the first name of Detective West in the police report of the Eddington murders. On a small police force like LJPD, it would have been a one-in-a-million shot to have two detectives with the somewhat uncommon first name of Hailey. Hailey Denton had been Hailey West. Divorce was hardly unusual for cops. Now her behavior made sense. She'd worked the Eddington murders and been the detective who found the blood evidence to seal Randall's fate. She had a vested interest in keeping the conviction righteous and Randall behind bars. And she'd been rattled enough to try to intimidate me off the case.

Something was wrong with that blood evidence.

Detective West/Denton had also been Bob Reitzmeyer's partner. If she'd worked the case, why hadn't he? Three detectives had been on the police report: Denton, now Police Chief Moretti, and Dan Coyote. The first two hated me. The third had been a friend once. The only one I'd had at LJPD after my dad had been forced out and Bob retired. But even that friendship had gone sour with the Windsor mess. Coyote had retired early after everything went down. Maybe time had healed our wound.

"Yeah. I found out she likes sugar in her coffee." I gave Castro his smile right back. "You two dream that up when you called her from Candlelight Drive?"

"I have no idea what you're talking about, Mr. Cahill." More smirk. Pleased with himself.

"I think you do. Maybe you can explain it to your boot, Officer Ives here, so he'll learn how the real police do it."

I looked out the window at the night and stayed quiet the rest of the way back to my car. I'd had enough of LJPD for a lifetime.

* * *

I pulled down my street and noticed for the first time that my house was one of the few without Christmas lights. It would just be Midnight and me this year. He didn't care whether I decorated or not.

He greeted me when I walked through the front door and led me through the living room to the sliding glass door that opened up onto the backyard. I let him out to do his business. He could hold it all day if he had to. He spent most days indoors when I was away at work. It wasn't fair, but life rarely is. Two years ago at another house, someone had thrown poisoned meat into my backyard and nearly killed Midnight. That person wasn't alive anymore, but I didn't want to take any chances. Midnight was my best friend. A cliché, but true. And that was all right by me.

I grabbed a beer from the fridge and joined Midnight outside. I sat down on a patio lounger. Midnight sat down next to me and leaned in. I scratched his head and we both looked out, past the rolling white-and-red lights of I-5, toward the sliver of ocean. It was barely visible during the day and now was just another shadow of the night. But I knew it was out there. Infinite. Forever. Unreachable.

Midnight's fur in one hand, a cold beer in the other. A constant low vroom wafted up from the highway. More a pleasant white noise than a distraction. I let it roll over me. The background hum of a life standing still. I thought of Colleen and the empty bedroom upstairs. The room that wasn't yet a gym and would never be a nursery. A shrine to an incomplete life.

The burr of my phone in my jacket pocket pulled me out of my thoughts. Good. I looked at the name on the screen. Kim. More thoughts, but I answered anyway.

"You needed a favor?" Not as gruff as the words, but not cheery, either.

"Sorry for the interruption earlier." Silence. "What did I interrupt?"

"Nothing."

This time I stayed silent.

"I'm moving in with Jeff." Soft, like it was a secret. I liked the silence better.

"I guess that would be the next logical step," I said. Magnanimous. Unfazed. Dishonest. "Congratulations."

"Thanks, Ricky." Warm. The "Ricky" hurt, but I wasn't sure why. She was the only person who I'd ever let call me that. It seemed too intimate now. Something from the past. Something I'd miss. Something I'd no longer earned.

"When's the big move?" I almost sounded like I was about to volunteer to help. Not quite.

"In the next couple of weeks. We want to be able to spend Christmas morning together."

Christmas was Kim's favorite holiday. It used to be mine too. She went into full, winter-wonderland decorative mode, right down to the Dickens' Village. She even decorated my house after we broke up. It would be up to me alone this year.

"Well, I'm happy for you." I wished I was. A better man would have been.

I warned her that Detective Denton might call and ask about me. Kim told me she wouldn't talk to Denton or anyone else at the Brick House. She had her own reasons and bad memories to dislike LJPD.

I gave her the addresses to the two houses where I'd seen the Raptor, Eric Schmidt, drop off the thin man. Well, where I'd guessed he'd dropped him off. Kim must have been in front of her computer because I heard the rattle of a keyboard. Ninety seconds later, I had the names of the owners of the two homes.

"Thanks, Kimmie. I owe you one."

"No, Rick. You don't owe me anything." Light. Like a stone had been rolled off her chest and she could breathe again. "Good luck with your case." She hung up.

Kim might as well have said "good luck with your life." She'd finally get the separation she needed to move on while I idled in neutral. Would she have changed her mind if I'd asked her not to make the move? Could I be that selfish? Or that smart? Apparently not.

I went upstairs to my office and dropped down in front of the computer. Donald Adam Briscoe was the first name Kim had given me. The names on homeowner deeds generally had the middle name included. Just like the press did with serial killers. I googled Donald Adam Briscoe and eight pictures of eight different men showed on the list. None looked like the man I'd seen tonight. I pulled the Adam out and got another eight pictures, only two of which were of men who hadn't been in the first set.

I tried the second name, Alan Wilson Rankin. Eight pictures again. Again, none of the thin man. I dropped the middle name and tried again. This time, all eight photos were of one man. The thin man.

I scrolled down the search lists and found a number of posts about Alan Rankin. I read them all. Alan Rankin was a criminal defense attorney and had defended a number of bad boys. Mexican Mafia soldiers and Carnales, Southeast San Diego crews, and biker-gang shot callers.

The Raptors.

I read and scrolled and clicked, oblivious to time. Newspaper links from the *San Diego U-T* and *Los Angeles Times* carried stories of a few of Rankin's high-profile cases. He got a Mexican

Mafia Carnal, a full-fledged member, three years for manslaughter instead of murder two.

A more recent article about him featured his defense of a Raptor captain named Raymond Oscar Karsten. Rankin hadn't been as successful this time. Five years ago, Karsten had gotten life without parole for beating a rival gang member to death with a tire iron. The article said he was doing his time up in Corcoran State Prison. Some outlaw website had gotten hold of crime-scene photos and posted them. Blood and bone and skin. None of it recognizable as belonging to a human being.

My pulse quickened. Not from the horror that I'd forced myself to look at, but from the modus operandi of the murder. Bludgeoned to death. Beyond recognition just like Thomas Eddington. The outlaw website had called the MO of the murder a Raptor signature. Could what the cops and I took for rage at the Eddington crime scene really been a Raptor signature? If we ever got Randall that second trial, this would be evidence in his favor.

When I finally moved my eyes from the Internet to the clock on the bottom right of the computer screen, I saw that it was after two a.m. I pushed my hands against the table, leaned back, and stared up at the ceiling. A big-time defense attorney who had defended a Raptor boss had apparently given Trey Fellows something out of his briefcase. Another jagged puzzle piece I didn't know where to put in the game Trey was playing on the side.

What was it? Money? Had Trey agreed not to testify against Raptor Steven Lunsdorf for cash? Was he waiting until the last minute to pull the rug out from under Randall Eddington for a few pieces of silver? I wanted to go back to Trey's hideout and squeeze him against the wall until some truth popped out. But Buckley would have to make the call on when to confront Trey. I just hoped he didn't wait too long.

I typed up a report about the night's events: my skirmish with LJPD and the visit to Trey by Raptor Eric Schmidt and Raptor lawyer Alan Rankin. It was almost three a.m. by the time I emailed the report to Buckley.

One more search to run before I called it a night, or maybe a morning. I hadn't gotten a match for a Brad Larson on a Google search earlier that fit the man in Trey's and Dianne Wilkens' photographs. This time I tried Brad Wilkens. Hundreds of names. None that linked with Trey or Dianne Wilkens. Brad Larson remained a mystery to be solved another day.

Time for bed. If not sleep.

I stared through the dark at the ceiling of my bedroom. I thought about Trey, Kim, Colleen, and the empty bedroom next to mine.

CHAPTER TWENTY-SIX

I bolted upright in my bed. The recurring nightmare hadn't awakened me this time. My own stupidity had. I jumped out of bed and ran downstairs to the kitchen. Midnight shadowed me, ears up, ready to protect and defend. I whipped out the camera from the backpack on the table and opened the slot that held the memory card. Empty. Shit. Sergeant Castro must have pulled the card from the camera when he stashed the bag of sugar in my backpack at the Brick House. The planted cocaine/sugar ruse had panicked me enough that I'd forgotten to check the camera for the memory card at the police station.

I grabbed my cell phone and called Trey. Voicemail. I called again. Voicemail again. Two more times. The same. Finally, on the fifth call, he answered.

"Bro, it's four o'clock in the morning." Groggy. "What the hell?"

"Where are you?"

"In bed, bro. Trying to sleep."

"Where in bed?"

"What's going on?" Now wide awake.

"Tell me where you are and don't lie."

"I'm at my sister's." Anxious. "Why?"

"Why are you at your sister's? Tell me the truth, Trey."

Silence. Then, "A couple of cops knocked on my door tonight and I got scared."

Probably Castro and Ives after they dropped me back at my car. Castro had seen the pictures of 5564 Candlelight I'd taken earlier that night after he stole the memory card from my camera.

"Did you talk to them?"

"No. I pretended I wasn't home. Why? What's going on?"

"This was at your house?" I wanted to see how long he'd keep up the charade.

A quick pause. "Yeah."

Now wasn't the time to call him on his lie. He was spooked enough already. "Where is your product?" The weed.

"I got rid of it like you told me to."

"Cut the shit, Trey. Where is it?"

Silent. "I left it..." The liar's pause. "...at home."

So, the weed was still at the Candlelight address. I'd figure out what to do about that later. "Leave it where it is until this thing blows over, and stay at your sister's at least through tomorrow."

"What's going on, Rick?"

"The police know you're a witness now, and they're going to try to discredit you if the case goes back to trial. As long as you don't do anything stupid, you'll be fine."

"But I need to make a living, man."

"I'll see if Buckley can get you something to live on until this thing's over. Go back to bed. I'll talk to you tomorrow." I hung up.

Sergeant Castro had stolen the memory card to my camera to find out who was staying at 5564 Candlelight Drive. Detective Denton had gotten her answers to her questions without me answering them.

Now they had photographs of the Raptor Eric Schmidt and the Raptor attorney Alan Rankin. I thought back to zooming in on the two with the camera. I'd only gotten profiles and the images hadn't been very clear. Hopefully, LJPD wouldn't be able to enhance the photos enough for anyone to recognize either of the men. If the cops started asking Schmidt or Rankin questions, they might find Trey again and force him to rabbit. If he hadn't already. And maybe it didn't matter if he was getting paid not to testify. I had to talk to Buckley first thing in the morning. Just a few hours from now.

I went back upstairs and stared at the ceiling until it was time to get up.

*＊＊

I left Buckley messages on his cell phone at 7:00 a.m., 7:30 a.m., 8:00 a.m., and 8:30 a.m. He returned none of them. I needed to talk to him about the events of last night, but he was ignoring me. He wasn't at his office when I got there at 9:00 a.m. I'd gone from pissed to worried.

I sat in the outer office where Jasmine ignored me too. She sat with her Doc Martens propped up on the desk, reading a *Rolling Stone* magazine.

"Jasmine, can you give me Buckley's home address?"

"No." She didn't look up from the magazine. I got the soles of her boots up on the desk and black eye shadow from her downcast eyes.

"He's not answering my calls and he should be here by now." I held my irritation in check for the greater good. "I'm worried about him. I need his address."

"That's against the firm's policy." No change in posture. "Sorry."

The sorry had a lilt in it as if she was enjoying herself.

"Then call him on his home line. I only have his cell phone number."

"Mr. Buckley doesn't like to be disturbed in the morning."

Somehow, I kept myself from slapping her feet off her desk. Instead, I went around to the keyboard of her computer, which was paused on Solitaire. Jasmine sprang out of her chair faster than seemed possible with her feet propped up on the desk.

"Get the fuck away from me!" Terror in her eyes. She whipped open a desk drawer and pulled out an oversized purse.

"Whoa." I put my hands up and spoke calmly. "I didn't mean to startle you. I was just trying to find Buckley's address."

"Stay the fuck away from me!" She pulled a small canister of pepper spray out and aimed it at me.

I knew what damage pepper spray could do. From firsthand experience. A canister malfunctioned on me back on the job in Santa Barbara. My eyes swelled shut and I blew snot bubbles out of my nose for an hour. I backed up with my hands out in front of me.

Buckley finally arrived in the middle of our standoff. "What in the G.W. Bush is goin' on?"

"He came at me." Jasmine kept the pepper spray pointed at me.

"No I didn't." I kept my hands in front of me to ward off flying pepper juice as long as she had the spray pinned on me. "I wanted to use her computer to find your address."

"Jasmine, darlin'." Slow Texas drawl. "Go ahead and put your pepper spray back in your purse. We'll get this all sorted out."

"I don't trust him." But she did put the canister away. "I don't want him here."

"Jasmine." I tried my calm tone again. "It was a misunderstanding."

"I'll handle this, Rick." Snappy, like he'd been on the phone about me questioning Jack Eddington. "Wait in my office and shut the door."

I went into his office, wondering what the hell had just happened. I paced the floor, the terror in Jasmine's eyes stamped into my mind. The fear was real. Was that how people saw me? Through fearful eyes?

Buckley came in a minute later, went to a pale oak credenza next to the window, and poured a cup of coffee. He held up the cup to me.

"No thanks." I continued to pace.

Buckley turned back to the credenza and opened a drawer. I caught a glimpse of silver, and it looked like he poured something from a flask into his coffee. A little hair of the dog. Or tail of the bull. Buckley drank from necessity, but necessity came from pain. Every alcoholic's did. My father's had. I knew his pain. I wondered what Buckley's was.

"Lemme hear your side." Buckley sat down behind his desk and took a sip of his spiced coffee.

I stopped pacing but remained standing and gave him my side. The only side. When I finished, he told me to sit down.

"Jasmine may seem tough, but she's quite fragile. She's had a hard life." The red spiderwebs in his eyes seemed to thicken and the corners of his mouth pulled down. "Harder than most. You can't get aggressive with her."

"Maybe I shouldn't have tried to use her computer, but I didn't get aggressive with her. She's disliked me from Day One and today was a wild overreaction. What's her problem with me?"

"She thinks you murdered your wife."

Now the fear in her eyes made sense. The reason most people hated me. Not the only reason for some, but the runaway winner for most. "What do you think?"

"Why, I like you, son." Another sip.

"That's not what I asked." My gut tightened. It mattered. A week ago, it wouldn't have. Now I cared what Buckley thought. Of me. "Do you think I killed my wife?"

"If you did, Rick, I figure you're already doing your time with the guilt that weighs you down every day like Atlas waiting to shrug."

"Do you think I did?" I searched his basset-hound eyes.

"I think you think you're responsible for her death in some way." He put the coffee mug down and leaned toward me. "But, no, I don't think you killed your wife."

The sense of relief I felt surprised me. But not enough to thank Buckley for believing in me.

"None of this would have happened if you answered your damn phone or returned a message, or if I knew where the hell you lived," I said.

"Oh. Thanks for reminding me." He opened a desk drawer and pulled out a cell phone. "Left the dang thing here last night." He wrote his home address on the back of a business card and handed it to me. Then he looked at the screen on his cell phone and probably saw my numerous calls. "Now what's got your chaps cinched so tight?"

"Did you read my report?"

"Not yet."

I recounted the events of last night: Eric Schmidt and Alan Rankin meeting with Trey, Rankin giving something to Trey, the police taking me to the Brick House, the planted fake drugs, the stolen camera memory card, Detective Denton/West questioning me and her implied threat, and Trey telling me he'd fled to his sister's.

I left out the picture of Brad Larson in the home of Trey's hideaway. He hadn't appreciated that thread earlier. I'd investigate that on my own. I also left out my suspicion that something was wrong with the blood evidence, and that I suspected that Bob Reitzmeyer had some connection to Randall Eddington's arrest.

Buckley was laser focused on the confession and the murder weapon. He was convinced those were what would get Randall a new trial. The rest was background noise for now. I let Buckley worry about the new trial; I worked best in the background.

Buckley sat quietly while I recounted the night, occasionally raising his eyebrows and writing a note on a legal pad. When I finished, he hit his hard coffee.

"I almost made a big mistake with you, son." He scratched his beard. "Thanks for talking me out of firing you. You can be a burr under my saddle, but you're a bulldog and a damn fine investigator. All you care about is the truth, and you're going to find it no matter what."

"Thanks, Buckley."

"Don't thank me. *No matter what* is a dangerous way to live." He tapped his head. "Without wisdom, you're gonna find your back against the wall more than the prettiest boy in prison."

"You calling me stupid or pretty, Buckley?"

"I'm telling you to be careful."

"Will do." I nodded. "What do you think we should do about Trey? What if the Raptors are paying him to recant his story?"

"That is an Albuquerque conundrum. Right now, we don't want to do anything to spook him. You and Ms. MacFarlane keep an eye on him and any visitors that show at his sister's. Once we get the DNA report from the lab, we'll decide how to proceed with Mr. Fellows."

"What do you know about Alan Rankin, the Raptor's attorney?"

"I've never had any dealings with him, but I watched him in court one afternoon. A mighty fine trial lawyer." Another sip of coffee that had lost its steam, but probably not its proof. "And I know a bit about his reputation outside the courtroom. He's shrewd, aggressive..." his voice trailed off.

"Yeah? What are you not saying?"

"I reckon he probably skates the edge a bit."

"Ethically? He's a lawyer. That's in his DNA."

"The edge of the law."

CHAPTER TWENTY-SEVEN

Former LJPD Detective Dan Coyote and I met on Torrey Pines Golf Course about four years ago. We'd both been singles and had been paired with a twosome. We got along well and ended up hitting the links together every few weeks for the next two years. That was before Dan found out that I was a never-ending person of interest in my wife's murder, and that my father had been forced off LJPD under murky circumstances.

He found all that out when the Windsor mess erupted and Detective Moretti zeroed his crosshairs on me. Dan lined up with all the other cops on one side of the thin blue line. I stood alone on the other. Even with all that, I don't think he liked the way Moretti handled things. I doubted the two traded Christmas cards.

I hadn't talked to Dan since he retired. We'd seen each other at Torrey Pines a few times, but pretended we hadn't. About time we finally talked.

I found Dan's phone number in my iPhone address book. I stared at the number but didn't punch it. Whatever had happened between Dan and LJPD aside, the Windsor case had turned Dan against me. I doubted that he'd be happy to hear from me, or be willing to set up an appointment to talk about the Eddington case. I needed to catch him off guard. At home.

Dan lived in La Mesa, a bedroom community twenty-five minutes southeast of La Jolla. La Mesa had the rolling hills of La Jolla and the same small-town feel. But fifteen degrees hotter in the summer and without the ocean views.

I'd been to Dan's house for dinner with his wife, Tracy, and young son, Tommy, once about three years ago. Neither Dan nor Tracy had accused me of killing my wife or called my father a bagman. Only because they had yet to learn about my past. Now they knew.

Dan lived up a windy hill just south of downtown La Mesa in a two-story house that would have cost over a million any-where in La Jolla. It probably cost him less than half that. His pickup truck sat in the driveway just under a basketball hoop. We had played a game of horse with little Tommy the last time I came here. I didn't think Dan would have to move his truck tonight.

I knocked on the door at 6:25 p.m. and waited, still not sure what I would say to Dan. Tracy opened the door. Petite and fit, she still looked like a college student, even though I knew she was older than me. Her blond hair, cropped in a youthful bob cut, had a red ribbon pinned above her left ear. She wore tights and a t-shirt and looked like she'd just returned from the gym. The smile she wore for front-door greetings dropped when she saw me.

"Hi, Tracy. Is Dan home?" I smiled like I was the next-door neighbor instead of a disgraced ex-cop and two-time murder suspect.

"Rick. What do you...Hold on." She gently closed the door on me. I figured she would have slammed it if she weren't com-ing back.

I waited. A minute later, Dan opened the door. Even less happy to see me than Tracy. PI work had been good to him. He'd dropped a few pounds since his LJPD days and, even though he was down to a dwindling half-moon of hair around his head, he looked younger than when I'd last seen him wearing a badge.

"What do you want, Rick?" Still no nonsense.

"About thirty minutes. I'll buy you a beer, then drop you back home. No damage done."

He looked over his shoulder, then stepped out onto the porch and closed the door behind him.

"You think you can just drop by here without calling ahead,

and we'll go have a beer like old times?" His Apache cheekbones flashed red under the porch light and he stabbed his chin at me. "After what happened? After everything you did?"

He was right. What the hell was I thinking? Nonetheless, Eddington case or not, I had to set the record straight. "What I did was try to help someone wrongfully arrested for murder and keep myself out of jail." I gave him a piece of my own chin. "Oh yeah, and try not to get killed."

"You don't even see it, do you?" He raised his hands and shook his head. "You are so self-involved that you can't even see what you did."

"What did I do?"

"People died because of you. If you had just come to me with what you knew instead of playing hero—"

"You worked for a corrupt police force. Remember? Or have you forgotten the reasons for your early retirement? I couldn't trust any of you." But he was mostly right. I could have done things differently. But so could have LJPD.

"Call next time, Rick. You'll save yourself a trip." He turned and opened the door.

"How come Bob Reitzmeyer isn't mentioned in the police report of the Eddington murders?"

"Eddington murders?" He closed the door and turned back to face me. "That was seven or eight years ago. Why the hell are you asking about that now?"

"Let's go get that beer and I'll tell you."

"You're not listening." He shook his head. "We're not pals anymore. I wouldn't be caught dead in public with a man who got away with murdering his wife."

I didn't think he believed that. Or maybe he did. It didn't matter.

"I'll wear a hat and we can sit in a dark corner." I shrugged my shoulders. "Believe what you want about me, Dan. I don't care. But I know, beyond all else, you care about justice. That's why you quit LJPD two years ago."

"Randall Eddington got justice."

"Then what's the harm if we have a beer and talk about it?"

He stared dark cop-eyes at me for what seemed like an hour. Finally, "I'll give you thirty minutes."

* * *

Dan picked the bar. A hole-in-the-wall pub with dim lighting and customers uninterested in anything but the drinks in front of them and their own sorrows. My kind of bar. Not Dan's. Except for tonight. I bet he picked the place because he'd never been in it before. If anyone recognized me because of my history, they wouldn't recognize him. We found a table in the back and settled in over a couple beers. I told him I was moonlighting with Timothy Buckley to try to get Randall Eddington a new trial.

When I finished, he said, "You've got twenty-four minutes left, Rick."

"I understand you think this is a waste of your time, Dan." I gave him a Clintonesque squint and tried to look earnest, then delivered the lie. "I'm just doing my due diligence. I've been stuck on the infidelity detail at LJI, and when Buckley came to me, I jumped at the chance to do something different. Now I wish I hadn't. The kid probably did it, but I owe it to the grandparents to cover all the bases. I'll try to be brief."

He studied me through dark eyes wedged between sharp cheekbones and a prominent forehead. Finally, "What do you want to know?"

"I know Bob Reitzmeyer was at the crime scene the night of the murders." I wasn't sure, but now was time to find out. "Why isn't he listed in the police report? Detective West was, and I know she and Bob were partners."

"They were partners, all right." The words and his raised eyebrows told me they were more than partners. Maybe the reason for West/Denton's divorce and one of Bob's three. "But why aren't you asking Bob this instead of me?"

"I'm walking a tightrope." I blew out a loud breath. "Bob allowed me to moonlight on vacation time, then got mad when he found out it was the Eddington murders. I'm trying to keep my real job and give the Eddington grandparents full value at the same time. I can't ask Bob anything."

Dan downed the rest of his beer. Good. His body language had loosened up. Maybe the beer helped. I waved for the waitress to bring us two more.

"Bob, Hailey West, and Chief Moretti were already at the crime scene when I got there." Dan air quoted "Chief" with his fingers. I'd been right about there being animosity between the two of them. "Randall Eddington arrived soon thereafter, and Denton, or West, whatever her name was before the divorce, and I took him back to the Brick House to question him. When I went back to the scene, Bob was gone."

"Any idea why he left?"

The waitress arrived with round two, and Dan took a healthy swig before he answered. "I see you're not taking notes, and I don't suppose you're illegally taping me with some hidden recorder."

"No tape recorder. This is all background."

"If you attribute to me what I'm about to tell you, I'll deny it and do my best to make it difficult for you to work as an investigator in San Diego." He hit his beer again.

"No attribution."

"You know your boss is a hound, right?"

"I'd be a pretty crappy PI if I hadn't figured that out by now." Three divorces and too many girlfriends to count. "So, he and Detective West/Denton were having an affair."

"Of course, but that's not why Moretti took him off the case."

"Why, then?"

"You claim to be a good PI, Rick." He downed the rest of his beer and stood up. "You figure it out. But when you do, it won't change the facts of that night. Randall Eddington murdered his family. He's where he belongs as long as hell isn't an option. Thanks for the beers. I'll take a cab home."

He walked out of the bar.

Bob Reitzmeyer had had an affair with Alana Eddington before she was murdered. That had to be it. Moretti knew and couldn't allow Bob to be a part of the investigation. If he was and the defense found out, they'd put Bob on trial in the courtroom.

The affair was plausible. Bob had gone to the Eddingtons' at Thomas Eddington's request to find out who'd been stealing jewelry and money from the house. Bob and Alana had probably met then. I'd seen Bob around attractive women. The charm oozed out of his pores, unforced. It was almost Pavlovian, as if he couldn't help it. And I'd seen dozens of women succumb to his charm. Alana Eddington must have joined the long list.

Had Bob and Alana still been involved at the time of the murders? If so, did it matter? I didn't believe he had anything to do with the murders, but how long had he been at the crime scene that night? Did he investigate the scene at all? And why did he retire within a few months of Randall Eddington's arrest?

I thought I knew of a way to get some answers, but there were other questions that needed answering first.

CHAPTER TWENTY-EIGHT

I got up at six the next day and drove down to Ocean Beach. I had the morning watch of Sierra Fellows' apartment, but not for another three hours. I had something else to do that Buckley didn't need to know about, and probably wouldn't be happy if he did.

Ocean Beach was elegant Point Loma's kid sister. Cute when you cut through the '60s hippie wardrobe. Sierra lived in a faded apartment building near Dog Beach. A yellow Volkswagen Bug parked in the mini-lot out front told me she was probably home. The local cops used to call the area the War Zone because of the drug deals done on the street and the belligerent bums. The area hadn't exactly been gentrified, but the streets were now mostly clean of discarded drug paraphernalia and discarded lives.

Moira had gotten a confirmed sighting of Trey last night when he answered the door of Sierra's apartment for a pizza delivery. Now he was probably sleeping off a buzz on the couch. Or, hopefully not, down by the Ocean Beach pier doing a stint with the surfing dawn patrol.

But he wasn't my concern right now.

Fog grayed the morning and briny breezes lolled inland off the ocean. I sat in my car a quarter block down from Sierra's apartment building and watched the door to her upstairs unit. She came out at 7:10 a.m. and trotted down the stairs to the parking lot. She wore black slacks, t-shirt, and shoes. The shirt had a red insignia over the left breast that I was too far away to read. Probably the logo of the Morning Cup restaurant where she worked.

I knew the restaurant. The best breakfast in La Jolla. I gave

Sierra and her yellow Bug plenty of room as I followed her onto Sunset Cliffs Drive and out of Ocean Beach. No need to push it and show her the tail if I knew her destination. The fog eased a bit but still kept a lid on the morning as we hit La Jolla.

The Morning Cup was on Wall Street, a block down from the Brick House. I hadn't been there in a couple years. Too close to the Brick House and bad memories.

I found a parking spot atop Park Avenue next to a grass circle that held a long-poled American flag. I never knew who ran the flag up the pole in the morning and down in the evening, but I always thought of my father when I saw it. The flag had been there even back when my dad patrolled the streets of La Jolla in an LJPD squad car twenty-five years ago. When we passed by it during the last ride-along I'd ever take with him, he pointed up at it and said, "That flag up there still means something. Honor still means something."

Liquid filled his eyes. On someone else, I would have called it tears. But I'd never seen my father cry. And he didn't that day. Not quite. I was too afraid to ask him what was wrong. I was ten years old and didn't want to believe there was a world where my dad wasn't the smartest, toughest, and most heroic man in it.

Two months later, he resigned from the police force under corruption rumors. Nine years after that, he'd be dead. Cirrhosis of the liver. By then, I'd learned all about that other world.

The Morning Cup sat in an old, white brick building that had avoided the trendy gentrification of other restaurants just a block away. This morning, it was full and had a wait-list. After I'd waited outside for five minutes, a hipster with the millennial generation's perennial five-day facial growth called my name. I asked him if I could sit in Sierra's section. He gave me a crooked smile like we were sharing a secret and said, "Sure, bro."

The Morning Cup wedged ten small tables in its rectangular toy-box interior. Exposed brick and ductwork coupled with hanging knickknacks gave it a cool vibe. Five-Day Growth sat me at a two-top in front of the window and went over to Sierra, who stood at the coffee station filling morning cups. He said something to her and nodded over at me. I hid behind my menu. He'd obviously told her that I'd requested her section. No problem. I had a reason ready for her.

Sierra made the rounds of her tables and stood in front of me a couple minutes later.

"Are you ready to order?"

She strained a smile. The real truth rested in her blue eyes, which wanted to know who I was and why I'd asked to sit in her station.

"I'll take the Rosemary Eggs, scrambled, sourdough, and a glass of OJ." I handed her the menu. "Thanks."

"Thank you." She hesitated and pondered the question in her head. When she didn't ask it, I answered it for her.

"I'm in town on business and my brother recommended that I eat here. He's an old surfing buddy of Brad Larson." Brad Larson. The lone picture on Trey Fellow's wall had Larson and Sierra in it. "He hasn't heard from Brad in a while and wanted me to ask you how he's doing."

"I'm sorry, I don't know a Brad Larson."

"Really?" I played it light instead of accusatory. "My brother told me you were Brad's girlfriend."

Sierra's face flushed. She had to feel the heat and know that her face betrayed her words.

"I don't know a Brad Larson. Sorry." She gave me a fake smile. "I'd better go put in your order."

Sierra spun and hurried to the wait station. I kept my eyes on her, but she didn't look back at me. Why the lie? She had dozens of pictures of Larson on her Facebook page for the whole world to see. I didn't take her for stupid. She must have realized it would be easy for someone to put her and Larson together. Maybe it was a reflex reaction and she hadn't thought it through. If that was the case, there had to be a reason the question caused a reflex.

Trey Fellows' puzzle pieces, the Raptor and the lawyer, Sierra's lie, and Brad Larson, all ran an itch up the back of my neck.

I wanted to put my fingernails to that itch, but Buckley wouldn't let me. Not yet.

I didn't know how long I could wait.

Ten minutes later, Sierra brought my breakfast over to me. She wore the smeared-on smile and wouldn't meet my eyes.

"Here you go." She placed a plate of scrambled eggs, rosemary-roasted potatoes, and a glass of orange juice down on the table in front of me and spun around to leave.

"Sierra, wait." I said it loud enough for the table next to me to look over. Too bad. I was tired of accepting things at other people's face value on this case.

"Yes?" Panicked eyes over the fake smile.

I lowered my voice, "Why are you lying about Brad Larson?"

She glanced around, and the couple at the next table went back to their own conversation.

"I'm not lying." Still wouldn't look at me. "I don't know a Brad Larson."

"I confess." I raised my shoulders in an "aw shucks" look and smiled. "I'm a curious guy in a Facebook world. When my brother gave me your name, I looked you up on Facebook and saw a bunch of pictures of you and Brad together."

Not a complete lie.

Her face burned a little brighter and the smile dropped. "You're the one who's lying. I don't know any Brad Larson and don't have any pictures of him on my Facebook page."

She spun around and went back to the wait station. It would probably take a subpoena to get her to tell me who the man was on her Facebook page and on the walls of her brother's apartment and Dianne Wilkens' house.

Who was lying now? Me, yes. Trey Fellows, probably. Sierra Fellows, maybe.

Five-Day Growth brought me the check when I was done with breakfast. He gave me a stink eye along with it. Couldn't argue with him. I left a large tip to buy off the guilt I felt about ruining Sierra Fellows' morning.

I'd followed Sierra to work to find out about the man who'd been featured in so many of her Facebook photos. Now I wasn't even sure I knew his real name. But his picture was still on the walls of Trey Fellows' cottage, Dianne Wilkens' house, and Sierra Fellows' Facebook page. My gut told me that "Brad Larson" was the corner piece of that other puzzle Trey Fellows was working on.

CHAPTER TWENTY-NINE

Buckley called me off my surveillance of Trey at noon and told me to meet him at his office. Uh oh, maybe my discussion with Dan Coyote last night or the one with Sierra Fellows this morning had somehow gotten back to him.

I was surprised to find Jasmine in the office on Saturday. She didn't cower in fear or point pepper spray at me. Instead, she ignored me. Progress. I quickly went into Buckley's office. Better his wrath than Jasmine's terror. Moira was there and actually smiled at me. Buckley did too. So, the meeting wasn't to chew me out. The day was looking up.

"Ya'll hungry?" Buckley put on his cowboy hat. "Follow me."

He led us downstairs to the restaurant across the street. Roppongi featured sushi and Asian fusion. I'd taken Kim there a few years ago. The food was excellent and expensive. I was glad Buckley was picking up the tab.

After we'd been seated and ordered, I raised my eyebrows at Buckley. "You expensing this one, Buckley? Did the Eddingtons cash out their last 401(k)?"

Moira rolled her eyes. Buckley shook his head and winced a closed-mouth smile.

"No, son. This one's on me."

"What's the occasion?"

"The results came back from the private DNA lab." Buckley smiled and lifted his hands up. "We go before an appellate judge next week."

"That's fantastic!" Moira smiled wider than I'd seen yet.

"Holy shit." I set down the beer I was about to hit. "How many strings did you have to pull for that quick a result?"

"Not too many. An old friend at the lab owed me a very big favor." Buckley took a swig of Maker's Mark neat. "Paid in full."

"So, Steven Lunsdorf's DNA was on the golf club along with the Eddingtons?" I asked.

"Not quite. There is DNA and blood from the three murdered Eddingtons, God bless their souls. There are some other DNA markers of an unknown person on the remains of the grip. Mr. Lunsdorf's DNA is not in the database, so it can't be compared. But the most important thing is that there is no DNA from Randall."

"What good is that? It proves the golf club was the murder weapon but nothing else."

"We have the affidavit from Trey Fellows stating that Mr. Lunsdorf told him that he hid the golf club he used to kill the Eddington family under some cactus down the hill behind their house. And that's where you found it."

"Will the affidavit stand up in court?"

"It will if it has to, but Mr. Fellows is going to testify anyhow."

"Have you forgotten that he met with the Raptor's lawyer the other night? Or that he's a drug dealer? And scared shitless."

"Rick, I appreciate your concern." Buckley laid a leathery hand on my arm. "But we're in tall cotton now, my boy. The work you and Ms. MacFarlane have done has made all the difference in this case. You two have given me the key to unlock that young man's cell."

"We have hearsay evidence and zero motive. I just can't believe that is going to be enough to make Eddington a free man."

"It's enough to free him from prison and get him a new trial. Motive is the DA's province."

A large slug of bourbon. "The Eddingtons will have to put up their condo for collateral on bail, but it's going to happen. The momentum is on our side, and the train's a rollin' down the track."

I still wasn't convinced, but I kept that to myself. I didn't want to ruin the party. Anyway, Buckley had been a lawyer longer than I'd been alive. He knew a whole lot more about the law than I did.

I'd been a cop. Not a great cop, probably not even a very good one. Not good enough for my lieutenant to stick up for me when the Santa Barbara Police Department booted me off the force. But, I'd been a cop long enough to develop a cop's gut, and my gut told me that Fellows couldn't be trusted. Somewhere along the way, he'd turn Buckley's defense to shit and doom Randall Eddington to life in his cell up at San Quentin.

Buckley looked at me after we'd all finished lunch and he'd polished off two more bourbons. "Now comes the tricky part." He kept his eyes on me. "As I said before, there were unknown DNA markers on the grip of the golf club. Not enough to identify anyone when matched against other DNA. However, it was enough to eliminate Randall as the owner of the DNA."

"The DNA doesn't necessarily have to belong to the killer," I chimed in when Buckley paused to hit his bourbon. "It could be from someone who borrowed the golf club and hit a few shots on the range, or the person who put the grips on the clubs. It could belong to anyone."

"You are right about all that, pardna." Buckley's eyes were more bloodshot than normal. "But it would make our case mighty strong if the limited number of markers matched those in Mr. Lunsdorf's DNA. There aren't enough markers to identify anyone, but there are enough to eliminate people. If Mr. Lunsdorf can't be eliminated, then that strengthens our claim."

"But I thought you said Lunsdorf's DNA isn't in any system," Moira said.

"We have to try to acquire some ourselves." Buckley trained his basset-hound eyes back on me.

"How are we going to do that?" Moira asked.

"Thus, the tricky part," I said before Buckley could. My ribs

and head began to ache. "I'm going to stake out the parking lot at
The Chalked Cue and snag one of Lunsdorf's discarded cigarette
butts."

"That was my plan, if you think you're up to it." Buckley
dipped his head.

"I'll be fine. I don't have to go inside the bar or confront any
Raptors. All I have to do is wait for the right moment."

"But will that even hold up in court?" Moira looked at
Buckley.

"Not at a trial. In a trial, we'd get a court order for the
DNA. But an appellate judge might accept it with the other evidence we offer regarding the murder weapon to help him make a
decision."

Moira and I walked Buckley up the stairs to his office a half
hour later. He'd had four bourbons and, judging from his wobble,
another two or three before he met us. He'd been celebrating victory before the final whistle, but I didn't begrudge him. There
was hurt hiding behind Buckley's bloodshot eyes and his smiles
mostly seemed like a lot of work. I didn't think he'd had many
victories in his life outside of a courtroom. Sometimes you had to
relish the moments that could never fill the emptiness.

Buckley stumbled through the door into his outer office and
I steadied him upright. Jasmine eyeballed us from behind her
desk. Thin black lips under goth eyes. She squinted at Buckley
and then shook her head at me like it was my fault.

"Timothy!" She stood up and swung around the desk toward
us. Latticed leather and knee-high boots.

Buckley hung his head like a scolded child. Suddenly, Buckley and Jasmine's relationship seemed familial. Father, daughter? It
was hard to see a resemblance under Jasmine's goth and Buckley's
beard. Still, there was a connection I'd never noticed before.

"Let me have him. You've done enough damage." Jasmine
grabbed Buckley's arm away from me and led him into his office.

I didn't bother to object. Her mind was made up. She knew
Buckley better than I did, but somehow I was responsible for his

condition. In her mind, I was a murderer and, apparently, an en-abler as well.

* * *

My car sat a block from Buckley's office. La Jolla Investigations was just another two blocks west. The job I'd taken a sabbatical from was there. The job given to me by Bob Reitzmeyer, my father's old partner and the only cop who went to the old man's funeral. Bob Reitzmeyer, the man who finagled the deal so that I could just af-ford to buy my new house.

Bob Reitzmeyer, who'd probably had an affair with Alana Eddington before she was murdered, and who told me he hadn't worked the case but had been at the crime scene.

I walked the three blocks to La Jolla Investigations.

The brass-and-copper facade on the building that housed LJI seemed shinier than when I was last there and its angles seemed sharper.

I'd only been gone a week, but I felt like a visitor when I used my key card to enter the building. The reception area was empty, so I went down the hallway past the conference room to Bob's of-fice. That was empty too. Probably for the best. I hadn't figured out what I'd say to Bob anyway. I'd gone to the office on instinct. Might be a good time to start using some of the wisdom Buckley had mentioned the other day. If only I knew where to find it.

I headed back down the hall toward the lobby and passed the storage room. I stopped. The storage room. Bob had taken me in there a couple times to show me some of the copies of files he kept from cases he'd worked on at LJPD. Would he have kept any notes he took from the Eddington murder the short time he was at the crime scene? One thing I knew about Bob, as messy as he was in his personal life, he kept his professional life regimented and organized.

I went back to Bob's office and found his office keys in a desk drawer. He rarely left his office unlocked, so he had prob-ably just gone to get some coffee. I didn't have much time, so I hustled back to the storage room and unlocked the door. I considered that I could be technically guilty of unlawful entry. That was the wisdom speaking that Buckley had mentioned. I ignored it and went to the corner of the room to the file cabinets where Bob kept the LJPD files. Locked, but I found a key on the key chain that unlocked them.

The file folders were alphabetical. There it was. A folder marked Eddington. I opened it and found a small notebook. Nothing else was in the folder. The files Bob had shown me of other murder cases had all contained copies of written reports from his LJPD "Murder Books," large blue binders he kept for each case at the Brick House. They'd also contained the original notebooks like the one in the Eddington file.

There weren't any written reports because Bob had been bumped from the case and never wrote up anything. The notebook read much like the Eddington police report in shorthand: what time Bob had arrived at the scene, who was there, the account from the neighbor who found the bodies, Randall's arrival on the scene. In every entry about Randall thereafter, he was referred to as "the suspect."

Bob had tabbed Randall as the murderer almost immediately, before he'd even been questioned by Detectives Coyote and West/Denton. I read through the remaining notes. The last entry sucked the air right out of me. Bob had written that he searched the suspect's car and had found a car registration, insurance card, and some music CDs.

No mention of a bloody sock.

Bob had searched Randall's car before Detective Denton and there had been no bloody sock. Someone had planted it in the car after Bob's search. If Bob's notes had been in the discovery evidence the DA was mandated to turn over to the defense before the trial, there wouldn't have been a trial. Except one for the cop who had planted evidence in a murder investigation.

Randall Eddington was going to be a free man.

I ripped out my cell phone and quickly took pictures of each page of the notebook, as well as the cover, the file, the file cabinets, and file room. Then I put everything away, locked the file room, and returned the keys to Bob's desk.

I'd just made it back to the lobby when Bob walked through the front door of the building carrying a cup of Starbucks coffee.

No hello, just, "How'd you get in here?"

"I have a key." I pulled out my key card. "I work here."

"Oh, yeah." Flat face. "Follow me to my office, and we can talk about work."

I did as told. Bob stopped at the door of his office and scanned the room. Probably looking for something out of place. I hoped I put the keys back in the correct part of the drawer. He finally went in and sat behind his desk. He pointed at a chair and I sat down.

He cop-eyed me like I was a crook. He was trying to sweat me. Maybe he knew what I'd done. No. Bob didn't have security cameras inside LJI, although he had some installed for the law firm upstairs, but not on our floor. I suspected that he didn't want there to be any video evidence of his late-night flings that sometimes took place at the office.

Finally, "Still working for Timothy Buckley?"

"Just the moonlighting that you okayed."

"How much longer?"

"I have another two weeks of vacation time left. It could be for that long."

"I need you for something tonight." Still cop eyes.

Bob had never given me such short notice to do a stakeout on a weekend before. This was strictly to get me off the Eddington case.

"I wish I could, Bob, but I already have something else to do."

He kept staring at me. The cop eyes slowly softened into sadness. "Your father was like a brother to me. He didn't deserve what he got. I tried to help him, but he wouldn't let me. Maybe I didn't try hard enough." His voice tightened. "I tried to do right by him when I hired you. You were broken when you started here, but I still saw a piece of the kid who used to sit at the dinner table and listen to cop stories. In a lot of ways, I saw you as the son I never had."

He wiped his eyes and stood up. "Wait here."

Reitzmeyer had me off balance. First the cop eyes and then the emotion. Emotion I'd never seen in him before. Guilt for the search of his files crept into my gut. If our positions were reversed, Bob would have asked me about the murder scene straight up. Too late. I'd already gotten the answers I needed from the notebook.

Bob walked back into the office carrying a large box. I thought it might hold some things of my father's that Bob had kept. He handed me the box. I looked inside and realized I'd been wrong. About too many things.

A framed photo of Colleen stared up at me. The one I kept on my desk there at LJI. Every other piece of personal property I'd kept at the desk was inside the box too. The air left my lungs like I'd been punched in the gut.

"I'll put a check in the mail tomorrow for whatever you're owed, plus a couple months' severance." Poker face. Flat voice. The emotion he'd shown earlier bottled back up. "Your father understood loyalty. You don't. That's not something I can teach."

My knees went weak. Down deep I knew this had to be the outcome, but it still hit me hard.

Bob had been my connection back to my dad during the good times before everything went to shit. Now all I had left were the old bad memories. And new bad ones. This was the result of living a "whatever it takes" life Buckley had warned me about.

"Goodbye, Rick." He didn't look at me, just shut the door behind me.

I lugged the box of all I had left from my two years at La Jolla Investigations the two blocks to my car. I'd gotten more than I could have hoped—a giant leap closer to making Randall Eddington a free man—but I'd lost a job.

I'd been fired by a friend once before. It didn't get easier the second time. I could find another job. Maybe even pay my mortgage. But I wouldn't be able to replace what I'd just lost.

CHAPTER THIRTY

The parking lot of the mini-mall that held The Chalked Cue hadn't changed in a week. I had. I didn't have a gun anymore and my ribs and head were sore. On the mend, but still sore. I sat in my Mustang parked in front of a Smart & Final store in an outer parking spot with a good view of The Chalked Cue. The store stayed open until 10:00 p.m., and it was now 8:05 p.m. I had another couple hours of cover until the cars cleared out.

I'd called Buckley after I left LJI with what I'd found. He explained to me what I already knew, that the evidence wouldn't be allowed in court because of how I'd obtained it. However, he agreed with me that once Randall was released, it could be a valuable tool in convincing the DA not to retry the case.

Buckley still wanted DNA from Steven Lunsdorf, if possible. Thus, I sat in my car with a zoom-lensed camera pointed at the front of The Chalked Cue. Moira had offered to ride shotgun, but I convinced her and Buckley that she should continue to stake out Trey instead. I wasn't going into the bar. Wouldn't even if I had my gun back. Not even with a howitzer. I'd stay safely outside, collect a cigarette butt, and flee the scene.

A full moon spotlighted the night, muscling out all but the brightest stars. The windows of my Mustang GT were tinted as dark as California would allow. They're opaque at night. Still, I ducked my head down whenever a car entered the parking lot. Couldn't be too careful. That was some of Buckley's wisdom talking.

I knew Lunsdorf was in the bar. His nickname was "Duke," and there was a Harley parked out front with that name emblazoned in orange flames on its gas tank. He'd come out sooner or later and light up. He'd had yellow smoker's teeth in his smirking booking photo. I doubted he'd started making healthy choices lately. I'd wait him out. I'd had a lot of practice waiting. I focused my camera on the front of the bar, not through the curtains of someone's bedroom. This was about murder and possibly freeing an innocent man, not broken marriage vows. As Buckley liked to say, this was a case that mattered.

A rumble pulled the camera down from my eyes. A beat-up Trans Am with a broken muffler or none at all pulled into the parking lot and parked near The Chalked Cue. What was it with these bikers and loud cars? Maybe after years of sitting atop 500cc engines they'd gone deaf, and only trusted a vehicle they could feel through the thundering woofer of life without a muffler.

I put the camera on the Trans Am and a mountain-sized man hoisted himself out of the muscle car. He could have been either the Raptor who cracked my head and ribs and stole my gun, or the guy who'd met with Fellows on the QT in the PB bar and then brought a lawyer to Fellows' Candlelight Drive hideout. Or it could have been just another Raptor side of beef with a buffalo head of black hair and a Rasputin beard.

I kept the camera pinned on him as he headed for the front door of the bar. The door opened before he got to it and a skin-head version of a Raptor came out. They said something to each other and the mountain turned his head in my direction as he finished the conversation. The light from The Chalked Cue neon sign caught his face and a scar across his eyebrow.

My attacker.

The man who'd pistol-whipped me and put a size 15 Timberland into my ribcage. My breaths came quick and through my nose and my gut turned over. Not because I was afraid. Because fight had kicked in over flight and I wanted revenge.

The man went into the bar and I sat in my car fogging the windows. I'd been hired to do a job, not to get even. But I didn't want even, I wanted one-up on even. And I wanted my gun back. I hadn't figured out how I could accomplish one or both yet, but

I was working on it. In the meantime, I kept the camera on the front door of The Chalked Cue and waited for a chance to complete the task I'd been hired to do.

I didn't have to wait very long. Fifteen minutes later, Steven Lunsdorf came out of the bar. Blond buzz cut, white t-shirt, and the rest, all leather. A woman was with him in matching attire. They didn't go to his chopper, but instead walked over to a eucalyptus tree in the corner of the parking lot. The orange flash of a lighter went up to a cigarette in Lunsdorf's mouth.

For the first time ever, I blessed the politicians up in Sacramento. Not even a gang as vicious as the Raptors wanted to take on the State of California and smoke in a bar. Or at least the bar owner didn't want to and was tough enough to make the Raptors comply.

I clipped off twenty or so shots with the camera without using the flash. The images would be a bit fuzzy, but the moon and the lights in the parking lot gave just enough illumination to make them identifiable. After a few minutes, both Lunsdorf and the woman flicked their butts into some ice plant that rimmed the parking lot.

Shit.

It would have been too easy if they'd just dropped the butts where they stood. Time to go to work. I put the camera away, took off my coat, grabbed a long-handled trash picker and paper grocery bag from the passenger seat, and got out of the car. Police always collect potential DNA evidence in paper bags because the evidence can collect mold in plastic. I didn't expect the cigarette butts to sit long, but I wouldn't take any chances.

The night had some bite to it, made that much colder without my coat. I wore jeans and a Dickies work shirt that had the name "Dave" above the left pocket. A Charger hat wore down low kept my head warm and gave me some cover.

I walked down the parking lot to the ice plant and zeroed in where Lunsdorf had flung his cigarette butt. There were at least fifty butts in the area, but only ten or fifteen that looked fresh. I plucked them up with the trash picker and smelled them for the scent of smoke. Only seven passed the smell test. Good. A small number for Buckley's friend at the DNA lab to test.

The good news was that, although Lunsdorf's DNA was not in any known database, his fingerprints would be. He'd been arrested a couple times and his prints would be in the FBI's IAFIS database. So, if I'd found the correct butt, his fingerprints would be on it, and the DNA on the butt could be linked to him.

I went back to my car and secured the paper bag with the cigarette butts in the trunk. While I was there, I pulled up the floor panel that covered the spare tire. Wedged next to the tire was a small duffel bag. The bag was gray, but it may as well have been black. It was where I kept my off-the-record tools. It held a lock-pick set, a blackjack, and a slim jim. For black-bag jobs. Bob Reitzmeyer didn't know about the bag. Neither did Buckley. They had never asked me to step over the line. That was my choice. I didn't use the contents of the bag often, but every time I did, I broke the law. I tossed the duffel onto the passenger seat.

I'd taken care of my professional task. Now I had a personal one to handle. I got into the Mustang, drove down the parking lot toward The Chalked Cue, and parked next to the Trans Am.

The man who owned the Trans Am had taken my gun away from me. A gun that I'd never fired and probably never would. Maybe never could. But I'd been a cop. Your gun was a piece of you. The man had taken my gun. A piece of me was missing.

Now was time to take it back.

My late father had told me long ago that sometimes you had to do what was right even when the law says it's wrong. Two years later, he was pushed off the police force for doing something wrong that I don't think even he thought was right. I didn't allow myself that cover. I just did what needed to get done. Tonight, I was just doing what I wanted done. No greater good involved.

I pulled out the slim jim and the lock-pick set from the duffel bag. The slim jim was a two-foot-long flat metal rod, about an inch and a half wide, with a plastic handle on one end and a hook cut out of the metal on the other. It was used by locksmiths to open car doors with keys locked inside. And by car thieves and rip-off artists. And by me. The slim jim only worked on older cars with the door lock on top. Like a '70s Trans Am. I could have used the lock-pick set on the car, but the slim jim was quicker. I'd need the picks if there was no latch for the trunk inside the car.

I put my coat back on against the chilled December night. The Trans Am was parked in the second row of cars in front of the bar, so I had cover from a pickup with oversized tires. I scanned the parking lot. Empty of people. I sidled up to the passenger side of the Trans Am where I had more cover, and checked the interior for a blinking light in the dash, signifying an alarm. Nothing. I tried the door handle. Locked. I slipped the hook end of the slim jim between the weather strip and the window near the lock, and gently wiggled it up and down during descent. I felt the hook latch onto something and saw the door lock move slightly. Bingo. I smoothly pulled up the tool and the lock clicked up.

I scanned the lot again, then ducked into the car. Empty Budweiser cans and fast-food wrappers were strewn on the floor below the passenger seat. This guy was a cheap date and a slob. The car smelled of stale beer, a combination of cigarette and marijuana smoke, and BO.

I'd only been inside ten seconds and I already wanted out. But I still had work to do. If my gun was in the car, I was going to find it. I opened the glove compartment and five years' worth of paper car registrations and take-out menus flopped out. I rummaged through the remaining debris. No gun. I looked under the passenger seat and sifted through more beer cans. Nothing. Same for under the driver's seat and in the backseat.

I went back into the front seat through the less-exposed passenger door to see if there was a latch for the trunk. I shimmied my torso across the seat and reached underneath the steering wheel in search of a trunk latch. Nothing. When I moved back to the passenger seat, the ashtray caught my eye. It was open a crack, and there was a small, folded piece of paper among smashed cigarette butts. I pulled it out and unfolded it. The address to Trey Fellows' hideaway was written on it. 5564 Candlelight Drive. Nothing else. I folded the paper up again and put it back in the ashtray, then exited the car.

Had Eric Schmidt, the Raptor who'd visited Trey with Alan Rankin, given the Trans Am owner the address, or had someone else? Someone on LJPD? I didn't have time to figure out who or what it meant now.

I went around to the trunk and pulled the pick set out of my pocket. I put the tension bar, a small, L-shaped piece of metal that looks like a flat Allen wrench, into the bottom of the key slot. Next the rake, another thin strip of metal that is shaped into a couple waves on the end, went into the top of the lock. I pulled the tension bar to the right while I moved the rake back and forth. One by one, the rake moved the lock pins into place and the key slot moved toward horizontal. I pulled out the tension bar and rake, replaced them with a flat-head screwdriver, twisted it up to vertical and the trunk lid popped open. The whole thing took less than a minute.

I pulled the lid up and looked inside. The trunk was more of a mess than the front seat. More crushed empty beer cans, a crowbar, a Phillips screwdriver, discarded newspapers, work gloves, a heavy chain, and a baseball bat with a small dark stain on the head that could have been dried blood. It could have been something innocent as well. My bet was on the blood.

On top of the mess were hundreds of fresh pine needles, like a tree had recently been shoved into the trunk. I guessed biker gangs celebrated Christmas too. At least the trunk smelled better than the rest of the car. I pulled up the floor panel and checked the spare tire well to see if the Raptor used my hiding place. Nothing. Just the tire. I closed the trunk.

I hadn't found my gun but I may have found something more valuable, the Candlelight address on the piece of paper in the Raptor's ashtray. If only I knew what it meant or what to do with it. I went back to my car and put the lock-pick tools back in the duffel bag, then went around to the trunk to put away the bag. A voice grabbed my attention as I opened the trunk. I peeked around it and saw the big Raptor with the scar talking to Steven Lunsdorf outside The Chalked Cue fifty feet away. Lunsdorf had been the Raptors' de facto shot caller since the real boss had been in prison. I wondered if Scarface was his enforcer. He fit the role.

I pulled the blackjack from the duffel bag, quietly closed the trunk, and crouched down behind my car. I had time to get into the Mustang and drive away before the big guy made it back to his car. That would have been the safe and smart thing to do. The pain in my ribs as I crouched down reminded me that I hadn't been safe and smart the last time I'd been to The Chalked Cue. It also reminded me of where the pain had come from.

I raised up a few inches so I could get a good look at the bar. The big one was still talking to Lunsdorf out front. I still had time to exit unnoticed.

I stayed put behind the car.

Lunsdorf handed something to the big Raptor, then went back inside the bar. The big dude held something between his thumb and forefinger. Maybe a small piece of paper. He studied it and then put it in the top pocket of his leather jacket. He scanned the parking lot and then headed in my direction.

I felt the blackjack's cool leather in my hand. The weapon was a leather strap with powdered lead in one end. I'd never used it before. Not even as a cop. If I did now, I could be looking at jail time if the Raptor pressed charges. It wouldn't matter that he had attacked me before. I was lying in wait. Serious time.

My life would be irrevocably changed by one stupid decision. I'd already made one of those decisions in my life. Ten years ago, I'd chosen not to pick up my wife from the library, and she'd been raped and murdered. I couldn't throw away the sliver of a life I had left.

I crouched back down and waited for the Raptor to get into his car and drive away. Five seconds later, I heard a key go into a lock and a car door open and shut. The engine didn't start right up, and I worried that the Raptor might have seen or sensed something wrong about the inside of his car. Maybe there'd been order in the mess. Maybe I hadn't put every empty Bud can in its proper place. Or maybe he was lighting up a cigarette or a blunt.

A footfall behind me told me I'd been wrong on all counts. "Waiting for somebody, motherfucker?"

I recognized his voice. I wondered if he recognized my back. Then I felt cold steel on my neck. The end of a round cylinder of cold steel. "Stand up slowly, asshole."

I'd felt the barrel of a gun pressed against my skin before. Two people had died that night, but not me. Had my luck run out? I did as I was told and the gun barrel stayed pinned to my neck. I kept the blackjack flat against my right leg.

"Think you can sneak up on me?" Apparently not. "Rock picked another dumb motherfucker to do his dirty work. Too bad for you. Start walking to the bar."

I didn't know who Rock was, but it didn't matter right now. I started walking slowly. If we made it into the bar, I'd either come out on a stretcher or in a body bag. I had to get the gun off my neck and make a move. Or just make a move and hope I was faster than his trigger finger. A quick movement would probably get me killed. I prayed a quick sound wouldn't.

CHAPTER THIRTY-ONE

I let out a sharp groan, stopped walking, and slowly hunched down and loudly hyperventilated.

The gun barrel lifted away, and I spun around and swung the blackjack at the Raptor's head just as the butt of the gun came down at my own. The blows landed at the same time. His had been a miss, hitting my left shoulder instead of my head. Mine, a direct hit to his forehead, just above the left eye. He staggered against his car, and I slammed the blackjack down onto the wrist of his gun hand. He yelped. The gun clattered to the ground, and he grabbed his dangling hand with his good one. I smashed the blackjack against his left temple. He hit the ground like a sack of cement falling off the back of a truck.

I grabbed the gun and pointed it at the Raptor. My hand shook. Not from the adrenaline coursing through my body. From fear. Not of the man lying below me. Fear that I'd have to fire a gun at a human being. Again.

Fear that I wouldn't be able to.

I lowered the gun. No need to fight the fear. The man was out cold. Blood oozed from a lump on his temple. He looked dead. I checked his throat for a pulse. Nothing. Shit.

I moved my hand and found it. Alive. Whew.

I examined the gun, then put it in my coat pocket. A wheel gun, but not my Ruger .357 Magnum. A Smith & Wesson .38 Special. Not as powerful as the Ruger, but deadly enough at close range. The serial number had been filed off. An untraceable gun for a biker hitter, or a throw-down gun for an unscrupulous cop. Or protection for a shaky PI who might never have the nerve to use it.

The adrenaline evaporated and left an empty echo inside me. My shoulder suddenly throbbed. Maybe it had throbbed all along but the adrenaline had covered it. I used my right shoulder, the good one, to lift the Raptor up off one ass cheek. I pulled his wallet from his back pocket, flipped it open, and found his driver's license. Wayne Delk, forty-two years old. I pulled out my iPhone and took a picture of the license.

I put the wallet back in Wayne Delk's pants. Then I remembered the piece of paper Lunsdorf had given him and pulled it out of his top pocket. The paper had been ripped from the bottom of a piece of notebook paper. An address was scrawled across it in masculine handwriting. 1635 Long Branch #6.

Sierra Fellows' address.

Voices came from the bar and moved toward the parking lot. I crouched down and slid around the Trans Am to my car, got in, and turned on the ignition. I backed out with the lights off. If I'd turned them on, they would have spotlighted Delk slumped up against his car. I eased my way out of the parking spot, pointed the car toward the exit, and turned on the lights.

It took more restraint than I'd shown all night to keep me from flooring the gas before I cleared the exit. My eyes stayed in the rearview mirror the whole way out. No commotion yet. I exited onto Clairemont Mesa Boulevard and gunned it for home.

Sierra Fellows' address on the piece of paper in Wayne Delk's pocket.

I whipped out my phone and called Trey Fellows. Voicemail.

"Trey, get you and your sister out of her apartment. Go to a hotel. Don't go home or back to Candlelight. Call me as soon as you get this."

I prayed he was still alive to hear the message.

Home would have to wait. I got onto 805 South, took it to I-8 West all the way to Ocean Beach. I had the accelerator pinned on eighty the whole way. Long Branch was just off Sunset Cliffs Boulevard, the main artery into OB. The street was away from the OB bar scene, but parking was still scarce. I had to park nearly a block away from Sierra Fellows' apartment building. I got out of my car and hustled down the street.

The night was cool and had the tang of an ocean breeze in it. My coat pocket felt heavy, and I remembered the gun I'd taken from Wayne Delk. With the serial number filed off, I didn't have to worry about Delk reporting a stolen gun to the police. I just had to worry about Wayne Delk. I wasn't even sure he'd gotten a good look at my face. If he had, I might spend the rest of my life looking over my shoulder and keeping my back to every wall.

The heft of the gun told me it was loaded, but I pulled it out and checked the cylinder to be sure. All five slots full. I hoped they'd remain that way when I checked on Trey and Sierra Fellows.

A couple of twenty-something dudes stumbled along the sidewalk across the street, high-fiving each other and uttering "bro" every third word. No one else on the street. No Choppers parked in front of Sierra Fellows' apartment building. At least, not yet.

Sierra's unit was the front one on the second floor. The building had five units on top and bottom and staircases at each end. I walked tight to the building underneath the second-floor balcony, all the way down to the far end. I wanted to approach from the back side in case someone was inside the apartment waiting for me or Trey to come up the nearest stairs.

I made it to Sierra's unit and peeked through the window where the blinds separated. No one in the living room. TV on. A shadow moved in the doorway of the lone bedroom. I shoved my hand in my pocket and felt cold steel. My breath caught in my throat. The shadow moved through the door and its human likeness followed. Sierra Fellows. Alone. She lugged a suitcase with both hands along her right side.

I backed away from the window and knocked on the door. Silence except for the sound of the TV. I knocked again and moved my face close to the door. "Sierra, it's Rick Cahill. I'm the guy who called Trey and warned him. Open the door. I'll take you somewhere safe."

I caught a slight movement of the blinds out of the corner of my eye. I stayed still so as not to spook her. The front door opened the width of a chain lock and Sierra's face appeared. Pretty, as I remembered. But scared. "You're that jerk from the restaurant. What do you want?"

"I'm sorry about that." I sounded sincere because I was. At times, my job called for me to manipulate and use people. Sometimes it didn't bother me. Sometimes it did. Looking into Sierra Fellows' frightened eyes, I now felt ashamed. "I was trying to get some information and should have been straightforward about it. But right now I want to get you out of here."

"How do I know you're who you say you are?"

I showed my PI's license. "I'm sure Trey's mentioned my name."

"He has." She nodded. "I just called a cab. It should be here in about ten minutes."

"I'll take you wherever you want to go. But we have to leave now." She unlocked the chain and let me in.

"Did Trey say where he was going?" His glass bong sat on a coffee table. He'd definitely fled in a hurry if he left behind his bong.

"No." She shook her head and looked down to her left. A lie.

"Sierra, I can help Trey, but you gotta tell me where he is."

"I don't know!" Shrill. Frightened.

"Let's go." I didn't have time to argue the truth out of her. Wayne Delk or some of his Raptor pals might show up any minute. I didn't figure to get lucky twice in one night.

I picked up Sierra's suitcase with my left hand and pain from my gun-butted shoulder almost made me drop it. I switched the suitcase to my right hand. Sierra grabbed a coat from a hall closet and followed me to the front door. I peeked through the blinds and didn't see anything threatening, then opened the door and stuck my head out. Clear.

"Leave the lights on and lock up," I said to Sierra, then sentried the balcony, looking down at the courtyard from the handrail.

Sierra locked the front door and met me at the rail. I heard a rumble from the street that sent a frozen buzz up my spine. The loud purr of an American muscle car. Like a 1970s Trans Am. A flash of black cruised by the parking lot of the apartment building. Wayne Delk's Trans Am, or its clone.

I turned to Sierra. "Is there a back way outta here?"

"There's a gate to the alley on the side." Big eyes. Tight mouth. Fear.

I grabbed her arm and shoved her toward the far staircase. "Go!"

She bolted for the staircase and I followed, lugging her suitcase and glancing over my shoulder at the street. No sign of the Trans Am, Delk, or any other Raptors. We shuffled down the stairs, and Sierra led me to the gate of an ivy-covered chain-link fence that separated the apartment complex from the alley. A car door slammed in the alley when we were two feet from the gate. And then another one.

I froze. Sierra grabbed my arm and pulled. I let her lead me around the back of the apartment building. We slipped in between two dumpsters and crouched down.

I pulled the gun out of my pocket. My hand trembled slightly. I put the gun down to my side so Sierra couldn't see it shake. Two sets of footsteps thundering up the staircase vibrated the apartment building. I glanced at Sierra. In the dark, I could only see the outline of her head and the huge round whites of her eyes. Fists hammering on a door upstairs shook the building and echoed through the courtyard. The Raptors had made it to Sierra's apartment. The whites of her eyes grew wider.

"Hey, you're shaking the—oh, sorry, bro." A neighbor's voice. Fear hung off the last three words.

"Where's Sierra and her brother?" Not Delk, but just as menacing.

"She just took off running down the stairs with some dude about a minute ago."

Footsteps pounded down the front stairs. I gripped the gun tighter in my hand. It still shook. The clomp-clomp of boots on cement. A car door opened and slammed shut. Just one. The two Raptors had separated. The Trans Am fired up and peeled out of the alley. Running footsteps faded away.

"Where's your car?" I whispered to Sierra.

"Trey took it."

"What's your phone number?" She gave it to me and I punched it into my phone. I gave her mine and had her do the same.

"I need to go get my car. I'll be right back. Do you have a friend here you can stay with for a few minutes?"

"I just moved in here a few weeks ago. I don't really know anybody."

"Then just stay here. I'll be right back. Put your phone on vibrate and stay here and wait for my call. If you think they've come back, call me and then call the police. I can get back here in less than a minute."

I stood up and Sierra grabbed my arm. "Don't leave me here alone. Let me go with you."

"I need to make sure it's safe first." The Raptors may have spotted my Mustang and been out on the street waiting.

"Please." She still held my arm, fingernails digging into my leather coat.

I pulled her hand off my arm and held it in my own. Then I put the .38 Special in it. "You ever fire one of these?"

She shook her head. "No."

"Just point and squeeze the trigger. It doesn't have a safety, so if you pull the trigger, make sure you mean it."

"I don't think I can." Her voice trembled like my hand had when I held the gun.

I didn't think I could, either. And I wasn't ready to force myself to find out. "You won't have to. They won't come back here. Not for a while. It's just a precaution. I'll call when it's safe."

I broke from Sierra before she could argue again and stayed close to the side of the building as I circled around to the front. I paused at the front edge of apartment #1 and scanned the courtyard, the parking lot, and then the street.

Clear.

But somewhere out there, Wayne Delk or someone just as dangerous was circling the streets in two thousand pounds of black death, and one of his men was on foot. Sierra Fellows now had the gun I'd pulled off Delk, but I still had the blackjack I'd used to take him down. I slipped my hand into my coat pocket just to be sure. Still there. I knew what damage I could do with it. A gun was still a question mark and might always be.

I eased through the lighted parking lot and then crossed the street to the darkened sidewalk.

Apartment buildings stood next to each other as the street pulled back away from the beach. Some with lighted parking lots. Most not. I stayed in the shadows, ears and eyes on high alert.

A half block from my car, I turned right on the next cross street, and jogged along it until it hit Brighton Avenue, which ran parallel to Long Branch. I hurried up Brighton to the next cross so I could approach my car from behind. If a Raptor was there, he'd expect me to come from the direction of Sierra's apartment building.

If I had to fight, I'd have the element of surprise and the blackjack in my pocket. A Raptor might have a gun. I gripped the blackjack and pulled it out. When I hit Long Branch, I stayed on the opposite side of the street from where my car was parked and walked slowly down the sidewalk.

Single-family homes had supplanted apartment buildings on this end of Long Branch. There were trees in front yards, hedges, and the occasional white picket fence. All possible hiding spots for Delk or his men. And for me.

I stopped behind an elm tree across the street and two houses down from my car. The house I'd parked in front of had a vine-covered picket fence about three feet high in front of it. I studied the fence and didn't see a head poking above it. That didn't mean there wasn't one attached to a Raptor hiding on the other side.

A large pepper tree grew in the next-door neighbor's yard abutting the picket fence. I focused my eyes on it, willing them to see through the dark, behind fences, and around trees. Nothing. Lights from a car rolled down the street. Not loud enough to be the Trans Am. I dropped lower behind the elm, but kept my eyes on the pepper tree. The car lights hit it, and I saw a flash of something dark, then it disappeared as the lights moved past. I kept staring at the tree. Nothing. No movement. The flash could have been a dark bit of bark, a shadow caught in the car lights, my imagination. Or it could have been a man's beard.

My bet was on the beard.

CHAPTER THIRTY-TWO

I angled across the street, well behind my car, eyeing the pepper tree the whole way. No movement, no beard, no nothing. My gut told me I'd seen a beard and there was a Raptor behind the pepper tree waiting for me to approach my car. I wasn't going to disappoint him. I silently walked toward the car and pulled my car key fob out of my pocket, careful not to let the keys jingle. Key fob in my left hand, blackjack in my right, I crept up to within fifteen feet of the tree. I stared at the back of the tree like I was trying to read the bottom line of an eye chart. Then the outline of a man snug against the tree slowly took shape.

Whoever he was, he was big. That's the way the Raptors grew them. I tried to locate his hands to see if he had a weapon. Too dark. I carefully took another step closer, but my foot caught a pebble and it scratched along the sidewalk. I jabbed the key fob twice to draw attention away from me toward the car. The Mustang's warning lights flashed and the horn sounded.

The outline jerked in the direction of the car. I bolted toward it and swung the blackjack down onto the back of the man's head. He crumpled down hard and a crowbar clattered across the sidewalk. I pounced on top of the man and turned him over onto his back. Unconscious. I didn't recognize him. Husky, black beard, leather jacket. A Raptor soldier. I rifled his pockets until I found a cell phone. I heaved the phone as far as I could and heard it crash down onto the street. The Raptor wouldn't be able to call Delk, or whoever was driving the Trans Am, or anyone else when he came to.

The porch lights flashed on from the house with the pepper

tree and the front door whipped open. I sprang up and dashed to my car and jumped inside.

"Hey!" A man's voice.

I throttled the ignition and tore down the street, then yanked out my cell phone and called Sierra.

"Hello?"

"Out front. Now."

I hung up and heard a low rumble in the distance behind me. Delk's Trans Am was out there somewhere searching for Sierra and me, just a couple blocks away. I slammed to a stop in front of Sierra's apartment building. No Sierra. The Trans Am rumble grew louder. Closer.

I fought the urge to hit the horn. Finally, Sierra trudged across the parking lot, both hands lugging her wheel-less ancient suitcase against her petite body. I jumped out of the car, ran over to Sierra, grabbed the suitcase, hustled her to the car, and threw it in the backseat. Just as Sierra and I slammed our doors in unison, I heard the siren.

Shit.

"Did you call the police?"

"No."

Must have been the man who owned the pepper-tree house. I prayed that he didn't get a good look at me or catch a glimpse of my license plate. Thank God for the dearth of streetlights on Long Branch.

After blowing my opportunity to lie in wait and assault Wayne Delk, I'd managed the deed against one of his minions. The fact that he'd been lying in wait for me and was armed with a crowbar might be mitigating circumstances if it ever went to trial. Cold solace.

I gunned the car down the street but eased the clutch enough not to squeal the tires. We made it onto Sunset Cliffs and out of Ocean Beach without a tail by either the police or the Trans Am. Safe. For now. I turned on my police scanner and listened for a possible 242: battery, what I did to the Raptor, or a BOLO, Be On the Look Out, for a black 2006 Mustang GT. Nothing.

Sierra sat quietly, staring at her side view mirror. When we hit Interstate 8, she turned and faced me.

"Maybe we should call the police," she said.

"We could, but I'm not sure what we'd tell them. That some bikers came looking for you and your drug-dealing brother? We don't really have enough to press charges and, without that, I doubt SDPD is going to use scarce manpower to guard you twenty-four/seven."

Not to mention the fact that, without too much twisting of the story, I could be arrested for assaulting two Raptors. I doubted that it would come to that, but I didn't want to take the chance. The Raptors would dole out their own brand of justice when they had the opportunity. That's what I really had to worry about.

"I guess you're right." She slumped down in her seat.

"Look, I know you're scared. I don't blame you. But I'll put you up in a hotel tonight where you'll be safe." I exited I-8 onto 805 North. I wasn't sure where we were going yet, but north felt safer than south. "The Raptors are after Trey, not you. They took a shot that he might be with you, and it almost worked. Now that you've disappeared, they'll focus all their attention on finding Trey. That's why I need you to tell me where he is, so I can help him."

"I don't know where he is." She looked out her window.

"Sierra, I can help him, but you have to tell me where he is."

"I told you. I don't know where he is!" Still wouldn't face me. Still lying.

"Then call him and tell him to meet us somewhere."

She turned from the window and looked down at her hands. She took a deep breath and let it out. "He threw away his phone. He said he's going to buy another one and call me when he can. But I don't know when. I don't know how to get a hold of him."

Trey had gotten rid of his personal cell phone and would buy untraceable burners in its place. No one could track him through the GPS from his cell phone. Smart. Trey was thinking. Good.

That would keep him alive for a while. I just had to find him before the Raptors did.

"But you know where he was going. Come on, Sierra. You gotta tell me. You know he's in danger. Where did he go?"

"He said he was going back to get the rest of his stash and then he was going to leave town for a while."

Bingo. Candlelight Drive.

Trey had gone from safe and smart to endangered and stupid in thirty seconds. If the police caught him with five pounds of marijuana, they wouldn't need a frame job to put him away for a while. And even if Timothy Buckley could get him released to testify in court on behalf of Randall Eddington, Trey's credibility would be shot.

On the other hand, if the Raptors caught up with Trey before the cops did, his whole body could end up being shot. The Candlelight address had been on a piece of paper in the ashtray of Wayne Delk's car. His men might be racing over there right now. Or, worse yet, they may already be there waiting inside the house. Trey could be heading into an ambush, and I had no way to warn him. I couldn't call the cops and send them over to find Trey walking out with five pounds of weed. I was his only hope.

By taking I-8 to the 805, I'd pushed us way east of where we needed to go. It would take at least ten minutes to get to Candlelight. Ten minutes Trey Fellows might not have. I gunned the Mustang up to eighty-five, hit Highway 52, and took it until it emptied into La Jolla.

"Where are we going?" Sierra asked, as we went up winding Hidden Valley Road to the steep serpentine climb of Via Capri.

"To find your brother." I didn't tell her that the Raptors might already be way ahead of us. She was scared enough.

We took Via Capri all the way up to the top of Mount Soledad and circled by the cross and war memorial. A favorite place to visit with my father as a child. Now forever a dark beacon of death inhabited by the man with the black staring eyes from my nightmares.

I pushed the nightmares aside and sped down the winding back side of Soledad Mountain. Three minutes later, I turned down Candlelight Drive. No sign of Sierra's yellow VW or Raptor trucks, Trans Ams, or motorcycles. Good. Unless the damage had already been done. I drove past 5564 and parked around the corner on Lamplight.

Sierra sat rigid. A statue. Her eyes, below blond bangs, round in permanent fear.

"You know how to drive a stick?" I asked her.

"Yes."

"Let me have your phone for a second." She handed me her phone, and I punched in Buckley's cell number but didn't hit send. "If I'm not back in five minutes, or if you see biker types coming down the street or a police car drive by, go check into a hotel. A nice one with a lobby and multiple floors. Call this number and tell the man who answers what happened tonight."

I handed her back the phone.

"Can't we just go now?" Eyes big and voice high pitched. "My car's not here, so Trey isn't either."

She was probably right, but I didn't want to tell her that I needed to make sure that Trey wasn't lying injured in the house. Or worse.

"Sierra," I gently grasped her wrists. "You're going to be fine, and I'll be back in a couple minutes. If for some reason I'm not, just do what I told you. Okay?"

She nodded her head.

"Okay. Now give me back the gun I gave you." I wasn't going into a possible Raptor ambush unarmed. I hoped I wouldn't have to find out if I could ever pull a trigger again.

"The gun?" Sierra's eyebrows went up. She shoved her hands into her coat pockets and pulled them out empty. "I...I think I left it back behind the apartment building."

The good news was that I wouldn't have to face my fears. The bad news was that I might have to face armed Raptors without a gun. I fingered the blackjack in my coat pocket. It had worked twice tonight. Would three times make me charmed?

"That's okay. I won't need it." I prayed.

"I'm sorry." She looked like she was about to cry.

"Don't worry. Remember what I told you. Now come around and get in the driver's side."

I got out of the car, and Sierra took my place behind the wheel. I walked along the sidewalk and turned left up the hill on Candlelight. No one else was outside and there were only a few lights on in the homes along the street. It was close to midnight and this was a hard-working, middle-class neighborhood.

One of the homes with lights on was Trey's old hideout. Good. If someone had been in there waiting to attack whoever came through the door, they would have wanted the cover of darkness. I felt better about not having a gun. But not by much.

I avoided the light coming through the kitchen window and went up to the front door, making sure no one in the neighborhood was staring out a window. Clear. I'd forgotten to grab my lock-pick set from the trunk of the car. Shit. Maybe I'd get lucky.

I tried the doorknob. Unlocked. Because Trey had left in a hurry and hadn't locked up? Or because the Raptors wanted to make it easy for him to walk into a trap? I took a deep breath and pressed my luck.

I pushed the door open six inches and realized I'd been wrong on both counts. The sickly sweet and rancid smell of un-discovered death wafted out of the house. I'd smelled it before back on the job in Santa Barbara. This wasn't overpowering like a cloistered old woman who'd been found a week too late. This was fresh. Certainly not someone who'd been killed in the last half hour like Trey would had to have been. There wouldn't yet be an odor. But probably no more than a day old.

I could either call the police or find out who it was on my own. Or I could close the door and leave right now. Candlelight Drive was in La Jolla and LJPD would handle the investigation. The dead body inside could have been planted there by the Raptors to set up Trey so he couldn't testify against their leader, Steven Lunsdorf. LJPD had their own reasons to keep Trey from testifying in a hearing to free Randall Eddington. They weren't likely to look past a murder rap against Trey dished up to them on a silver platter.

But Trey might still be in the house. Alive. Or dead.

I pushed the door open and went inside.

CHAPTER THIRTY-THREE

The stink pressed against me like a sheet of chain mail. The reason for it lay in the foyer that led to the living room. A large man was splayed out facedown on the floor. A halo of dried black blood circled his head. A black hole, smaller than a penny, stared out from behind his left ear. Black stippling from gunpowder dotted the bare skin around the hole. He'd been shot at close range. Like the killer had been waiting behind the front door and shot the man when he entered the house. The dried blood around his head came from what must have been a gaping exit wound out the man's face. I didn't have to or want to see it. The man wore a black leather Raptor jacket.

I'd only seen him twice before, and I now could only see him from behind, but I felt fairly certain that the dead man was Eric Schmidt, the Raptor who'd met in secret twice with Trey Fellows. Once at the bar in Pacific Beach, and the second time with the lawyer Alan Rankin two nights ago.

Who had killed him? Trey? Could he have possibly done it? No. Sometimes people surprise you, but Trey Fellows wasn't a killer. Besides, I was pretty certain that he'd spent the last forty-eight hours holed up in his sister's apartment.

Then who? A fellow Raptor at Steven Lunsdorf's behest? My pal, Wayne Delk? Maybe somebody at LJPD leaked that Trey Fellows had signed a sworn affidavit stating Lunsdorf had confessed to the Eddington murders, and Lunsdorf found out about it. Schmidt and Rankin must have been working against Lunsdorf and someone ratted them out. A power play at the top? Whatever the reason, Lunsdorf found out, and Delk had the Candlelight address in his car. Thus, the dead body. If Lunsdorf could pin the murder on Fellows and discredit him as a witness in the Eddington case, he'd get a twofer.

Just by staying here for a day, Trey's DNA and fingerprints were in the house. Now, by walking inside, there was probably a tiny trace of my own DNA too. A few dead skin cells, a hair, a drop of sweat. I was now a part of the crime scene. When they discovered the body, the police crime-scene techs would test for fingerprints everywhere. Trey had a conviction for drug possession, so his prints would be in the FBI's IAFIS. When the prints were run against IAFIS, some would have Trey's name on them.

IAFIS had my prints too. Because of my arrest for my wife's murder, even though I was never tried, much less convicted. But they didn't have my DNA in IAFIS, and I was going to make sure they didn't find my fingerprints here.

But I still had to find out if Trey was lying somewhere else in the house. Injured or dead. I went into the kitchen, grabbed a dish towel off the handle of the stove, and went back to the front door. I opened it a crack and peeked outside. No cop cars. Yet. I wiped down the outside doorknobs, closed the door and locked it, then wiped down the inside doorknobs. I carried the towel with me in case I had to open any doors and checked the living room, two bathrooms, and three bedrooms downstairs. No Trey. First good news of the day.

Upstairs was just one room, the master bedroom. No Trey on the floor or in the bathroom. Something on the bedside table on the far side of the unmade bed caught my eye.

A gun.

A Ruger .357 Magnum SP101. I walked over to the table and picked up the gun to check the serial number on the barrel. But I knew the number even before I read it.

My gun. I checked the cylinder. Four bullets. One empty

shell. The one that had held the bullet that went through Eric Schmidt's head.

My phone vibrated in my pocket. I pulled it out but didn't recognize the number on the screen. Then I did. Sierra.

"I'm on my way," I said.

"A police car just drove by." A desperate whisper. "It turned up Candlelight!"

CHAPTER THIRTY-FOUR

My body went nuclear and my heart bongoed against my chest. No way would I be able to get back downstairs and out the front door before the police cruiser pulled up in front of the house. Walking outside with my hands up and telling the cops the truth wasn't an option. Not on LJPD's turf. Neither was shooting it out over a crime I didn't commit.

I jammed the gun in my coat pocket and spun my head looking for an escape route. I might have found one. The upstairs master bedroom must have been an addition to the house. A window looked out over the roof of the lower floor and probably had a tiny daytime view of the ocean miles away. I opened the window, removed the screen, leaned out and gently set it on the roof.

A loud triple knock on the front door echoed up the stairway. "La Jolla Police Department. Open the door."

Had I locked the door? Couldn't remember. Shit.

I slipped through the window onto the roof and closed it behind me. The roof sloped away from the window toward the next-door neighbor's house. I could see the cruiser parked on the street, but not the police under the eaves of the front door. The car's headlights were on but not the rainbow light bar on the roof. Good. Must not have been a "shots fired" radio call. Maybe the cops would just knock and walk. It was almost midnight. Near the end of the shift. I crouched down and waited.

Another triple knock. This one I heard from outside.

"La Jolla Police Department. We have a report of a disturbance. Please open the door." Urgent, but not out of control.

If the cops barged through the door and found me on the

roof, I'd be toast. If they found me with the murder weapon, I'd be burnt toast. If I threw the gun into the backyard or the yard of a neighbor, the cops might hear it thump down. I needed to hide it somewhere. Now. Not many options on a roof.

A small chimney vent stuck out of the roof about five feet away from me. Probably to the hood system from the stove in the kitchen. The beam of a flashlight strafed over the fence into the backyard below me. They weren't giving up. I crawled down the slope to the chimney vent on my stomach, took the gun out of my pocket and wiped it down with the dish towel, then wrapped the towel around it. I eased the circular rain cover off the vent and wedged the gun down into the chimney vent. The towel muffled the sound of the gun rubbing against the vent. Quietly, I slid the rain cover back down onto the vent, then used the tail of my shirt to wipe off my prints.

I crawled up the sloped roof back to the edge of the master bedroom. My phone vibrated in my pants pocket. I put my hand over it to further muffle the faint sound. The beam of the flashlight pulled back over the fence to the front yard. Another three-bang knock on the front door and the cop demanding the door be opened.

A dog in the far side neighbor's backyard barked. A barrel-chested woof. More dogs added on. Lights popped on in windows of the neighbors north and south. Then across the street.

The cops discussed something down below on the front porch. I couldn't make out the words but it sounded like a disagreement. More windows lit up along the block. I scanned the roof, looking for the best escape. Sweat stung my eyes. The side yard had a concrete patio. A broken ankle and arrest waiting to happen. I hadn't seen the backyard, but the front had a lawn. A softer landing and then outrace a cop car? Or bullets?

The cops were still arguing when a man walked across the street through the patrol car's headlights toward the cops. I caught a flash of gray hair and a polo shirt. He walked with the confidence of a man used to being in control. Used to getting his way. I lost sight of him when he crossed under the eaves above the front porch.

Cops' voices, then his. I could make out a few of his words, but not the cops. "Hawaii." "Next month." I guessed he told them that the owner was out of town. Good. Maybe no need to break in and investigate. A little more discussion and then the man strode back across the street. His life back in control. The cops appeared from under the eaves and walked back to their squad car. They got in and their radio squawked. One of them said something into it and they drove away.

A gust of breath erupted from my mouth and my body felt the cool December night for the first time since I'd been on the roof. It chilled the sweat along my forehead and down my neck. The chill felt good, like the first relief after fighting nausea and then vomiting. But more nausea always followed. I had to get off the roof and back to the car. I hoped Sierra hadn't done what I told her to do and fled the area.

I checked my phone. The call had been from her. I listened to her voicemail, the volume turned low.

"Rick! Are you all right? Please call me. I'm still parked around the corner. Please call. I'm scared."

I texted her to drive back up Candlelight past the house and circle around at the top of the hill. I'd meet her two houses below 5564 Candlelight. Ten seconds later she texted back, "Ok."

A few dogs continued to bark and most of the windows in the neighborhood still burned light. I didn't have time to wait until everybody went back to bed. If there were eyes in those windows looking at the house, I figured most of them would be targeting the front door. That wouldn't be my exit. I stood up, hunched over, and Quasimodoed to the front of the house. The wooden fence that I'd peeked through two nights ago stood an inch-and-a-half wide and four feet below the roof.

Sierra drove past up the hill in the Mustang. She'd be back down in less than twenty seconds. I didn't want to make her wait and have my car sitting on the street two houses down from where the police had answered a call.

I got down on my belly and shimmied blindly backwards

down the roof, my legs dangling in midair. I clutched the bottom on the eaves below me with my left hand and splayed my right against the roof as I inched further down. My ribs cried out, but I didn't listen. Finally, my shoes caught the top of the fence, and I balanced myself holding onto the roof.

Sierra drove past and the brake lights flashed as she pulled to a stop below. No time to scale the fence. I jumped down onto the front lawn, hit, and rolled to my feet. I hustled down to the Mustang and whipped open the door. I peeked over the roof of the car as I got in and saw the man in the polo shirt standing in his driveway.

If he caught a glimpse of the Mustang's license plate I might have two BOLOs out on it from two different police departments.

"Drive."

Sierra pulled away from the curb and let the clutch out too fast. The car bucked and almost stalled, but she finally smoothed it out.

"Make a right at the first street and then another right up the hill."

"What happened with the police?" Panic. "You didn't find Trey, did you?"

"Trey's not there." I didn't tell her that one of his associates was. Facedown. She was scared enough already. "I avoided the police. Everything's okay."

Not even close.

"Where are we going?"

I had no idea, but we had to keep moving. Wherever we went, there'd still be a dead body that someone would discover sooner or later. When it was, Trey Fellows would be in even deeper shit, and the chance for a new trial for Randall Eddington would follow him right down the shit hole.

"Just stay on this road for a while."

Sierra's phone rang before we hit the top of La Jolla Mesa. The ring startled her so much that she jerked the steering wheel and almost hit a parked car.

"Whoa."

She pulled out her phone and almost hit another one.

"Pull over."

She did and let out the clutch and the car lurched to a stop. I'd do the driving for the rest of the night.

Sierra looked at the phone.

"The number's blocked."

"Answer it." I turned off the police scanner to cut the background noise.

She answered. "Trey! Yes, I'm fine. Where are you?"

I grabbed the phone from Sierra's hand and put it on speaker.

"I'm on my way to LA. I need to hide out up there for a while. I'll call you when I've settled somewhere. You be careful."

I mouthed to Sierra to tell Trey that I wanted to talk to him. I figured if he heard my voice or anyone else's without introduction, he'd hang up.

"Trey, Rick wants to talk to you."

"The PI? No!"

"He wants to help. He saved me from those biker guys. Please talk to him."

"No. I gotta go."

No time left for niceties. "Trey, it's Rick. Listen. Pull over somewhere and we'll meet you. Let's be smart about this."

"I am being smart. I'm getting the hell outta town. Those... they...they killed Smitty, man!"

Sierra sucked in a huge gust of air and her eyes went giant. I took the phone off speaker and put it up to my ear.

"Look. We'll hide you in a hotel tonight and then get you under protective custody." Wasn't sure how I could do that, but I thought Buckley would be able to figure something out. When he did, I'd also find out Trey's connection to the dead Raptor and the lawyer. "If you run, you'll look guilty."

"Those fuckers want to kill me, man!"

"That's why you have to let me protect you. Tell me where to meet you."

"Let me talk to my sister."

I put the phone back on speaker and handed it to Sierra.

"I'm here, Trey," she said.

"Do whatever Rick tells you to do to stay safe. I'll call you tomorrow from another phone. I love you." The line went dead.

Sierra stared down at the phone. A tear ran down her nose and splashed down onto the screen of her iPhone. More followed. I didn't give her a hug and I didn't tell her that everything was going to be all right. I didn't believe it and I didn't have the time.

I had to get Sierra somewhere safe and get rid of my car.

CHAPTER THIRTY-FIVE

I took Sierra up to the eighth-floor room I'd rented for her at the La Jolla Marriott. I'd chosen the Marriott for a couple reasons: it had way too many rooms for the entire Raptor gang to scope out searching for Sierra, and I could get a price break from the night manager. Plus I didn't have to use my or Sierra's ID to get the room. Rachel, the manager, saw to that. No one would know Sierra was staying there.

I knew Rachel back from my days managing Muldoon's when she'd come in to listen to jazz. About a year ago, I'd done her a solid off the books and pro bono. She'd been dating a frequent out-of-town guest to the hotel, an act that could get her fired. Rachel had really fallen for the guy, but something in the back of her mind told her that something about him was off. She'd been right. I did a background check and a little digging, and found out that not only did he have a wife back home in San Jose, but he had girlfriends in every city where he traveled to for business.

Thus Rachel had gone from breaking a big rule for love to breaking a couple little ones for me.

I unlocked the door to room 812 and lugged Sierra's over-packed suitcase to the lone bed. She'd packed for a life on the run. I hoped it would only be for a couple days.

"I'll call you in the morning." I handed Sierra the key card. "You'll be safe here. If Trey calls again, please try to get him to call me. Failing that, try to get him to tell you where he is. Okay?"

Fear crept back into Sierra's eyes. She took my hand in both of hers. "Please stay with me tonight. You say it's safe, but what if someone followed us. I can't stay here alone. Please."

Her eyes pleaded more than her words. I didn't know much about Sierra, but what I did know didn't mesh with a life on the run. Thirty-three years old and, like so many people nowadays, working hard just to make ends meet. She had two jobs, an apartment, and a car. Now she was in a jackpot because she'd tried to keep her drug-dealing brother from getting killed.

Sierra didn't deserve any of it. But she might hold the key to solving that other puzzle I was still convinced Trey Fellows was working on. Her ex-boyfriend. Brad Larson. Or whatever his real name was. If I stayed tonight, maybe I'd learn the truth.

"Where am I supposed to sleep?" I looked at the lone king-size bed in the room. There was a desk chair and an upholstered chair. I guessed I could pull them together and sleep sitting up.

She looked around the room, apparently realizing for the first time that it only had one bed. "We can share the bed. It's big."

It wasn't an invitation to something else. It was a desperate plea to keep me there tonight.

"Okay. But I have to get rid of my car first. If the Raptors are still out there searching hotels, which I don't think they are, I don't want my car to be seen in the hotel parking lot." Plus I didn't want the police to see it if they were after me too.

"Okay." Eyes still big. "But you're coming back?"

"Yeah. I'm coming back. First I have to park the car somewhere else and borrow a friend's car." I hoped I could still impose on that friend. Probably for the last time.

* * *

Kim met me at an underground parking structure on Herschel Avenue in La Jolla. She hadn't been overjoyed when I asked for yet another favor. Maybe I'd finally used up her deep well of goodwill. I couldn't blame her. I wasn't proud of myself for calling her when I was in yet another jam. It was too late to get a rental, so I didn't have a choice.

Like always, she was the answer to my needs. She'd held onto her Toyota RAV4 when she leased the BMW. The Toyota came in handy when she had an open house that needed extra signage and extra goodies.

Kim drove me to her house to drop herself off. The drive was only a couple minutes. Neither of us spoke. She'd always asked me about the case I was working on when she'd helped me in the past.

Tonight was different.

She pulled to a stop in front of her house and we both got out of the car. I walked her up to her front door. She folded her arms and held her elbows in her hands like she was cold. But her coat looked warm enough. She wouldn't look at me, but I sensed she wanted to say something. Something I knew was coming but didn't want to hear.

"Rick, you know I always want to help you when I can and that I'd do anything for you." She stared at my chest.

"I ask for too much."

"No. It's just that Jeff doesn't understand our relationship." She unwound her arms and looked at me through beautiful, but sad, emerald eyes. "I won't be able to do things like this when I'm living with him."

At least Jeff and I had one thing in common. Neither one of us understood Kim's and my relationship.

"Do you love him?"

She blinked like the question startled her. It startled me, as did the feelings welling up inside of me. I'd kept them hidden from both of us for so long. To acknowledge them would have been cheating on Colleen. A woman dead for ten years who I loved better in death than I had in life.

None of it was fair to Kim. Now she'd finally realized it. Just as I finally realized that I loved her.

She dropped her eyes back to my chest. "I love the man he is, and he loves me without qualification."

"Is that enough for you, Kimmie?" I put my fingers on her chin and gently raised it so she'd look at me. "To be with a man you admire who loves you?"

"Yes." Tears pooled in her eyes. "Better than to be with a man I love who admires me."

"I do love you." The words tumbled from my throat.

"Why? Why now?" Angry tears ran down her cheeks. "It's too late, Rick. It's too late."

"It's not, Kimmie." I held her shoulders, wanting to pull her toward me and start anew. "It's not too late."

"You have to do the right thing, Rick. Please. That's how you live your life, trying to do the right thing." She forced the words out between sobs. "Keep the car as long as you want. Save the world. But when you're done, do the right thing, Rick. Walk away. Please just walk away."

"Okay." The word, a croak. Painful as it left my mouth. I blinked through liquid and looked down at Kim. "I'll just drop the keys through the mail slot when I bring the car back. We won't have to see each other."

She stepped into me and wrapped me in a hug. Her face against my chest, jerked by sobs. I hugged back. Hard. She smelled clean and fresh scrubbed like she always did. I breathed her smell in and held it, trying to hold onto a piece of her for as long as I could. I kissed her on the forehead and let her go.

CHAPTER THIRTY-SIX

The thirty-foot walk back to the street seemed like a mile. The adrenaline that had pulsed through my body all night sucked out of me and left me deflated. Inside out. I got into Kim's RAV4 and my left shoulder throbbed where Wayne Delk had hit me with the gun. I put on the seat belt and his kick from a week ago echoed along my ribs.

Kim had waited for me to come back to her in full and realize that I loved her. Now that I had, it was too late. I'd taken Kim's love for granted for so long that I'd forgotten that I didn't deserve it. It had always been there, even when we weren't together. Like air I needed to survive, never realizing how precious it was. But she wasn't Colleen, and I never forgave her or myself for that. Now she only had to worry about living up to herself. That was more than most men and, certainly, more than I deserved.

There were plenty of bars between me and the La Jolla Marriott up in the Golden Triangle. I could call Sierra and tell her that she'd be safe and had nothing to worry about. Or that I'd be back at the hotel in an hour. I thought about calling Buckley. Not to tell him about the dead body and everything else, but to ask him if he had any room left in that bottle he crawled into every night. I didn't know the source of his pain, but I knew the ache. The bars and Buckley's bottle would have to wait. There was one last woman I'd made a promise to whom I wouldn't disappoint. At least, not yet.

I got back to the hotel room around one-fifteen a.m. Sierra greeted me at the door barefoot, wearing a bathing suit bottom and a Charger sweat top. She'd obviously packed for all contingencies.

Even the summer. My guess was she usually slept naked and got as close as she could without looking too enticing.

Failed.

She had beach-volleyball legs to go with her beach-blond hair. If I wanted to go "This Ol' Cowboy" by the Marshall Tucker Band and "kiss the lips of another woman and forget all about" Kim, tonight would have been a nice place to start.

But that was the wolf in me that was in every man, and I kept him on a short leash. Off leash, regret usually followed. For me and for the woman. Besides, I needed answers from Sierra tonight. Nothing else.

Sierra slipped into bed, and I sat down in the upholstered chair diagonally across from her.

"I have to be at work at the Morning Cup at seven-thirty tomorrow." She looked at the clock radio on the bedside table. "Or I guess I should say this morning. Can you give me a ride there?"

"Sure."

"And maybe make sure no one, ah, tries to hurt me?"

"I'll make sure you're safe. I promise." Without a gun.

"Thanks for everything you did tonight. I don't think I could have made it through alone." She rolled over onto her side. "Good night, Rick."

I walked over to the bed and sat down on the open side that Sierra now faced. She smiled at me.

"Sierra, I need to get some things straight so I can protect Trey."

"Okay." She sat up and wrapped her arms around her blanket-covered knees.

"Trey has only one picture in his house and it's of you and the man he called Brad Larson. There are plenty of pictures of you alone that he could've hung on his wall, but he chose one of you with the man who is in a lot of your Facebook photos. The same man whose picture is on the wall at Dianne Wilkens' house where Trey hid out. This guy is obviously important to you, but he's important to Trey too. Who is he? And don't pretend that you don't know who I'm talking about."

"His name is Brad Bauer." Her eyes fell to the bed.

"Why doesn't he have the same last name as his mother, Dianne Wilkens?"

"He'd been a foster child when Dianne and her late husband adopted him. He kept his family name."

"Where is Dianne now?"

"She's in Hawaii. She gave me her keys so I could water her plants while she was gone."

"Why did you lie to me about knowing Brad Bauer this morning?"

"I didn't lie." Her head came up, lips curled. "You did. You asked about some guy I'd never heard of."

"True." I squinted at her. "But you knew who I was talking about."

"Say I did, why should I tell anything to some guy I've never met who is lying to me?"

"Good point. That was stupid of me. I should have just told you who I was and asked you straight out. I apologize." I loosened the squint. "But I need to know everything now. Who is Brad Bauer, and why did Trey lie to me about his name?"

"He's my boyfriend."

"I already figured that one out, Sierra." I shook my head. "Where is he now, and why would Trey lie to me about him?"

"Do you think Brad has something to do with all of this?" Her eyebrows lifted and she squeezed her knees tighter.

"Maybe." Probably.

"Why?"

"Call it a cop's gut instinct." That's really all I had.

"You're not a cop."

"I used to be." I inched slightly closer to her and raised my chin. "Sierra, where is Brad now?"

She rested her right cheek on her knees and sighed. A sad, lonely sound. "He's in prison."

Now I knew why Trey had lied to me about Bauer's name. He didn't want me to know that Bauer was in prison. He'd blurted out the real first name, realized he'd made a mistake, and then made up a last name. But why didn't he want me to know the truth about Bauer? He was a drug dealer, I was a PI who'd been a cop. Surely Trey knew I wouldn't be shocked to hear that he had a friend in prison. It was something else.

"What was he busted for?"

"Selling drugs."

"Weed. Must have been a lot?"

"Cocaine. He got caught in a sting." Sierra let out a long, sad sigh. "He'd been selling pounds of weed to this guy for months and everything was cool. Then the guy asked Brad if he could get him some cocaine. He said Brad could make $20,000 on a one-time deal. The guy was an undercover cop. The cop set him up, but the judge didn't care."

"Was Trey involved?"

"No." She looked down at the bed. A lie.

"Did Brad take the fall for Trey, Sierra? You've gotta tell me everything. Now."

"No." A tear pooled in the corner of her left eye, then broke free and slipped down her face along her nose and onto the blanket. "Kind of. Brad wouldn't tell the police about Trey and the other..."

"Other what?"

The tears streamed now. Sierra put her face in her hands and rested them on her knees.

"Other people? Brad wouldn't tell the police about who supplied him with the coke? Is that it, Sierra?"

Her head bobbed up and down on her knees.

Brad wouldn't rat out his partner or his supplier to get a lesser sentence. A stand-up guy. As crooks go. And if he was Trey's partner, then his suppliers were the Raptors. A smart decision not to rat them out.

The itch I'd first felt when I'd seen Trey look at the picture of Brad Bauer and his sister on the wall of his apartment ran all the way down my spine. He'd been nervous and glanced at the

picture when I'd asked him if he'd testify against Steven Lunsdorf in court. The glance had been a tell. I'd sensed it at the time,
but didn't know what it meant. I still didn't, but I was more convinced than ever that it meant something.

Bauer in prison. Wouldn't rat out Trey or the Raptors. The
Raptor Kingpin, Raymond Oscar Karsten, in prison. Defended by
Alan Rankin, the lawyer who'd visited Trey with murdered Raptor, Eric Schmidt. The Raptors asking me if "he" had sent me
before they roughed me up at The Chalked Cue the first time.
Wayne Delk telling me that "Rock" had sent another dumb motherfucker to sneak up on him when he stuck a gun in my neck tonight.

He.

Raymond Oscar Karsten.

R. O. K.

Rock.

The Raptors thought I was working for their old boss. Now
their enemy. That made me more than a nuisance who poked
around in their bar looking for answers. That made me a target. I
wished I had the gun that Sierra lost back at her apartment building. Or my own Ruger that I'd hidden at the Candlelight murder
scene. I couldn't take the chance of getting stopped by LJPD with
a murder weapon on me. Now I'd forced myself to take a chance
on my life unarmed.

Hopefully I could remedy that tomorrow. Tonight I still had
a puzzle to put together.

Brad Bauer was a piece to Trey Fellows' other puzzle. The
one I always felt he was working on. Separate, yet connected to
the Eddington case. Somehow. And the rest of the puzzle pieces
were the Raptors. Bad blood between the old boss and the new
boss. Eric Schmidt picked the wrong side and ended up dead.
Bauer was the link to the Raptors. To Rock Karsten. But what did
it mean?

Why had Trey met with the lawyer, Alan Rankin? Was
Rankin paying Trey to testify against Steven Lunsdorf? To lie?

Why? Randall Eddington was innocent of murdering his family. I knew it. I now had proof. The police had planted the blood evidence. Maybe Rankin was paying Trey to tell the truth. Rankin knew that Trey was afraid to testify against the Raptors and he paid him to make sure that he would.

But where did Brad Bauer figure in? Was he doing time with Rock Karsten? A liaison between Karsten and Trey?

I whipped out my iPhone and googled the story about Alan Rankin and Raymond Oscar Karsten to find out where Karsten was incarcerated. Found it. Corcoran State Prison.

"Sierra, where is Brad serving his time?"

"San Quentin."

CHAPTER THIRTY-SEVEN

San Quentin? "Are you sure?"

Sierra lifted her head off her knees and pointed bloodshot eyes at me. "Yes. I know what prison my boyfriend is in. He's been there for three years."

I looked up the California Department of Corrections and Rehabilitation website on my phone and logged on. I found the inmate locator page and typed in Raymond Oscar Karsten. Just like the article I'd read. Corcoran.

I looked at Sierra. "And he wasn't transferred to Corcoran in the last few weeks?"

"No." Arched eyebrows. "Why? What's going on?"

"I don't know."

I didn't know. I'd let my imagination run wild and it nose-dived off a cliff. Maybe there was no other puzzle. Maybe Trey Fellows was just trying to do the right thing.

"One last question." I pinned my eyes on Sierra's. "Why do you think Trey came forward with the information about the Eddingtons?"

"I've asked him the same question a million times." She shook her head and looked down at her knees. "He says he wants to do the right thing."

"And you believe him?"

Her eyes went up to the right like she was looking for an answer. Then she looked at me like she'd found it. "Yes."

"I know Trey's your brother and I think he's a decent guy, but risking his life to do the right thing seems a bit out of character." Like Arnold Schwarzenegger playing Hamlet.

"You don't know Trey." She shook her head. "Sometimes, I wonder if I do. Right when I'm convinced he's just a stoned-out loser, he'll surprise me and do something wonderful."

She was right. I didn't know Trey. Not very well. Just the stoned-out loser part of him. I wasn't yet convinced he had any other parts.

"Good night, Rick." Sierra reached over to the nightstand and turned off the light.

I stretched out on the bed on top of the comforter and closed my eyes on a night that I hoped to wake up the next morning and find had all been a nightmare. But I knew it couldn't happen. My nightmares were real.

* * *

The ceiling closed down on me and I bolted upright. I was alive. The man in my nightmare was dead. Until he'd be alive again in my dreams tomorrow night.

"Are you okay?" Sierra, a frightened voice out of the night.

"Yeah. Bad dream. Sorry."

I'd slept with a few women over the last couple years but never long enough to fall asleep. I'd always gone home to sleep alone. And wake up in the middle of a nightmare the same way. It wasn't fair to make someone else have to deal with it. Certainly not Sierra, who'd already been through enough.

"Get under the covers. You don't have to sleep like that."

"I'm okay. Thanks."

"No, really. You're making me feel bad. You went out of your way to help me tonight and then I made you stay with me. You should at least be able to sleep under the covers in the bed you're paying for."

Actually, Buckley was paying for the bed and, ultimately, the Eddingtons were. I was too tired to explain or argue.

I slipped off my jeans and shirt in the dark and got under the covers. I turned away from Sierra and hoped she'd fall back asleep. I hoped I would too.

"This is going to seem weird." Sierra wasn't ready to go back to sleep yet. "But could you just hold me for a couple minutes? Nights are still hard without Brad. This whole thing is scary. I just need someone to hold me tonight."

I flipped over and put my arms around Sierra. Her body was warm and felt good against mine. I hadn't held a woman in bed that I hadn't just had sex with in years. I'd usually be in my car within fifteen minutes. I wasn't going anywhere tonight.

Sierra's breathing grew deep and steady.

I fell asleep and slept through the night.

* * *

I circled the block around the Morning Cup a couple times before I dropped Sierra off for work at seven-thirty a.m. She'd pleaded with me to come in with her, but I told her she'd be safe inside and that I'd check by every couple hours.

I doubted the Raptors would make a brazen move for Sierra in public. I doubted they'd make any move at all. They'd put their other plan in action. The dead body in Trey's hideout. The murder weapon now would never be found, but the body would. Maybe it already had. I'd transferred the police scanner from my car to Kim's last night and had it on during the drive. No mention yet of suspicious circumstances, possible DB or a 187, possible homicide.

Either way, I needed to talk to Buckley right now. I called him as I drove out of downtown La Jolla and headed onto La Jolla Boulevard toward Pacific Beach. Of course, he didn't answer. Morning before eight a.m., he'd still be sleeping off last night. I left a message and warned him that I was on the way. The morning air was damp and thick and collected on the windshield of the car. An occasional swipe of the wiper cleared the view. Huge Monterey cypress trees canopied the street as La Jolla turned into Bird Rock. A shady respite from the sun on most days. This morning with the fog, a dark claustrophobic ceiling.

Buckley lived in Pacific Beach, just a stone's throw down

from Bird Rock. PB often got a bad rap for being a dusty, twenty-somethings' playground. Especially from me. But that was just the strip of streets downtown. The rest was family friendly, with lots of homes having either a view of Mission Bay or the Pacific Ocean. Buckley's rested on a hill that offered a little piece of both. The house was modern, with sloping peaks and big bay windows. I'd expected a ranch house. Or a log cabin.

I grabbed the grocery bag with the cigarette butts from The Chalked Cue parking lot and walked up to the house. I knocked on the door and waited. Knocked and waited some more. Then rang the bell and pounded on the door. I knew it wouldn't be easy to pull Buckley out of the bottle he'd poured himself into last night, but I didn't have time to be mannerly.

Finally, a gray head peeked through a latticed window next to the front door. The door opened and Buckley stood slumped over in a white terrycloth robe. Gray hair loose from his ponytail stretched out in all directions like a broken halo. He looked like Jesus, had Jesus grown old and not been the son of God. And drank too much.

"Rick, what in the hell is this all about? Do you know what time it is?"

"Yes, I do." I stepped inside his house, though he hadn't offered. "It's about the time people who work are already up and starting their day."

"Well, come the hell in, then." He shut the door, realizing I was already in. "Let me get some coffee before you give me what can only be bad news at this time of the morning."

He was right about that. He wasn't going to be happy about how right. I followed him into the kitchen as he shuffled bare feet along dark hardwood floors. The kitchen had top-notch appliances, Wolf oven, Sub-Zero refrigerator. Buckley liked to cook, but he was messy about it. The sink was full of dirty dishes and an unwashed, cast-iron skillet sat on the stove.

He pointed to a wooden stool in front of a granite island and walked over to a coffeemaker on the counter. I took a seat and set the paper bag on the island. A bottle of Maker's Mark bourbon lay opened on its side on top of the granite. There wasn't enough bourbon left in the bottle to spill out. Remnants from last night.

"It's so damn early, my coffee machine hasn't even started yet." Buckley punched buttons on a drip coffeemaker. He walked over to the Sub-Zero and opened it. "Get you some orange juice? Water?"

"I'm good. Thanks."

He grabbed a bottled water out of the fridge and sat down across from me at the island. He righted the upended Maker's Mark, glanced at me, then moved it aside. I was pretty sure that if I hadn't been there, he would have finished it up. Was this how he started every morning?

"Now, what brings you to my house at this god-awful hour?" He took a sip of his water and looked at me through morning bourbon eyes. "Is the bad news in that trash bag?"

"No. That's the good news. Steven Lunsdorf's cigarette butt with fingerprints and DNA...and a few others."

"Good work. What's the bad news?"

"Before I tell you, I may need to hire you as an attorney."

"Does this involve something you did, son?" Buckley set the water down on the island.

"Something I found when I entered a hou—"

"Stop right there!"

I stopped talking.

"Be right back."

Buckley left the room and came back with a document, sat down and slid it across the island to me. He handed me a pen. "Sign it. Says you're hiring me as your attorney. That way, whatever else you tell me is privileged. Judging by you droppin' by before the rooster crows and the look on your face, I'm guessing it best be privileged."

He was wrong about the rooster, but right about the rest. I picked up the pen.

"Wait." Buckley stopped me. "Slide that back here with the pen for a second."

I did as told. Buckley crossed something out on the contract, then wrote something down and slid it and the pen back to me. "Changed $400 an hour to a dollar. Could get a little pricey. Plus, gonna have you write it off as an expense anyway, and we don't want the IRS to think we're laundering money."

Buckley gave me back the contract, and I signed and initialed where he directed me. Coffee began to drip from the maker down into the decanter, sizzling on the hot glass.

"All right, now you can tell me your story." Buckley eyed the splashing coffee, then the Maker's Mark, and licked his lips.

I told him about Trey fleeing town, Wayne Delk in the parking lot of The Chalked Cue, Sierra Fellows, the Raptor by the pepper tree, Eric Schmidt's body in Trey Fellows' hideout on Candlelight Drive, the police coming to the house, and the murder weapon being my stolen gun.

Buckley didn't interrupt me or say anything when I finished. He got up and poured himself a cup of coffee, tasted it, then sat down and grabbed the Maker's Mark. He poured the remaining two ounces of booze left in the bottle into his coffee.

I didn't say anything. Buckley had a routine. I trusted him enough to let him follow it. I just hoped he'd change the routine before it killed him.

Finally, Buckley spoke. "Son, you wade into more horseshit than anyone I've ever met. If someone gave you a prize stallion, you'd dig around in the stall picking through its shit."

I couldn't argue with him.

"Problem is." He hit his hard coffee. "You're pulling this case right in there with you."

"I saved this case, Buckley. If I hadn't gone after Wayne Delk, we wouldn't know about any of this, and Trey and his sister would be dead. Just like the Raptor murdered with my gun in the house on Candlelight."

"Where is the gun, by the way?"

I told him. "Son, I'm not going to tell you to break any more laws than you already have." Buckley looked me dead in the eyes like Bob Reitzmeyer used to when he was about to give some fatherly advice. "But for your own good, that gun can never be found."

"They can't pin the murder on me." I tried to convince myself, but my voice caught in the back of my throat and tumbled out dry. "I reported the gun stolen a week ago."

Buckley grabbed the contract and ripped it up.

"Why the hell'd you do that?"

"I can't be your lawyer."

"Why not?" My body flashed hot and clammy at once.

"Because I can't work at cross purposes. I've got too many dogs in one fight. A lawyer who was only concerned with your best interests would advise you to go down to LJPD right now and tell them everything you know about the death of that biker and who stole your gun."

"First you tell me the gun can never be found, and now you tell me to tell LJPD where it is." I threw up my hands.

"I'm rethinking the situation." He took another slug of the coffee. Maybe the booze made him more focused. Or sloppy. "Going to the police and telling the truth might be the only way to keep you out of jail."

"I should have told the truth when I went in to report the gun stolen. But now it's too late."

"Why?"

"Because the Raptors might have a mole at LJPD. Lunsdorf and Delk had to get the Candlelight address from someone and I doubt it was Eric Schmidt or Alan Rankin. That leaves LJPD. But we don't know who the mole is or how high it goes up the ranks." Buckley narrowed his eyes, grunted, got up and walked out of the kitchen. He returned a minute later with another contract.

"I guess we're going to ride this one out." He made the same changes on the document he'd made earlier and slid it over to me to sign. "We go before a judge in four days. We need to get Mr. Fellows back here and ready to testify."

"What happens after he testifies before the judge?"

"What're you getting at?"

"If the judge throws out the first conviction and we get a second trial, how do we protect Trey from now until the trial?"

"I'm working on that." He took a sip of his morning-after coffee and looked down at the granite island.

"You mean you haven't figured it out?"

"Not yet." He looked up at me. "I'm also figuring out how to keep you out of jail. When that body on Candlelight Drive starts to reek enough for the mailman to smell on his daily rounds, the police are gonna come a-calling on you."

I was worried about the police showing up at my house. But I was more worried about the Raptors getting there first.

CHAPTER THIRTY-EIGHT

I needed a gun if the Raptors came calling. If I went to a gun store and bought one, I'd still have to wait California's ten days before I could take it home. That might be nine days too late. I'd been in a similar situation two years ago. The gun had arrived too late then. But I'd gotten lucky. Considering the turns my life had taken recently, counting on luck didn't constitute a plan.

I knew where to find a gun. Two, actually, but the one I'd bought two years ago would have to remain hidden. The Ruger .357 that I'd never fired but someone else had. Once. To put a bullet behind Eric Schmidt's ear. That gun was too hot to carry, and I'd have to climb on a roof to retrieve it anyway. But there was a second option in Ocean Beach. The gun I'd taken off Wayne Delk that Sierra had left behind her apartment building last night. I needed to get down there before some kid found the gun and thought it was a toy, or some homeless dude did who was looking to get even.

I drove down Ingraham Street out of Pacific Beach. The white noise of the police scanner, background music to the images of last night playing roulette in my mind. I crossed over the Ingraham Street Bridge that bisected Mission Bay and watched a lone kayaker smoothly stroke through the water. Then I heard the police dispatcher's call on the scanner, but it didn't register at first. Possible DB at 5564 Candlelight Drive. Then it slapped me in the face.

DB, dead body.

5564 Candlelight Drive.

Trey's hideout.

The house where the body of Eric Schmidt lay inside de-composing.

Shit.

Whoever called the police last night hadn't given up. Either that, or Dianne Wilkens had come home from Hawaii and found a horrible surprise.

The morning closed in on me. The fog hung low and pressed down on the RAV4's windshield. I pulled off the road into the Hospitality Point parking lot and turned up the volume on the scanner. A two-man squad car took the call. I listened and wait-ed. I didn't realize I'd been holding my breath until I let go a long exhale. Minutes passed like hours as I listened to the background chatter of cops answering calls, but nothing on 5564 Candlelight Drive.

Finally, the squad checking the call on Candlelight Drive radi-oed dispatch. Nothing suspicious to report. No sign of possible DB.

What? They must not have gone inside.

The dispatcher asked if anyone had been home. The patrol-man responded "no," but that the front door had been ajar, and he and his partner entered and checked the house for fear that someone might be injured inside. An old trick for an eager patrol-man. If the door is unlocked, the cop goes inside and writes up in his report that the door was open. I'd done it myself back in Santa Barbara. The patrolman reported a slight odor of decomposition and said it may be due to a dead mouse or rat in the walls.

Either someone had moved the body of Eric Schmidt or the cops were lying. Both options were hard to believe, but one of them had to be true. I ruled out lying cops. It didn't make any sense. Sooner or later, the body would be discovered and then the cops would have some explaining to do.

That left the first option, which was almost as ridiculous but had to be true. Someone had taken the body from the house and the only thing remaining was the decomp odor. Whoever had moved the body must have mopped up the blood or the cops would have seen it. But the smell of death lingers, grasping onto carpet fibers and furniture fabric. A persistent reminder that a life had ended. This one, violently.

Who could have moved the body? Who even knew about it? Trey Fellows, the Raptors who killed Eric Schmidt, their captain, and me. Now Buckley too, but way after the fact. Trey and I were the only ones with a motive to move the body. Trey had claimed to be on his way to Los Angeles last night. He could have been lying, but he couldn't have moved the body by himself. Schmidt had to have weighed at least 230 pounds. Minus a quart of blood.

Lifting a dead man was different from lifting a barbell. Too many loose parts that give into gravity. Even if Trey could have somehow hoisted the body up into a car, where would he put it in Sierra's Volkswagen Beetle? The trunk? You can't even fit a golf bag back there. Strap the body into the front seat? No. Someone else had moved the body. The Raptors? Why? They had to have been the ones who murdered Schmidt at the Candlelight address, specifically to frame Trey. And if they had moved the body, who called in the tip to the police?

Someone else had to have known about the body and moved it. But who?

I called Buckley, and told him about the radio dispatch call and the missing body.

"Sure you heard correctly?"

"Come on, Buckley."

"Sorry, son. It's so dang strange."

"You think the attorney, Alan Rankin, could have had anything to do with this?"

"Hell, no. Why?"

"Because other than Trey moving the body, and I don't think he did, I'm all out of guesses. And Rankin and Schmidt met with Trey at the Candlelight house. Call it guilt by association."

"Alan Rankin has more bends than a coiled rattlesnake but I don't think he'd cross this line."

"Then who?"

"I don't know, son. That can't be our concern right now. You need to find Trey so we can go forward with Randall Eddington's case, and for Trey's own safety."

I hung up, got back on the road, and called Sierra on my cell phone. No answer. I called again. "Rick, I'm buried. I can't talk now."

Buried. Restaurant lingo for hopelessly behind. I could sympathize but needed answers now.

"It won't take long. Go into the bathroom so we can talk."

"Dammit." A rustling noise, like she'd put the phone in her apron pocket. Ten seconds later, "Okay. Hurry."

"Has Trey called?"

"No."

"Do you have any idea where you left the gun last night? Under one of the dumpsters? In one?"

"No. I just got up and went to your car. It must be on the ground between the dumpsters." Her voice quivered high. "I don't know. I'm sorry."

"It's okay." Actually, a big problem. "You told me that Trey threw away his cell phone. Do you know where?"

"I'm not sure. But..."

"But what?"

"It was weird. He didn't pick up your call last night, but listened to the message right after you hung up."

"How do you know the call was from me?"

"He looked at the name of the caller and said, 'I don't want to talk to that asshole private dick.'"

That would be me. "What's the weird part?"

"After he listened to your message, he called somebody and went into the bathroom."

"Could you hear any of the conversation?"

"No. He had the fan on." She spoke quickly, still riding the anxiety of last night. "But when he came out he was panicked. He told me to leave the apartment right away, and he said he had to get rid of his phone and would call me from another one later. Then he said he had to take my car, and he grabbed his duffel bags and left."

"Who do you think he called on that last call?"

"I don't know. Lately, he's been making calls in private and answering some in private too."

"Just in the last two days, since he's been staying with you?"

"No." Anxious. "Ever since this whole Eddington murder thing happened."

"One more thing. Does Trey have a girlfriend?"

"Yes."

"What's her name?"

"Kelsey something, ah..." I gave her time to search her brain. "Santos. Yeah, Santos. She lives somewhere in Mission Beach."

"Do you have a phone number?"

"No. Sorry. Gotta go."

* * *

Nine o'clock. Still early for Ocean Beach. Especially on a Sunday. The morning fog wouldn't burn off for another couple hours and everything was draped in a bleached-out gray. The Dawn Patrol surfers had taken up most of the parking spaces in the lot at Dog Beach, but there were still a few available spots waiting for winter tourists. I left them one less and walked the two blocks to Sierra's apartment building on Long Branch.

No cop cars, Raptor Trans Ams, or Choppers. I went around the back of the building where Sierra and I had hidden last night. I searched between the two dumpsters. Nothing. Got down into a push-up position and looked underneath them. More nothing. I doubted Sierra had tossed the gun into the dumpster, or that anyone who found it would have. Trey wouldn't have thrown in his phone either. He would have bolted straight for Sierra's car, and not gone all the way around the building to ditch the phone. I called his number on my phone anyway. Straight to voicemail, and no ring coming out of a dumpster.

Maybe he left the phone in the apartment. If I could find Trey's phone, I'd have all his recent calls, contacts, and texts. I'd have at least the phone number of the call he made after mine last night. At best, a name to go with that call.

I went back to Kim's RAV4 and dug out my lock-pick set from the duffel bag I'd transferred over from the Mustang last night. Right before Kim asked me to do the right thing and walk away. The adrenaline of the case had pushed the end with Kim to the background for now. I'd find out how to live without her when the case was over.

Nobody came out of their apartments during the sixty seconds or so it took me to pick the lock on Sierra's door. I slipped inside and everything looked the same from last night. I called Trey's phone again. No rings on the phone or in the apartment. I checked all the trash cans in the apartment. No phone. I looked under the bed, the sofa, in cabinets, even in the refrigerator. No phone. Trey must have thrown the phone away somewhere else.

I scanned the apartment one more time to see if there was something else that could give a clue to where Trey was. Nothing. I grabbed the doorknob, then something clicked in my mind. Something was missing. I looked back at the coffee table. No bong. I remembered seeing it last night. Now gone. Sierra had locked the door when we left last night. Unless some stoner in the complex as skillful with a pick set as me had broken in and stolen the bong, Trey had come back for it.

When? Between the time Sierra and I left the apartment and he called Sierra to tell her he was on his way to Los Angeles? That would have been a period of twenty to twenty-five minutes, tops. No way would he have gone back there then when the heat was still on broil. He wouldn't have come back for hours. Maybe even this morning.

Trey had lied to Sierra about going to Los Angeles. He was still somewhere in San Diego. Could he have been stupid enough to stay with his girlfriend? If I could find out about her, so could the Raptors.

CHAPTER THIRTY-NINE

I got lucky with the online white pages on my cell phone and found a Kelsey Santos, single, age thirty to thirty-four, living on Mission Beach Boulevard. There was a phone number to go with the address. Most people don't know that their address, and sometimes their phone number, are waiting to be found on the Internet for free. Just like the old days with phone books. Couple that with social media, and you can learn all you want and more about almost anyone. Great time to be alive if you're a stalker. Maybe that's why there are so many.

Ten a.m. on a weekend in the winter, Kelsey Santos might still be home. Most days in Mission Beach got off to late starts. But I didn't want to drive over there and spend a half hour looking for parking, only to discover she wasn't home. I called her phone number from my car.

"Hello?" A woman's voice.

"Is this Kelsey Santos from the University of Nebraska, class of 2003?" I didn't want to hang up once I knew she was home, or try a ruse that might make her suspicious. I doubted that if she went to college, it would be at Nebraska. No beaches.

"This is Kelsey Santos, but I didn't go to the University of Nebraska."

"Sorry. I must have the wrong one. Thanks." I hung up and hustled out to my car.

* * *

Mission Beach is a sliver of a town south of Pacific Beach, built on a sandbar between the Pacific Ocean and Mission Bay. It features a boardwalk along the beach and Belmont Park, a mini-version of Coney Island. A bit run-down, the park did most of its amusing back in the 1920s and 1930s, when land developers envisioned roller coasters with ocean views rather than hotels with the same. Belmont Park still had the Giant Dipper roller coaster from its 1925 birth. The wooden coaster was frightening, not because it went fast or very high, but because you had the sense that it could break down any moment and send you shooting off into space on your final ride before the hard landing.

Kelsey Santos lived on Mission Boulevard, kitty-corner from Belmont Park. The parking in Mission Beach made La Jolla look like the Qualcomm Stadium parking lot on a Charger off-day. I circled the block three times in turtle traffic, every driver's neck straining to locate a car exiting a spot on the curb. After fifteen minutes, my turn came up in the rotation, and I parked a block down from Kelsey Santos' apartment.

I walked down the block, passing a couple of bamboo bars, a sandwich shop, and a lot of bundled beach types with faded tans waiting for winter to end and spring to spring. In San Diego, that could happen in five minutes.

The apartment door opened up two steps before I could get to it. A woman stepped out, dressed in jeans and a blue Puma sweatshirt. Polynesian roots and a year-round tan. Sharp cheekbones pushed up to black-coffee, almond-shaped eyes. Full lips under a straight nose blew an "Oh" when she turned from closing the door and saw me. I'd startled her. She hadn't been expecting a man to creep up on her porch. Or maybe she had, and I was the wrong man.

"Kelsey Santos?" I smiled against the sun that had just peeked through the morning fog and poked me in the eyes.

"Yes?" She elongated the word and her eyebrows pinched together. Wary.

"I'm hoping you can help me." Still smiling.

"I was just on my way out. Maybe another time. Do you have a business card? I'll call you."

"It's about Trey Fellows." I dropped the smile and let my words echo my genuine concern.

Her eyes went half-lidded and her mouth micro-expressioned into a frown. She caught herself and gave me a beautiful, but false, smile. "I don't think I know that person."

"Kelsey." I looked at her until she held my eyes. "We both know Trey is in danger. I can keep him safe, but I need your help." I showed her my PI license. "Trey has probably mentioned my name to you. You can trust me."

Kelsey dropped her eyes and her shoulders slumped. I stepped toward her because I thought she might drop to the ground. She stayed upright and leaned against the door of her apartment.

"I don't know where he is." She kept her voice low and her eyes darted over my shoulder. "He's supposed to call me tonight at six."

"When did you last talk to him?"

"Late last night."

"What did he tell you?"

"That the Raptors were after him and that he had to lie low." Almost a whisper.

"Where?"

"He wouldn't tell me. He said it would be safer for me if I didn't know."

"I need to be with you when you get the call tonight."

"Why should I trust you?"

"Because I kept Trey from getting killed last night and his sister from being kidnapped by the Raptors. And because I'm the only person left on his side." I gave her my business card with my cell phone number and told her to call if she heard from Trey before the six o'clock call.

My phone rang on the drive back up to La Jolla. I didn't recognize the number or even the area code. I answered.

"My name is Max Greenfield. I'm a producer for the *48 Hours* television series."

I didn't hear what he said next. My mind had gone back in time to Colleen's murder. My blood flushed heat to my face. Ten years ago, *48 Hours* producers had chased me around for an interview to get the husband/killer's side of the story. I didn't give them one and they told the story the way they wanted to. I was the killer either way. Just not in front of the camera.

"Mr. Cahill?"

"You had your chance." I snapped my words out like left jabs to the face. "You already told the story. Can't you let Colleen rest in peace?"

"I'm sorry, Mr. Cahill." He sounded young and confused. "You must have misunderstood me. We're covering the possible new trial for Randall Eddington and we'd like to get an interview with you."

"How did you get my number?"

"From Mr. Buckley's office."

I hung up and hit Buckley's cell phone number. He picked up on the third ring.

"Why the hell didn't you tell me about *48 Hours*?"

"Pull the reins back in, son. Now, what are you talking about?"

"I just got a call from a *48 Hours* producer who is doing a piece on Randall."

"That's true. I contacted them and they are going to cover the hearing, and, hopefully, the new trial. This can only help us."

"It didn't help me ten years ago." I fought the urge to mash the gas pedal to the floor to see how far and how fast one tank of gas could take me. But no matter where I ran, the memories would stay with me. My shadow at high noon.

"That's because you wouldn't talk to them. All due respect, if I'd been your lawyer, I'd have had you cooperate with them. You let them tell your story. We're going to do our best to shape the story with Randall."

"You can do whatever the hell you want. Just tell me about it first. And ask the next time you want to give my phone number to an organization that did a hit piece on me."

"I didn't give them your number." Honest surprise in his voice.

"They said they got it from your office."

"Oh..."

We both came to the same conclusion at the same time. Jasmine. Buckley's assistant and my biggest fan. She knew my whole story and had accepted the *48 Hours* version. Plus, she just didn't like me. She hadn't been able to pass up the chance to make my life a little more uncomfortable. Score one for her.

"Well, I don't want a damn thing to do with them, so please tell the producer to leave me alone."

"Son, I think you're coming at this from the ass end of the donkey."

I hit La Jolla Boulevard and noticed a cop three cars ahead of me. I lowered the phone, switched it to speaker and eased off the gas. "Translate, Buckley."

"As soon as this case is over, you're gonna have to nail up your own shingle. I'll get you as much work as I can, but it ain't gonna pay your mortgage."

"So you think I should go on air for a little free publicity?"

"Now you're coming correct." He sipped something. Probably his 100-proof coffee. "When we free that poor young man, people are going to take notice, and I'm going to tell them how indispensable you were in making it happen."

"You think *48 Hours* would interview me, and miss the opportunity to talk about a ten-year-old unsolved murder in which I was the only suspect?"

"I talked to Mr. Greenfield, and I think they'll play it differently. A wrongly accused man helping to free another."

"A Hollywood ending." I pulled to a stop in front of the Morning Cup. "Tell them I'm not interested."

CHAPTER FORTY

I met Kelsey Santos at the grassy park near the parking lot at Belmont Park at five forty-five p.m. I walked up to greet her like I'd just arrived, but I'd been there since four, surveilling her apartment. If she'd run, I'd have been right behind her. Invisible. I almost wished she had run. Straight to Trey. That would have been too easy. Now I had to try to figure out where he was, or try to convince him to come in.

I gave Kelsey instructions on what to say when Trey called. We sat at a picnic table and waited. The cool winter day had just left the stage and pulled down the sun behind it. Kelsey sat rigid. Hands in the pocket of her mini-parka. Hood up. The winter night pulled the residual warmth out of the day, but it still wasn't cold enough to be so bundled up. Her phone lay on the picnic table between us.

"It's going to be fine, Kelsey. We're going to make sure Trey is safe."

"Then what?" Head down, but the hint of an edge hanging off the corners of her words.

"What do you mean?"

"What happens after Trey testifies?" An accusation more than a question, chin thrust out like a spear. "You think Steven Lunsdorf's biker friends are just going to let bygones be bygones after Trey calls him a murderer in court?"

"After he testifies, things will die down. He may have to lie low for a while, but not too long." I hoped Buckley had come up with a better plan than that.

But Kelsey was right. Trey's post-trial safety was the elephant in the room that Buckley and I had tap-danced around. Theoretically, that was Trey's and the police's concern. But this was real life. LJPD was trying almost as hard as the Raptors to keep the trial from happening. That left Trey. Alone.

"Right." Angry.

"You're right. He'll probably have to move somewhere else."

"Where is he going to move? He's lived in San Diego his whole life. He doesn't know anyone anywhere else." She shook her head. "And it's not like he has any marketable skills."

"You can sell weed anywhere. Doesn't he have some friends in Los Angeles?"

"No."

"He told his sister he was on his way there last night."

"He didn't go to LA."

"I know. You have to get him to tell you where he is."

"So he can testify and then get murdered."

Her phone rang on the picnic table and we both froze. The phone number on the screen was blocked.

She looked at me. I nodded. She answered the phone and put it on speaker.

"Trey?"

"Yeah, it's me, Kelse." Calm. None of the panic that had been in his voice last night.

"Are you okay?"

"I'm fine. Are you on speaker? I can barely hear you."

Kelsey put the phone closer to her mouth. "Bad cell. Is this better?"

"Yeah. Listen. Be careful. This will all be over in a few days and then we can chill."

"Where are you?" She looked at me for confirmation. I nodded. "I want to see you. Can we meet somewhere, just for a little while?"

"Not yet, baby. But I'm okay."

"Why won't you tell me where you are? I'm worried about you."

"I can't. It's safer this way for both of us. But I have some protection, so don't worry."

"What do you mean?" Kelsey raised her eyebrows and she looked at me. "What kind of protection?"

"A couple dudes are guarding me. Everything is fine."

"Who? I've talked to all your friends. They don't know where you are."

"It's one of my customers. A rich dude. He's cool, so don't worry. Everything's cool."

"I want to come see you." On script, but the longing in Kelsey's voice wasn't faked. "Or at least give me your phone number so I can call you when I want to talk, instead of having to wait for you all the time."

A voice in the background came out of the phone. The words indiscernible, but the voice belonged to a man.

"I gotta go, babe." Nervous. "Bye."

"No. Not yet." But he'd already hung up.

I hadn't found out where Trey was, but I had learned something. A rich customer was protecting him or confining him. Or both. From the tone of his voice early in the conversation, I doubted it was the Raptors. A friendlier situation. But the voice at the end had proven that whoever it was, they were in control, not Trey.

Kelsey put the phone down on the picnic table like it had suddenly caught fire. She looked at me with more concern than before the call. "I don't like this. Who was the guy talking at the end?"

"I don't know." If I did, I'd have Trey. But I didn't like it either. "Do you know any of Trey's wealthy customers?"

"No. I know he has a couple, but I don't know who they are."

Could they have made the body at Candlelight Drive disappear? Somehow, someday, I'd get answers out of Trey. First I had to find him and make sure he testified. Then Buckley's kid gloves would come off.

"I'm sure he's fine." I smiled like I believed it. "You did great."

"Don't patronize me." Anger mixed with fear. Black-coffee eyes wide. "You think Trey is just some small-time drug dealer that you can use to get what you want. But that's the least of who he is." She got up from the picnic table and shoved the phone in her coat pocket. "He's a good person. Better than you."

She spun and walked across the park to her apartment. I let her go. She'd done what I'd asked her to and had gotten all Trey was willing to give. And I'd gotten all I could out of her. Used her just like she said I used Trey.

I told myself it was all in the name of a good cause.

A case that mattered.

CHAPTER FORTY-ONE

I picked up Sierra from her second waitressing job of the day at ten p.m. This one was in the ground-floor restaurant in a luxury hotel in downtown La Jolla. Buckley had agreed to let her stay at the Marriott for the next few nights until after Trey had testified at the hearing. That is, if I tracked Trey down in time to get him to the hearing or he showed up on his own.

The police scanner crackled in the background as we drove down Prospect Street. I'd had it on all day and had yet to hear the discovery of a dead body or a BOLO out for my Mustang or me. Eric Schmidt's corpse was out there somewhere waiting to be found. Unless it was buried in the East County desert, cut up in little pieces and scattered in dumpsters around San Diego, or feeding the fish off La Jolla Shores.

"Trey called me about twenty minutes ago," Sierra said, her voice surprisingly bubbly.

"What?" I almost slammed on the brakes. "Why didn't you call me?"

"He wouldn't tell me where he was, so I didn't learn anything that would help you find him. And I knew I'd see you soon anyway."

"That wasn't the plan." A long day had put some broken glass in my voice.

"I know. Sorry, but I didn't think it would matter." A little hurt, like disappointing me upset her. "But he told me to tell you and Mr. Buckley that he was going to testify and that he is being protected."

Protected. Same as he'd told Kelsey Santos. The declaration to testify was new. Just trying to keep me at bay, or telling the truth? Could his "protectors" have a vested interest in Trey testifying?

"Did he tell you who was protecting him, or why?"

"No." She shook her head. "But he told me it was one of his customers."

At least he was consistent with that. "A customer in Los Angeles?"

"No. He decided to stay in San Diego."

No more lies to his sister. Maybe Trey did feel safe.

"Do you know any of his customers? Any wealthy ones?"

"I know a couple surfers who buy from him, but I doubt they're wealthy."

"How about somebody new? Maybe some new friend. Do you remember him talking about any new people in his life?"

She thought for a second. "No."

"Did you hear anything or anyone else's voice in the background?"

"No. But he sounded really good. Relaxed. He's safe now and everything is going to be okay."

I nodded like I agreed with her. But I doubted everything was going to be okay.

I drove to the garage where I'd parked the Mustang and transferred my gear from Kim's RAV4. The police didn't seem to be looking for me or the car. Fine by me. Sierra followed me in the Mustang to Kim's house.

Kim's BMW was in the driveway and the lights were on in the house. She was home and awake. I took the keys up to the front door and stood staring at it. My body, my heart, and my mind begged me to knock. I could win her back. I was fully committed now. This time it would work. Then I thought of Kim and what she had asked me to do.

I slipped the keys through the mail slot and walked away.

* * *

Buckley called me at nine-fifteen the next morning. Early for him.

"Son, you can call off the search for Mr. Fellows." Clear voiced. Neither hungover nor drunk.

"Why? Is he there with you?"

"Not yet. But he will be. He called and said he'd meet me at the office the morning of the hearing. He's going to testify." There was some Texas yahoo in Buckley's voice. I'd never heard him sound so happy.

"Wouldn't you still like to know where he is?"

"In a perfect world." No more yahoo. "But heaven's not on earth yet. So, you need to leash the bulldog right now. Okay, son? I don't want that boy spooked."

"Can I at least be at your office when he gets there?"

"I don't think that would be a good idea."

"I'll be on my best behavior."

"I'm sure you would, but we're so close right now." Hopeful emphasis. "I don't want to take any chances. Besides, the hearing's closed, so there's no reason for you to go with us to court. Other than your scintillating personality."

If the DNA from Lunsdorf's cigarette butt had already come back from the lab, I would have testified about its collection to the judge. But Buckley had used up all his favors with the lab, so we were in the normal rotation.

"Your loss, Buckley. I'll have to scintillate somewhere else. Call me when the judge makes his decision. Good luck."

I told Buckley I wouldn't come to his office for his meeting with Trey before the hearing. I didn't say anything about waiting for Trey to arrive outside. Not that I'd confront him. Or even let him see me. I was more interested in seeing who dropped him off. Trey's car was still parked on his street in Pacific Beach, so he wouldn't be driving it. I'd follow whoever dropped him off long enough to figure out who they were and which puzzle they fit into.

* * *

I parked down the block from Buckley's office the morning of the hearing for a new trial for Randall Eddington. An hour later, a taxi dropped Trey Fellows off at the office. Damn. No mysterious guardian to follow back to Trey's new hideout. I still had a plan *B*;

follow the cab Trey took after the hearing.

Trey, Buckley and his associates, Melinda and Jacob, exited his office building at noon for the one o'clock hearing. Buckley must have given Trey a crash course in trial prep and appropriate apparel. Trey had entered Buckley's in jeans and a sweatshirt and came out wearing a perfectly tailored gray suit. His dreadlocks were tied back in a ponytail. He looked respectable. I hoped he wasn't stoned.

Jacob stowed a file box in the trunk of Buckley's Cadillac, and the four of them got in the car. They could have walked the two blocks to the courthouse and made it on time, but why not take the Caddie?

I gave them a full minute before I drove the Mustang over to the courthouse. Buckley parked in the courthouse parking lot reserved for court business. I circled until I found a spot a half block away with a view of the entrance to the courthouse. I scanned the area, looking to see if the Raptors had gotten wind of the hearing. No Choppers or old American muscle cars in sight.

Two hours later, Buckley, Melinda, and Jacob exited the court-house. No Trey. Maybe he stayed behind a second to take a leak. I called Buckley anyway and watched him put the phone up to his ear.

"Rick." He sounded happy. "Everything went well, and the judge said he would render a decision by this evening. Trey did a fine job. Handled the cross by the prosecution with flying colors."

"Where is he?"

"He left the courthouse after he testified about a half hour ago." Buckley looked around, probably realizing I could see him. "Why?"

"I just wanted to thank him for standing up."

Trey must have left the courthouse via a side exit. He wasn't taking any chances with the Raptors or with me. Plan *B* hadn't worked. I didn't have a plan *C*.

Yet.

CHAPTER FORTY-TWO

Buckley called me at my house at six p.m. I'd just sat down with a beer and pizza to watch a college bowl game. The Aqua Velva Bowl, or Old Spice, or Trojan. Hard to keep track.

"Well, son." Happy. "All the work we've done paid off. The judge vacated the conviction and ordered a new trial, providing the DA wants to proceed."

"That's fantastic, Buckley. Let me buy you a Maker's Mark or three."

"How about a rain check, pardna. Jack, Rita Mae, and I are flying to San Francisco tonight so we can post bail for Randall tomorrow and bring him home." His voice filled with emotion. "I can hardly believe it's happening."

"You made it happen, Buckley." Some of Buckley's emotion caught in my throat. "Thanks for sticking with me when I made things difficult." Santa Barbara PD hadn't. Neither had Bob Reitzmeyer. Not even Kim, in the very end.

"There'd still be room on the last flight to San Francisco tonight. Why don't you join us, son?"

"Thanks, but I'll meet up with everyone when you get back." San Francisco had too many good memories gone bad.

* * *

Randall's release led off all the local five o'clock news telecasts the next night. All the San Diego TV news stations had reporters outside the gates of San Quentin. Buckley must have made a few calls last night before he got onto the plane. The crew from *48 Hours* was there with one of its highly recognizable reporters.

I sat alone in my living room in front of the TV, and felt guilty for not feeling happier for Randall and his family. I thought of Colleen. Gone forever. I thought of Kim. Just gone. Bob Reitzmeyer, friend to enemy. Jasmine, just enemy. Timothy Buckley, boozy brother of broken lives. A mortgage that I could no longer afford. This was the life I'd made. There had to be something in me that liked it this way. Something crooked that I couldn't make straight. Or didn't want to.

Midnight sat next to me, his head under my hand that didn't have a beer in it. He didn't know that he'd probably soon be moving to a rental with a tiny yard, but he sensed something was wrong. He could see it in my eyes and sense it in my touch. Just as I could feel his anxiety in mine.

I heard a news anchor set the scene at San Quentin and a reporter take it from there. I turned away from the view and self-pity and looked at the flat screen mounted on the wall. A beautiful Latina with big eyes and a wide mouth had just asked Randall Eddington what it felt like to be a free man, then stuck her microphone ahead of five or six others in front of Randall's face. He looked down at his grandmother, enveloped in his right arm, and a huge grin grew on his face.

"Unbelievable."

Reporters machine-gunned questions, and Randall looked at Buckley, then took a step back.

Buckley filled the void. "The family wants to thank everyone for coming out as well as the hundreds of well-wishers who have supported Randall and his grandparents throughout this ordeal. But we're only halfway home, folks. Randall is not yet free. He is out on bond and will get a new trial. While we are confident that Randall will be exonerated, we hope the new district attorney of La Jolla will right the wrong of the previous DA, and drop all charges so this innocent young man can get on with his life, which has been maliciously delayed for eight years."

The reporters continued to press Randall with questions as Buckley held up his hands. "Folks, Randall does not have anything else to say at this time. Please give him some privacy to be with his grandparents. You will all get a chance to talk to him back down in San Diego. He's anxious to get back there. His home."

A stretch limo picked its way through the crowd, and Randall, his grandparents, Buckley, and the *48 Hours* reporter and cameraman all got in. Buckley had brilliantly given access to enhance favorable treatment on the show and put pressure on the DA not to retry the case. The limo slowly Y-turned, then sped away from the crowd on the way to the airport and a homecoming for Randall.

Seeing Randall happy and free from prison, at least for now, made my beer taste better. Like Buckley had said, we were only halfway home, but it sure beat showing a two-timed wife pictures of her husband naked and ugly with another woman.

Buckley was right. It did feel good to work a case that mattered.

CHAPTER FORTY-THREE

Randall's release had blown up nationally on every news channel that had covered his original trial seven years ago and condemned him even before the judge did. Now they all sang his praises and attacked a criminal justice system that could allow an innocent young man to go to prison for life.

Three days after the homecoming, Buckley had the defense team assemble at Jack and Rita Mae Eddington's condo at three p.m. Rita Mae answered my knock on the door and, as soon as I saw her face, I knew what the meeting was about.

I stepped inside and saw the *48 Hours* film crew and reporter. A man with a close-trimmed black beard nodded to me. I didn't nod back. I suspected him to be the producer Max Greenfield. I'd told him on the phone, as well as Buckley, that I didn't want to be interviewed. Luckily, the camera was pointed at Randall, who sat on the couch next to Jack and Rita Mae, reseated after letting me in. If the camera swung around to me, I'd hit the door and not look back. But I knew that today, I was a minor character in reality TV. That was fine by me.

Buckley's young associates, Melinda and Jacob, stood behind Buckley, who took center stage in the middle of the living room. Now that I'd arrived, the event could proceed. Buckley turned to the Eddingtons, but still left enough profile to be caught on camera. I knew what he would say before the words left his mouth. Not because I had foreknowledge, but because Rita Mae's face was a fleshy mood ring.

"We all have to head down to the courthouse for a press conference at four-thirty p.m. But I wanted to let everyone know in private what it's gonna be about. District Attorney Franklin will not be seeking a second trial at this time."

The Eddingtons burst up off the couch all at once. Randall hugged Rita Mae, who couldn't hold back her joyful tears any longer. Jack patted Randall on the back and put a hand to his own watery eyes. Melinda and Jacob took turns hugging Buckley and then each of the Eddingtons. Randall, dark eyes glistening, shook Buckley's hand and then bear-hugged him so hard I feared for Buckley's ribs. Rita Mae took over when Randall finished and sobbed uncontrollably into Buckley's shoulder. The *48 Hours* crew let the camera roll, and were smart enough to know that the scene would play out best without their interruption.

I watched it all from the corner of the room near the door. My heart swelled to know that I'd had a part in freeing an innocent man. It also ached a bit for not having such a definitive moment to lift the cloud of suspicion off me for Colleen's murder. Buckley, released from Rita Mae's grasp, smiled at me, and I chased the selfish thought from my head.

"Come on over, son." Buckley held out his hand. "You're a damn big part of this."

Rita Mae didn't wait for me to move. She strode over and wrapped me in a hug. I sensed the TV camera swing over to us, and I turned Rita Mae toward the door, giving the camera my back.

"God bless you, Rick, for all you've done to help free Randall." Her voice choked on joy and pain. She still smelled of vanilla and baby powder, and reminded me of my late grandmother. We hugged long and hard, and I fought the moisture gathering in my own eyes.

Rita Mae took my hand and led me across the room to the teary-eyed group. I kept my back to the TV camera. Randall stepped toward me and gave me the handshake/one-shoulder bro hug.

"Mr. Cahill, I can't tell you how much your belief in my innocence means to me." Sunlight cutting through the glass door from the balcony reflected off his glasses, hiding his eyes. "You know what it's like to be accused of something you didn't do and have the whole world against you. That's why I wanted you to work with Mr. Buckley. I knew you'd find the truth."

Buckley had told me that Jack and Rita Mae had chosen me. They probably had told Randall about me, and he'd gotten on board after the fact. Still, it was a nice thought.

Jack shook my hand and thanked me. He seemed sincere, without any residue of anger from my mistaken accusation at the golf course. The associates hugged me. I enjoyed Melinda's hug more than Jacob's. Buckley slung an arm over my shoulder, his long, gray hair in a ponytail braid.

"Rick Cahill, you are one ornery sumbitch. But, you're a bulldog for the truth." His breath had an afternoon nip of Maker's Mark in it. No judgment. He'd earned it. "Without you poking 'round where no one wanted you to, this day might never have come about."

I passed on the "aw shucks" moment. My "poking 'round" had cost me my job and the friendship of the one man left on earth I'd looked up to. But today, it was worth it. Randall Eddington was free, and his grandmother could smile again. I curved a pinch-lipped smile and nodded.

"Feels good, don't it?" Buckley pulled me close so I got a whiff of last night's Maker's Mark on top of today's. "Being on the right side."

"Yes, Timothy." I slapped him on the back and squeezed his neck. "It sure do."

The *48 Hours* reporter moved toward Randall and the cameraman followed. Restraint over, time for interviews. Buckley followed the camera. He knew today's victory would up his client load and he'd milk that cow dry. As he should. I slid back into the corner of the room. When the producer worked to get everyone seated, I eased out the front door.

Five steps down the hall to the stairs, I heard the Eddingtons' door open and close. "Rick."

I turned and saw Max Greenfield striding toward me. Young, thin, with curly black hair above black, horn-rimmed glasses. He looked like a grad student studying for his MFA. I kept walking.

"Rick." I heard his steps quicken into a trot. "Just give me a second. Please."

I stopped above the staircase and waited for him to catch up.

"I'm Max Greenfield. We spoke on the phone. I know you didn't have a good experience with our show ten years ago." He gave me a concerned look. "But things have changed. Heck, I wasn't even working for *48 Hours* then. And you helped free an innocent woman from jail two years ago, and now an innocent man from prison."

He'd done his homework, but he'd only read the *Cliffs Notes* version. My story read more like a senior thesis. And not one that would grade out any higher than a *C*. I gave him nothing, but let him say his piece.

"Just give me five minutes in front of the camera and you can tell all of America your story. The real one. How being wrongly accused has made you a crusader to free others in your situation. It will be free publicity for your new agency." Buckley had obviously gotten in his ear. "And it will be great TV."

I couldn't blame Greenfield for wanting to make "great TV." But, five minutes wouldn't be enough and ten seconds would be too much. Either way, it wouldn't be great TV. Especially for a family up in Mill Valley, still grieving the murder of their daughter and sister ten years later. For them, it would be salt in an unhealable wound.

"I'm not on a crusade, kid. Too many innocent people die on those."

I fled down the stairs to my car.

Buckley called me a half hour later when he realized I'd left. He tried but couldn't convince me to come down to the press conference. I'd spent enough time in front of cameras and on the front pages of newspapers when Colleen had been murdered, and again when I stuck my nose in the middle of a murder investigation two years ago. Things hadn't turned out well either time.

I watched the local news at five p.m. Every station led off with a tape of the four-thirty news conference in front of the old

Episcopal Church that had been converted into La Jolla's only courthouse forty years earlier.

A stern-faced La Jolla DA, Candace Franklin, stood at the podium. She wore a no-nonsense business suit to go with her no-nonsense expression. She said that, due to new evidence, she would not retry Randall Eddington for the murder of his family, but that the search for justice would go on.

Translation: At a time when the existence of La Jolla's District Attorney's Office and Police Department teetered on the constant threat of a voter ballot initiative, it would be best not to hold a trial that would expose the underhanded and illegal tactics of both. Especially with a network news organization hanging around.

A reporter shouted a question as to whether Randall Eddington was still a suspect in his family's murders.

Candace paused long enough to belie her answer. "No."

Translation: We still think he did it, but there's not a chance in hell we'll try him again for reasons already stated.

Chief Moretti replaced DA Franklin at the podium and gave his own justice speech. He wore his dress blues instead of one of his Italian suits to give an air of authenticity to his quest for justice. He first introduced himself so everybody would know he was in charge.

"New evidence has come to light that, while not completely exonerating Mr. Eddington, has led the investigation in a different direction. The La Jolla Police Department will pursue all leads in the murders of Thomas, Alana, and Molly Eddington until the murderer is brought to justice. The people of La Jolla can be confident that LJPD is on the case."

Translation: We still think Randall is guilty, but will not pursue a case against him for reasons listed above. Hopefully, there will be enough evidence to arrest the biker, or there will be another murder to take La Jollans' minds off the Eddington case.

When asked, Moretti declined to describe the new evidence.

Buckley took the podium next. He thanked everyone for coming, then thanked DA Franklin for siding with justice as opposed to political expediency. Of course, she'd done just the opposite, but Buckley was a Texas gentleman and too smart a man to imply that any attempt to retry Randall would be pure politics.

Buckley then thanked his defense team by name, including me, saying that I'd risked my career to help free an innocent man. Good to his word, as usual. Finally, he pulled Randall, Jack and Rita Mae up to the podium. "Randall will say his piece in a moment, but I just wanted you all to meet Jack and Rita Mae Eddington, Randall's grandparents. Without their love and unrelenting faith in their grandson, young Randall would still be in prison. These are two of the finest people I've ever met."

Jack nodded and Rita Mae blushed. Buckley then introduced Randall. Broad shouldered with prison muscles, he filled up the TV screen and looked bigger than he did in person. The falling winter evening light softened his thousand-yard prison stare, and he looked like a large man happy to be alive. He thanked his grandparents, Buckley, and his team.

"And I want to thank someone who is not here today, but should be here front and center, Rick Cahill. Mr. Buckley mentioned him, but I wanted to single him out because of the courage he showed in helping to free me. Not only did he lose his steady job to work on my case, he was assaulted by a criminal biker gang that is protecting the real killer of my family, Steven Lunsdorf."

Buckley quickly wedged himself between Randall and the microphone. Nervous smile under his ten-gallon hat. "We'll leave the La Jolla Police Department to handle the investigation. I'm afraid, as you can see, it's getting dark, so that will be all we have time for tonight. Please respect this wonderful family's privacy as they take time to get reacquainted after eight long years."

Buckley hurried the Eddingtons away from the podium toward a limo parked at the curb. Reporters chased them, firing questions about Steven Lunsdorf and the purported new evidence. Buckley ignored all and herded the family into the limo, then jumped in after them.

I sat back in my recliner and took a long slug of beer. Randall had just ripped the scab off the investigation and put Lunsdorf and LJPD right in the middle of the blood. He may have also put a target on his own back, but I didn't think even the Raptors were bold enough or stupid enough to put a hit on a man who had just told the world they were murderers on TV.

Buckley obviously had not been ready for Randall's declaration. Randall was a free man and had a mind of his own. I doubted Buckley would advise they do any more press conferences. Freeing your client was one thing. Embarrassing the police and DA who put him in prison was another. But I had to admire the kid. He wanted the police to go after the man who he believed had slaughtered his family.

My house phone rang. Midnight looked at me, waiting for me to answer the phone. I stayed seated and let the call go to the answering machine. A few minutes later, another call. Three in the next five minutes. I finished my beer and went into the kitchen for another one. The house phone and answering machine sat on the granite kitchen counter across from the fridge. I hit the message button on the machine. Each call had been a different reporter asking for an interview.

I changed my favorable opinion about Randall speaking up.

CHAPTER FORTY-FOUR

Sierra Fellows had moved back into her apartment after she bought a German shepherd. The dog took my place as a guard. The Raptors left her alone. So did everyone else. Her brother came out of hiding the day after the press conference. To me, at least. Not to the general public. Or the police. DA Franklin's decision not to retry Randall and the ensuing press conference was all over the local news, print and TV and radio, the next day. Trey called me in the morning.

"Bro, you think the Raptors still want to kill me?" Not quite conversational, but not panicked, either. Maybe he'd gotten used to having a target on his back. Or maybe he felt confident that his rich stoner buddy could keep him safe indefinitely. Had worked so far.

"I doubt it. After Randall Eddington outed them on TV last night, they're probably keeping their heads low. I'd bet Lunsdorf is either lawyering up or going underground."

"Yeah, well, that Randall dude wants to meet me. Shake my hand and all that. I just want to make sure it's safe."

"Where are you going to meet?"

"My house." He was silent for a couple seconds. "Buckley's going to be with him. I just don't want to get ambushed by the Raptors when I go back out in public."

"I'll pick you up and take you to meet Randall. Make sure everything is safe."

"Sorry, bro. My friend is serious about his privacy. He doesn't want anybody to know who he is."

"I'll be discreet. I don't care who he is." Yes, I did. "I'm just looking out for you."

"I know, man. You're a good dude. You took care of Sierra when I couldn't. I'm in your debt, bro."

"We're square, Trey." I'd risked injury, maybe my life, to keep Sierra safe. But it had been in service to a case I was paid to work on. At least, it had started that way. Trey risked his life to free an innocent stranger and try to bring the murderer of a family he'd never met to justice. All for no other reason that I'd been able to figure out, than it was the right thing to do. Maybe Kelsey Santos had been right. There was a helluva lot more to Trey than just being a stoner.

"What time is the meeting?"

"Tonight at six."

The meet was a bad idea. I was surprised that Buckley had agreed to it. If the DA ever decided to try Randall again, his meeting with Fellows could look like collusion or a conspiracy. One man accused of murder meets with the man who would testify in his defense that someone else confessed to the murder. The DA could use the meeting to weaken, if not destroy, Trey's testimony. A bribe for friendly testimony. Coercion. The DA could take her pick.

On the other hand, the meet could help me discover where Trey was holed up and who his protector was.

"I'll surveil the area around your house beforehand to make sure no Raptors are watching. I'll call you on this number if there's a problem, so make sure you hold onto this phone. No more burners."

"Cool, bro. I'll keep this phone for a while. I owe you one."

I hung up without repeating that we were even.

* * *

Jasmine greeted me with dagger goth eyes when I walked into the lobby of Buckley's office.

"Is he in?" I didn't bother with niceties. Any form of pleasantness from me to Jasmine came back at me in inverse venom.

Jasmine kept the daggers on me, picked up the handset to

her office phone, and stabbed a button with a black-nailed finger. "Rick."

She made my name sound like the *F*-word. She listened to the receiver, hung it up, then said, "Okay."

I took that as it was okay to go into Buckley's office.

"Rick, my boy, I think Jasmine is slowly coming around." He smiled from under his cowboy hat, boots up on the desk, leaning back in his chair, staring out at the ocean a half mile away. The sun had eaten through the morning haze with a bright voracious appetite, making winter in San Diego feel like spring anywhere else.

I ignored the jab. "You sunning yourself in the afterglow of victory, Buckley?"

"Son, I've been a criminal attorney for forty-plus years. I believe in the law and the role of the defense attorney in the greatest system of jurisprudence that man has ever conceived." He tilted his head further back to let the sunlight bathe his neck. "But I don't think I've had an innocent client more than a couple dozen times, if that. Now, I've had plenty of clients who were innocent of the crimes they were charged with, but guilty of many others. No, a truly innocent client is a rare thing. And to be able to get justice for a young man who has been treated so unjustly for eight years is something worth savoring."

Buckley was right, of course. His belief in Randall's innocence had been what convinced me to take a look at the case. That, and Rita Mae Eddington's chocolate chip cookies. The case had turned my world upside down, and lost me most of what little in life I had left. But it set me on a new direction. It had shown me the soul-cleansing grace of working a case that mattered. I was grateful to Buckley for showing me the light and for giving me the opportunity.

But I'd already thanked him once.

"That's beautiful, Buckley. Now come back down to earth." I sat on one of the two leather chairs that faced his desk. "Why in hell are you allowing a meeting between Randall and Trey Fellows?"

Buckley dropped his boots onto the floor and leaned forward. "Son, you are ice cubes down the underpants after the first kiss with a childhood crush." He scratched his permanent, two-week-old beard. "But you do have a point. I can't talk young Randall out of it. He's determined to meet Trey and thank him for being so courageous."

"It's a bad idea."

"Well, of course it is. But Randall's very persuasive, and after having eight years stolen from him by the great State of California, he deserves to act on a bad idea with good intentions. The meeting will be quick and under the radar. There will only be four people that know about it, and each of us understands the importance of secrecy."

"Hell, Trey isn't being too secretive. He told me about it on the phone."

"Trey trusts you like I do, Rick. Implicitly."

I didn't know what I'd done to deserve all the trust. I'd defied Buckley's orders more than once, and what I had planned for Trey after his meeting with Randall would ruin any trust he had in me.

"I don't trust anyone implicitly." Maybe Kim, not that it mattered anymore. "But some good could come from the meeting."

"I see the wheels turning behind your eyes, Rick." Buckley squinted at me. "What do you have in mind?"

"I'm going to put a GPS tracking device on Trey's car at the meeting and track him back to where he's been holing up."

Buckley's brow creased and he shook his head. "Why in hell would you do that?"

"I want to find out who this mysterious man is who's been 'protecting' Trey." My turn with the air quotes. "You have to be curious too, Buckley. There's still a dead body floating around out there yet to be discovered, and I think this guy is responsible for making it invisible."

"And to what greater good is all this, Rick?" He raised his hands up. "Whoever this person is, he's looking out for Trey's best interests and has kept Trey alive for the last week and a half. Kept him from being framed for a murder he didn't commit."

"And thus helped you free Randall from prison."

"Yeah. Sure. I had selfish reasons for looking the other way about Trey's protector. But all for the greater good. An innocent man is free from prison, and a courageous man is free from harm. Surely, you can see this, Rick. Why peek behind the curtain when you already have the ruby slippers?"

"Because I have to know the truth."

CHAPTER FORTY-FIVE

I arrived in Trey's neighborhood at five p.m. and did a few laps around it in my Mustang. No Choppers, black Trans Ams, or any signs of Raptors. I parked a block down from Trey's house and walked the neighborhood. The sun had already set, so I peeked in hedges, behind fences, and even under cars. Clear. I made a few more rounds on foot, then went back to the car and did the same on wheels. Finally, I found a spot closer to Trey's house near the intersection with the cross street. I parked and waited.

At five minutes to six, a late-model, silver Ford Focus circled the block. Too dark to see the driver inside. The Focus parked in the spot I had given up a half hour earlier. The driver walked down the block toward Trey's. A streetlight caught him, and I saw that it was Trey, himself. His head was on a swivel. Nervous to be out in public unprotected. Or so he thought. But he was mostly right. I wasn't armed. Not with a gun, anyway. The blackjack that had served me so well of late weighted down my bomber jacket pocket.

Trey had left his parking spot in the main house's driveway open. Smart. Even though he wasn't driving his own car, he didn't want to make it look like anyone was home. I waited until he slipped around the back to his cottage, then got out of my car. I went over to the Ford Focus and pulled a tracking device out of my jacket pocket. The device was roughly half the size of an iPhone and had a magnetic strip on the back. I made sure there weren't any eyeballs on me, then bent down behind the bumper and attached the tracker to the chassis of the Focus.

Headlights bisected the intersection, and Buckley's Cadillac turned onto Trey's street in search of a parking spot. I slowly walked to Trey's, making one last round peeking into the dark. By the time I got to his cottage, Randall and Buckley were already there.

The tiny cottage could barely hold four adult men, especially when one of them was the size of Randall. He could easily fill out the uniform of a Charger linebacker. When I went inside, he and Trey had just decoupled from the obligatory bro-hug. Randall only had a couple inches on Trey in height, but looked twice as wide and outweighed him by at least sixty pounds. All muscle.

"Trey, I'll never be able to thank you enough for risking your life to come forward with the truth." The single overhead light in the room caught Randall's eyes and all of the thousand yards had disappeared, leaving them vulnerable, yet warm. "After everything dies down, when LJPD finally gets off their butts and arrests Steven Lunsdorf for...for..." Randall took a double deep breath, fought back tears. "...for the horrible things he did, I want you to come work for us at Eddington Golf. I know things have been hard for you the last couple years, and I think you'd be an asset to our team."

Buckley's face pinched and a low groan escaped his mouth. He quickly tried to cover. "In due time. You're right, Randall. Once the DA charges Mr. Lunsdorf."

Trey looked shocked. Even stricken. Maybe he'd gotten used to living on the dole and dealing marijuana to get by. Or better yet, living under the wing of a sugar-daddy pal. Whatever it was, I doubted working for Randall was in his top three choices of what to do with the rest of his life.

"Yeah. Cool." He worked up a tight smile. "That would be great."

Randall gave him back a closed-mouth smile, seeming to understand that he'd never have to worry about someone having to teach Trey how to glue the head of a nine iron onto a steel shaft. He slipped past Trey and went over to the lone photograph on the wall of the cottage. The one of a smiling Brad Bauer and Sierra Fellows together.

"Is that your sister?" Randall turned and asked Trey.

"Yeah." Trey blinked a couple times.

"She's very pretty." It was complimentary and not predatory. "Is that her boyfriend?"

Seemed like a genuine question, but at least three people in the room knew that the prison that Randall had just been freed from was the home to the man in the picture for the last three years. There were four different cell blocks and over 5,000 inmates in San Quentin. It would probably be more unusual if Randall did know Brad Bauer than if he didn't.

Trey probably ran through the same thoughts in his head because he didn't answer right away. Finally, "Yeah."

"Well, he's a lucky man. They look very happy together."

Nobody volunteered that Brad Bauer lived in the same zip code that Randall had just fled. Everyone but Randall seemed anxious to end the awkward meeting and have Trey and Randall go their separate ways. Forever.

"Well, son, we best be going." Buckley put his hand on Randall's massive back. "I know Mr. Fellows has some things to attend to. Now, this meeting needs to stay between just the four of us, right?"

Buckley looked at each of us individually, and we all nodded our heads.

Randall thanked Trey again and squeezed him in a full bear hug this time. Beyond awkward, it looked painful. Randall, Buckley, and I left together, then split off to our cars. I waited in mine while Buckley drove off with Randall in the Caddie.

I activated the app on my iPhone that tracked the tracer I'd put under Trey's car. A red light blipped in place right where the Focus was parked on the little map. Trey finally left his house and got into the Focus. I put the phone into a holder attached to the inside of the windshield. I waited until Trey was a half mile away before I started the car and followed him using the blinking red dot on the map on the cell phone.

It only took me a few minutes to figure out where he was going.

CHAPTER FORTY-SIX

The red dot went down La Jolla Boulevard, then through La Jolla, down Torrey Pines Road, and onto La Jolla Shores Drive. I didn't have to watch the red dot to know that it would turn onto La Jolla Farms Road and stop in front of Alan Rankin's gated home.

Alan Rankin. Lawyer for imprisoned Raptor kingpin, Rock Karsten.

Trey's protector. The man responsible for hiding the corpse of Eric Schmidt? What was the connection between Rankin and Trey? A small-time drug dealer and the lawyer for the leader of the biker gang that supplied him the drugs. Drugs and money. Was that what this was all about? That simple? No. It wasn't business. It was something more. Whatever it was, I doubted Rankin was protecting Trey out of the goodness of his own heart.

I parked up the street from Rankin's house and debated about what to do. Half of me, most of me, wanted to go bang on Rankin's front door and demand that he and Trey tell me what the hell was going on. The sliver of restraint left in me that I'd ignored too much lately finally won an argument. I'd have better luck with Trey alone when I confronted him with proof that he'd been staying with Rankin. I'd wear him down, and use his sister if I had to. Plus, I now could track him wherever he went. I made a Y-turn in a driveway and drove home.

Every half hour or so, I checked the tracking map on my phone. Trey, or at least the Focus, didn't move all night. I decided to drive back over to Rankin's street early in the morning and wait until he went to his office, then confront Trey. Otherwise, Trey might stay holed up inside the house all day. All he needed was a bong and something to put in it.

My cell phone vibrated in my pocket and woke me up. I'd

crashed on the couch watching TV. Midnight raised his head from his spoon position behind my legs. I pulled the phone out. 2:17 a.m. No name attached to the phone number on the screen. I answered.

"Is this Rick Cahill?" A woman's voice. Familiar and urgent.

"Yes."

"This is Kelsey Santos. You gave me your card and told me I could call you anytime."

Two-seventeen in the morning certainly qualified for anytime. "Sure, Kelsey. What is it?"

"Trey's missing." Near panic. "He was supposed to meet me at my apartment at midnight after I got off my shift. He never came over and doesn't answer his phone."

The last time I'd checked the tracker map had been around ten-thirty p.m. I must have fallen asleep sometime shortly after. Maybe Trey had done the same and left his phone somewhere where it couldn't wake him.

"Give me a second." I wondered if Kelsey knew about the Alan Rankin situation. Doubt it. If she had, in her current panicked state, she probably would have driven over to Rankin's house. I tapped the tracker app open and saw the red dot still blinking in one place. I was about to tell Kelsey that she had nothing to worry about, when I noticed that the dot's location had changed since I last looked at it. It now blinked in place at Trey's address.

"When did you talk to him last?" I sounded calm, but inside, concern tugged at me.

"About ten-thirty."

"What time did you call after he didn't show up at your apartment?"

"Quarter after twelve, and every fifteen minutes since." Now the panic, a fever pitch.

"Did you go by his house?"

"No. I know he's not staying there and I want to be here in case he shows up." Tears in her throat now. "Do you think I should?"

"No. Listen, everything is going to be okay. I'll try to find him." Calm, but the concern in my gut now yanked with both hands. "Call me if Trey finally shows up or calls you. Otherwise, I'll call you back in about a half hour."

I called Trey's latest phone number. Automated voicemail. I left a message to call me right away. I grabbed the coat that had the blackjack in the pocket and wished again that I still had a gun as I ran to my car.

Trey's rental Ford Focus was parked in the front driveway. I fought back the growing sense of dread gnawing at my body. I parked behind the Focus, the Mustang's ass hanging out into the street. I jumped out of the car and ran back to Trey's bungalow and pounded on the front door. "Trey!"

Nothing. I tried the doorknob and it turned. I pushed the door open and rushed inside, slipped on something wet, and nearly fell down. The scent of iron hung in the air. I flung up the light switch and saw red.

Blood. Streaked castoffs on the walls and ceiling. Wet, pooled on the hardwood floor under my feet. Two bodies strewn on the floor.

Trey Fellows lay face up to the left of the door. What was left of him. I recognized the tan board shorts and gray sweatshirt he'd worn earlier that night. Now both were red with only a few dry patches of the original color. Trey's head, a broken eggshell. Half of it beaten jagged with brain and blood oozing out, one eye socket empty, the other holding one dead, staring eye.

The other body was prone in the middle of the room, its lower extremity blocked by the loveseat. It was a man, or had been. His skull gashed open, brain matter and blood congealing in light-colored hair now turned pink from the blood. Then I saw it. A caved-in cowboy hat on the floor a few feet from the body. I took a step forward and my eyes cleared the loveseat. Cowboy boots beneath Levi jeans. The gray end of a ponytail curled under a shoulder.

Timothy Buckley.

Tears boiled out of me and I ran outside as my stomach emptied out my throat. I fell to my knees and retched until the only thing left in me was stomach acid. I staggered to my feet and called 911 on my cell phone. The dispatcher told me to wait there and the police would arrive in less than five minutes.

I stayed back by the bungalow and guarded the empty, broken bodies.

CHAPTER FORTY-SEVEN

I heard the siren three or four blocks away. I walked out to the Focus and snatched the tracking device I'd planted under the car earlier. I hid it and the blackjack back under the spare tire in the trunk of my car. Hard to explain either to the police.

I waited for the patrol car to arrive. It did, lights flashing and siren wailing, ten seconds later. The driver whipped open his door and jumped out of the car. Another cop calmly got out of the passenger side. He walked over to me with the younger driver right behind him.

The older cop asked the questions. I told him everything about the night back to the phone call from Kelsey Santos that woke me up. The cop's first concern was if the suspect or suspects were still in the area. I told him the scene was quiet when I arrived.

"Where did you find the bodies?"

"In the cottage around back. It's...it's a massacre."

"Stay with Officer Lewis. I'll be right back."

Officer Lewis was the driver. Twenty-four, twenty-five. Thin. Baby face.

"Pretty bad back there, huh?" A little too eager.

I'd been young and eager once. Back on the job in Santa Barbara. Eager for action, never for blood. "Fuck you."

The young cop's face pinched mean and his eyes seemed to be searching his mind for what to do. I hoped he'd make the wrong decision so I could make a wrong one too. A night in jail with scraped knuckles and black eyes fueled on adrenaline would be welcome if it would give me some relief from the images of mutilation strobing through my head.

My cell phone rang. The cop kept staring at me. I pulled the phone out of my pocket. Kelsey Santos' number. My stomach sank again. A different kind of dread this time, but just as painful as the first. I answered the phone.

"Rick, did you find him?" Excruciating hope.

"It's not good."

"What! What! Tell me!"

"I'm sorry...Trey's...Trey's dead."

A screech and wails. I listened. All I could do. I wished I could have found a way to comfort her. And myself. But there wasn't one. Death was without comfort. Unless it ended unbearable suffering. Unexpected death was its own suffering for those left living.

"Where, where is he? I have to see him."

"You can't see him. He's gone. Please call family or friends and have them come stay with you. Can I call anyone for you?"

"You've done enough! You and that fucking lawyer, Buckley. You got Trey killed. You used him and then you left him exposed! You killed him!" She hung up.

Buckley had died for his sins. I had to live with mine.

The night swirled around me. Buckley and Trey's slaughtered bodies, Kelsey's anguish, and then her vitriol. My knees deserted me, and I sat down hard on the asphalt next to the cop car.

"Whoa." The young cop's face hovering over me. A smirk pulling at the corners of his mouth. "Not so tough, after all. Deep breaths. All that blood, huh?"

A pair of homicide detectives arrived a half hour later. This was the San Diego Police Department's turf, so I didn't have to worry about Detective Denton or Chief Moretti. No complaints.

I told the detectives all I knew. The whole story about Trey as the key witness against Raptor Steven Lunsdorf in getting Randall Eddington out of prison, the Raptors' pursuit of Trey and Sierra Fellows, Trey holing up at Alan Rankin's house. Trey, Buckley, Randall Eddington, and I meeting at Trey's house earlier that night.

I left out my physical altercations with the Raptors, and discovering Eric Schmidt's body at the Candlelight Drive house and its subsequent disappearance. Maybe I should have copped to the laws I'd broken and given the detectives the complete story. But my history with police and my survival instinct wouldn't allow me.

The cops were done with me by three forty-five a.m. I drove home in a haze. Midnight greeted me at the door and sniffed at the dried blood on the soles of my shoes. I took a shower and scrubbed at blood that wasn't there, then went to bed.

The images of Buckley and Trey pressed down on me, forcing out all else. Kelsey's accusation, the soundtrack playing behind the horrific images. I prayed for sleep. I welcomed the nightmare of the dead man with the gun that woke me almost every night. Anything but what I'd seen tonight. Anything to shield me from the truth of Kelsey's words.

I was culpable in Trey's death. So was Buckley, but he had paid the ultimate price. Buckley and I had gotten what we needed from Trey and left his security in the hands of a stranger. A stranger who turned out to be linked to the imprisoned Raptor kingpin. Had Alan Rankin used Trey for his own purposes and then had him murdered? Or had he given Trey up to Lunsdorf and his crew? The body bludgeoned beyond recognition was a Raptor signature. Why had Trey gone back to his house, and why was Buckley there? The Raptors murdering Trey, as horrible as it was, made sense. Buckley being at Trey's and ending up collateral damage did not.

The police would investigate and, hopefully, bring those responsible to justice. But not all of those responsible would go on trial. Not in Kelsey Santos' eyes.

And not in mine.

CHAPTER FORTY-EIGHT

The murders were all over the TV news. A news camera had gotten a shot of me standing next to the police car and talking to the detectives. My landline started ringing as soon as the shot of me aired. I let all the calls go to the answering machine. No doubt, reporters who saw the shot of me on the news recognized me from my fifteen minutes of infamy over the years.

A few hours later my cell phone rang. I allowed a glimmer of hope to seep through the darkness that it might be Kim. I pulled out the phone and the glimmer burned out.

Randall Eddington.

"Mr. Cahill, are you okay?" Subdued.

"I'm okay. What about you and your grandparents? I know they'd gotten pretty close with...with Buckley." His name came out jagged and broken.

"We're all in a state of shock. Grammy is really taking it hard." His voice tightened. "She thought Mr. Buckley was my guardian angel. Thinks you are too. Anyway, Mr. Buckley spoke very highly of you, and I wanted to tell you I'm sorry for your loss."

"Thanks, Randall. If there is anything I can do for you or Rita Mae, let me know."

"Will do, Mr. Cahill." He paused without saying good-bye, like he was waiting for me to say something or he had more to say. "The police came by my grandparents' condo today and questioned mc about visiting Trey last night with Mr. Buckley. Did you tell them about that?"

"Yeah. I know we all agreed to keep it a secret, but the

crime-scene lab techs will be all over Trey's house. If they turn up our DNA, I want the detectives to understand why it's there."

"Horrible to have to think about such a thing. But that was very smart of you, Mr. Cahill. I wouldn't have thought of it."

"Did the detectives seem suspicious?"

"Not really. I think they were just doing their job and eliminating suspects. But..." He paused again. "I do feel somewhat responsible for what happened. If Trey hadn't come forward with the confession, and Mr. Buckley hadn't taken my case, they'd both still be alive."

Of course, he was right, but he wanted a denial to feel better. I hadn't lied to myself, but Randall deserved a reprieve. All he'd done was go to prison for seven years for a crime he didn't commit. He couldn't help it if the truth coming out had gotten people killed.

"You didn't do anything wrong, Randall. The cops, the old district attorney, and the State of California were wrong in the first place. If they'd all done their job better, Trey and Buckley would still be alive, and the man who murdered your family would be in prison."

All true, but none of it mitigated my responsibility for not realizing how vengeful the Raptors were.

"It has to be the Raptors, right?"

"Yeah."

"Do you think...ah." Low, timid. "Do you think my grandparents and I are in danger? That the Raptors would want to kill us?"

"I don't think so." But I'd already been horribly wrong once. "The DA isn't retrying you. If they bring charges against Steven Lunsdorf, you won't be called as a witness. You don't have anything to do with the Raptors. But be careful anyway."

"I guess I shouldn't have called Lunsdorf a killer on TV the other day. Not very smart in retrospect. But I wanted to put pressure on the police department."

"You did." Images of Trey's and Buckley's mangled bodies

pushed their way back into my head. "The pressure is on now more than ever."

"My publisher offered to put me and my grandparents up in a hotel for a couple weeks until the police arrest Lunsdorf."

"Your publisher?"

"Yes. I'm writing a memoir."

Barely twenty-six and writing a memoir. But he'd lived enough for two lifetimes in his short time on earth. And suffered enough for many more. The story of his life would, no doubt, be a *New York Times* best seller. Probably become a movie too. Youth and tragedy sold in today's America. Put both together and you had a blockbuster. I wouldn't judge Randall for cashing in on his tragedy. He'd already paid a debt to society he didn't owe. No harm in society paying some of it back.

"You should probably take up your publisher on their offer. Just to be safe."

"I think you're right." An exhale, like he had more to say. Finally, "I know you probably also feel somewhat responsible for Trey's and Mr. Buckley's death."

No argument.

"I know that's the kind of man you are. But you shouldn't feel guilty." The words were peeled of emotion. Matter of fact. "Trey understood the danger when he came forward, and Mr. Buckley did, too. If you hadn't investigated his claim, someone else would have. Maybe not someone as determined as you, but the outcome would have been the same. I believe that with all my heart."

His words didn't make me feel better. I'm not sure they were meant do. Sounded more like a statement of fact. How the world worked. That was fine by me. I didn't want a pep talk. Or any more talk at all.

"Good night, Randall." I hung up.

I spent the next three hours sitting in front of the TV. The TV couldn't block the images in my head or the voice of Kelsey Santos. I fought the urge to call Kim. She'd made the decision I always knew she should. It wouldn't be fair to try and pull her back now. And it hurt that she hadn't called me after my cameo on the news. She'd asked me to walk away, and I had. Now she'd closed the door behind me.

I glanced toward the kitchen and the liquor cabinet. A crutch to hold me up or push away the truth. Too easy. Too cheap. And the truth would still be there in the morning, along with a headache and regret.

Midnight sat close and gave me big-eyed Lab concerned looks. I scratched his head. The one sentient being I could reassure and comfort. He let out a contented sigh.

Someone knocked on my door about nine. Midnight growled and bolted upright. I quieted him and went to the hall closet and grabbed a baseball bat. Hickory. I went to the front door with Midnight at my side, ready to pounce. I looked through the peep-hole, then set the bat down and opened the door. Midnight waited for an attack command. He wouldn't get one.

Scott Buehler, reporter for *The Reader*, a free local paper, smiled up at me. "Rick. You didn't return my calls, so I thought I'd try to talk to you directly."

"How the hell did you find out where I lived?"

"Like you, I have my sources. Could I come in and ask you a few questions about the Fellows and Buckley murders?"

Buehler had been the only reporter in San Diego who'd gotten things right in the murder case I'd been involved in a couple years back. Well, mostly right. As right as LJPD and I were willing to admit to. He'd made me look like some kind of hero. I hadn't been. But the rest of the press had made out LJPD to be a hero, and it hadn't been one, either. Even less so than me.

"No." I didn't want to be mislabeled a hero again. I started to close the door.

"My editor wants to call the murders a drug deal gone bad." He spit the words out before the door closed in his face.

I held the door open just enough for my head to stick out. "Is that what the police told you?"

"They haven't told me or anyone much of anything." He looked me straight in the eyes. "That's not what happened, is it?"

"Look, I can't give you anything better than the police can."

"Is that how you want Trey Fellows to be remembered, as some small-time criminal who was murdered in a drug deal gone bad, with Timothy Buckley getting caught in the middle?"

Somehow, he knew how to get to me. I opened the door and let him in.

We sat at the kitchen table. Buehler balding, studious, looked fifty, but I figured he was ten years younger. He started to ask a question, but I beat him to it.

"Tell me what you know or think you know, and I'll guide you as best I can."

He told me about Trey's suspected Raptor drug connections and that Brad Bauer, Trey's best friend and Sierra's boyfriend who had gone to prison for dealing cocaine, was thought to be supplied by the Raptors too. He didn't say anything about Trey coming forward with evidence incriminating Steven Lunsdorf in the Eddington family murders. LJPD was keeping that info secret for now, probably so Lunsdorf wouldn't run. He obviously hadn't run after Randall called him out at the press conference the other day. Or, if he had, he'd left behind some animals to do his killing for him.

"Why does your editor think it was a drug deal gone bad, other than Trey and the Raptors having a supposed connection? Were there any drugs or a suitcase of money found at the scene?"

I hadn't seen any evidence of either, but everything I remember was outlined in blood.

"The police haven't conceded or denied a drug connection. But my editor thinks the viciousness of the attack was a warning to other business partners not to step out of line. That's the Raptors' MO."

"That seems like quite a leap, without any evidence to prove it."

"I know. He thinks it's too coincidental that Brad Bauer and the Raptor chief, Rock Karsten, are in the same prison, and that the connection between both of them was murdered. He thinks maybe Bauer was ready to give up some of the Raptors for a deal to get the cops who arrested him to speak on his behalf at his parole hearing."

I froze. "What did you say?"

"That maybe the Raptors had Trey Fellows murdered as a warning to Brad Bauer to keep him from talking to the cops."

"No. You said Rock Karsten and Bauer were in the same prison. When was Bauer transferred to Corcoran?"

Buehler frowned. "He wasn't. He and Karsten are both doing time in San Quentin."

"Karsten is in Corcoran. I checked the CDCR website."

"No." Buehler shook his head and ran his finger on his computer tablet from left to right over and over again, scrolling back over notes. He stopped. "Karsten has been at San Quentin for the last seven months. The state transferred him earlier this year. The CDCR website is notoriously slow to update. I talked to someone in records on the phone."

A chill ran up my spine and the dread from early this morning attacked my insides.

"What block? At San Quentin." I could hardly push out the words.

He scrolled a bit more. "I believe North."

North cell block. The same block I'd visited Randall Eddington in when I agreed to take on his case. Alan Rankin, Rock Karsten's lawyer, secretly meeting with Trey Fellows before he testified against Steven Lunsdorf. Lunsdorf, the man who took over the Raptors from Rock Karsten, and became his enemy when Karsten went to prison. Alan Rankin, the man who had been secretly "protecting" Trey Fellows right up until he was murdered.

"Scott, it's been a long day. The weight of it just hit me. Call me tomorrow and we can try again."

"We go to press tomorrow. Unless you can give me something more, my editor is going to run with the drug angle."

"He can run with whatever the hell he wants."

The drug angle wasn't the truth, but I didn't care about other people's truths anymore. I'd thought I'd known the real truth about Trey's and Buckley's murders right up until now. But I didn't. I knew where to find the man who did. And I was going to make him tell it to me.

By any means necessary.

CHAPTER FORTY-NINE

At ten-thirty p.m., I climbed the fence outside Dianne Wilkens' house on Candlelight Drive. The December moon shined a crescent spotlight on the night. The house looked empty, like the owner was still away on vacation. I didn't care whether she was or not. I wouldn't be there long. Teetering on top of the inch-and-a-half-wide wooden fence, I grabbed the eaves of the house, pushed off with my legs, and smeared my torso on the edge of the roof. I slowly brought my right knee up onto the roof. Same with my left and then I was on. Up to my feet and quickly over to the small chimney vent where I'd hidden the gun. I pulled off the vent cover and found what I needed but still feared.

I put the Ruger .357 Magnum in the pocket of my bomber jacket.

* * *

I parked on the street in front of Alan Rankin's home. I pushed the intercom button on the piled-rock pillar that connected to the wrought-iron gate then looked up at the closed-circuit camera staring down at me.

"Yes." A voice that sounded like it came out of a bass drum. Not Rankin, his muscle. That's okay. I was ready for the muscle.

"I'm Rick Cahill." I continued to stare at the camera. "The cops are all over me about the Eric Schmidt murder. They think I had something to do with it, but they know you're involved too. Disposing of the body and all that."

Long silence. Then the gate swung open.

I left my car on the street and walked the fifty yards down the winding flagstone driveway. A mansion loomed at the end of it. Tuscan style, if homes in Tuscany took up entire blocks. Crime paid well and being a criminal lawyer paid even better. At least, in La Jolla.

I rang the doorbell to a teak door that rose to the clouds. The door opened and the silhouette of a giant blotted out the light trying to leave the house. A Gold's Gym rat, if they made rats six-foot-three, two hundred-thirty pounds of flexed muscle and no hair.

He sneered. I hit him with the blackjack on the forehead. His legs folded like a cheap card table, and his ass then his head hit the marble floor in the foyer. Out cold. I jump-straddled him, cinched-cuffed his hands behind his back, and patted him down for a weapon. I pulled a Glock 9mm out of a holster above his ass. Ejected the magazine, put it in my pocket, and threw the gun out the front door.

The whole event took less than ten seconds. I moved past Gold's Gym into the massive house. The sound of a TV suddenly went silent.

"Buck?" A hint of anxiety echoed down a long hallway.

I ran to the voice down the hall into the living room. Alan Rankin dressed in a silk bathrobe, stood with his phone to his ear, eyes wide. I knocked the phone out of his hand and shoved him down into a puffy leather recliner. I grabbed the phone off the floor and hit the end button.

Rankin calmly eyed me from his chair. He crossed one leg over the other. In control, despite my invasion. I grabbed the lapels of his robe and yanked him up to my face. Still no fear in his eyes. I needed fear to get answers.

"Who did you call?"

"Do you know who I am?" Aristocratic with an edge.

He wasn't the first La Jollan to ask me that. The rich ones all thought they were someone and that you should already know it.

I slapped him in the face hard enough to leave my handprint. "Who did you call?"

"Adding battery to breaking and entering." He winced, then

gave me the calm eyes. "Why don't you threaten to kill me and we'll make it a triple header?"

I slapped him again and he cowered, then caught himself and straightened back up. "Who did you call?"

"More like the one who answered the door."

"Will they call back or just show up?"

His phone rang in my hand before he could answer. I looked at the number. The same one he'd just dialed. I handed him the phone, took the gun out of my pocket and let it dangle at my side. I hoped Rankin didn't notice the slight tremor of my hand.

"Tell them it was a false alarm."

He hit answer on the phone. "I want you to pick me up tomorrow at seven. Buck's not feeling well." He hung up.

I put the gun back in my pocket. "Very nice. I won't hit you again if you cooperate just like that."

"You can play tough guy all you like, Mr. Cahill, but you're not tough enough to deal with some of my other friends."

I slapped him harder than the first two times and he stumbled over the chair and fell to the floor. I kicked him in the stomach, then pulled him up and threw him down into the chair. He balled up again and fought for air.

"Your other friends are why I'm here." I stood over him, fists at my sides. "The next one won't be a slap. Nod if you agree to play nice."

He nodded.

"How is Rock Karsten involved with Randall Eddington?"

"I don't know what you're talking about." He covered up, chin into his chest, left hand protecting his flushed face and right arm guarding his belly.

I pulled out the blackjack and hit his left elbow. Not hard enough to dislocate it, but hard enough to keep him from playing golf for a couple months. He yelped and his face went crimson. He grabbed his elbow and rocked back and forth. I grabbed his chin with my left hand and held the blackjack over his head with my right.

"How is Rock Karsten involved with Randall Eddington?"

Tears streamed out of Rankin's eyes from the pain. No sob-
bing. He was tough and determined, but not unbreakable.

"Randall saved Rock from getting shivved in the cafeteria in
San Quentin right after he transferred there. Rock took the kid
under his wing after that."

"Where do Brad Bauer and Trey Fellows come in?"

He kept rocking, but didn't say anything. I showed him the
blackjack.

"Rock got word to Trey that Bauer would be killed unless
Trey went to the kid's lawyer with the confession from Lunsdorf
about murdering the kid's family."

"Got word to Fellows, meaning you told him."

"Yeah."

"How did Karsten know about the confession?"

Rankin raised his eyebrows like I was the slow kid in class.

I was.

My knees wobbled and my breath left me like I'd made it
leave Rankin. I took a step back, then regained control.

"There was no confession." My throat went dry and the words
were jagged in my mouth. "Randall murdered his family and he
and Karsten made up the confession." I'd helped free a murderer
from prison. A monster who'd slaughtered his own family.

Rankin nodded.

"So Rock Karsten concocts a story about Lunsdorf murdering
the Eddingtons just to do Randall a favor and get back at
Lunsdorf? Seems pretty far-fetched." I shook my head. "Who's
to say Lunsdorf doesn't have a solid alibi for the night of the
Eddington murders? And why go to so much trouble to frame the
guy when Karsten could have just put out a hit on him?"

Rankin went quiet again. Sharp, intelligent eyes staring daggers at me. I grabbed his elbow and squeezed. He screamed and
I waited. He rocked like a Hare Krishna in mid-chant. I slowly
moved my hand toward his elbow again.

"Rock and Lunsdorf were down in Mexico setting up a meth
connection the week of the Eddington murders." He spit the

words out fast between ragged breaths. "Rock is Lunsdorf's alibi. When Rock learned that, he and the kid concocted the plan."

"But why not just hit Lunsdorf?"

"Rock would much rather torture him in prison. The Mexican Mafia, the Raptors, and Aryan Brotherhood run the California prisons on the inside. They also control the outside crews from there." He tested his arm, then groaned through clenched teeth. "Lunsdorf took over the local Raptors when Rock went inside. Didn't wait his turn. Rock loved the idea of getting Lunsdorf in the system for a crime he didn't commit, and have him know that Rock put him there. Once he got tired of having him tortured, he'd put him down. Plus, he and the kid had worked out a way to launder money through Eddington Golf when the kid takes over the company."

"If you lie to me, I'm going to take the blackjack to your other elbow, both wrists, your knees, and your ankles. Do you understand?"

"Yes." The fear returned to his eyes.

The look made my stomach turn over. The malevolence of my actions finally caught up to me. I'd acted like the kind of person I'd reviled my whole life. Take what you wanted through force and intimidation. I felt justified. Those with the power always did.

Too late to turn back now.

"Why did you set up Trey and Timothy Buckley to be murdered by the Raptors?"

"Hear me out before you hit me again. Please." His eyes begged me.

I'd broken him. Nausea tugged at me. I nodded.

"Trey got a phone call and went into the other room. He came back and said he was going to meet Randall and Buckley. He looked afraid. I told him to take Buck with him, but he said he couldn't." Rankin shook his head. "I should have figured it out."

Three people met at Trey's and only one left alive. "Randall killed them both."

My face flashed hot then cold. Icy sweat clung to the back of my neck. Bile climbed my throat. I'd helped free Randall only so he could kill again. A harmless druggie and a man I respected who had become my friend.

"The kid is a stone killer. I've defended plenty like him, but none nearly as smart. Rock told me the kid had ice water in his veins. Trey Fellows was a loser, but a decent guy. He didn't deserve to die like that."

Neither did Buckley.

"You think Karsten told him to do it?"

"No. Randall's cleaning up loose ends."

"You're a loose end, Rankin."

"I know."

"You can't call the police because you're in too deep. Possible accessory to murder. Best-case scenario is you do some time and never practice law again. Worst case, you share a cell with your boss, Rock Karsten. And LJPD is not going to touch Randall Eddington again without a locked-down case. And you can't have Randall killed without Karsten's say so. That's not going to happen. You put yourself in a shithole and got a friend of mine murdered. A good man."

I handed him his phone. "Call Randall and tell him you need to meet him tonight. Make it for midnight at La Jolla Recreation Center." I'd head right over there and get the jump on Randall.

Rankin did as he was told. He did more listening than talking at the end of the call. "He says he'll be at Windansea Beach beneath the Surf Shack in an hour. I think he knows something's up."

"He may, but he doesn't know what it is."

I told Rankin to give me his cell number. He did. I called it to make sure. His phone rang.

"You better answer that phone if I call, or I'll come back and finish what I started." I waited until he looked at me. "You send your boys after me, I'll still come back. But I'll be in a bad mood when I get here."

Rankin nodded, but his eyes were on the muted flat-screen TV on the wall opposite him. I followed their gaze and saw Chief Moretti standing in front of reporters.

"Turn it up."

Rankin grabbed the remote off the side table next to his chair and unmuted the television. Moretti continued to speak.

"...known to be armed and dangerous. La Jolla Police Department is working hand in glove with other law enforcement agencies to pursue Mr. Lunsdorf, and we will not relent until he is apprehended."

The shot cut back to the studio and the anchor summed up: Steven Lunsdorf was on the run and the main suspect in the murders of Trey Fellows and Timothy Buckley. Unspecified incriminating evidence was found at the murder scene and in his house.

"Looks like LJPD has wrapped the murders up in a tidy bow." Rankin hit the off button on the remote. "You still going to meet with Randall?"

"Yep."

Gold's Gym struggled to get to his knees as I went into the foyer. I kicked him over onto his side, then went out the front door.

Back in the car, I pulled out the mini-recorder that was wirelessly connected to the microphone I'd taped to my chest before I left my house. I rewound a few seconds and hit "play." The end of my conversation with Rankin was crystal clear.

That was just the preliminary.

Randall Eddington was the main event.

CHAPTER FIFTY

Windansea was a small but famous surfer's beach in La Jolla. Many local surfers had made their name on the waves rolling off a reef break. I drove past the small parking lot above the beach. The lot was empty. I parked two blocks past and took the stairs down to the beach from the Westbourne Street entrance. The Surf Shack was an open, four-poled hut with no side walls and a palm-frond-thatched roof.

The Shack had been made famous in literature and local lore, and was now a San Diego landmark. Tonight, the meeting place for a five-time murderer.

The moon slashed a silver triangle down on the whomping shore break. The tide was low and I stayed up against the sandstone cliffs and slowly made my way toward the Surf Shack 200 yards away. My eyes peered through the shadows made by the night, moonlight, and crevices of the cliffs. No Randall yet. I'd driven to Windansea directly from Rankin's house and arrived forty minutes early. Enough time to get the lay of the land and find the right place to lie in wait.

I inched along the beach, flush against the sandstone walls, the Surf Shack still 100 yards away. Waves crashed thunder every thirty seconds. Residual foamy white water of the last wave sucked back out into the ocean. A sound behind me. I whipped around and saw a hulking shadow, backlit by the moon. Larger than Gold's Gym back at Alan Rankin's house.

"Hello, Mr. Cahill." Randall's voice came out of the massive shadow. "Are you here on behalf of Mr. Rankin?"

"I'm here on behalf of Timothy Buckley and Trey Fellows." I slipped my hand into my jacket pocket and onto the handle of the Ruger .357 Magnum.

"That's an odd thing to say, Rick." A taunting laugh in his voice. "You don't mind if I call you Rick, do you?"

I didn't say anything.

"Seems like we're past the formalities. If you're here on behalf of your dead friends, God rest their souls, you're in the wrong place. Didn't you hear the news? Chief Moretti said Steven Lunsdorf killed your friends."

I slowly moved my right foot back to position a shooter's stance. "You met Trey at his house yesterday evening so you'd have an explanation if the crime lab techs found your DNA there, right?"

"I'm afraid you're not quite up to date." Jovial. Enjoying himself. "The techs found some rolling papers at Trey's house with Lunsdorf's fingerprints on them, and a pair of socks with Trey's and Mr. Buckley's blood on them at Lunsdorf's house. Socks. Kind of ironic, huh?"

"You didn't intend on killing your sister, did you? Your tears for her were real when I visited you at San Quentin."

"I miss my sister very much." The joy left his voice. "Please don't mention her again."

"That helped sell me on your innocence during my visit. I wasn't quite convinced when you talked about your parents, but you convinced me with your tears for Molly. I wish I'd been smart enough to realize that you were crying because you'd killed her, not someone else."

"You're a cruel man, Rick." Menace.

"From you, that's a compliment." I kept my eyes on the shadow that was his right hand in the front pocket of his dark, hooded sweatshirt. "Molly walked in when you were butchering your parents and you had to kill her. If she just hadn't woken up, she'd still be alive, right?"

A blur from his left side. I yanked the gun free from my pocket, then something hard exploded onto my right wrist. My gun dropped to the sand and pain screamed along my arm, my right hand dangling immobile. His arm moved again. I spun to my left and ducked my head. The iron crowbar bounced off my shoulder and banged my head behind the right ear. I splatted face-first down onto the sand.

"You didn't know I was ambidextrous, did you, Rick?" He chuckled. A reverb from hell. "Gun in my right hand, crowbar in my left, snug against my leg. Old magician's trick. You watched the wrong hand, Rick."

I tried to push up off the sand but collapsed back into it. Crippling pain swelled in my head. The world tilted on its axis, spinning me off its edge. I sensed Randall next to me and caught him swiping my gun off the ground. He shoved it in his waistband behind his back. I fought the spinning in my head and tried not to pass out.

"Make a move and your life ends now, Rick."

Randall grabbed my jacket and yanked me up into a sitting position. The back of my head slammed against the sandstone cliff. The pain vibrated in my ears. Randall put the barrel of a gun to my temple and checked my jacket pockets with his free hand. He pulled the blackjack out of my left pocket and the moon caught his grinning teeth.

"Old school, huh? Nice, but just a bit behind the times, Rick. Just like you've been a few steps behind me the whole way." He patted down my pants and found the wireless recorder. He shoved it and my cell phone into his jeans pockets. "Must be a microphone here, somewhere." He stuck his hand down inside my coat and shirt and ripped out the microphone taped to my chest.

"Thought you were going to get me to confess and take the recording to the police?" The devil's laugh again. He took the gun from my head and stepped back. "Never would have thought of that."

I was going to die on the beach tonight. The cops weren't on the way. Neither were Rankin's men. Bob Reitzmeyer wasn't backing me up. Unless I somehow stopped armed, prison-fit Randall Eddington—without a weapon, with a broken right wrist, and a spinning head—he would pound my skull jagged like he had Trey Fellows', Timothy Buckley's, and his family's. I wouldn't be able to trick him. He was smarter than me. The fact that he wanted me to know just how smart was the only thing I had going for me. All I could do was try to prolong my life and hope for a miracle.

Or make one happen.

"Why me?"

"Oh, come on, Rick. I thought you were supposed to be a tough guy. You're not going to go out begging for your life, are you?"

"No. Why did you choose me to work with Buckley on your case?" I fought the pain in my head that told me to lie down and let it be over. "You let that slip at the celebration the other night."

"You know, Rick, it's a good thing you never went to prison for your wife's murder, cuz you wouldn't have survived. Not smart enough." The moon caught his smile again. I felt time and my life ticking away. "I didn't let that slip. I put it out there to see if you'd react or catch on. A little game to make things interesting. In prison, you have a lot of time to try to make things interesting."

"Why me?"

"Like I told you the other night, you know what it's like to be accused of something you didn't do. That made you sympathetic to my plight. A lot of ex-cop PIs wouldn't believe a man could be convicted of murder if he didn't do it, or they wouldn't care either way. Once I hooked you in, I knew you'd do whatever it took. I also did my research. Every hour I had of computer time in the joint, I researched you and Buckley. I knew that you worked for Bob Reitzmeyer, who fucked that whore of a mother I used to have. He was close to the investigation. I hoped he might know something about the planted evidence and you'd find out about it. And you did, then your hero complex kicked in, and everything fell into place."

"Planted evidence that helped convict a guilty man."

"Guilty or not, LJPD cheated, and you caught them. Because of that, and a little cheating on my side, I'm now a free man. Thanks again, Rick."

"Why did you have to kill Buckley? He didn't know the truth about you."

"Collateral damage. Felt badly about it." The demon's smile.

"For a good second or two. Trey wouldn't see me alone. He was smart enough not to trust me. I coaxed Buckley to go with me. Told him Trey had new evidence to show us for a civil case against LJPD. When we got there, I opened up my backpack, took out my crowbar, and that was it. I wanted to meet back at Trey's because it was a tight space. Nowhere to run. A quick tap to incapacitate Trey. A couple to kill Buckley, then back to kill Trey. And, finally...ah, the finishing touches to make it look like a Raptor murder."

"You think Lunsdorf is just going to roll over for the murders? How do you know he doesn't have an alibi for Trey and Buckley?"

"He does. He was dead at the time. Now the police are chasing a dead man's shadow. Too bad they'll never find him." The laugh. "Or what's left of him."

Randall had demonstrated his brilliance. There wasn't anything left to say. He'd attack soon without warning. I had to attack first. "You forgot about Rankin. He knows everything."

"He'll never say a thing. He's under Rock Karsten's thumb, and I'm Rock's boy."

"He already told me everything. About you and the concocted confession. The threat to kill Brad Bauer. It's on the recorder you took off me."

In a slip of moonlight, I saw uncertainty in Randall's eyes. He took the recorder out of his pocket. I waited for his eyes to look at the recorder to turn it on.

"I recorded the recording on my voicemail—" He looked down. I bolted up from the sand, pushing off the cliff with my one good arm, and sprang at Randall. His reaction with the crowbar whooshed just behind me as I exploded into his chest with my left shoulder. He clamped his massive right arm around my neck, but I kept churning my legs and slammed him into the lone boulder behind him at the shoreline, before his left arm could match his right. The air whumped from his body and he dropped the crowbar. We bounced off the rock. His hold loosened an instant, and I ducked down and reached my left hand around his back and found the Ruger in his waistband.

His hold on my neck vised again, and he tightened it with his left arm. I yanked out the Ruger and jammed it into his ribs as my throat started to close off. The hold went slack. I sucked air into my lungs.

"Step back." I held the gun on him in my left hand. My right, useless, dangling from a broken wrist. I willed my gun hand not to shake and fought the dread from my nightmares. My hand trembled slightly, but I didn't think Randall could see it in the darkness.

He took a small step back, but his smile returned. "Nicely done, Rick. You saved yourself. But it doesn't change things for me."

I backed up three paces.

"Slowly take the gun out of your sweatshirt pocket by the barrel with two fingers and toss it over here." He tossed the gun at my feet. "Now, hands behind your head."

He did as told. "You think you're going to walk me into LJPD and tell them you caught the killer of poor Mr. Buckley and the drug dealer, Trey Fellows?"

"Kneel down."

He ignored me.

"I'm untouchable. The press loves me. Nationwide. You think LJPD wants to arrest me again on some crazy story of yours? You taped Alan Rankin without him knowing. Your supposed tape is inadmissible, my dim-witted friend. And you're not exactly LJPD's favorite citizen. Besides, the cops have all they need to chase the ghost of Steven Lunsdorf for the murders."

Everything he said was true. Even if the Rankin tape could be admitted, it was all hearsay and speculation. I'd needed a confession by Randall on tape, and I'd failed.

"Kneel the fuck down!"

"How are you going to hold that gun on me and call the police with your broken hand?"

The devil's laugh. "Tell you what. We'll call this one even. We stay out of each other's way and get on with our lives."

He moved his head slightly to the left and moonlight spot-lighted down on me. And my trembling left arm.

"Rick, your hand is shaking. Lost your edge after being off the force for ten years? Put the gun down now and we'll go our separate ways."

His mother, father, and sister. Timothy Buckley and Trey Fellows. Steven Lunsdorf. Randall had murdered them all to serve his purposes. No other reason. Obstacles in the selfish life he'd chosen to live. And he was going to walk away a free man to live that life and eliminate other obstacles. Evil has no conscience.

A wave crashed down onto the beach. My hand held steady. I pulled the trigger.

CHAPTER FIFTY-ONE

I dialed a number on Randall's cell phone. When someone picked up on the other end, I hit the "play" button on the recorder and Alan Rankin's voice came on. I let it run about ten seconds, then turned it off.

"Who the fuck is this? Randall?" Alan Rankin.

"Not Randall."

"You're resorting to blackmail now, Cahill?" Rankin knew that in the hands of the bar association, the tape could cost him his law license. In the hands of the police, it could cost him his freedom. In the hands of Rock Karsten, it could cost him his life. "That's a very dangerous game. How much do you want?"

"I want you to send down your cleaning crew. The same ones that made the body disappear from Candlelight Drive." I told him where to send the men.

"Why don't you just go to the police and claim self-defense?"

LJPD might even believe me. But that didn't matter. All that mattered was what the people of La Jolla believed. Right now, they, and the rest of America, believed Randall Eddington was a saint who'd been cheated out of eight years of his life and forced to grieve the loss of his family from a prison cell. Any story that contradicted that could get the voter initiative to disband LJPD on the ballot. LJPD wasn't about to commit professional suicide.

Certainly not for me.

"Send your team now or a copy of the recording goes up to San Quentin. I'm sure Karsten can find another lawyer. One that's alive." I hung up.

I drove home, stopping every few miles, and dropped individual pieces of the Ruger .357 Magnum, which I'd disassembled and wiped down, into sewer drains. The same with the single remaining bullet and four empty shells; three from the bullets I'd put into Randall Eddington, and one that someone had used to kill Eric Schmidt. I used a file from my tool kit in the trunk to file the serial number off the barrel of the last piece I threw down a sewer.

I left puzzle pieces around La Jolla for a puzzle harder to put together than the one that Trey Fellows had worked on and gotten he and Timothy Buckley killed.

* * *

Rita Mae Eddington called me the next evening. Worry hung off her voice. "Rick, have you talked to Randall today or last night?"

"He called me early last night. Why?"

I hadn't felt guilty last night when I put three bullets in Randall Eddington's chest. Nor when I'd had Alan Rankin make his body disappear. I'd played God and broken his most cherished commandment. And it hadn't bothered me. But it did now. Not because of what I'd done, but because of the pain it would bring a nice old lady who'd already endured more pain in her life than she or anyone deserved.

"He didn't come home last night and he isn't answering his cell phone." Fear in her voice that I'd put there. "Did he tell you that he was going somewhere?"

"No. We just talked about Timothy Buckley and Trey Fellows."

"Oh, dear, that is so horrible. So much evil in the world. Are you okay?"

No. Even though I'd rid the world of an evil that Rita Mae loved but never saw. I hadn't seen it either, until it was too late. For Buckley and Trey. And almost too late for me. "I'm hanging in there."

* * *

Two days later, Randall's disappearance was all over the news. Local and network reporters called me day and night, wanting an interview with the private detective who'd helped set Randall free, only to have him now disappear. I ignored them all.

*　*　*

The day of Buckley's funeral, Detective Denton showed up at my front door. "Mr. Cahill, Chief Moretti would like you to come down to the station and have a brief talk."

"I'm going to a funeral today. Maybe tomorrow." I started to close the door, but Denton stuck her foot in the jamb. I fought the urge to slam the door on it.

"It will only take a few minutes. I'll bring you right back."

"I'll follow you down there." I could call a lawyer to come along, but the only lawyer I trusted was dead. Besides, I needed to find out what game Moretti wanted to play.

Denton gave me cop eyes, like it was her decision whether or not I went in her car or mine. Finally, she nodded. I walked next to her down the walkway from my house.

"Detective Denton." I stopped walking. "I lost the memory card to my camera, can you lend me one?"

She stopped and looked at me, but didn't say anything.

"Also, I'm looking to buy a motorcycle. I know you have a direct line to experts in the field where information is sometimes leaked. Let me know if you hear about any deals." Someone at LJPD had told the Raptors that Trey was hiding out on Candle-light Drive. Detective Denton had had the most to gain if Trey never testified. Her plan had failed, but Randall Eddington's hadn't.

"Get in your car before I put you in the back of mine." Taut eyes, snake hiss of a voice.

*　*　*

Moretti sat behind a grand mahogany desk in a raised chair with pictures of he and *B*-list celebrities in golf attire on his desk. He pointed to a chair in front of the desk. I sat down and was forced to look up at him, perched on his throne.

"I'm sorry for your loss, Rick. I know that you and Timothy Buckley were friends." He sounded sincere. Maybe he'd just gotten better at acting like a decent human being since he'd become police chief.

"Thanks."

"Timothy Buckley and Trey Fellows. Two more people who spent time with you and ended up dead. How many is that now? Three? Actually, four, if you count your wife." Couldn't hide his true personality for long. "Might make a man question some of the decisions he's made in his life."

He'd gotten something right. Not that I'd ever let him know.

"Is that why you had your tainted detective escort me up here? To give me a body count? I know exactly how many people I've lost in my life." I pushed the anger up front. But only to cover my growing anxiety. Moretti was playing a game. He was the cat and I was the mouse. I knew the claws would come out soon.

"All those bad decisions. All those people dead." He gave me the smirk he'd given me two years ago, when he thought he knew something about me that he shouldn't. "Might make a thoughtful man reevaluate his life. Might make a rash man angry and want to seek revenge."

"I have to go to a funeral today, Moretti." I stood up. "Call me when you're done philosophizing."

"What happened to your arm, Rick?"

I had a cast on my broken wrist and had to keep the arm in a sling for a few more days.

"Got drunk and fell down some stairs."

"Sorry to hear that. Seems to happen to you a lot." He studied me with double-barrel coal eyes. "Sit back down. I'm almost through with you."

I stared at him, and saw handcuffs and a jail cell in my future with one more bad decision. I sat down.

"No doubt you've seen the news about the disappearance of Randall Eddington?"

"Yes." I kept my voice under control.

"We're investigating the disappearance and looking at all angles."

I controlled my breathing and didn't say anything.

"You know people all over La Jolla have security cameras on their property." More smirk. "Everybody is afraid of home invasions. Some of those cameras catch things all the way out on the street."

No home-security camera could have filmed Randall and me on the beach. We were thirty feet below street level. But Moretti had something. I was about to find out what.

"It turns out that a camera on Neptune Drive down at Windansea caught a shot of Jack Eddington's Volvo driving by the night Randall Eddington disappeared in that very car. At eleven ten p.m."

Alan Rankin's cleanup crew had found the Volvo and disposed of it somewhere. But this was before that. Back when Randall arrived early to get the jump on me. When he was still alive.

"That's great, Moretti. You have a lead. Why am I here?" Sweat beaded under my arms.

"Well, twelve minutes later, another security camera filmed a black Mustang GT with your license plate park on Westbourne Street, and someone who looked just like you get out of the car and return thirty-one minutes later and leave. Westbourne runs right into Neptune. Coincidence?"

"Sometimes I go down and look at the ocean at night, like hundreds of other San Diegans."

"So that was you?"

Nowhere to run. "Yes. And I'm sure you know that the Eddingtons live on La Jolla Boulevard, just a couple minutes away from Windansea."

"Of course." Moretti leaned across the desk and his smirk flattened out into a silent accusation. "Did you happen to hear any gunshots while you were down at Windansea Sunday night between eleven twenty-two and eleven fifty-three p.m.?"

"No." His eyes bored into mine looking for a tell I didn't think he needed. I gave him nothing. "The waves were pretty loud that night."

"That's what the man walking his dog above the beach said. But he also thought he heard gunshots. Three of them."

"All I heard were the waves."

Moretti slid back and smiled his non-smirk version. "Okay, but let me know if you remember anything else."

"Will do." I got up to leave.

"Because we're going to solve this disappearance. No matter how long it takes. Even if it turns out that some Good Samaritan killed that murdering son of a bitch." He gave me the hard eyes again and they struck home. "You and I both know that son of a bitch was just about untouchable for law enforcement. He was a hero in the public's mind. Whoever killed him might think he was doing LJPD a favor. He wasn't. The public will demand that the killer be brought to justice and take Randall's place up at San Quentin. And I'm going to make that happen. Count on it."

"I thought Randall was missing, Moretti." I fought against the tickle of sweat running down my underarms. "You calling it a murder now?"

"Not yet. You'll be the first to know when it changes." He gave me a smile that frightened as much as his words had. "Have a nice day, Rick. And take care of that arm."

My legs felt like they were stuck in tar. I had to force them to carry me out of Moretti's office.

* * *

Jasmine spoke at Buckley's funeral. She wore black, but this time she didn't match it with her makeup. Without the Goth look, you could clearly see the resemblance to Buckley. As I'd suspected, she was his daughter. She gave an eloquent, heartfelt speech that had everyone in tears.

Including me.

I went up to her after the service to give her my condolences. A mistake.

"Where were you when he needed you?" Tears flowed, but her

voice held anger instead of sorrow. "You should have been with him. You should have protected him. You're not welcome here."

I didn't argue. I made my way through shocked mourners and out of the church to a beautiful December day. The sun stared down at me with its own judgment.

I'd been to two funerals ten years apart, and both families of the deceased held me at least partially responsible for the death of their loved ones. They hadn't been exactly right, but they hadn't been too far wrong, either.

Something about the Eddington case had always gnawed at me. Gently nibbling at first, then deep gashing at the end. I'd followed its lead at first, but looked past it when the chance to be a hero presented itself. I'd listened to men who I'd once respected tell me that Randall was a stone killer, and had shunned their gut instincts and my own when I'd found out they'd let their ends justify their means. I'd ignored my father's credo, the one I'd adopted two years ago for my own, when I'd seen it in action by Bob Reitzmeyer.

"Sometimes you have to do what's right, even when the law says it's wrong."

Reitzmeyer had followed that credo to help put a murderer behind bars. I'd ignored it to free him so he could murder three more people. I'd done it because I thought I was right, but also because I wanted to make a difference. I wanted to come out on the winning side of a case that mattered.

EPILOGUE

Jack and Rita Mae Eddington hired me to find Randall. They weren't happy with the progress that LJPD was making. Moretti hadn't shared with the press or the Eddingtons what he'd shared with me the day of Buckley's funeral.

I tried to convince myself that prolonging the fiction was much less cruel than revealing to the Eddingtons the monster that was their grandson. But survival instinct had played a bigger role. If I didn't investigate the disappearance, someone else would, and they might find the truth that Chief Moretti was searching for. Truth or fiction, both were unfair to people who deserved some joy at the end of their lives after so much sorrow.

I'd check in with them once a month and report no progress. I wouldn't accept any pay except for Rita Mae's chocolate chip cookies. After each meeting, I'd take the cookies home and give them to the next-door neighbor's daughter who sometimes watched Midnight.

To eat them would be too much of a betrayal, even for me.

I sleep through most nights now. The nightmares left me the night I killed Randall Eddington. Like the man in my earlier nightmares, he'd deserved to die.

Now the only nightmare I fear is a waking one. The day that Chief Moretti knocks on my door with an arrest warrant for murder.